FOR RENT

LARGE ROOM. 20 meters × 15 meters. Room to swing a cat. Bring own cat. Rats provided. Room includes VU, but without intrusive searchlights at night. SECOND STORY, avoiding intrusions by prospective tunnelers. Two floors below roof, preventing annoyances from guards on roof, escapers on roof, rats on roof, or rain, considering roof only semipresent. INCLUDES: Remains of four beds. Ruins of desk. V/thick walls. POWER: Single bulb from ceiling, apparently wired into circuit. WATER: A close walk to nearby dispersing point. A REAL FIXER-UPPER. *Once visited, never left.*

By Allan Cole and Chris Bunch
Published by Ballantine Books:

The STEN Adventures:

STEN
THE WOLF WORLDS
THE COURT OF A THOUSAND SUNS
FLEET OF THE DAMNED
REVENGE OF THE DAMNED

A RECKONING FOR KINGS

REVENGE OF THE DAMNED

ALLAN COLE
and CHRIS BUNCH

A Del Rey Book
BALLANTINE BOOKS ● NEW YORK

A Del Rey Book
Published by Ballantine Books

Copyright © 1989 by Allan Cole and Christopher Bunch

Library of Congress Catalog Card Number: 88-92138

ISBN 0-345-33173-7

Printed in Canada

First Edition: February 1989

Cover Art by David B. Mattingly

To
Frank Lupo
Scholar, bon vivant, gentleman
and
part-time werewolf

Note

The titles of the books are taken from the Earth nation of Japan, which at one time in its feudal history formalized the art of sword fighting, much as it formalized all else. It was called *kenjutsu*. *Ma-ai* is the threshold where the combatants meet. *Suki* is the opportunity to begin the fight. *Kobo-ichi* describes the offensive and defensive engagements. *Zanshin* is final domination.

—AC and CRB

MA-AI

MA-AI

CHAPTER ONE

HE TUGGED AT the last piece of rubble, wincing as rough masonry bit into soft fingertips. Straining under the weight, he lifted it to knee height, then staggered a few paces and dropped the mass onto a pile.

Senior Captain (Intelligence) Lo Prek stepped back to review his work. Only a large, twisted steel door remained. The Tahn officer had labored for hours clearing that door. Beyond it, he hoped, was the key to the puzzle he had been fitting together for more years than he cared to remember.

He hesitated a few minutes as if afraid that he would be disappointed. Almost daintily, Prek wiped his face with a silk handkerchief, which he then returned to his uniform sleeve. For a Tahn, Prek was a tall man and painfully slender. His body was all angles of jutting bone topped by a long horselike face with small eyes set too far apart and a short nose that left him with an overly long upper lip.

Prek unclipped a small laser torch from his harness and began cutting through the door. Prek was not the kind of man who hummed to himself while he worked or who used a string of favorite obscenities when the task became momentarily difficult. At his former post, where he had worked for almost his entire career, he had been notorious—even among Tahn—for insisting on absolute silence and complete dedication to even the smallest job. He did not allow his mind to wander when performing rote and insisted on the same from his underlings. The joke at his old bureau was that if Prek had his way, every intelligence clerk would have a monitor surgically implanted in his brain as a requirement for employment.

Prek had heard the joke, and although he did not see any humor in it, he acknowledged its truth. Captain Prek knew he had an obsessive personality. He did not particularly like it or dislike it. It was just so. It was a character weakness that he had learned to use to his benefit.

There was a shriek of metal as the door sagged under its own weight and then crashed to the floor. Prek reclipped the torch and stepped inside the record center of the Imperial Navy's defeated 23rd Fleet. If the Tahn had gods, Prek would have whispered a prayer. He had traveled very far and taken many chances to come to this point. If Prek was correct, in this room he would pick up the trail of the man who had murdered his brother.

STEN, (NI). Commander Imperial Navy. Last known post: OIC, 23rd Division TacDiv, asngd Imperial 23rd Fleet. Prev: Cmdr, Imperial Personal Bodyguard. Prev: Records show assigned to various Guards units. NOTE: IntelEst these records fraudulent, prob Cat. 1. STEN actually assigned various Imperial Intelligence duties. GENERAL DESCRIPTION: Species: Human. Sex: Male. Age: Unknown. Records destroyed. Estimated first quarter of life span. Place of Birth: Unknown. Height: Slightly below Imperial norm. Body: Well formed, low body fat, high muscle ratio. Hair: Blk. Eyes: Blk. General Health: Excellent. Distinguishing Marks or Characteristics: None. Family: Unknown. Interests: Unknown. Friends: Unknown.

Prek was not dismayed when he saw the shattered ruins inside. File vaults had been twisted into bizarre shapes by intense heat. There were large spots of white ash scattered uniformly about where office dividers and furniture had once stood. As he walked, his boots stirred up a fine dust that drifted upward and clogged his nose and throat. He fitted a rebreather into place and began combing through the litter of what had once been the 23rd Fleet.

Once his heart jumped when he found a tiny scrap of microfilm lying under a steel joist. He slid it into the slot of his reader and then felt like crying when he saw that it was nothing more than part of a bill for general office supplies.

Prek berated himself for his reaction. Yes, his mission was personal. But his only hope for success was if he behaved like a complete professional.

Prek reorganized himself. He went all the way back to the

beginning—to the outlines of what might have been the desk of the chief clerk of the records center. He began sifting through the rubble, starting in the middle and slowly working out to the edges. He was looking for much more than the chance minutiae of one man's life, he reminded himself. Even more valuable would be to discover the pattern of record storage. Prek knew that every office had its own individual logic. Things might have changed over the years as chief clerks came and went, but there would always be the trace of the first being who had received and filed the first and then the second and then the thousandth document.

The Tahn captain was convinced that once he had determined the procedural map, he would find his man.

Although they had worked in private industry, Prek's parents had also been lifelong bureaucrats. They had been equally dull in personality and unattractive in appearance. True, they had both been intelligent people, but their intelligence was what a personnel psych might have called "highly focused." Prek was ten years old when his brother, Thuy, was born. From the moment the infant had drawn its first breath, the family knew it was blessed with a golden boy.

Thuy was everything his family was not. To begin with, he was beautiful. Blond, curly hair. Blue eyes. And a physique like an Adonis even as he entered puberty. He was quick-witted and consumed with curiosity about everything. Thuy also saw humor in nearly any stituation. It was hard to be around him long and not be infected by his cheery outlook on life.

Far from being jealous, Lo had loved his young brother more than anything in the world. He had lavished all his attention on him, going so far as to strap himself financially so that the boy could have the benefit of the very best education the Tahn System could offer.

The investment had proved to be well placed. Thuy was instantly snapped up by the diplomatic corps, a situation that allowed him to blossom even more. The only arguments any of his superiors had ever had concerning him was who the young Tahn's mentor *really* was.

And so, when the delicate peace negotiations with the Eternal Emperor were undertaken, Thuy had instantly been assigned to accompany Lord Kirghiz and the other Tahn representatives as a junior diplomatic officer. It was to be a career assignment, which everyone agreed would be just the beginning of a rich career.

The Imperial and Tahn fleets met under the blinding pulsar shadow of NG 467H. The initial negotiations went quickly and well. Everyone believed that an agreement beneficial to the Tahn was only a formality away. The Eternal Emperor had invited the Tahn dignitaries aboard for a treaty celebration. Lord Kirghiz had quickly picked the Tahn who would accompany them. Included among them had been Thuy.

No Tahn knew what exactly had transpired next.

Prek believed the facts spoke for themselves.

Every Tahn who had boarded the *Normandie* died in a horrible bloodbath as they sat at the Emperor's banquet table.

The Eternal Emperor, through his toady judges and special prosecutors, had claimed that the Tahn had merely been the tragic victims of a plot against himself. As far as any Tahn—especially Prek—was concerned, that was too obvious a lie even to comment on. And the only answer to the lie and the treachery was a war of vengeance. It was a war to the death, to the last ounce of air and the last drop of blood.

It was a war that Prek believed in as intensely as did every other Tahn. But the larger war merely underscored his own private battle.

Prek did not remember when he had learned of his brother's death. He had been sitting in his office at Tahn Intelligence headquarters, and his superior had entered. The next thing he knew, Lo found himself sitting up in a hospital bed. Four months had passed. During that time, he was told, he had been a virtual catatonic. War was at hand, and so Lo had been declared "cured" and sent back to work.

It was then that his private war began. Prek examined every dot of information surrounding the deaths of his brother and the other Tahn diplomats. And gradually he had determined which beings had been responsible. He had not included the Emperor. That would be pointless. To go for the Emperor would be not only impossible but the act of an insane man. No. Go for the possible: the men who had actually wielded the knives or fired the guns. Sten, Prek firmly believed, was one of those men.

He had obtained a copy of Sten's military record, a tissue of lies, he was sure, but at least a beginning point in forming a profile of the man. The official record showed a man who had held a series of slightly above average posts, who had won a little more than his share of military awards and honors, and who had been promoted regularly. Then, suddenly, for no apparent reason, his career had taken a sharp upturn. For no readily apparent reason, he had been appointed head of the Emperor's bodyguards. That had been followed by another sudden shift from the army to the navy and a promotion to commander.

Prek believed the promotion was because of special service to the Emperor. Sten's record was a fake. Actually, Prek thought, Sten had been a valued intelligence agent. The shift to the navy and, ultimately, to his command of four tacships had been a reward for services rendered. Those services, Prek was sure, included the murder of his brother.

Prek had tracked Sten forward to the final battle for Cavite City, where enormous casualties had been suffered on both sides. Tahn records indicated that Sten had probably died in that battle, although his remains had never been found. There had been some out-of-the-ordinary official effort to determine Sten's fate because of "criminal actions instigated by said Imperial officer" prior to the battle for Cavite.

Prek did not believe Sten was dead. His profile showed him to be a man who would do anything to survive. Prek also did not believe that Sten was serving elsewhere. He was an officer who would always be in the forefront of battle, and he was also the kind of hero the Eternal Emperor liked to feed into his propaganda machine.

No. Sten was alive. And Prek was determined to run him to the ground. He would find the man and then . . . The Tahn brushed that thought from his mind. He could not allow emotion to interfere with the hunt.

Senior Captain (Intelligence) Lo Prek was right.

Sten *was* alive.

CHAPTER TWO

TWO EMACIATED, SHAVEN-HEADED men crouched, motionless, in the thigh-deep muck.

One of them had been Commander Sten, formerly commanding officer of the now-destroyed Imperial Cruiser *Swampscott*. Sten had assumed command of the obsolete rustbucket in the final retreat from Cavite and had fought a desperate rearguard action against an entire Tahn fleet. One ultramodern Tahn battleship had been destroyed by the *Swampscott*'s missiles and a second had been crippled beyond repair, even as the Tahn blasts shattered the cruiser. In the final moments, Sten had opened his com and sent a surrender signal. He had collapsed long before the Tahn boarded the hulk that had been a fighting ship. That almost certainly had saved his life.

Seconds after Sten went out, Warrant Officer Alex Kilgour, a heavy-world thug, ex-Mantis Section assassin, and Sten's best friend struggled back to consciousness. He bloodily registered, on the *Swampscott*'s single functioning screen, Tahn tacships closing in. He foggily thought that the Tahn, barbarians, "ae th' Campbell class," would not properly honor the man who had destroyed the nucleus of a Tahn fleet. More likely, Sten would be pitched out the nearest lock into space.

"Tha' dinnae be braw nor kosher," he muttered. Kilgour wove his way to a sprawled body, unsealed the suit, and tore away the corpse's ID tags. He checked a wall-mounted pressure readout. There were still a few pounds of atmosphere remaining in the CIC. Sten's suit came open, air hissing out, and his ID tags were replaced. Kilgour heard/felt the crashing as the Tahn blew a lock open and decided that it might be expedient for him to be unconscious as well.

Fewer than thirty gore-spattered, shocked Imperial sailors were transferred from the wreck of the *Swampscott* to the hold of a Tahn assault transport. Among them was one Firecontrolman 1st Class Samuel Horatio.

Sten.

Fed and watered only as an afterthought, their wounds left untreated, twenty-seven survived to be unloaded on a swampworld that the Tahn had grudgingly decided would be a war prisoner planet.

The Tahn believed that the highest death a being could find was in a battle. Cowardice or surrender were unthinkable. According to their belief, any Imperial soldier or sailor unlucky enough to be captured should have begged for instant death. But they were also sophisticated enough to realize grudgingly that other cultures felt differently and that such assistance to the dishonored might be misinterpreted. And so they let their captives live. For a while.

The Tahn saw no reason why, if prisoners were a burden to the Tahn, that burden should not be repaid. Repaid in sweat: slave labor.

Medical care: If the prisoners included med personnel, they had a medic. No supplies were provided. Any Imperial medical supplies captured were confiscated.

Shelter: Prisoners were permitted, on their own time, using any nonessential items permitted by the camp officers, to build shelter.

Working hours: At any task assigned, no limitations on hours or numbers of shifts.

Food: For humans, a tasteless slab that purported to provide the necessary nutrients. Except that a hardworking human needed about 3,600 calories per day. Prisoners were provided less than 1,000. Similar ratios and lack of taste were followed for the ET prisoners.

Since the prisoners were shamed beings, of course their guards were also soldiers in disgrace. Some of them were the crafty, who reasoned that shame in a guard unit was better than death in an assault regiment. There were a few—a very few—guards who had previously been trusties on one of the Tahn's own prison worlds.

The rules for prisoners were simple: Stand at attention

when any guard talks to you, even if you were a general and he or she was a private. Run to obey any order. Failure to obey: death. Failure to complete a task in the time and manner assigned: death. Minor infractions: beatings, solitary confinement, starvation.

In the Tahn POW camps, only the hard survived.

Sten and Alex had been prisoners for over three years.

Their rules were simple:

Never forget that the war cannot last forever.

Never forget you are a soldier.

Always help your fellow prisoner.

Always eat anything offered.

Both of them wished they had been brought up religious—faith in any or all gods kept prisoners alive. They had seen what happened to other prisoners, those who had given up hope, those who thought they could not filter through animal excrement for bits of grain, those who rebelled, and those who thought they could lone-wolf it.

After three years, all of them were long dead.

Sten and Alex had survived.

Their previous training in the supersecret, survive-anything Mantis Section of the Empire's Mercury Corps might have helped. Sten also knew clotting well that having Alex to back his act had saved him. Kilgour privately felt the same. And there was a third item: Sten was armed.

Years earlier, before he had entered Imperial service, Sten had constructed a weapon—a tiny knife. Double-edged and needle-sharp, hand-formed from an exotic crystal, its edge would cut through any known metal or mineral. The knife was sheathed *in* Sten's arm, its release muscle-controlled. It was a very deadly weapon—although, in their captivity, it had been used mostly as a tool.

That night it would assist in their escape.

There had been very few escapes from the Tahn POW camps. At first those who had tried had been executed after recapture, and recaptured they almost always were. The first problem—getting out of a camp or fleeing from a work gang—was not that hard. Getting off the world itself was almost insurmountable. Some had made it as stowaways—or at least the prisoners hoped the escapees had succeeded. Others escaped and went to ground, living an outlaw existence only marginally better than life in the camps, hoping that the war would eventually end and they would be rescued.

Within the last year there had been a policy change—prisoners attempting an escape were not immediately murdered. Instead they were purged to a mining world, a world where, the guards gleefully told them, a prisoner's life span was measured in hours.

Sten and Alex had made four escape attempts in the three years they had been prisoners. Two tunnels had been discovered in the digging, a third attempt to go over the camp wire had been aborted when their ladder was found, and the most recent had been abandoned when no one could come up with what to do once they were beyond the wire.

This one, however, would succeed.

There was movement in the reeds nearby. Alex pounced and came up with a muddy, squirming, squealing rodent. Instantly Sten had the small box he held open, and the water animal was popped inside and closed into darkness. Very good.

"You two! Up!" a guard's voice boomed.

Sten and Alex came to attention.

"Making love? Sloughing?"

"Nossir. We're hunting, sir."

"Hunting? For reeks?"

"Yessir."

"We shoulda killed you all," the guard observed, and spat accurately and automatically in Sten's face. "Form up."

Sten didn't bother to wipe the spittle. He and Alex waded out of the paddy to the dike, into line with ten other prisoners. The column stumbled into motion, heading back toward the camp. There were three guards, only one of whom was carrying a projectile weapon; they knew that none of those walking dead were a threat. Sten held the box as steady as possible and made soothing noises. He did not want his new pet to go off before it was time.

The reek—an odoriferous water animal with unusable fur, rank flesh, and spray musk glands below its tail—was the final tool for their escape.

CHAPTER THREE

THE PRISONER-OF-WAR camps had two command structures. The guards were the most visible. But the camp was actually run by the prisoners. In some camps the commanders were the strong and the brutal. Those anarchies were deathcamps, where a prisoner was as likely to die at the hands of his fellows as by a guard.

Sten's camp was still military. He and Alex were at least partially responsible for that.

The two had fought their way back to health during long delirium months. Then one day Sten was well enough to make a major discovery—not only was he known by the rather clottish name of Horatio, but Warrant Officer Kilgour outranked him. Somehow, he knew that had been carefully plotted by Alex back in the CIC of the *Swampscott*.

But regardless, rank would prevail. Those who felt the "war is over" or they "don't have to listen to any clottin' sojers who got us in the drakh in the first place" were reasoned with. If that did not work, other methods were applied. Sten might have been a skeleton, but he was one who knew many, many degrees beyond the third. And Kilgour, from the three-gee world of Edinburgh, was still the strongest being in the camp—even including the camp executive officer, Battery Commander (Lieutenant Colonel) Virunga.

The N'Ranya were not particularly civilized-looking primates who had developed as tree-dwelling carnivores. They had recently been recognized as the Empire's preeminent artillery experts—their ancestry had given them an instinctual understanding of geometry and trigonometry. Their 300-kilo-plus body weight did not hurt their ability to handle heavy shells, either.

Colonel Virunga had been badly wounded before he was captured and still hulked around the compound with a limp and a cane. Very few people who survived Sten and Alex thought it wise to argue with the colonel's orders. The Imperial camp commander was a thin, wispy woman, General Bridger, who had reactivated herself out of retirement when her world was invaded and led the last-ditch stand. Her only goal was to stay alive long enough to see the Imperial standard raised over the camp, and then she would allow herself to die.

At dusk, after Sten and Alex had forced down the appalling evening ration, she and Colonel Virunga said their good-byes.

"Mr. Kilgour, Horatio," she said, "I hope I shall never see either of you again."

Kilgour grinned. "Ah hae th' sam't dream, ma'am."

Virunga stepped forward. It took a while to understand the N'Ranya speech patterns—they thought speech mostly a waste of time and so verbalized only enough words to make the meaning clear.

"Hope . . . luck . . . When . . . free . . . do not forget."

They would not. Sten and Alex saluted, then began their moves.

Under orders, without explanation, other prisoners had begun what Sten called "two in, one out, one in, three out." In small groups they filtered toward one of the camp's few privies, one that "coincidentally" sat less than three meters from the inner perimeter. Sten and Alex joined them; the small box with the reek inside hung around Sten's neck, concealed by a ragged towel. It would be impossible for either of the guards in the towers nearby to keep track of how many prisoners went into the privy and how many came out.

The privy sat over a deep and dank excrement-filled pit. The building itself was a shed, with a water trough down one side and the privy seats—circular holes cut into a long slab-cut lumber box—on the other. Sten and Alex clambered *into* one of those holes. On either side of the box, on the inside, they had hammered in spikes a few days earlier.

Both of them had root fiber nose plugs stuffed in place. The plugs did no good whatsoever. Just hang on, Sten thought. Do no faint. Do not think whether that arachnid that's crawling up your arm is poisonous. Just hang on.

Finally the curfew siren shrieked, and the prisoner sounds subsided. Footsteps thudded, and one privy door opened. The guards, for olfactory reasons, only checked cursorily.

It would have been best for Sten and Alex to wait until the middle of the night before moving, but they had kilometers to travel before dawn. At full dark, they levered themselves out of their hiding places and grimaced at each other.

The next step was up to Colonel Virunga.

It started with shouts and screams and laughter. Sten and Alex saw the searchlight sweep over the cracks in the privy roof, toward one of the barracks. They slid out the privy door.

In theory, they should not have been able to go any farther. The camp was sealed with an inner barrier of wire, a ten-meter-wide "no-go" passage, and then the outer wire.

The tower guards swept the compound with visual search-lights, far more dangerous light-amplification scopes, and fo-cused-noise sensors. By assignment, one guard should have been on each detector.

But the guards were lazy. Why, after all, was it necessary for three men to work a tower, especially at night? There was no escape from the camp. Even if one of the Imperials man-aged to get out, there was nowhere for him to go—the peas-ants surrounding the camp were promised large rewards for the return of any escapees in any condition, no questions to be asked. And even if an Imperial managed to slip past the farmers, where would he go? He was still marooned on a world far inside the Tahn galaxies.

And so a bright guard had figured a way to slave all three sensors to a single unit. Only one guard was required to moni-tor all three of them.

So when Virunga ordered the carefully orchestrated ruckus to start inside one of the barracks and a guard swung his spot-light, all sensors on that tower pointed away from the two scuttling blobs of darkness that went to the wire.

There were three strands of wire to cut before Sten and Alex could slip through into the no-go passage, three razored strips of plas. Sten's knife would make that simple. But those dangling strands would be spotted within a few minutes. And so, very carefully, Alex had collected over the past several cycles twelve metalloid spikes.

Sten's knife nerve-twitched out of its fleshy sheath. Very gently he punched two holes side by side on a razor strip. Alex pushed the spikes through them, then used his enormous strength to force the spikes into the plas barrier posts. With the strip thus nailed in place, Sten cut the wire. One . . . two . . . three . . . slip through the gap . . . repin the wire . . . and they were in the no-go passageway.

Across that, and again they cut and replaced the wire.

For the first time in three years Sten and Alex were outside the prison camp, without guards.

The temptation to leap up and run was almost overwhelming. But instead they crawled slowly onward, fingers feathering in front of them, expecting sensors and screaming alarms.

There were none.

They had escaped.

All that remained was getting offworld.

CHAPTER FOUR

"NOW . . . WHERE THE hell is that clottin' sentry?" Sten whispered.

"Dinna be fashin' Horrie, m' lad," Alex growled.

Horrie. Somehow Alex not only had managed to make Sten a lower-rank but had found a diminutive for Horatio.

"You'll pay."

"Aye," Alex said. "But th' repayment ae a' obligation dinna be ae gay ae th' incurrin't ae it."

Sten did not answer. He stared at the dispatch ship, sitting less than 100 meters from their hilltop hiding place.

Sten and Alex had discovered a potential way off the planet

when they were assigned to a work detail on the prison world's landing field. They had both observed and noted a small four-man dispatch ship, once state of the art but now used for shuttle missions between worlds. The ship might have been obsolete, but it had both Yukawa and Anti-Matter Two drives. All they had to do was steal the ship.

Once Sten and Alex were beyond the camp's wire, it should have been simple for them to sneak the few kilometers from the camp to the landing field. But it took more hours than they had allowed. Neither of them realized that one of the corollary effects of malnutrition was night blindness.

And so, in spite of their Mantis skills, they found themselves stumbling through the dark as if they were untrained civilians. Only their reflexive abilities from Mantis on night and silence moves kept them from being discovered as they crept past the peasant farms surrounding the prison camp.

"While we be hain't ae sec," Alex said, "whidny y' be likin't Ae tellin't th' aboot th' spotted snakes?"

"If you do that, I shall assassinate you."

"Th' lad hae nae sense a' humor," Alex complained to the sleeping reek in the tiny box in front of them. "An' here com't thae ace boon coon."

Below them, the sentry ambled across their field of view.

The airfield security was complex: a roving sentry, a wire barricade, a clear zone patrolled by watch animals, a second wire barricade, and internal electronic security.

With the sentry's passage logged and timed, Sten and Alex went forward. They crawled just to the first wire barricade. Alex patted the small box.

"Nae, y' wee't stinkard, go thou an' earn th' rent."

He flipped the top open, and the reek sprang out. Fuddled by its new environment, it wandered through the wire, into the clear zone. Then it sat, licking its fur, wondering where water would be, and waking up. Its slow thought processes were broken by a snarl.

The caracajou—three meters on three dimensions of fur-covered lethality—waddled forward. The skunk bear was angry, which was the normal disposition of its species. But the crossbreeding and mutation to which the Tahn had subjected its forebearers made the mammal even angrier. It dully reasoned that two-legs was its only enemy, and somehow it was forced to be kindly to those two-legs who fed it yet destroy any other two-legs. Also, it was kept from breeding and from finding its own territory.

This caracajou had spent five years of its life walking up and down a wire-defined corridor, with nothing to release its anxieties.

And then, suddenly, there was the reek.

The skunk bear bounded forward—according to instincts and general piss-off.

The reek—also according to instincts and general piss-off —whirled, curled its worm tail over its back, and sprayed.

The spray from its anal glands hit the caracajou on its muzzle. Instantly the creature rose to its hind paws, howled, and, trying to scrub the awful smell from its nostrils, stumbled away, one set of conditioning saying find shelter, the second saying find the two-legs that can help.

The reek, satisfied, hissed and scuttled off.

"Th' stink't tool work't," Alex whispered.

Sten was busy. Once again the barrier wire was drilled, pinned, and then, after the two crawled past, replaced.

The ship sat in sleek blackness, less than fifty meters away. Neither man went forward. Alex slowly reached inside his ragged tunic, took out four segmented hollow tubes, each less than one centimeter in diameter, and put them together. That made a blowpipe nearly a meter long. At its far end, Alex clipped on a pierced fish bladder, which was filled with finely pulverized metal dust.

Kilgour put the tube to his lips, aimed the blowpipe at a bush, and blew. The invisible dust drifted out, collected around the bush, and settled. Both men went nose into the dirt and thought *invisible*. Minutes later, the Tahn patrol charged up. Then they stopped and milled about.

In their initial casing of the escape, Sten and Alex had noted that inside the field's perimeter were electronic detectors. They theorized that from a distance the detectors would be fairly simple: probably radar-based. This was, after all, a world far behind the front lines.

The Tahn corporal commanding the patrol lifted his com.

"Watch . . . this is Rover. We are in the suspect area, clear."

"Rover . . . Watch. Are there any signs of intrusion?"

"This is Rover. Hold."

The overage and overweight corporal used his torch to scan the ground. "Rover. Nothing."

"This is Watch. Are you sure? Sensors still show presence in area."

"Clot if I know," the corporal complained. "But there's clottin' nothing we can see."

"Rover, this is Watch. Maintain correct com procedure. Your inspection of site recorded . . . your report logged that no intrusion has been made. Return to guard post. Watch. Over."

"Clottin' wonderful," the corporal grumbled. "If there's nobody out here, we done something wrong. If there's somebody out here, we're gonna get the nail. Clot. Detail . . . form up."

The Tahn guards doubled away.

Very, very good, Sten thought. The metallic spray that Alex had blown onto a bush had obviously registered on the nearest sensor. An alert squad had been sent out and had found nothing. Yet the sensor continued to show the presence of something alien. Therefore, that sensor's reports would be ignored until a repair person fixed that sensor.

And Sten and Alex had free passage to the dispatch ship.

The port was not locked. Alex went to the rear of the ship, while Sten headed for the control room. The unanswered question was whether he could fly it.

The controls were very, very simple.

Sten was in the pilot's chair, touching controls, when Alex rumbled into the tiny command center.

"Tha's nae fuel," he said.

Sten muttered four unmentionables and touched computer keys. Yes, there was fuel. Enough to lift them off into space. Enough to boost them into stardrive. Enough fuel to . . .

He fingered keys on the navcomputer. Enough to take them out of Tahn space?

Negative.

He slammed the control panel off and spun. "And all of this is for nothing."

"Nae, nae, lad," Alex said. "Ah hae checked the fuelin't records. This ship'll gae a' topoff in three days. All we hae t' do is seal it, gae back through th' wire, an' then home, an' wait f'r it aye beat. Can we noo come back again?"

Go back through the wire. Go back through the paddies. Go back to the three-year-long hell of the prison camp.

They could not.

But they did.

Sten and Alex slid through the wire, through the guards, and into the camp and their barracks close to dawn. All they wanted was to drift back among the sleeping prisoners and get a few moments of sleep. Instead, they found the prisoners awake.

The explanation came quickly.

The furor that Colonel Virunga had set up to cover their escape had provoked revenge. Revenge was a surprise roll call for all prisoners, with the guards checking each Imperial by name, finger- and poreprint, and visual recognition. There was no way for Virunga or any other prisoners to be able to cover that intensive a check.

Of course, the guards knew, Sten and Alex could not have escaped—their check of the perimeter proved that. But the two must be hidden somewhere, preparing to escape. Perhaps digging a tunnel.

It did not matter.

Colonel Virunga gave Sten and Alex the word: When they reappeared, they were to be purged. Along with Colonel Virunga—he somehow had to be connected with their nonappearance.

Sten and Alex eyed each other. They would never be able to make the second attempt to get that dispatch ship. Their next destination would be the mining world and death.

They were wrong—courtesy of the supreme rulers of the Tahn.

CHAPTER FIVE

THE TWENTY-SEVEN MEMBERS of the Tahn High Council slumped in bored inattention as their elder secretary droned through another day's legislation.

"... HCB No. 069-387. Titled: Negative Pensions. Arguments for: A graduated tax on guaranteed incomes for retirees —not to exceed 115 percent—will relieve a heavy burden on the state and result in key military enlistments. Arguments against: None."

The elder secretary did not bother to look up as he asked the routine question. "Opposed?" There was the usual silence. "Then it's unanimous."

"Next. HCB No. 434-102. Titled: Fuel Allotments. Subsection Medical Emergencies. Arguments for increase: The commandeering of private emergency vehicles for military use without compensation is proving an undue hardship on an already overburdened civilian health care system. Staff recommendation: No increase."

Once again the routine question. And once again silence indicated unanimity. It was the way the business of governing had always been done. However, the lords and ladies of the Tahn High Council were hardly mere rubber stamps for their chairman, Lord Fehrle. On the contrary, each member had very strong opinions and powerful allies. Otherwise, they would not have been named to the council.

Lord Fehrle was their chairman as the result of a delicate balancing act. Over the years he had shored up his position through key appointments. For instance, he had recently raised Lady Atago from associate status to full member. True, she was a military hero. Still, she had her detractors.

He glanced over at Colonel Pastour as the secretary mumbled on. Sometimes he thought his decision to support the old colonel's appointment a mistake. It was not that the industrialist was outwardly difficult. He just seemed to have a way of asking innocent questions that were difficult to answer. More importantly, he was, as time went by, becoming a voice Fehrle could not always depend on.

Hmmm. How to deal with Pastour? The problem was that Pastour not only was a successful industrialist, he was also a miracle worker in finding new bodies to hurl at the Empire. He also carried the expenses of many regiments out of pocket. Perhaps it would be better to live with the old man for a while longer.

Then there was Lord Wichman. Absolutely loyal. Absolutely committed. That was his problem. He was an absolutist who knew nothing of the art of compromise. It was a fault that several times had nearly upset Fehrle's balancing act.

Compromise was the key to Tahn politics. All proposals were discussed in labored detail before any meeting. All viewpoints were considered and, whenever possible, included in the eventual program under consideration. With rare exceptions, all decisions were therefore unanimous.

Unanimity was as necessary to the Tahn as breathing. They were a warrior race who had suffered humiliating defeat in their ancient past and had been forced to flee across eons past the fringes of the Empire to their present home. It was a place no one wanted except for the natives, who proved reluctant to move aside for the Tahn. Genocide convinced them of their faulty logic.

Slowly the Tahn rebuilt themselves, and in the rebuilding of their warrior society they created a new racial purpose. They would never again flee. And someday they would revenge their humiliation. Meanwhile, it was necessary to prove themselves.

They turned to their neighbors. First one, then another, and then more and more fell to the Tahn. They used two skills for those victories: a native genius for negotiation as a screen for bloody intent, and a resolve to win at all costs. At times their wars required a sacrifice of up to eighty percent of their military. After each war the Tahn quickly regrouped and struck out again.

It was only a matter of time before they bumped into the Eternal Emperor. The result once again was war.

"...HCB No. 525-117. Untitled. No arguments. Opposed?"

The silence was broken.

"Not opposed, exactly. But I do have one question."

The other twenty-six members of the council were startled out of their boredom into absolute shock. First, an untitled High Council bill was always a personal proposal from a council member. Such a bill would not even be presented if there was the slightest controversy. Second, and even more shocking, was the identity of the questioner.

It was not Pastour for once. It was Wichman. And the number 525 meant that it was Pastour's bill. All the members of the council leaned forward, eyes glittering in anticipation of a battle of a different sort. Only Fehrle, as chairman, and Lady Atago remained aloof. Atago had a soldier's disdain for politics of any kind.

Pastour leaned back in his seat, waiting.

"Now, as I understand the proposal," Wichman said, "we are creating a program in which we will rely on prisoners of war to build our weapons. Am I right so far?"

"Poorly put," Pastour said, "but basically correct. What is your question?"

"Simply this: A soldier who surrenders is a coward. True?" Pastour nodded in agreement. "Cowardice is an infectious thing. I fear we may be taking a grave risk with the morale of our own work force."

Pastour snorted. "There is no risk at all," he said. "If you had bothered to read my plan, you would not have asked the question."

"I read your proposal," Wichman said flatly. "And I still ask it."

Pastour sighed. He realized that Wichman was intentionally putting him on the spot. He wondered what kind of compromise he would have to offer and whether it would doom the success of his plan.

"Then you certainly deserve an answer," he said, trying and failing to keep an edge of sarcasm out of his voice. "The problem we seek to address is simply described but thus far difficult to solve.

"We have factories and material in barely sufficient quantities to fight this war. But we have less than half of the work force required to man the machines.

"I'm mainly a businessman. I see a problem, I immediately assume there is some way to fix it. A lot of times the solution is found in another problem. And with luck, you can fix two things at once."

"Such as?"

"I looked for a surplus of people. I found it in our prisoner-of-war camps. But that is only the tip of the matter. Our worst shortages are in the technical skills. So, not just any POW would do. Where to find the largest pool of untapped skills? Among the troublemakers, of course. Especially the habitual troublemakers."

"Where is the logic in that? A difficult prisoner equals a skilled being?" Wichman asked.

"The logic is simple. If these prisoners are still alive after all this time, then our prison officials must have had good reason not to have them killed. Those were my instincts, and after study, my instincts proved correct.

"Regardless. I'm satisfied, and as far as I know, my lord, so are the other members of the council."

Wichman ignored that. "So you're guaranteeing us that this program of yours will solve the problem."

"I'm not guaranteeing anything," Pastour gritted out. That was one trap he would not spring. "First off, the program is experimental. If it doesn't work, it affects nothing, especially since I am paying for it out of my own pocket."

"Good. Very good. You have answered almost all of my questions. But I still have one small worry."

"Which is?"

"The staffing of the first prison. I note a lack of hard experience in this field."

Here it is at last, Pastour thought. Wichman wanted a man in some key position. Was it someone Pastour's people could live with? There was no time to find out. He had to make up his mind quickly.

"Perhaps you could help in that area, my lord," he purred.

"Delighted," Wichman said.

There was immediate relaxation around the table.

"Once again," the elder secretary said, "is anyone opposed?"

In an instant HCB No. 525-1717 was law. Lady Atago put another check mark on her agenda. There were half a dozen items to go before it was her turn to face the Tahn High Council. Although it would be her debut report as a full member of the body, she was not nervous at all.

Atago had a list of facts to present on the war. It did not matter to her whether the facts underscored gloom or optimism. The emotions the report elicited from her colleagues was not her concern.

It was plain to her that they were quickly approaching a crucial point in the war. And it should have been equally clear to the others that the way events played out in the near future would determine the eventual winner and loser. She was confident, however, that the plan she and Lord Fehrle had already partially implemented would assure the Tahn of final victory.

"... a special report from Lady Atago ... I'm sure we will all ..."

Atago did not bother listening to the routine platitudes from the elder secretary. When she heard her name, she stood.

She was an imposing figure even among a group of beings not easily impressed, and she was well aware of that fact. She was much taller than most Tahn, and she wore her hair in a dark spill almost to her waist. Her eyes were large, her lips generous, and she had a lush body set off perfectly by her tight-fitting uniform.

Only the very stupid were fooled by her sensuous looks. Lady Atago's sole passion was war.

"My lords, my ladies," she said. "You will have my full report before you shortly, so I won't bore you with a lengthy summary of its contents. You can review the facts later at your leisure. Here, in brief, is where we find ourselves:

"From the beginning, we have managed to always take the war to the enemy. We have won vast areas from the Empire.

"There are two key reasons for our success. First: We are always willing to risk all. Second: The very size of the Emperor's military machine has worked to our advantage. By the time his forces react, it has been too late. This is an advantage we are about to lose."

That got Lady Atago the full attention of the council.

"Here are the basic reasons," she went on. "One. At this moment in time, each success brings an equal burden. Our supply lines are stretched well beyond any safety factor. We are wasting valuable resources garrisoning new territories. Two. The Emperor's intensive efforts to shift from a peacetime to a wartime industrial economy are about to bear fruit. Soon we will not only be outgunned but outmaneuvered because of the sheer size and number of his fleets."

She paused to let that sink in. Then it was time to spell out the plan.

"Before this can happen, we need to find a place to sink our knife. Lord Fehrle and I are confident we have found it."

Atago palmed a switch, and the far wall shimmered into a vidscreen. The council members leaned forward when they saw the starmaps. They were looking at two systems in relative proximity. There was nothing that unusual about them— except that they were deep inside the Empire.

The first system, Lady Atago explained, was called Al-Sufi, a major depot for Anti-Matter Two, the fuel that powered the Empire—and the Tahn. It was not necessary for Atago to explain that the Eternal Emperor's control of all AM2 made him the ultimate ruler.

"Obviously, Al-Sufi is a prime target," she said. "For some time now, we have been building up our forces in that area. And if we captured it, the setback to the Emperor would probably be fatal."

"Isn't that also obvious to the Emperor?" Pastour asked.

"We hope so," Lady Atago said. "Because the buildup I spoke of is only on paper. It is a shadow buildup. A fake."

"I don't understand," Wichman said.

"Without arousing suspicion, we have allowed the Imperial Forces to believe that we intend to attack Al-Sufi. And we have confirmed reports that the Emperor is responding with an equal buildup at Al-Sufi. Now, let me show you our *real* target!"

They saw a tight view of the second system, Durer. It was also a well-known area, as important to industry and transport as Al-Sufi was to the handling and storage of AM2.

"As you can see, the buildup at Al-Sufi has left Durer exposed. It is ours for the taking."

It was not necessary to explain to the others what that would do. A warrior race could instantly see when the enemy had been outflanked.

From Durer the Tahn High Council could see the beating red heart of the Empire. All they had to do was give Lady Atago permission to use her dirk.

The vote was unanimous.

CHAPTER SIX

GENERAL IAN MAHONEY hobbled down the long paneled corridor, gritting his teeth in pain as he tried to keep up with the two Gurkhas who were escorting him to the quarters of the Eternal Emperor. He imagined he could feel the plas and metal brackets grating against the bones they were supposed to support.

A door hissed open, and someone rushed out, almost colliding with Mahoney. He cursed at his clumsiness as he nearly fell. Ian, he told himself, you have the gait of a three-legged horse at a steeplechase. Mahoney recovered and moved on. He was deep in the bowels of Arundel Castle, or what was left of it, anyway. Aboveground what had once been an oversize replica of a graceful Earth castle was blackened ruins—victim of a surprise nuclear attack by the Tahn. Even now, there were still pockets of intense radiation.

The Tahn had hoped to wipe out the Emperor with one daring attack on Prime World. They could not know that the castle was an elaborate facade for the bombproof Imperial nerve center many kilometers beneath the surface. The Emperor ground their failure in many times a day. Every news broadcast emanating from Arundel began and ended with a shot of the ruins. Two flags fluttered bravely overhead. One was the shining standard of the Empire. Beneath it was the Emperor's household banner: gold, with the letters "AM2" superimposed over the null element's atomic structure. Mahoney could almost imagine the Emperor's chuckle over that far from subtle bit of propaganda.

He had mixed feelings about seeing his old boss and, he guessed, friend. Careful, Mahoney, he warned himself. Being a friend of the Eternal Emperor was a decidedly mixed blessing. It was friendship, more than duty, that had led him to his present rotten state of being.

The Tahn's final assault on Cavite had left him shattered and nearly dead. He had no idea how he had survived, although he expected it had something to do with his protégé, young Sten. Mahoney had come to woozy consciousness many months later and immediately had had second thoughts about the highly overrated business of living. Over the next few years he went under the surgeons' laser scalpel more times than any being ought to have to remember. He supposed they had performed what any casual observer would have called a major medical miracle, piecing him back together to a semiwhole.

Despite their efforts, Mahoney felt many more years than his middle age. What was hardest to get used to was not the nagging pain. It was his face. One side displayed what he had once believed to be the dignified gullies and edges of a long and interesting life. The other was baby-bottom smooth. The doctors had assured him that the plasflesh was programmed to gradually match the elder side. Mahoney did not believe them —although he had to admit that four months ago his jaw had not worked, either. Now it did, after a painful fashion.

Mahoney did not have the faintest idea why the Emperor had requested his presence. He suspected they were still friends enough that the Emperor might want to personally break the news to him that he was getting the old heave-ho into early retirement. What the clot, half pension for a two-star general was not bad. Besides, he could always get another job, couldn't he?

Give it a rest, Ian. Killing people is not considered one of
the more desirable skills in private industry.

He came back to reality when the Gurkhas stopped in front
of an unmarked door. They motioned for him to place his
thumb against the security beam. It beeped satisfaction, and
the door hummed open.

Mahoney stepped into the Emperor's suite. There was no
one there to greet him, just gray walls and Spartan furniture.
Mahoney figured his first guess had been right. He was for the
old heave-ho.

Then another door opened, and Mahoney was suddenly
overwhelmed by kitchen smells and kitchen heat. It was like
being inside an immense Irish meat pie. And there was the
muscular figure of the Eternal Emperor standing in the doorway. He looked Mahoney up and down as if measuring him
for the pie. Old soldier's habit tried to pull Mahoney's creaking bones to attention. Then the Emperor smiled.

"Mahoney," he said. "You look like a man who could use a
stiff Scotch."

* * *

"I tell you, Mahoney, this Tahn business has given me a
whole new outlook on life. When I finally get them out of my
hair, things are going to be different. I don't know if you
know it or not, but the job of Eternal Emperor is not all it's
cracked up to be."

Mahoney grinned a crooked grin. "Uneasy lies the head,
and all that," he said.

The Emperor looked up from his chopping board. "Do I
detect a note of cynicism?" he asked. "Careful, Mahoney. I
have the power of Scotch."

"Beg your pardon, boss. My most grievous error."

They were in the Eternal Emperor's kitchen, which looked
like a ship's wardroom mess area. The Emperor was not
happy about that, preferring his old kitchen with its mixture of
antique cooking gear and redesigned modern equipment. But
this, he had told Mahoney, was adequate for his current needs.
Besides, he had not had much time lately to fool around with
cooking.

Mahoney was sitting at a stainless-steel table, a double shot
glass in his hand. The Emperor was on the other side, prepar-

ing a dinner that he had promised Mahoney was perfectly suited to a war motif.

He called it "nuked hen." Between them was a quart of the home-distilled spirits that the Emperor thought might be pretty close to Scotch. The Emperor topped their glasses up and took a sip before going back to his task. As he worked, he talked, shifting back and forth between subjects with a logic unique to him.

"I don't remember the real name of this dish," he said. "It was part of a whole phony Louisiana cooking fad that went back even before my time."

Mahoney guessed that Louisiana was a province on ancient Earth.

"Apparently some people thought food wasn't food unless you burned the clot out of it. It didn't make sense to me, but I've learned over the years not to be too quick about judging folk beliefs. So I tried a few things."

"And it was all delicious, right?" Mahoney asked.

"No. It was all terrible," the Emperor said. "First, I thought it was me. I burned everything. My granddad would have killed me if he had seen all the food I wasted. Finally, I worked out a few ground rules. You just can't go around burning *anything*."

"Like potatoes," Mahoney said. "A man wouldn't want to burn a potato."

The Eternal Emperor gave Mahoney a strange look. "Who was talking about potatoes?"

Mahoney just shook his head. He lifted his glass and worked the edge between his lips. He tilted his head back and drank it down. He was beginning to feel a lot better. He re-filled his glass.

"I was just being silly," he said.

The Emperor grew silent for a few minutes, going on automatic. Using his fingers and the hollow of his palm as measuring spoons, he dumped the following ingredients into a bowl: a pinch of fresh cayenne; two fingers of ground salt, ground pepper; a palm of dried sage, and finely diced horse-radish. He moved the bowl over to his big black range. Already sitting beside it was a bottle of vodka, fresh-squeezed lime juice, a half cup of capers, and a tub of butter.

The Emperor took a fat Cornish game hen out of a cold box and placed it on the metal table. He found a slim-bladed boning knife, tested the edge, and then nodded in satisfaction. He turned the hen over, back side up, and started his first cut alongside the spine. He paused for a second, then laid the knife down.

"Let me run something down to you, Mahoney," he said. "See if it comes out to you the same way it does to me."

Mahoney leaned forward, interested. Maybe he would finally learn why he was really there.

"You familiar with the Al-Sufi System?"

Mahoney nodded. "Big AM2 depot, among other things," he said. "We've got, what, maybe one-third of all our AM2 stored there?"

"That's the place," the Emperor said. "And lately I've been getting reports of a big Tahn buildup in that area. Not all at once. But a real gradual shifting of fleets from one sector to another. We're also picking up a lot of radio chatter from supply ships."

Mahoney nodded in professional sympathy. "Those buggers are all alike," he said. "Tahn or Imperial. Can't follow even the simplest rules of security." He worked on his drink, thinking. "So, what's the problem? If we *know* they're going to hit us, then we've got the fight half-won before the first shot is even fired."

"That's so," the Emperor said. Then he picked up his knife again, leaving the whole subject hanging. "You might want to watch this, Ian," he said. "Boning a hen is easy when you know how, but you can chop the clot out of it and yourself if you don't."

Very carefully, the Emperor cut on either side of the spine. He pushed a finger through the slit and pulled the bone up through the carcass. Next, he laid the hen flat, placed a hand on either side of spine, and crunched down with his weight.

"See what I mean?" he said as he lifted the breastbone out.

"I'm impressed," Mahoney said. "But never mind that. I've got the idea *you* aren't too impressed with this intelligence you've been getting on the Tahn."

The Emperor moved over to his range and fired up a burner.

"You guessed right," he said. "But I don't blame my intelligence people. I think the Tahn have something entirely different in mind for us."

"Such as?"

"Al-Sufi has a neighbor. Durer."

"I've heard of it, vaguely."

"You put a dog's leg on Al-Sufi," the Emperor said, "and you'll find Durer on a bearing just about at the dog's big toe."

Mahoney remembered and grunted in surprise. "Why, that's only . . ."

"If you stood on Durer," the Emperor said, "you could just about reach here with a good healthy spit."

That would have been one mighty spit, but Mahoney basically agreed.

"Assuming you're right," Mahoney said, "and the Tahn are trying to make us respond to shadows, then if they took Durer, we could kiss any forces we have at Al-Sufi a fond but regretful farewell. To say nothing of the fact that we'd have zed between us and the Tahn."

"Interesting, isn't it?"

"What do you plan to do about it?"

"First, I'm going to burn the clot out of this hen," the Emperor said, turning to his range. "The whole trick is getting your pan hot enough."

Mahoney leaned closer to watch, figuring that what was on the menu had everything to do with the Emperor's plans for the Tahn.

The Emperor turned the flame up as high as it would go and then slammed on a heavy cast-iron pan. In a few moments, the pan began to smoke, and fans in the duct above the range whirred on. A few moments more, and the pan stopped smoking.

"Check the air just above the fan," the Emperor said. "It's getting wavery, right?"

"Right."

"As the pan gets hotter, the air will wave faster and faster until the whole interior is a steady haze."

The haze came right on schedule.

"So it's ready now?" Mahoney asked.

"Almost. But not quite. This is the place most people foul

up. In a minute or two, the haze will clear and the bottom of the pan should look like white ash."

As soon as the ashen look appeared, the Emperor motioned for Mahoney to duck back. Then he dipped out a big chunk of butter, dumped it into the pan, and moved out of the way. Mahoney could see why as flames flashed above the pan. As soon as they died down, the Emperor moved swiftly forward and poured the spices out of the bowl and into the pan. He gave the mixture a few stirs in one direction, then the other. Next he tossed in the Cornish game hen. A column of smoke steamed upward in a roar.

"I give it about five minutes each side," the Emperor said. "Then I spread capers all over it and toss the hen into the oven for twenty minutes or so to finish it off."

"I sort of get the idea," Mahoney said, "that you're in the process of heating up a pan for the Tahn."

The Emperor thought that was pretty funny. He chuckled to himself as he dumped the thoroughly blackened hen into a baking dish. On went the capers, and into the oven it went— at 350 degrees. He cranked the flames down on the range, shoved the pan of drippings back on the fire, and stirred in two Imperial glugs of vodka and a quarter glug of lime juice. He would use the mixture to glaze the hen when it came out of the oven.

"You're right," the Emperor finally said. "I've been playing the same game with them. On paper I've been moving forces from all over the map to the Al-Sufi region."

"But actually, they'll be waiting for the Tahn at Durer," Mahoney said.

"That's the plan," the Emperor said.

Mahoney was silent for a moment.

"Question, boss. What if there really is a Tahn buildup at Al-Sufi? What if we're wrong?"

The Emperor busied himself with some spears of asparagus. He planned to steam them in a little thyme butter and dry white wine.

"I've been wrong before," he said.

"But can you afford to be wrong this time?"

"No," the Eternal Emperor said, "I can't. That's why you're here."

He fished into his pocket and handed over a small black jewelry case. Mahoney opened it. Inside were two rank tabs —the rank tabs of a fleet marshal.

"When the attack comes," the Emperor said, "I want you leading my fleets."

Mahoney just stared at the stars resting on velvet. He could not help but remember the last time he had gotten his orders straight from the Emperor. Those had been the orders that had led him to Cavite.

"Will you do it for me?" the Emperor pressed.

Fleet Marshal Ian Mahoney had difficulty finding his voice. He assumed command of the fleets at Durer with a simple nod.

CHAPTER SEVEN

THE HUGE TAHN prison transport ship hissed down onto Heath, the capital world of the Tahn systems. After proper security was set, ports whined open and the prisoners debarked.

Sten and Alex marveled as they clanked down a gangway wearing heavy, archaic, and useless leg and arm irons, with weighted plas chains between them. They had expected to be unloaded onto the Tahn mining deathworld. Instead—

"W' been here before," Alex whispered, using that motionless mouth and jaw whisper that all professional prisoners learn.

"Yeah."

Lord Pastour's dictate might have come from the all-highest, but the Tahn bureaucrats still found a way to take their half kilo of flesh. A single Tahn transport was dispatched to all the prison worlds to pick up those incorrigible war prisoners who were to be purged into the new prison. It was a slow, filthy transport.

Therefore, when the transport unloaded, the best and the sneakiest did not appear such as they clanked out, smelling like drakh, unbathed, uncombed, surly, and snarling.

The only measure of respect they had, although none of the prisoners realized it, was that armed Tahn soldiers flanked their passage through the streets of Heath at five-meter intervals. Those guards were the combat element of an entire Tahn assault division whose deployment to a combat zone had been delayed by three weeks merely so that a motley 1,000 scruffy men, women, and beings could be led to their new prison.

Sten clanked forward, head down, hands down, shuffling as the chains clanked—the perfect picture of a properly programmed prisoner. But his eyes flicked from side to side, observing as subtly as Alex's commentary had been delivered.

"Clottin' Heath," he whispered.

"Na," Alex whispered back. "Th' last time we bein't on this world thae were gladdins an' parties."

"Try war, you clot."

And Alex observed the city with new eyes.

The last—and only—time they had been on Heath had been under cover, with instructions to find a murderer and extract him. But that had been years before, and just as Sten had suggested, war had ground Heath into grayness.

There were few vehicles to be seen—fuel was restricted to necessary military movements. The streets were deserted. Shops were boarded up or, worse, had few items in their windows. The rare Tahn civilian they saw either disappeared quickly from the streets or, seeing the solidiery, raised one ragged, whining cheer into the cold air and then scurried on about his or her business.

Their route led them through narrow streets, the streets climbing upward.

Sten's psywar mind analyzed: If you have the worst enemy scum in your hands, would you not arrange a triumphal parade? With all your citizens spitting and cheering because we have the barbarians in our hands? With full livie coverage? Of course you would. Why haven't the Tahn done that?

Exploratory thinking: They don't think like I do. Possible.

They can't muster the citizens on call. Wrong—any totalitarian state can do that. Maybe they don't want to show how badly the war is hurting them if they are presenting Heath as being the proud center of their culture and don't want offworlders to see the reality. Most interesting, and worth considering—

Sten's analysis was cut off as the column of prisoners was shouted to a halt and screaming Tahn soldiers ordered them to attention. Sten expected to see a float of combat cars move across the street in front of him. Instead, there was one cloaked officer, with flanking guards on foot, riding some kind of animal transport.

"What's that?"

"Clottin' hell," Alex whispered. "A bleedin' horse."

"Horse?"

"Aye. A Earth critter, w' nae th' brains ae a Campbell, tha' bites you an' is best used ae pet chow."

Sten was about to inquire further, but the officer in charge of the column ordered them forward again, and for the first time he looked up the cobbled narrow street.

His guts clamped shut.

At the top of the rise was a huge stone building. It sat atop the hill like a great gray monster, its towering walls reaching upward, capped by a ruined octagonal pinnacle that still reached some 200 meters toward the overcast sky.

Alex, too, was staring.

"Lad," he managed. "Ah dinnae think't th' Tahn are takin' us to church. Tha' be't our new home!"

CHAPTER EIGHT

KOLDYEZE CATHEDRAL HAD not been constructed by the Tahn. Their only religion was a vague sort of belief, unworshiped, in racial identity and racial destiny.

Koldyeze had been the Vatican for the first settlers on Heath, monotheistic, agrarian communards. They had spent nearly two centuries building their church atop the highest hill in their tiny capital.

Those settlers stood less than no chance when the first Tahn, then more roving barbarians than the self-declared culture they later became, smashed down on them. They were forcibly absorbed by the Tahn, their language forbidden to be spoken, written, or taught, their dress ridiculed, and their religion driven underground and finally out of existence.

The Tahn might not have been religious, but they were superstitious. No one quite knew what to do with the looming cathedral, and so it was surrounded with barbed fencing and posted for hundreds of years. Seventy-five years before, an out-of-control tacship had smashed off the spire's crown, and storms had battered the ruins.

But Koldyeze Cathedral was still a mighty work of man.

It was cruciform in design, stretching along its longer axis nearly two kilometers and along the shorter axis one kilometer. The center of the cross was the sanctuary and, above it, the remains of the bell tower. The shorter arms of the cross were roofed, but the longer arms held courtyards in their centers.

Koldyeze had been built as a self-sufficient religious community, even though the churchmen were not at all withdrawn from their society. When the Tahn had ordered Koldyeze abandoned, the pacifistic communards had systematically closed it down, sealing passageways and chambers as they went.

To the Tahn, Koldyeze seemed ideally suited to become a prison. Activating it required no drain on scarce building materials. The power drain from Heath's grid should be minimal. The assigned prisoners would provide the work crews to make the complex livable.

The northernmost short arm, where the main entrance to Koldyeze had been located, was sealed off from the other wings, and the chambers around its courtyard were set up as guard and administration quarters. The passage from the guard courtyard into the center sanctuary was set with detectors and triple gates.

Four rows of fencing with mines and detectors between each row surrounded Koldyeze.

Then, even though the security precautions were not complete, Koldyeze was ready for prisoners. The outer perimeter, after all, was sealed—and none of the Imperials could fly. Further antiescape measures would be added as time went by.

The Tahn believed that Koldyeze was escapeproof.

The Imperial prisoners straggling through the thick stone and steel gates looked about them and believed that somehow, somewhere, a clever being could manage to find freedom.

And there was no reason at all why it could not be one of them.

CHAPTER NINE

INSIDE THE COURTYARD, the Imperial prisoners were shouted and pummeled into a formation. Most interesting, Sten thought, as he analyzed the guards.

They looked much as he had expected and experienced in his previous camp: overmuscled bullyboys, semicrippled ex-

combatants, and soldiers too old or too young to be assigned
to the front.

Their obscenities and threats were also the same.

But none of them carried whips. They were armed with
truncheons or stun rods—which seemed mere pattypaw
weapons to the thoroughly brutalized prisoners. No projectile
weapons were being waved about. And no one had been
slammed to the ground with a rifle butt, which was the standard Tahn request for attention.

The main shouter wore the rank tabs of a police major. He
was a hulk of a man whose broad leather belt was losing its
battle with his paunch. As he roared orders, one hand kept
creeping toward his holstered pistol, then was forced away.
The man's face was amazingly scarred.

"Tha' be't ae screw," Alex whispered, lips motionless,
"thae hae plac'd second in a wee brawl wi' ae bear."

Eventually the formation looked adequate, and Colonel
Virunga limped to his place at its front. That had been one of
the few cheery notes of the long crawl through space on the
prison ship: Virunga was senior Imperial officer and would
therefore be in command of the prisoners in the new camp.

Virunga eyed his command and started to bring them to
attention. Then he caught himself.

Standing ostentatiously away from the prisoners was a single defiant being. He—she? it?—was about a meter and a
half in height and squatted on his thick lower legs as if early in
his race's evolution there had been a tail provided for tripodal
security. His upper arms were almost as large as his lower
legs, ending in enormous bone-appearing gauntlets and incon-
gruously slender fingers.

The being had no neck, its shoulders flowing into a taper-
ing skull that ended in a dozen pink tendrils that Virunga
guessed were its sensory organs. The being had once been fat,
with sleek fur. Now its ragged pelt draped down in togalike
folds over its body.

Colonel Virunga had been denied access to the prisoners'
records aboard ship, and of course there had not been time to
meet every one of the purged prisoners. But he wondered how
he had missed that one.

"Form up, troop."

"I am not a troop, and I shall not form up," the being squeaked. "I am Lay Reader Cristata, I am a civilian, I endorse neither the Empire nor the Tahn, and I am being unjustly held and forced to be a part of this machinery of death."

Virunga goggled. Did Cristata think that any of them had volunteered to be POWs? Even more wonderment: How had that paragon of resistance managed to survive in a prison camp so long?

The police major trumpeted incoherently, and two guards leapt toward Cristata, batons ready. But before they could pummel him to the ground, a large man wearing the tatters of an infantryman's combat coveralls grabbed Cristata by his harness and dragged him bodily into the formation. Evidently the use of force satisfied Cristata's objections, because he then remained meekly where planted.

"Formation . . . ten-hut."

Virunga about-faced, leaned on his cane, and stared up at a balcony on the third level. He could see two faces looking down at him from behind the barred, clear plas doors.

He waited for the prisoners' new lords and masters to make their appearance.

CHAPTER TEN

POLICE COLONEL DERZHIN was, in his own mind, despite his rank, neither a cop nor a military officer. Many years before, long before the war with the Empire, he had been a junior lieutenant in the Tahn ranks, assigned to a survey ship. Somehow one of the emergency oxygen containers on the ship's bridge had exploded, killing all four of the ranking officers and, worse, destroying the ship's navcomputer. Derzhin, the sole surviving officer, had taken command and managed—mostly by luck, he thought—to limp to an inhabited world.

The Tahn livies must have been hurting for a hero that week, because they made much of the lieutenant. Derzhin received a couple of hero medals and a promotion, but that did not aim him toward a career in the military. A year later, after the publicity had been forgotten, Derzhin quietly bought his way out of the service. His medals got him a lower-management job in one of Pastour's corporations.

Dezhin was promoted rapidly as he showed a rare talent for the proper utilization of personnel and available resources. Pastour once said that Derzhin could be put on an asteroid with six anthropoids and two hammers and, within a year, would have a prototype ship in the sky and three variant models on the production line.

Derzhin maintained his commission in the inactive reserve for the social clout it gave him in the business community. He was not, of course, antimilitary. He *was* a Tahn. He never questioned his race's moral recitude or the rightness of the war.

But he would rather not have been brought back into the military by the general call-up at its beginning. Nor was Pastour happy to lose his talents.

When Pastour realized that a very valuable, highly trained resource—the Imperial prisoners—was being wasted through high-principled flummery and saw a proper utilization for that resource, he immediately set out to get Derzhin to run the project.

He recognized that no executive, no matter how qualified, could instantly become a warden, and so he gave Derzhin backup.

His backup was Security Major Avrenti. Avrenti, too, was not a warden—experienced prison administrators were in high demand. Avrenti was one of the Tahn Empire's most skilled countersabotage specialists. Anyone who could prevent the planting of a minuscule bomb or the contamination of a war material or who could identify a potential saboteur long before he became active should have had no trouble keeping known malcontents imprisoned within a known and heavily guarded area.

Avrenti was physically unremarkable. Anyone who met him casually would forget his face minutes after his departure.

He would have made an excellent spy. He was soft-spoken and nonargumentative, preferring to win through reason and persistence. His one affectation was his wearing of archaic eyeglasses. When anyone asked why he had never had corrective surgery, implants, or replacements, he professed a dislike for medicos. Actually, he had vision very close to normal. He used his glasses as a stall, giving him time to consider the proper answer or policy, just as other beings used fingering devices, writing instruments, or the careful preparation and consumption of stimulants.

The two men looked down at their charges.

"I imagine," Derzhin said finally, "that I am expected to make some kind of speech."

"That seems to be requisite for a warden," Avrenti agreed.

Derzhin smiled slightly. "You know, Major, that part of business requires an ability to speak publicly."

"One of the many reasons I preferred to remain what I am," Avrenti said.

"Yes. I have spoken to lords and drunken roustabouts, but I cannot recollect ever having addressed war prisoners."

Avrenti did not comment.

"Actually," Derzhin mused, "it should be quite simple. All I need to do is suggest that they are here to work for the greater glory of the Tahn. If they perform, they shall be rewarded with seeing the next sunrise. If they resist, or attempt to escape . . . even an Imperial should see the logic in that."

Again Avrenti was silent.

"Do you agree, Major? Is that the correct approach? You are more familiar with military thinking than I."

"I can be of little assistance," the major said. "I do not understand the mind of a soldier who can find himself in the hands of the enemy and not seek self-extinction at the first opportunity."

Derzhin kept his expression and tone of voice quite neutral. "There is that, of course."

And he opened the balcony doors and stepped out.

Police Major Genrikh slammed back into his quarters, wanting to feel out of control.

He held the solid wood door ready to crash closed—then

caught himself. He pushed it shut softly. Then he tore off his Sam Browne belt, intending to hurl it. Again he stopped.

He had just witnessed a nightmare.

But should he give in to it? What was the likelihood that his quarters were not bugged? None. Genrikh would have bugged himself.

Instead, he carefully hung his harness over a chair, opened a cabinet, extracted a bottle, checked the bottle to see whether its level had been marked, drank deeply, and sank back on his bunk.

This was going to be a disaster.

Then he cheered himself. Hadn't he been warned? Hadn't he been told, first by Lord Wichman's cutout, then when he was duly if privately honored by a presence with the lord himself?

But still.

Genrikh ground his teeth against his bottleneck, producing a singularly unpleasant noise. He had spent half a lifetime as an expert penologist. He knew the way to handle the subbeings that committed crimes. Crime to him was anything that contradicted the Way of the Tahn, which he defined as anything that his current superior ordered.

Genrikh's mother was a whore; his father was a question mark. He had fantasized, growing up, that his father was a rising officer whose forced marriage had made him seek happiness in other quarters. That did not mean that he saw his mother as a fairy princess—but Genrikh's dreams were never very coherent.

Genrikh grew up feeling himself an outcast and fearing that someday he would be revealed for what he was and scorned. He was indeed scorned by his compatriots—scorned for being the first to toady to the newest bully, for being the first to inform on any minor offense, for being the first to volunteer for any superior-suggested idea.

He was the ideal prison official.

Genrikh, in spite of his obsessive concern with others' morals, had no problem acquiring anything and everything he could within the prison system. He was in his own dim-witted way a truly immoral being.

Needless to say, he rose rapidly in the Tahn prison system, so rapidly that he was chosen for greater things. Before the war, the Tahn Council had seen the emergence of unions among their exploited workers and had instantly realized the necessity to destroy anybody that did not represent their own best interests.

Genrikh was a natural choice to head company unions or to act as a strikebreaker or an informer.

But even the embryonic unions within the Tahn systems had eventually put out the word: Anyone matching Genrikh's description was pure trouble—trouble that, if it was convenient, should be deposited in the nearest paddy with many, many puncture wounds.

Genrikh's ultimate controller, Lord Wichman, chose not to discard his thug. Instead, he made him head of his personal bodyguard while trying to find a new place to deploy the man. Wichman knew that Genrikh was absolutely loyal to him. The man was ideal to insert into Pastour's scheme, no matter what it *really* was.

Genrikh, now calm, sipped from his bottle and considered what he would have done had he been appointed commandant of the prison. A good thing to think about. He smiled to himself. Because very, very soon he *would* be the commandant.

Yes.

You are in front of an assemblage of not only criminals but cowards and traitors, he told himself. Genrikh thought that anyone who did not kowtow to the Tahn was a traitor.

All right. You want technicians, he mused. But first you must bring them under control. Yes. Bring them into the courtyard at attention. Then select, at random, 100 of the Imperials—there were a thousand in that courtyard—and have them beaten to death.

No, he corrected himself. Select that 100 and then require the *others* to kill them. Kill them or be killed. Yes. That would produce the correct attitude.

Housing? Food? Nonsense. Let them live in fields and eat roots. Wasn't the clotting Empire rich with people, none of whom would *really* fight until they died? The resource should be exploited like cattle—use them until they drop, because there are many, many possible replacements.

Ah, well. Very soon Colonel Derzhin would learn his error and disappear.

Major Genrikh closed his eyes and began planning just exactly how he would be arranging *his* prison.

CHAPTER ELEVEN

AFTER COLONEL DERZHIN'S speech, the prisoners were marched from the guards' courtyard through the shattered sanctuary into their own area, brought to attention, and dismissed. They exploded out into the cathedral, exploring their new home.

For the first time in their long captivity, they were in a prison too large for them. The worst thing about jail to noninstitutionalized beings was the complete lack of privacy. There was never a moment to be alone. But now 1,000 malnourished beings, quartered in a complex intended to house 15,000 individuals, scattered to the winds.

Sten and Alex held a conference in the courtyard.

"Mr. Kilgour?"

"Aye, Firecontrolman Horrie?"

"Where's the best way to get out of this tomb?"

"Ah hae nae certainty. But Ah'd hazard th' east or west wing, or aught near th' sanctuary. Best luck, th' west wing, bein't near'st th' cliff edge."

"Right."

And they started looking for their own quarters in the southernmost, longest arm of the cathedral.

Escapers they were. Experienced escapers. Experienced enough to realize that under no circumstances did they want to have their own living quarters near the center of activities. They had once started a tunnel in their own bunkroom and learned the impossibility of peace and quiet when every twenty minutes bags of dirt, tunnelers, or guards were busting through.

After some searching, they found the place.

"Dinnae tha' be bonnie?" Alex asked happily.

Sten looked around the room. It was perfect. He mentally wrote the "For Rent" ad:

LARGE ROOM. 20 meters × 15 meters. Room to swing a cat. Bring own cat. Rats provided. Formerly office of moderate-level religious official of probably now-defunct order. Room includes VU, but without intrusive searchlights at night. SECOND STORY, avoiding prospective tunnelers, sports players from floor below, yet also two floors below roof, preventing annoyances from guards on roof, escapers on roof, rats on roof, or rain, considering roof only semipresent. INCLUDES: Remains of four beds, which possibly may be reconstructed into two bunks. Various dangling pieces of plas and metal. Ruins of desk. V/thick walls, not only soundproofed but may contain interesting passageways. POWER: Single bulb from ceiling, apparently wired into circuit. WATER: A close walk to nearby dispersing point. A REAL FIXER-UPPER. *Once visited, never left.*

Yes, Sten thought, and stopped being cute. Now, how the clot are we gonna get out of here? Alex was tapping the walls, checking for bugs. There were obviously none, and there was no way a shotgun mike could be trained on them through the chamber's tiny windows.

"Hae y' a call, Horrie, on our wee head screw?"

"Not yet."

"Ah. Noo, thae's why Ah be't a' warrant an y' be't a low firecontrolman. Ah ken th' man."

"I never argued you've got a future career in prisons," Sten said.

"Ah'm wee, nae slickit nae cowerin't, an Ah can still smash y'," Alex said. "Close th' yap, an listen: We're goin't t' be treated nice, ae long a' we dot-an'-carry f'r th' man. Now, m' question be: Do we cooperate?"

Kilgour was suddenly serious, and Sten was no longer a firecontrolman named Horatio. And he spoke as a commander and as Alex's CO.

"Yes," he said. "The clot is talking about using us in war industry. That's the stupidest idea I've heard lately."

"We can hae fun wi' that," Alex agreed.

"And as soon as we can, we're going out."

"We?"

"I don't know anybody here but you and Virunga. There may be doubles, there may be stoolies, there may be agents."

"Thae e'en may be Campbells."

"Don't bet on it. Even the Tahn have some standards."

"Y' hae ideas on how we'll blow th' place?"

"That's what you're for, Mr. Kilgour. That's why you're a warrant and I'm a clottin' firecontrol man."

Alex grinned, and the two fell back into their roles just as there was a thud on the door that might have been a gorilla knock. It was just about that—and it was also the senior officer, Colonel Virunga. Both men came to attention.

Virunga had little time for preambles.

"Tahn have made it . . . clear . . . cooperate. Drakh. Promise under duress . . . meaningless."

Sten and Alex did not need to show their agreement.

"Drakh. Drakh."

Sten's eyebrows lifted. He had never heard the N'ranya repeat a word. He must be quite angry.

"Duty . . . soldier . . . escape. Resist. Am I correct?"

A repeat—and a full sentence!

"Yessir."

"Knew . . . agree. Why you're now Big X."

Alex started to say something, and Sten waved him to silence.

"Colonel. You can't do this to me!"

"Just did."

"Goddammit. Why?"

The chain of command in any prison was complex and often unspoken, even in a military prisoner-of-war camp. Big X was part of that secret command link. The title was eons old, dating back to a time even before the Empire. Big X was the head of *all* escape attempts in a camp. His authority was absolute. Part of the hypno-training that all recruits into Imperial service received was "how to behave if you are captured." That conditioning included the obvious: Reveal nothing of military value until physically or mentally forced; do not volunteer services unless ordered; remember that although you are a prisoner you are still at war and are expected to continue to fight by any means available.

Continue to fight.

Escape.

Big X's orders, within the very narrow confines of escape attempts, superseded all others, including those of the senior Imperial officer. And once he was appointed, his authority was absolute. Big X, the head of the escape committee in any camp, could be any rank, private to fleet marshal. It was a dubious honor. If Big X was revealed to the captors, of course he would be skedded for immediate death, brainburn, or, at the very least, transport to a death-camp.

That was not Sten's objection.

The real objection was that Big X was normally picked because he or she was the most accomplished escaper or resister in a camp. But because all escape attempts had to be registered with his committee, he or she was honor-bound *not* to personally participate in any escape.

Colonel Virunga, by appointing Sten, had also ensured that he was doomed to be a POW until the end of the war. Or until the Tahn discovered the identity of Big X and had him killed.

Virunga answered Sten's question. "Because . . . trust. Known quantity. These others? Unknown."

There was no possible argument. Virunga saluted once more and left. Sten and Alex looked at each other. Neither of them could find any obscenities sufficient to the occasion, and neither of them felt that tears would be appreciated.

Very well, Sten thought. If I can't be a personal pain in the

butt to the Tahn, I'm going to create me 999 surrogates that'll
give the Tahn a rough way to go.

Nine hundred and ninety-eight, he corrected himself, looking at Alex. If I'm gonna be stuck here in this clottin' ruin for
the rest of the war, I'm gonna have at least one other clot for
company.

CHAPTER TWELVE

SENIOR CAPTAIN (INTELLIGENCE) Lo Prek stared at the battered
mail fiche on his desk.

A normal human being might have cheered, exulted at
closing on his enemy, or snarled in happy rage.

But to Prek, the mail fiche merely verified what he had
known: Commander Sten was not only still alive but within
Prek's reach.

He had come up with a unique method to check his theory,
a method that did not require either approval from his superiors or any out-of-the-ordinary efforts from Intelligence. He
had merely prepared a letter.

The letter was packeted in a routine drop to one of the Tahn
deep-cover agents within the Empire. The agent was instructed to deposit the letter normally and use a return address
of one of his safe houses.

The agent followed orders.

The letter purported to be from one Mik Davis. It was quite
a chatty missive.

Davis, according to the letter, had gone through basic
training with Sten. "Of course you don't remember me," the
letter began.

I got washed real quick and never got to the Guards. Instead they made me a baker. Guess, probably, they were right.

Anyway, nothing much happened to me. I served my term, making dough, and got out before the war started.

Got married—got three ankle-biters now—and started my own business. Guess what it is—prog you do—a bakery.

Compute you're laughing—but I'm making a credit or six. Guess I can't kick on what bennies I got from the service.

Anyway, here I am out in nowhere and I saw this old fiche, talking about some captain named Sten who's up there running the Imperial bodyguards. I always knew you were gonna rise to the top like yeast.

I told my lady, and she thought I was blowing smoke when I said I knew you back when. I decided I'd drop a line, and maybe you'd have time to get back to me.

Do me a real favor, if you would. Just scribble out a mininote so my lady doesn't think I'm a complete liar.

No way I can do paybacks, unless you show up on Ulthor-13, and we'll take you out for the best feed this planet's got. But I'd really appreciate it.

Yours from a long time back,
Mik Davis

That letter put Prek in a no-lose situation. If the letter was answered, he knew that Sten was still in the ranks of the Empire. If it went unanswered, he knew the same. It would have been delivered at least. Prek had a far greater faith in the Empire's mail system than did any of its citizens.

Instead, the mail fiche bounced, being returned to the Tahn agent in a packet with a very somber, very official, and very formal note.

Dear Citizen Davis

Unfortunately your personal letter to Commander Sten is undeliverable.

Imperial records show that Commander Sten is carried on Imperial Navy records as Missing in Action, during Engagements in the Fringe Worlds.

If you desire any further information, please communicate with . . .

Sympathetically . . .

Captain Prek felt that he had begun his self-assigned mission in an adequate manner.

Sten was not only alive but within reach.

A prisoner.

Prek refused to admit that Sten could have died of wounds or been killed in captivity. He was still alive.

He *must* still be alive.

Prek keyed his computer to begin a directory search for the records of all Imperial prisoners of war captured in the conquest of the Fringe Worlds. He felt he was getting very close to the murderer of his brother.

BOOK TWO

SUKI

CHAPTER THIRTEEN

THE FIRST ESCAPE attempt was go-for-broke.

Captain Michele St. Clair had watched closely for two weeks as the first working parties were formed, assigned tasks, and marched down into Heath. She thought she saw a possibility.

The procedure was rigid: After morning roll call, Major Genrikh would order X number of prisoners for Y number of outside duties. They would be broken down into gangs inside the prisoners' courtyard, and Tahn guards would take charge. Each detail would have, on the average, one noncom per ten prisoners and three guards per five POWs. The Tahn were being very careful.

The ethics of the work gangs were still being debated by the prisoners, a debate that St. Clair took no part in. The debate ran as follows: Participation, even unwillingly, contributed to the enemy. Nonparticipation, on the other hand, could contribute to the prisoner's own death. St. Clair thought both points nonsense—she knew that the eventual boredom of being in the prison would make people volunteer for any detail that was not actually pulling a trigger. And personally she was all in favor of the outside gangs. Once outside the cathedral, the possibilities of successful escape would be . . . she did not try to work out the exact odds, but she did not have to.

Michele St. Clair had grown up with an instinctive appreciation for the odds and was quite content with the comfortable, if somewhat hazardous, living a "gambler's share" gave her.

St. Clair, very young, had considered the various careers available on her native world, one of the Empire's main trans-shipment centers. Whoring or crewing on a spacecraft she saw as a mug's game, and running a bar kept one from being a

53

moving target. St. Clair had been a professional gambler from
the time she was tall enough to shove a bet across to a crou-
pier.

She learned how to play a straight game against the suckers
and how to shave the odds if she was playing with cheaters.
She knew when to get her money down, when to cut her
losses, when to fold a bet and get offworld, and, maybe most
importantly, when to stay out of the game itself. She was
broke many times and rich many more. But the credits themselves were meaningless to her, as to other professionals.
They were just markers on how well she was doing.

She had a hundred names on a thousand worlds, and nick-
names, as well. All of them related her to the same sort of
animal—a sleek, good-looking minor predator.

But for some years the odds had been coming back on her.

Since she preferred to gamble with the wealthy, she maintained a host of identities, all of them well-to-do if a little
mysterious. She was very fond of one of them—that of a
purchasing agent for the Imperial Navy. Since she had a certain respect for the laws of the Empire, she actually was an
officer in the Empire. Standby reserve, of course.

Unfortunately, St. Clair paid no attention to politics. When
war broke out, she was systematically cleaning out an upper-
class tourist world in her military role, a tourist world with a
medium-size garrison on it. St. Clair grudgingly admitted that
she might have done too good a job setting up her various
identities as unblowable, because no one would believe that
she was not actually a first lieutenant, Imperial Navy. Her
cover was so well constructed that three months later she was
promoted to captain and reassigned as executive officer on a
transport.

The convoy her ship was part of was ambushed by a Tahn
deep-strike destroyer force, and Michele St. Clair found herself a prisoner of war.

Fortunately, St. Clair was, like all gamblers, an inveterate
optimist. In the first prison camp she started running the odds
again. What were the odds of surviving as a POW? She saw a
gravsled carrying away bodies, shuddered, and estimated
ninety–ten against.

What were the odds of improving her lot by collaborating?

Two other calculations were required: Could the Tahn win the war? Sixty-two–thirty-eight—against. The Empire: sixty–forty—in favor. Now, collaboration: seventy-three–twenty-seven—against.

Option: Escape.

St. Clair did not run odds on the likelihood of her getting free. That would have meant factoring in the failed escape attempts of others, and she knew damned well that she was superior to any of those other clots. Proof: They were soldiers or sailors, and she was not.

Michele St. Clair found a new career. And a new nickname—the Lucky Eel. She had made more than twenty attempts to escape, almost all of them solo. And while she had never succeeded in being free longer than four days, she also had never been executed. Somehow the commandant was feeling kindly, she had a convincing excuse for not being where she should have been, or she managed to get away from the chaos before the sorting out started.

Captain St. Clair was ready for her twenty-first attempt.

Observing the work details, she had noticed an absolute consistency to their actions. Buried in the middle of a thirty-man work gang, she hummed happily to herself, watching that routine play out once more.

Shuffle . . . shuffle . . . then wait as each work gang was singly processed through each of the three gates in the center sanctuary, being swept and counted at each gate. Then each detail moved across the guards' courtyard to the outer gate and waited until that gate came open.

Her gang started through the process. As they were herded across the inner courtyard, St. Clair worked her way to the outside of the knot of prisoners.

The outer gate was opened, and the gang went through. It was time.

St. Clair had noticed that as each gang exited the cathedral, the Tahn guards would turn, come to attention, and salute the colors hanging on either side of the Koldyeze's entrance.

Five seconds of inattention.

More than enough.

As the guards saluted, St. Clair elbowed a prisoner aside and darted for the edge of the path that wound downward toward the city. Six to three, she had thought, they won't see me. Five to two there'll be an incline I can scramble down. Eight to one, even if it's a cliff I can spot a ledge or something I can drop to and get out of the line of fire.

One meter short of the edge, St. Clair realized that she had made another sucker bet and slid to a stop.

The edge of the path dropped straight down for more than 100 meters. All the outcroppings she could see were obviously rotten. St. Clair had no interest in ostentatious suicide.

There were shouts behind her, and a projectile *snap-CRACK*-D past her head. St. Clair put her hands straight up, turned around, and looked at the guards hurtling toward her.

"And sixteen to three I'll never learn how to fly," she managed before a rifle butt drove into her stomach and sent her down.

Sweat beading on his forehead, Alex fiddled at the lock, trying for what seemed the hundredth time to coax the strange-looking eyehook key his people had fashioned over the little nipple of metal he could feel inside. He had already turned three wheel gears, and according to theory he had just one more to go.

The key slipped, and it was all Alex could do to bury an almighty great shout of "Clot!" Instead, he wiped the sweat sting out of his eyes, bent his creaking spine, and eased the key back inside.

Behind him, his two companions chatted on, presumably critiquing Alex's efforts. He did not know that for sure, because the entire conversation was taking place in silence.

"Patience, lads," Alex said, although he had not heard anyone complaining. "Ah'm a wee tickle away."

"Not to worry," the big blond man said aloud. "Kraulshavn and I aren't the hurrying kind."

Kraulshavn looked up at his largish friend, Sorensen, waiting for a translation. Sorensen's fingers signed swiftly, and Kraulshavn nodded his head in vigorous agreement. Alex shifted his attention momentarily from the lock to Kraulshavn. There was more finger wagging.

"Whae's he sayin'?"

"That if you are even close to being correct about the contents of the room, the wait will be well worth it."

Alex grunted his answer and tickled on with his eyehook key.

Kraulshavn and Sorensen were hands down the strangest pair that Alex and Sten had thus far roped into their growing organization.

Sorensen was the epitome of a corn-fed farm boy, with slabs of muscle, pale skin that flushed at the least effort, and a grammar-book way of speaking. He also did not appear to be blessed with a great deal of native brightness. But Alex knew from his days in Mantis how strange a breed Sorensen was. Beings like him had made up a valuable part of several Mantis teams Alex and Sten had been on. They were living battle computers. Their innocent looks and surface slowness concerning immediate things about them hid a massive calculating brain. In fact, Alex strongly suspected that Sorensen *was* a surviving member of a blown Mantis Team or maybe still active on a deep-cover run. There was no sense in asking, because Sorensen would not answer. Even more nagging than that was the fact that if Sorensen was Mantis and Alex knew the being's private code word, they would have themselves the damnedest walking, talking battle computer. Which might help on the odds a bit. He shot Sorensen another sizing-up look.

Like his brothers and sisters, Sorensen knew zip about his fellow beings. His people were perfect marks for any con man or traveling carny. In fact, the Imperial governor-general of their homeworld had been forced to pass strict laws forbidding carnivals, circuses, or anything even vaguely connected with hustle artists. On the other hand, if Sorensen was shown a distance point, he could instantly calculate the range, trajectory, wind speed, and relative gravitational tug that any projectile might encounter on its way to its target.

Those talents made Sorensen a valuable find. Doubling his value was the man's friendship with Kraulshavn.

Alex felt the eyehook catch. Gently he twisted and felt the gear wheel sliding smoothly until it clicked into place with its gearmates. Inside, the gears should have been lined up, exposing the pie-shaped wedge cut into them. Quickly, Alex pulled out the eyehook and inserted a heavy bar key. A few minor fumbles and the gears fell back with a heavy *thunk*. On the other side of the door Alex could hear a counterweight shift, and he stepped back to let the door creak open on its heavy hinges.

Kraulshavn signed what Alex took to be a "congratulations" at him. A little dip at the end by the being's nimble fingers, however, looked suspiciously like "dummy." Alex shot Sorensen a glance. The big man was looking blandly innocent.

"Ah'm sussin' a wee joker frae y'r mate," Alex said.

"There was not one single joke in anything he said, Mr. Kilgour," Sorensen protested.

He turned to Kraulshavn, spelling out Alex's comments. Kraulshavn's mouth opened in a round merry O. He covered it with a delicate furry hand, hiding his silent giggle. Alex had to grin.

"Na. He's nae a joker. Noo our Kraulshavn. 'Kay. Waggle thae a' th' lad. In yon room thae may be't a wee haunt."

"Ghosts?" Even Sorensen was incredulous at that. Kraulshavn signed back what was a blatant suggestion where Alex could put his "wee haunt."

Alex just shrugged. "Aye. Ye be't doubters. But th' Tahn hae tales thae'll kink y'r curlies."

With that, he walked inside. Despite their strongly expressed doubts, Sorensen and Kraulshavn hesitated a long moment before they followed.

Kraulshavn had particular reason to hesitate.

Like any reasonable and sophisticated adult Struth, Kraulshavn viewed stories of the spirit world with imperious amusement, as something to look down one's beak at. Even so, ghost stories were an important and ancient signing tradition in his society. Nestlings barely able to put a few symbols together were told simple tales of ghastly elegance. In the deep past, fear of the unknown had been a valuable tool for a hen to keep her featherless, spindly hatchlings safe.

The Struth had originated on a barren and hostile world that to a nervous observer might have seemed to be entirely populated by creatures with fangs and claws and talons and sharp beaks. That was just true enough to require some fairly tricky skills to avoid being on someone else's menu.

In Struth prehistory, they had once been a species facing extinction. Originally beings of the air, they were a little bit too large to hide and too small to defend themselves. The Struth were also handicapped by poor hearing—limited to the ultrafrequency sounds the leaders and guards of the rookeries used to guide their brothers and sisters. The advantage of that was they could not be heard by any potential enemies. Unfortunately, that meant the Struth also could not hear said enemies approaching.

The Struth were down to a few great rookeries when they finally fled to a small subcontinent. It was a place of small animals with sweet flesh, luscious fruits, and no natural enemies at all—a Struth paradise. And as contented Struth generations passed, they became much larger and heavier and lost the ability to fly. Their small wing claws developed into graceful feathered "hands," good for mutual grooming, plucking fruit, wielding a large stick or rock to fell game, and, more importantly, speaking.

Paradise, however, could not last forever. Maintaining a large rookery in their new homeland became quickly impossible as the sheer size of the Struth suggested a brighter future in small cooperative groups that would put far less stress on the food supply. That also meant that a sophisticated communication system was essential.

Signing was born. At first it was limited to a few basics: *Tasty creature under rock. You lift. I take. We share.* Soon, however, it became a swift and complex language. A superior signer had greater status than a Struth with a beautiful tailfeather display. Eventually, a Struth philosopher could collapse the most intricate idea into a few symbols of great simplicity. The gentle Struth were on the verge of evolving their signing language into written form when disaster struck.

A land bridge had formed between their paradise and a much greater landmass. At first only a few weaker animals fled across it. They were soon followed by a trickle and then a flood of grazing creatures. The carnivores were right behind. The Struth were easy prey. After thousands of years of relative safety, they were a top-of-the-menu item again. Once again they faced extinction.

But that time they had greater resources to fall back on. The two key talents they had developed post migration were cooperation and language. The Struth split into even smaller groups. They learned to build their nests in the most difficult terrain. They formed two-Struth teams to gather food. That proved to be an ideal number with which to deal with any enemy. One Struth would always be at watch while the other worked. If escape was impossible, the two of them together could kill the attacker.

Smaller rookeries, however, meant that the hatchlings had to be left unguarded for long periods. The question was how to keep the young in their safe nests. The answer was simple: Scare the clot out of them. The ghost story was invented. Struth tales of the spirit world always involved a young hatchling who ignored the warnings of his parents and more cautious siblings and ventured out of the nest. He was always eaten. A favorite villain was the Talon Thing that swooped out of the sky and carried away the little Struth to its own nest, where smaller Talon Things waited to eat the little Struth alive. Another was Big Fang. That beast, it was said, hid in the brush all day, waiting for groups of disobedient Struth young. Big Fang would catch them at play, quickly eating his fill and then hamstringing the others so they could not run away. Big Fang could then seek out his pack mates and return for a feast.

The ghost stories worked. The hatchlings stayed in their nests until they were old enough to bond with other Struth. Eventually the Struth grew tired of hiding in rocky hills from creatures they had realized were not nearly as bright as themselves. The Struth came out of the hills and began killing the carnivores. They killed them until there were no more left. Then they crossed the land bridge and began killing all over again. In two centuries, the Struth were kings of their small planet. Unlike many other races on countless other worlds, when the Struth had run out of common enemies, they did not begin seeing a replacement among their own numbers. Instead, they returned to being the peaceful Struth again, whose greatest joy was in the elegant symbols—both written and signed—that they used to communicate with.

When they were finally discovered by the Empire, the

Struth language had reached the giddy heights of the purest of pure maths. Their computer hardware, for instance, was primitive compared with Imperial standards. But the programs they wrote were so simple that they barely taxed the capacity of the most dim-witted Struth machine.

As software artists, they were instant hits, commanding premium salaries and the most luxurious perks. There was one requirement, however, written into every Struth contract with the outside. They must always be hired in twos. Otherwise, they would have no one else to sign with. Struth had been known to die of loneliness.

Kraulshavn was not near death when Sorensen found him at their previous prison camp. But day by day he was wasting away. Kraulshavn had been working as a civilian on an Imperial military contract when the Tahn had invaded. His companion was killed in the first fighting. Somehow Kraulshavn had survived.

Sorensen thought the little Struth was the most mournful being he had ever met. Sorensen's great calculating brain and Kraulshavn's elegant way of thinking made them natural friends. It was easy for a being like Sorensen to learn the signing language, and soon he was wagging away with Kraulshavn like a native Struth. Kraulshavn began eating again and taking an interest in life.

They soon teamed up permanently and made one nearly successful attempt to escape. They were just getting ready for another when they were transported to Koldyeze.

When Kilgour found them, he knew instantly that they were the solution to a seemingly impossible problem. What the organization needed more than anything else was a computer capable of reducing endless years of calculating drudgery to a few hours. With such a computer, the chances of escape would soar geometrically.

Sorensen and Kraulshavn had assured him that the solution was simple. All they had to accomplish was two things. Step one: Reinvent the chip. With that, they could build a tiny-brained computer. Step two: Invent a language that said little brain could deal with without blowing its circuits.

When Alex stumbled upon the large room with the tricky

sliding gear lock, he was pretty sure that among its contents was the answer to step one.

When the creators of Koldyeze had considered the early plans for the cathedral, they had paid particular attention to the stained-glass windows that would grace the structure. They quickly discovered that it was an art form that had been lost thousands of years before. Yes, they could create adequate stained glass with modern scientific techniques. But no matter how much they experimented, what they produced paled when compared with the great works of the past.

So it was to the ancient past that the monks of Koldyeze went to find their answer, and find it they did in the writings of a goldsmith named Rugerus. They carefully copied every detail of the methodology. They disdained modern glass-cutting lasers for a tool of heated iron. To smooth the edges of the glass designs, they used a notched tool called a grozing iron. For color, they included in their palette gold and silver salts and precious gems ground to dust.

The room to which Alex had led Sorensen and Kraulshavn was one of the workshops the monks of Koldyeze had labored in for many generations. It was cloaked in dust and cluttered with hundreds of bewildering objects and substances. But little by little they began to pick them out.

Kraulshavn wagged his fingers excitedly when he pulled aside a tarp and revealed neatly stacked sheets of thick glass. He pulled one sheet from a stack and kept pushing it in Kilgour's face. Alex gently brushed him aside.

"Thae be glass. Ah've peeped glass afore. Why's th' feathery one all flutter, young Sorensen?"

"He says glass is what the Struth used in some of their early computers."

Alex considered that for a moment. "Aye. Thae'll be a decent breadboard. 'Tis a start."

As the other two beings continued their search, he wondered how they could etch the glass to hold the circuitry. He would have to get the scroungers busy coming up with a decent glass-eating caustic.

There was sudden excited motion from Kraulshavn. Kilgour found him trying to tug a small barrel from beneath a teetering mess of other barrels. Alex added a little heavy-world weight, and they soon had it out. They popped the lid, and Alex's mouth gaped. Inside was what had to be flakes of pure gold.

"Clottin' figures. Shake down a wee monk, and ye'll find gold about." Kilgour had always been an instinctive anticleric. He was even more so after his and Sten's dealings with the three pontiffs of the Lupus Cluster.

Kraulshavn signed at the flakes and then pointed to the glass. Alex had to chortle. They had found their circuitry.

When they were done, they might have a dullwit for a computer, but it surely was going to be a clotting valuable dullwit.

But before they could scrabble through the mounds of dust and debris to see what other treasures they could find, what seemed like every alarm on Heath went off.

By the time Alex joined Sten on a battlement overlooking the prisoners' yard, he had managed to retrieve his stomach and somewhat untangle his nerves. Sten motioned him over, and he saw what all the shooting and shouting had been about.

The two of them watched as the bloody and limp figure of St. Clair was dragged through the three gates and toward the area that the Tahn had already designated as a "punishment chamber."

"Who is it?" Sten asked.

"Dunno. Ah'll find out. She looks t' be still alive."

Neither of them paid much attention to the prisoner. They were waiting for the next whiplash.

It was not long in coming.

The prison speakers crackled. "All prisoners! Your immediate attention. This is Colonel Derzhin. One of your number has attempted to escape. She was completely unsuccessful. As I guaranteed when I spoke before, this attempt shall not go unpunished."

Sten held his breath.

"The prisoner shall be kept in isolation for thirty days. Diet shall be minimal.

"But this is not sufficient."

"Now's th' clanger," Alex said.

"All prisoners are ordered lockdown in their cells for twenty-four hours. Since no work can be performed in that time, no rations shall be issued. You have ten minutes to return to your cells. At the end of that time, any prisoners outside their cells shall be fired upon."

The speaker went dead.

Sten and Alex looked at each other.

"Clottin' hell," Alex marveled. "A bleedin' philanthropist."

"Yeah," Sten agreed as the two men doubled toward their chamber. "All the same. I want the word out. The next hero that tries a cowboy run like that won't have legs to run on."

"Ah'll see thae's nae mistranslation, Skipper."

CHAPTER FOURTEEN

BUT THERE HAD to be more to Sten's plans than just ordering, "Back off, Buckwheat." Because if he did not get the camp's escape efforts organized very soon, the provable crazies in the cathedral would ignore his orders.

Escaping as an art form—and given the nature of Koldyeze, any escape would have to be pretty arty—required a great deal more than punching a hole in the ground or lashing a ladder together. It required a formidable conspiracy.

Drawn out, an escape organization would resemble two equilateral triangles set point to point. At the top of the first were the watchers and security people. Then a lesser number of carpenters, tinbashers, and so forth. After them, a still smaller number of artists and specialists.

Probably none of them would be among the escapers.

All their work would go to Big X—the escape organization's head. He would filter material down through the ranks of the actual escapers to the tunnelers or the people working on the physical escape.

And security had to be perfect. Not only did each level have to be protected from exposure, the manner of escape itself had to be a total secret to almost everyone.

As Alex put it: "I' y' ken me strollin' aboot th' compound wearin' a purple chemise wi' a light standard stick't oot m' arse, Ah dinnae wan' to hear anybody say aught but how bonny the weather is."

The biggest problem was not with the Tahn guards—Sten had already allowed for their presence. The danger lay in those prisoners who were unknown. Having a measure of respect for Tahn Intelligence, Sten was absolutely sure there would be at least one double among the prisoners. Probably more. But he—or they—must be found quickly and disappeared. The Imperial prisoners would define that death as execution for treason—the Tahn would call it murder and make reprisals. Sten was forced to use Alex and his hooligans as a cutout, even though there was a good possibility that he might be putting his friend very decidedly into harm's way. But he had to start recruiting.

Another problem: There would be prisoners who for their own reasons would want nothing to do with whatever Sten planned as the main escape attempt: claustrophobes, solitaries, or simply prisoners who had figured out a single-person way to get out. All those attempts had to be registered to make sure escapers did not cross each other's routes and destroy two or more plans at once. Sten thought he would be lucky if he heard about half the plans—he was just as unknown and suspect to the other prisoners as they were to him.

Sten was glooming over evening rations in their cell and was very glad to hear the shuffle at the door that interrupted him. He was not so glad when he turned and saw who it was.

Lay Reader Cristata crouched in the doorway.

Cristata, since that initial formation, had not become any less of a pain in the fundament. At every formation he insisted he was a civilian and did not belong in the prison, and at every formation he had to be plopped into place. He refused any work detail; *any* task assigned by a uniformed person was assisting the war effort. Naturally, he refused to salute any

Tahn guard as required. So far he had not ended up in isolation, but sooner or later . . . Not that Cristata was disliked. The squat being was the first to volunteer to mess-cook. He set up the ludicrous assemblage of medical gear available as a dispensary. He had no objection to latrine cleaning whatsoever. Any sick prisoner would have Cristata hovering over him or her night and day.

Sten wondered what he wanted. Probably he had just discovered their rations were issued in uniform packs and felt that was military. But why was he not ruining Colonel Virunga's meal?

"Yes?"

"May I enter?"

Sten waved him in. Cristata closed the door behind him.

"I understand you are the individual in charge"—Cristata shuddered a bit—"of the escape attempts."

Sten mumbled neutrally. Could *Cristata* be a Tahn agent? Not a chance.

"My beings have decided that I should be the one to reserve an area."

"*You* want to escape?"

"Why not? How else can I remove myself from this abhorrence of uniforms and regulations? There are four of us who plan to depart this place of testing for freedom."

"How?"

"We are constructing a tunnel."

"A tunnel?" Sten looked at Cristata's slender, delicate fingers.

Cristata caught his glance. He extended the armor gauntlet of his wrist, and muscles bulged—very hefty muscles, Sten noted. The fingers retracted, and thick claws slid out.

"In my necessities in dealing with the material world," Cristata said, "I function as a mining engineer."

Sten grinned. "The Tahn don't know that, of course,"

"I thought, since they forced me to obey their ludicrous orders, there was little sin in not disclosing my mammon-profession and the excavating implements the Great One gave my race."

"Where are you planning to go out?"

"We have removed a section of paving from the ground level of the east wing. We plan to dig directly out from there."

Sten mentally pictured Koldyeze. "That is going to be a very long tunnel. That's just about the farthest point from the cliff edge."

"That is also our observation. We estimate, and have prayed for guidance to be correct, the location gives us a place unlikely to be examined too closely."

"How long until you go?"

"Soon, I think. The digging has been easy, and since we are tunneling under the foundation of the cathedral most of the way, not much shoring has been necessary. At the moment I estimate we are nearing the inner wall."

Sten was jolted. The progress was incredible. "Clotting great!"

"I wish you would not use obscenities in my presence."

"Right. Sorry. What support do you need?"

"None."

"None? Assuming that you get out, what comes next? You aren't exactly—no offense—a look-alike for any Tahn I've seen."

"We shall proceed directly into open country. There we propose to dig a shelter and slowly make the farmers of the area aware of our presence."

"What makes you think they won't dump you for the reward?"

"You must have faith," Cristata said. "Now . . . may I return to my dedications? We have four new sick ones in the bay."

"Sure. Let us know if you'll need a diversion or anything."

"I doubt it."

"Oh. Yeah. May your, uh, Great One be with you."

"He is."

And Cristata ambled out.

Platoon Sergeant Ibn Bakr was perfect, Kilgour thought, especially considering the still-underfed state of the prisoners. He marveled at the infantryman's bulk and repressed the urge to check the man's teeth as if he were buying a Percheron or to

look at his pads to make sure he could support the full weight
of a howdah. Ibn Bakr could, Alex thought, have fit into any
combat livie as the ultimate hero/crunchie, or maybe the
hero's first sergeant.

"Mr. Kilgour," the bulk said.

Clottin' hell. H' can e'en talk.

"I want to volunteer for the committee."

The word "escape," of course, was never spoken by anyone unnecessarily under threat of bashing.

"An' we accept, lad," Alex said heartily. He had fond
dreams of maybe finding three more like the sergeant, and
they would just rip the old pinnacle off the cathedral and use it
as a battering ram through the gates. *All* the gates. "We'll be
needin't a braw tank like you. Digging...carrying...
holding up the world."

"Umm...Mr. Kilgour, that wasn't what I wanted to do."

Alex's dreams wisped away. "Aye?"

"I assume," Ibn Bakr went on, "that we'll be altering uniforms to look like civvies, screwsuits and that, right?"

"You want to be a clottin' *seamstress*!"

"Is there something wrong with that?" The ham that hung
at the end of Ibn Bakr's arm knotted into a fist.

Kilgour, deciding the sergeant might be a handful even for
a heavy-worlder like himself, regrouped. "Nae a' all, nae a'
all."

"I can do needlepoint, knitting, crewel, petit point, cross-
stitch, featherwork, lace, Carrickmacross, quillwork, broidery
anglaise—"

"Tha'll do, Sergeant. Ah'm appalled—tha's nae th' word
—o'erwhelmed ae thae talents. Be standin't bye, an' we'll
hae materials f'r ye in a wee bit."

The sergeant saluted and left.

Kilgour stared after him and sighed mightily.

The evening formation stunned the Imperial prisoners.
They had assembled at the siren blast, counted, and stood
warily, staring at a five-meter-high stack of plas crates nearby
and wondering what new Tahn screwing the crates presaged.

Camp Commandant Derzhin had taken the count from Colonel Virunga and said he had an announcement. It was short and shocking.

"Prisoners, the Tahn find your work to be acceptable."

Clot, Sten thought. We'd better step up the sabotage program.

"As a reward, I have authorized the issuance of your Prisoner's Aid parcels. That is all. Colonel Virunga, take charge of your men."

Virunga saluted like a being in a trance.

The prisoners were equally amazed.

"I din' know there *was* parcels," somebody muttered ungrammatically.

Sten knew what they were; in the three-plus years of captivity, a softhearted camp officer—who had been quickly shipped off to a combat unit—had issued the boxes once.

Prisoner's Aid was a neutral society, overseen by the ostensibly neutral Manabi and intended to give POWs on both sides some rights, some method of appeal, and most importantly support. The Tahn ignored the first two goals of the society but encouraged the latter. Each parcel contained supplementary rations, vitamins, minerals, and replacement clothing for ten prisoners. Sten wondered if the kindly little old ladies—that was how he pictured them—ever realized that those scarves, gloves, and tidbits in the parcels almost never reached the prisoners they were meant for. If the parcels were not sidetracked by the Tahn supply system itself, the prisoner guards would ensure that the prisoners never saw them. The one parcel that Sten had seen had been most thoroughly picked through long before it was sent into the gates.

"Food," someone whispered.

The formation swayed forward a little.

Virunga blinked back to awareness only seconds before his military formation turned into a food riot.

"Formation! Ten-hut!"

Military discipline took over—at least for a moment.

"Three volunteers . . . break down . . . parcels. Cristata . . . Kilgour . . . Horatio!"

Lay Reader Cristata muttered but evidently decided that

task was allowable and waddled forward, Sten and Alex behind him.

"Sir," Sten said. "Request that—"

Virunga interrupted him. "Quite right . . . forgot . . . task. One more being! Sarn't Major Isby!"

The supply specialist swung out on his crutches toward Virunga. In an age when few injuries were permanent, Isby was a man with only one leg. That he had lost it through medical inattention was one atrocity to be chalked up to the Tahn. But it could be explained away as an excusable oversight during wartime. There could be no explanation for not providing him with a new one. The only war crime trials the Tahn were counting on would be overseen by them.

"Rest . . . dismissed! Distribute parcels . . . two hours."

The formation broke up, but none of the prisoners left the courtyard. They intended to watch—very closely—just how the parcels were divided. At least all three of the "volunteers" were trusted by the prisoners—more or less.

Sten glanced at Alex, who nodded. Alex would take Colonel Virunga aside and give him a very interesting piece of information that had been learned during his and Sten's pre-Tahn War Mantis training. If that bit of information still applied, those Prisoner's Aid parcels might prove very useful.

Sten, thinking hopeful thoughts about the continuity of sneakiness, saluted Virunga and hurried away. He did indeed have another task.

The two guards snarled at Sten. He kept well back. They unlocked the cell door and snarled once more. A moment later St. Clair walked out, squinting at the light—walked, not tottered or stumbled. During the month of isolation, her bruises had mostly healed. She was even skinnier than before—half rationpaks and water had done that—but, Sten noted, must have maintained some kind of exercise regimen in the cramped isolation cell.

"Next time," the Tahn said, "it'll be worse."

"There won't be a next time," St. Clair said. The guard pushed her away, down the corridor, and banged the cell door closed.

St. Clair stopped in front of Sten. "My welcoming committee."

"Call it that," Sten said.

"What's been happening in the big wide world?"

"Not much worth talking about."

"So the war's still not over. And by the way, why aren't you calling me by my rank, Firecontrolman."

"Sorry. Captain."

"Forget it. I'm just up to here with clottin' screws. Thanks for the welcome. Now I want to see if the 'freshers are on yet."

They were in a deserted section of the corridor.

"We have something to talk about first," Sten said.

"GA."

"You tried to get out solo. A real cowboy move."

"So?"

"No more. Any escape attempt's gotta be registered and approved by the committee."

"Not mine," St. Clair said. "Committees screw things up. Committees start war. I like my own company."

"This isn't a debate, Captain. It's an order."

St. Clair leaned back against the wall. "You're Big X?"

"You have it."

"Nice meeting you. But as I said—"

"Listen to me, Captain. Read my lips. I don't give a damn if you want to try a single run. Anybody who's got any way out of this coffin has my blessings. But I am going to know about it and approve it—before you go."

St. Clair allowed herself six deep breaths before she said anything. She smiled. "Again, my apologies. I'll follow orders. Of course. Whatever you and your committee want."

"Cute, Captain St. Clair. And I think you're blowing smoke at me. Those are my orders. You will follow them!"

"And if I don't?"

Sten spoke very quietly. "Then I'll kill you."

St. Clair's face was impassive.

"One more thing, Captain. Just to keep you out of trouble, I'm appointing you my chief scrounger."

"Scrounger? I'm not familiar—"

"Thief."

St. Clair bristled. "I am a gambler. Not a clotting burglar!"

"I don't see the difference."

Again St. Clair buried her anger. "Is there anything else, Firecontrolman?"

"Not right now."

"Then you're dismissed!"

Sten came to attention and saluted her.

St. Clair waited until Sten had rounded a corner, then gave herself the luxury of a silent snarl of rage. Then her face pokered, and she started looking for her long-overdue shower.

Outside in the courtyard, the distribution of the Prisoner's Aid parcels was under way. Sten noticed that as each crate was opened Alex would remove one or maybe two packs and set them unobtrusively aside. Good. Then he saw, leaning against one of the half-ruined columns, what had to be the Empire's oldest warrant officer. The man looked like the grandfather Sten had never known. He was holding a small pack of what Sten guessed were biscuits and an equally tiny pack of fruit spread. Part of his share from the parcels. The man was crying.

Sten shuddered.

It was time they all went home.

CHAPTER FIFTEEN

BIG X WAS flexing his muscles.

Through his cutouts, Sten had deployed the surveyors. The surveyors were reluctant prisoners who were given improvised metric rules and told to measure everything and anything. Sten was trying to find out what he had to work with and work from. Since there were no plans that he could find or steal for Koldyeze, he would make his own.

The details reported back. A hallway measured so many meters wide, long, and tall. The rooms branching off that hallway measured B meters wide, long, and tall. The wing itself measured C meters wide, long, and tall. And none of the figures matched in Sten's mind. He wished desperately that Alex and his team could move a little faster on the computer. What the clot! Probably wouldn't work, anyway.

Sten tossed aside the bits of paper he had been figuring on. Later for that drakh. In the meantime, which meant on the morrow, he was on a work detail.

The work detail was commanded by someone who seemed to be the first of the Tahn quislings.

Chief Warrant Officer Rinaldi Hernandes seemed to call everyone "my friend"—except the Tahn guards, whom he referred to, with a completely obsequious bow, as "honorable sirs."

"My friends," he cajoled. "Come, now. Lift together. We can do this."

"Doing this" was muscling a huge generator that should have had a McLean sled to raise it up a ramp into a cargo ship.

"You aren't trying, my friends," he said. "I am disappointed that I shall have to report you to our commandant when we return. Remember, we are being given a fair day's ration, and we should be prepared to deliver a fair day's work."

Sten grunted, along with twenty others, and slowly the generator groaned up the ramp into place. He, like the others on the work crew, hated Hernandes. Suddenly Sten realized that in spite of the constant threat, no one assigned to Mr. Hernandes's work crews had ever been reported for anything.

Interesting.

The generator loaded, the prisoners sagged in exhaustion. Hernandes walked among them, patting, joking, and ignoring the muttered obscenities he heard.

"That wasn't bad, my friends. Come on. The shift's barely begun. Come on. We've got to show our honorable masters we're as good as they are."

The prisoners groaned to their feet. The next task was simpler: loading crates into another offbound ship.

Sten realized he was spending less time watching Hernandes than watching Heath's spaceport. Which ship could be stowed away on? Which ship was outbound for where? What were the security measures taken once a ship was loaded?

He humped a crate up a laddered ramp. Hernandes was standing at the ship's cargo door in his typically baggy over-sized coveralls.

"Hi-diddle-diddle," the officer chanted. "Right up the middle, friend. We've got to get this ship loaded and offworld."

Definitely, Sten thought, a traitor. But isn't he a little obvious to be an agent?

"There are troops freezing on an arctic world," Hernandes went on. "We've got to make sure they have what they need."

Sten glowered at the warrant officer and continued on, part of the antlike procession, into the ship's hold, where he dumped the crate he was carrying. And then he stared at the loading slip on its side: *Uniforms, tropical, working dress*.

He quickly scanned some slips on other crates: *Recreational equipment, E-normal environment (low-caloric); Rations, beasts of burden (not for Tahn Consumption); Livies, medical, educational, avoidance of social diseases; Livies, counselatory, what to do when your mate leaves; Spores, seedable, rock garden, for issue to general officers and above.*

That should have had an interesting effect on any Tahn crunchie—on whatever frozen world the ship was bound for —who had to unload or consume any of the crates.

As he made his way back toward the ramp, Sten looked at Mr. Hernandes a bit differently. To make sure, he bumped against him. Mr. Hernandes's coveralls clanked.

"Careful of what you're doing, my friend," the grandfatherly warrant officer cautioned.

"See me tonight," Sten ordered in a low voice.

"I beg your pardon?"

"Big X," Sten said. What the clot. If he was blown, he was now thoroughly blown.

* * *

He was not.

In case Hernandes was wired, Sten had him strip searched and then, finding he was clean, took him for a long and aimless walk down one of the wing's corridors.

Rinaldi Hernandes was a building tradesman, a general contractor who had been a master plumber, carpenter, plasman, ceramic specialist, and so forth, who had joined the service at the beginning of the conflict. He had been assigned to the Imperial construction units—for once the grinding bureaucracy that was the military had put a square peg into a square hole.

Hernandes desperately hated the Tahn. His only grandchild had been killed at the beginning of the war. Then Hernandes himself had been captured. He had survived and, during the years of his captivity, resisted—resisted in ways that would keep him alive until the time came when he had a weapon in his hands and could kill.

"Although, my friend," he said sheepishly, "since I've never killed anyone in my life, I really don't know what I would do."

In the meantime, he had learned the Tahn worlds and sent shipments intended for garrisons to the front, and vice versa. He had stolen and then destroyed any protruding bits of military hardware that he could. He had surreptitiously tugged connections loose wherever he could when he was permitted aboard any Tahn ship.

Hernandes hated the Tahn so thoroughly that he was willing to sacrifice the opinion of his fellow prisoners. So they believed he was a quisling, a traitor, a double. Perhaps they might even kill him. That was the risk that Hernandes was willing to take. In the meantime, he was as trusted by the Tahn as any Imperial prisoner could be. He often wondered, he told Sten, how many—if any—Tahn he had killed. He had never seen any of them die.

Maybe he was not really accomplishing anything.

Sten thought that perhaps Mr. Rinaldi Hernandes had killed more Tahn than any Imperial battleship.

And now he had his jack-of-all-trades.

Big clottin' deal, Sten thought. I'm assembling all these troopies. Giving them a mission.

But so far I haven't come up with any mission.

CHAPTER SIXTEEN

L'N THUMBED BACK on the joystick. There was a soft whirr as the feeder machine came to life and then two sharp clicks as the tubes dropped into the slots in front of her. She gave a quick double-check glance to make sure there was a pos and neg symbol on each of them, then toggled the joystick forward. The tubes slid slowly toward each other, then gave a quick jump as they mated.

She bent closer to look at the seal. It was so apparently perfect that she could barely see the nth of a hairline where the tubes joined.

All those movements were accomplished in nearly absolute darkness. In fact, it was so dark in the testing room that any other being would have started feeling like a claustrophobe after a few minutes. He would have felt completely cut off from the rest of the world, sensing only the form of his own body. To L'n it was a little bit better than twilight.

She toggled left to apply stress to the seal, pressing down to activate an electric field. Outwardly the seam was still apparently perfect, but L'n's light-actinic eyes could see a dark red stain. The seam was badly flawed. L'n giggled and toggled right to drop the tubes into the discard bin. After only a few hours on shift, the bin was nearly full of rejects. So much for the Tahn's boasts of superefficiency.

L'n liked to think that someday far in the future a really bright historian would trace the Tahn's eventual defeat at the hands of the Emperor right back to the discard bin under her worktable. For the hundredth time L'n smiled at her little private joke, then toggled back to call for the next two pipes. Her small, delicately pointed left ear turned to catch the sound of the machine whirring into life. Instead, there was a loud shout just outside the room. Her ear curled back on itself in pain. What the clot? The shouting went on. It was Cloric, the Tahn work boss. She could not hear what was being said, but somebody was definitely getting it. If Cloric held to form—and she had no reason to believe that he would not—the shouts would eventually lapse into incoherence, followed by heavy blows.

Whoever it was, L'n felt very sorry for him. Still, what could she do about it? She turned back to her work, trying to push the sounds outside her mind. It was a process that seemed to be getting easier every day. That frightened L'n more than anything else—more than Cloric, or the other Tahn, or the war itself. Because until a few years before, violence had not even been a word in L'n's vocabulary.

It was not that L'n came from a race of pacifists. On the contrary, on a scale of amoebic jelly to outright beasts, the Kerrs rated fairly high on the fierce side. They were a slender, soft-furred folk with large, limpid eyes; delicate, highly sensitive ears; and a long, agile balancing tail. The Kerrs' original homeworld was mostly covered by dense forests. They inhabited the middle levels, where light was as scarce as the food supply on the top tier.

Like many forest beings, L'n's forebearers were intensely jealous of their privacy. The only time a Kerr experienced a feeling even close to loneliness was during estrus. It was a trait that would stay with them through the ages, just like their passion for light.

An artist, L'n had been nearing the height of her powers when she decided to emigrate from her home system. It was a very bold—or foolish—thing for a Kerr to do. She was abandoning the warmth of personal privacy for what seemed to her friends and family a hostile and patently ugly life on the outside. But the artist side of L'n knew—as sure as she knew the conceptual beauty of polarized light—that the price of continued privacy was too high. To reach the next level in her art, she needed knowledge, a knowledge that could be found only in the great "outside."

L'n thought she was just on the verge of finding her way,

when the Tahn struck. She was in her biaxial period, and her strange light paintings were beginning to find a wider audience.

Audience. That was a strange word. There was no equivalent in the Kerr language. It made a being think of large, smelly crowds, pushing in, closer and closer . . . L'n learned to deal with audiences. In fact, she was even starting to like being the center of one.

She had also made her first "outside" friend. His name was Hansen. Lance Corporal Hansen, a very large and, at first, very frightening human. When she had met him and Hansen had grasped her small hands in his and grunted on in his ugly low-toned human voice about her light paintings, it was all she could do to keep herself from taking a shrieking leap for the studio's rafters. But she had steeled herself, listened as politely as she could, and then ushered him out the door. L'n had spent hours that night trying to comb the smell of him out of her fur.

Months later, it was one of the things she liked about him the most. He was with her every minute he could spare, admiring her work, criticizing it in ways that turned out to be helpful, and hovering over her when she had a showing— keeping the crowds at a more comfortable distance.

When the Tahn had invaded, Hansen had fought his way to her studio, dragged her from it, and then fought his way back to his lines. They reached safety only moments before the battle-shocked Imperial Forces surrendered. Even then, the Tahn had kept their missiles thundering in.

Hansen and L'n were caught in one such explosion. Sometime later, L'n came to. How very odd. She was barely wounded—while Hansen was messily dead.

L'n had learned many things since she had left her home system. One of them was lying. The Tahn had mistaken her for a member of the Imperial Forces. L'n did not correct them. Out on the streets she could hear them killing the civilians.

The last thing she learned was after Hansen died. L'n learned what it was like to be lonely.

The seam on the next pair of tubes glowed a faint orange. Adequate. Clot! She toggled it to the appropriate bin.

Outside, the shouting had stopped. Instead of heavy blows, she could hear muttering. What was going on?

Chetwynd had heard the brouhaha clear across the hangar-sized factory. He quickly checked his guards and their work parties. Everything *seemed* okay. Wait. Something or someone was missing.

He maneuvered his enormous bulk around a chattering machine and took off at a dead run. Chetwynd dodged the waving jaws of a forklift, skittered around a corner, and came to a stop. It was Cloric—again. The man's face was flushed with anger, and his eyes were bulging out from the intensity of his shouting. It was almost orgasmic. The object of his affection, Chetwynd noticed, was a much smaller man—an Imperial prisoner of war. The reason for Cloric's anger was instantly apparent. The two men were standing in the middle of a large jumbled pile of hydraulic tubing that spilled across the floor. Behind them was the bank of doors to the test labs. On one lab a red light burned, showing that it was in use.

Chetwynd assumed a casual pose and strolled over. Whether he intervened would depend on only a few simple factors. On the one hand, the prisoner might have done something wrong or, even worse, sneaky. In which case Chetwynd would shrug his shoulders and abandon the prisoner to his fate. On the other hand, Cloric had a reputation even among the most callous of the guards as a person who lashed out for no apparent reason. Not that anyone really cared; it was just considered unprofessional. Chetwynd had a more important reason to be concerned. As he was the shift commander, the prisoners were ultimately his responsibility. And the word had come strongly down that there was a severe shortage of labor, and therefore the prisoners had suddenly gained value. They were not to be wasted. If Cloric were allowed to run amok, they would quickly run out of people for the work parties.

There was one other reason. Chetwynd knew firsthand what it was like to be a prisoner.

Cloric finally spotted him and went on the defensive without a pause.

"I can handle this, Chetwynd."

"Snarl at me once more, Cloric, and I'll show you what *I* can handle."

Cloric took in the mastodon that was Chetwynd. Cloric was big but not *that* big. Chetwynd had at least fifty kilos on him, a great deal of which was muscle. And although as the boss of the work gangs he was not Cloric's immediate superior, Chetwynd had a great deal of clout, even with the muckity-mucks of factory security. The source of the clout was a bit of a mystery, although talk was that Chetwynd was a dispenser of many favors. As for what he got in return, even Cloric was not dumb enough to ask.

All those thoughts took a great deal of time to lumber through the man's mind. Chetwynd waited patiently and was rewarded with a slump of shoulders and a stubborn but still hangdog expression.

"He was tryin' somethin'," Cloric muttered, waving at the prisoner and the jumble of tubing. "See. He's got all the good ones mixed up with the bad ones."

Chetwynd did not bother letting Cloric finish explaining. It would take much too long and consist mostly of lies. The prisoner, he was sure, would be much more creative. He turned to the man, who had been looking back and forth as they talked, obviously wondering what was going to happen to him. The prisoner was Sten.

"What do you have to say for yourself?" Chetwynd asked.

"It was sort of an accident," Sten said. "See, I was moving the reject bin out of the way, and the officer grabbed my shoulder. Scared the clot out of me, I can tell you. Knocked over that bin and the other—"

"That's a lie," Cloric protested. "I was watchin' him the whole time. He was gonna mix 'em together. I could tell."

"But sir," Sten said. "Did you actually *see* me doing anything like that? Where were you standing?"

Cloric was so confused by Chetwynd's presence that he found himself actually discussing the matter with the prisoner instead of smacking him for his insolence. He pointed to a position about twenty meters away; he had obviously been lurking behind a gravlift. Sten studied the indicated spot with great seriousness. After a moment, he shook his head.

"No, sir. I hate to disagree with you, but I don't think you could have seen much over there. Those plascrates would have been in the way."

"They were at first," Cloric said, "but I moved some, see?" He pointed at a gap in a large stack of crates waiting for shipment.

"Gee, sir. That is pretty good," Sten reluctantly admitted. "But wouldn't my back have been turned to you, sir?"

Chetwynd waved them both to silence. The discussion was not getting them anywhere. Besides, there was something else preying on his mind. The prisoner looked very familiar. He could not quite put his finger on it, but he was sure he knew the man from someplace. And that someplace was cop!

"Don't I know you?" he asked.

Sten peered up at him. He, too, saw a vague kind of familiarity, but he kept it hidden. "No, sir. The prisoner doesn't believe so, sir."

Chetwynd looked closer. He could not shake the feeling that somewhere, sometime he had seen the man in the uniform of a Tahn cop. But what was he doing there acting like an Imperial prisoner? If Chetwynd was right, then the man was a snoop, and he and Cloric could find themselves in deep drakh.

"What's your name?"

"The prisoner's name is Horatio, sir," Sten said.

He was worried. Chetwynd's face had finally clicked into position. It was when he and Alex had been on the trail of that little bomber, Dynsman. Sten remembered clearly the attack of the gurion. The thing had rushed through the surf at them on its six legs, its tooth-lined stomach reaching out of its body at them. And the whole time, the man in front of him had lolled laughing on the beach, surrounded by a score of lovely female prisoners. Sten and Alex had been posing as Tahn prison guards, so they really could not blame Chetwynd for his lack of concern for their fate. He wondered how Chetwynd had ever gotten off the prison planet. More importantly, how in the clot had he gone from prisoner to boss guard?

Wars produced strange things, Sten had noticed. He had also noticed that those things were rarely funny.

"Okay, Horatio. We'll let this go. This time. Next time your butt is ground meat!"

"Thank you, sir," Sten said with some amazement.

Before Cloric could protest, Chetwynd raised a hand to silence him.

"Get these parts loaded," he told Sten. "We'll run 'em back through again."

"Yessir. Right away, sir."

Sten was a blur of eager motion as he began picking up the scattered tubing as Chetwynd and Cloric walked away.

"Whyn't you let me thump him?" Cloric asked. "He deserved it."

"Probably," Chetwynd said. "But do us both a favor. Keep your eye on him. But your hands off. Got me?"

Cloric nodded. He did not know what was going on, and he was pretty sure he did not want to find out. As for Chetwynd, he still thought he recognized Sten. But the cop business was probably pure foolishness. Probably. Still, he was not taking any chances.

L'n went at her rote tasks with new interest. She even hummed a Kerr lullaby to herself as she worked. She had been startled and badly frightened when the man Horatio had slipped into her lab. She almost had not flipped on the small blue light that was just barely comfortable to her eyes but would have allowed Horatio to see. For a moment she had almost let him bump around in the dark while she found a place to hide.

But the man had stayed perfectly still and whispered her name. Finally, she had responded. Without hesitation, the man walked directly to her, as if he could see in the dark as well as she could.

Horatio seemed to understand her right away. He made soothing noises at her and talked about things that interested her, like the geometric pattern and colors produced when light was refracted in a certain, special way. He said he had heard about her art, although he had not actually ever seen one of her light paintings. He promised to help her set up a studio at the prison.

He had also asked her for help. Not in *return* for any favors he would do. Of that she was quite sure. L'n had the idea that Horatio would provide the studio no matter what she did.

Why did she trust him? Well, he had trusted her, hadn't he?

He had confessed that he was Big X. That information alone was a death warrant in her hands. And the things that he had asked her to do also depended on his absolute trust in her.

She would be the forger. She would use her many skills as an artist to produce fake Tahn documents and ID cards and a host of other things the prisoners would need when and if they escaped.

L'n had only one hesitation. There was no way she could escape with them. In the Tahn sunlight, she was blind.

Hansen had said— No. Not Hansen, she corrected herself. Silly me. Horatio had said that as Big X he could not escape, either. So they would work together and help the others.

L'n liked that. She also liked the second thing he had asked her. It also involved danger, but not as much. He wanted her to do a little sabotage, to approve as many sections of flawed tubing as she could. *That* would be a pleasure. In fact, she had thought about it before but had been afraid to try it.

Since she had met Horatio, she was not afraid anymore.

CHAPTER SEVENTEEN

THE THIRD GATE in the center sanctuary opened, and Security Major Avrenti stalked into the prisoners' courtyard.

The base of the triangle—the support for the escapers— went into operation.

Sergeant Major Isby leaned on his stool and lifted the bandage away from the stump of his leg to get a little more of the dim sun above.

Lance Corporal Morrison, on the second-level balcony, dropped his propaganda leaflet.

Major F'rella, at the far end of the prisoners' courtyard, curled one tentacle under—another Tahn recorded as entering —and, with her second brain, continued puzzling over whether that unusual archaic Earth tune written by someone named Weill could be polyphonically hummed using six of her eight lungs.

Technician Blevens yelped—supposedly at the heat of the caldron he had just touched—and dropped the caldron on the floor of the prisoners' kitchen.

The *klang* rang through the courtyard.

And the word was out.

"Great One protect us," Cristata said. "And now it is time to go."

Instantly Markiewicz dropped her improvised spade and began slithering backward, away from the face of the tunnel. She, like any sensible tunneler who might have to pass inspection at a moment's notice, worked naked.

Cristata grabbed her legs and helped yank her back toward the nearest way station. He looked at her body, interestedly. He was wondering why some of the religious humans he had met saw shame in a body without covering. And suddenly he had a flash. Of course. They realized that their bodies should have been fur rather than pale flesh. They were ashamed of what they should have been instead of what they were.

Cristata, finding that thought worthy of his next meditation with the Great One and thanking the Great One for one more enlightenment, scurried back up the shaft after Markiewicz.

Markiewicz tugged on her coverall, and then they burst out of the tunnel, into the courtyard, as the paving stones slid away and then closed. Two soldiers dropped a very smelly basket of lichens over the stones and busied themselves peeling them for the evening meal.

Sorensen was lowering the eighteenth plate of glass into position, with Kraulshavn waggling final instructions, when the boot thudded against the door. The plate came back up and went hastily down onto the table beside them while Kraulshavn signed frantically for clues.

Tahn. They're approaching.

Clots!

Kraulshavn pulled at the cord hanging close to him, and

the ties of a mattress cover, fastened to the rafters above them, came open. Dust clouded down around them.

All the pieces they had worked on that day would have to be laboriously cleaned and sterilized before the project could continue.

Sorensen swore as the two beings slid out the door of the workshop, into the corridor, and closed the door behind them. Their waiting watchman relocked the door, then covered it with more dust blown from a small bellows. He took one final precaution: Just in case the Tahn checked the corridor with heat detectors, he drooped a length of live lighting wire from the overhead so that it dangled across the cell door. Burn marks had already been artistically painted on the door, and the wire occasionally spit sparks. Any heat pickup would, everyone hoped, be attributed to that continuing short.

The watchman wondered what the clot the two beings were doing inside that workshop. But as Mr. Kilgour had reminded him, that was na' his t' fash aboot. He headed for the courtyard.

What was going on inside the workshop was the slow, laborious construction of the computer that Sten needed.

Dreamers often wondered what would happen if they could appear in another, earlier time and build some sort of common tool that would make them gods, or even kings. The problem they never considered was that almost all technology required six steps of tooling before that trick item showed up.

And so Sten's computer had to begin with a chip—a series of chips.

No one would have recognized what Sorensen and Kraulshavn were constructing as a computer chip, however.

Their "chips" were cubes, almost a third of a meter to any side. For simplicity's sake, they had decided to use a basic design of a twenty-four-layer chip. Each layer was a slab of glass. Each slab had the circuitry scratched on its surface and then acid-etched. Where each resister, diode, or whatever belonged, an open space was left. Full-scale components were either built or stolen by the working parties. The circuitry was then "wired" as molten silver was poured into the acid etching. The chips' connecting legs were hand constructed of gold and wired in. Twenty-four of those plates made up each chip.

They had twelve chips ready and were about a third of the way through their task.

Both Sorensen and Kraulshavn wondered where Alex planned to put together their computer. He had not told them, and they recognized that as yet they had no need to know. They also wondered what Kilgour was planning to use for a storage facility. Another impossibility—but somehow they thought that there would be, when the time was right, an answer.

Security Major Avrenti paced through the prison corridors. He growled at the prisoners, ignoring greetings and the obligatory shouts as the Imperials ordered themselves to attention as he entered each chamber.

He imagined himself a psychic octopus, each strand of his being wisping out, trying to get the feel of his charges.

Were they hostile—indications of a potential riot? Were they smug, hiding a secret joke—indications of an escape in the planning? Were they sullen—hope abandoned? Avrenti continued his tour.

Kilgour watched the Tahn stroll down a corridor and stepped back out of sight.

"What's he doing?" one of his cohorts whispered.

"Ah dinnae ken," Alex replied. "Hae y' aye rec'lect tha' any ae th' Tahn be psychic?"

"Clottin' hope not."

"We'll dinnae take th' chance," Alex decided.

Avrenti finished his inspection and exited the prisoners' quarters into their courtyard. He paused a moment, waiting for some kind of impression. Then he saw, in the courtyard's center, a medium-sized—each way—Imperial painting the courtyard. His paint had been made from wallplaster soaked in water. His brush was a knotted rag. He was painting what appeared to be a star.

Avrenti walked up to him.

The Imperial—Avrenti searched his mental fiche and remembered him as one Kalguard or Kilgour, a minor, unimportant being—seemed oblivious to the Tahn.

"What are you doing?"

The Imperial bolted to attention, whitewash splattering.

Avrenti frowned—some of the droplets had landed on his tunic.

"Ah 'polgize," Kilgour stammered. "Ah dinnae ken y' creep."

Avrenti barely understood what the Imperial was saying but took it as an apology. "What are you doing?"

"Keepin't th' Campbells off."

"The Campbells?"

"Aye."

"What, may I ask, are they? Or it?"

"Thae'll weird, dread six-leggit beasties whae live on treacheries an' soup."

"Nonsense," Avrenti snorted. "I've never seen anything like that."

"Aye," Kilgour agreed. "M' star's ae worker, ain' it?"

Avrenti looked closely at the Imperial. There was not a trace of a smile on the prisoner's face. "Yes. Carry on."

"Aye, sir."

Kilgour went back to painting his star, and Avrenti went out through the three gates, his mind intent on whether he should alert Commandant Derzhin to the possibility that some of the Imperials might need psychiatric care.

Alex finished his paint job, walked three times around it, then started back for his quarters. Very well, he thought. Tha' Avrenti's noo psychic. He's just most intent. He'll hae two watchers on him when'ever he com't through th' gates frae noo on.

CHAPTER EIGHTEEN

TANZ SULLAMORA WAS at his repose. He sat confidently in the anteroom to the Emperor's suite, waiting patiently and confidently to be summoned. Back straight, legs crossed, brow furrowed in thought, he was the definite portrait of a great industrial baron. A man to be reckoned with. A man who had the ear of the mighty.

The Eternal Emperor strode into the room and, without even glancing at Sullamora, walked over to the small service bar and pulled out a bottle and two glasses.

"Tanz, old friend," the Emperor said. "You need a drink."

Sullamora was startled. He felt his careful pose starting to collapse about him. He had sworn to himself that he would set the tone of the meeting. Sullamora had definite ideas about what constituted Imperial behavior. Unfortunately, the Emperor did not go along with him.

"Uh . . . no. I mean, no, thank you. It's a little early."

"Trust me, Tanz. When I say you need a drink, I mean it."

Numbly, Sullamora took the glass. "Is there some, ah, difficulty?"

" 'Difficulty' isn't the word I had in mind. 'Disaster' would be better. Ship production has gone all to hell."

Sullamora sat up even straighter. That was a serious charge. He had been put in charge of all shipbuilding in the Empire for the duration of the war.

"But that isn't so," he sputtered. "I mean—uh, the latest figures, Your Majesty, uh . . ."

"Bull. I say ship production is dangerously off. And it's no wonder. All that labor unrest at the six plants in the Cairenes.

88

Slowdowns. Wildcat strikes. I tell you they're endangering the progress of the war, and it has to stop!"

That really startled Sullamora. The factories of the Cairenes were his most efficient. He started to protest, but the Emperor waved him to silence.

"I'm not blaming you, Tanz. My lord, no one could expect one man—even a man as efficient as you—to keep abreast of *all* the developments. And I plan to say so at the livie news conference tomorrow."

"News conference? What news conference? I wasn't informed—that is to say. . ." Sullamora stumbled into muteness.

He choked down his drink, all his confidence gone. Maybe the Emperor was right. But how could he have missed something like that? The Cairenes. Labor unrest. Wildcat strikes. Slowdowns. Profits in peril. It was a capitalist's greatest nightmare.

Watching him closely, the Emperor refilled the man's glass. He let Sullamora torture himself just a little longer. There was absolutely nothing the Eternal Emperor did not know about the military-industrial establishment and how to keep it under his very heavy thumb. "You gotta keep them off balance," he had once told Mahoney. "To them, cost overrun is just another word for paradise."

Finally he took pity on the man—but just a little bit. He started laughing. Sullamora looked up at him, totally bewildered and unmanned.

"Don't you get it, Tanz? This is just one of my little ploys."

"You mean it's a joke?" Sullamora sputtered.

"No joke. I've never been more serious. Look. I lay this out at the news conference. Announce that I've called for an investigation by the Imperial Labor Commission."

"What labor commission?"

"Clot, you're thick sometimes. There's no such animal. I'm just saying there is. Like the labor unrest and declining shipbuilding figure stuff. By the time the Tahn figure out that I'm lying through my teeth, you should be able to crank out minimum twelve more ships that they won't be aware of."

Sullamora lifted his eyebrows. "Ah, now I understand." It had something to do with the rumored buildup, he realized. Where, no one was sure. Although, now that he thought of it, maybe the rumors were also part of the Emperor's unroyallike and very slippery planning.

"There's something coming, isn't there, sir?" he asked. "Something big. Is it anything you can tell me about?"

"No offense, Tanz, but that's a negative. I've got to play these cards *really* close to my chest. If the Tahn get even a hint, we're in a world of drakh."

That was something Sullamora finally could understand. He was an old hand at playing shadow games with business rivals, although rarely did those games result in more than a little bloodshed.

"This much I can tell you," the Emperor continued. "If this works out, the war will be over in four years. Five tops. If I can smack them, and smack them good, they may never really recover.

"Oh, they can keep fighting for a while. But it'll be all over but final surrender. On *my* terms."

Even Sullamora's frigid soul had to shudder at that thought. He would hate to be on the receiving end of a contract dictated by the Emperor.

"Of course, I *do* expect a few immediate benefits. Such as the signal that will be sent to any of my wavering allies and the fence sitters."

After a moment he added in a near whisper, "I think it's the fence sitters that irritate me the most."

Sullamora felt his mouth go dry. He felt he should say something, but for some reason he was suddenly afraid. And then the moment passed. The Emperor took Sullamora's glass and put it and the bottle away. Sullamora was being dismissed.

"Plan on a five-minute speech tomorrow, Tanz," the Emperor said. "My flack can get together with your flack tonight. Put what I want you to say in your own words."

Sullamora rose. He started to say his good-byes, then paused. With some amusement, the Emperor watched the other man screw up his courage to speak. He kept silent, deciding not to help him.

"I've, uh...Ah. Your Majesty, I've been wondering," Sullamora finally got out.

"Yes?" The Emperor's voice was flat; he was still not helping.

"After the war, uh...What do you plan to do?"

"Get very drunk," the Emperor said. "It's a good habit to get into before you count the dead."

"No, sir. That's not what I meant...uh, sir. See, I've been talking to the other members of the privy council, and... What I mean to say is...What do you intend to do with us?"

The Emperor had created the privy council just after the outbreak of war. On it he had placed Sullamora and several other beings important to his cause. In theory they were supposed to advise him. The Eternal Emperor had never meant to listen to them. It was just his way of making them feel important and keeping them out of his hair. Like the Imperial Parliament. The Eternal Emperor was a great believer in the trappings of democracy. It was one of the essential underpinnings of an absolute monarchy.

He pretended to consider Sullamora's question.

"I don't know," he said. "Disband the council, I guess. Why?"

"Well, we think that if we've been of use to you during war, then think what we can do during peace. I mean, there are certain concerns we have, Your Majesty, that it would be impossible for you to be aware of."

Riigght, the Emperor thought. I'll bet you'd just love that. No way was he going to have an advisory body with any kind of official recognition. But why tell Sullamora that? He also tucked aside the man's comment that the privy council members had even been suggesting such a thing among themselves. Perhaps he had better start keeping closer track of them.

The Eternal Emperor smiled his most charming smile. "That *is* a thought, Tanz," he said. "I'll be sure to keep it in mind."

He wore the smile until Sullamora had exited. The smile disappeared when the door closed.

CHAPTER NINETEEN

THE TAHN HAD unwittingly provided the prisoners of Koldyeze with the ideal hiding place for their reinvented computer: the general-purpose sanitation facility. The Tahn had approached the problem of sanitation for so many prisoners with typical single-minded efficiency. Thirteen cells had been turned into one huge room by the simple application of sledgehammers to the walls. One area was devoted to lavatory facilities. Another contained half a dozen gigantic and ancient industrial washing machines. A third was to be used for showering. And on another were nearly 100 washbasins. Above those were an equal number of large mirrors sunk into the stone wall.

Alex had replaced thirty-six of them with the mirror-surfaced chips that made up the computer. They swung out on hinges designed by Hernandes after pictures he recalled from a course he had taken on "Ancient Engineers" in his student days. They were linked together by cryogenic wire scavenged by St. Clair from the motor coils of abandoned gravsleds.

Next problem: software. Despite the size of the computer, it was a basic pea brain. It would not be able to handle too many facts at a time, much less compare and analyze them against a mounting pile of data being gathered by Sten's surveyors, scavengers, and work-party spies.

The solution required two very different but equally elegant minds: Sorensen and Kraulshavn. The big farm boy boiled everything down to the smallest possible level of expression. That reduced everything by about eighty percent. Still too much. Then Kraulshavn performed the impossible. He created a symbol language in which a single squiggle might represent a hundred screens of data. The written lan-

guage of the ancient Chinese was a mere glimmer of Kraulshavn's art.

Next came the difficult problem of communication with
the electronic moron. In such primitive conditions, how did
one send and receive symbols? Oddly enough, the answer
came rather simply. Why not a spark transmitter? Sten had
asked. Alex had just gaped at him a moment and then put
his little team to work on it. They quickly broke Kraulshavn's symbol language down into dots and dashes. A simple key—a spring device manipulated by hand—was used
to transmit. A tiny speaker was used to receive the computer's buzzing response.

The memory banks had created the biggest problem. No
one had been able to offer even a silly suggestion for stor-
ing the data. Alex had lied to Kraulshavn and Sorensen,
telling them that he had the solution in mind and urging
them to press on with the computer. As the on-line date
grew closer and closer, Alex found himself growing increasingly frustrated.

Ibn Bakr gave him the answer. The big tailor needed to age
cloth to make Tahn peasant costumes. He used a mild caustic
in near-boiling-temperature water and washed the cloth over
and over again in one of the huge industrial washing machines. One day Alex found himself considering the problem
as he stood in front of the machine, hypnotized by the twin
agitators chugging back and forth. His jaw dropped as he realized he was staring at the answer. If he played with the
gearing . . . spooled wire from one spindle to another . . .
reversed the polarity of the wire . . . then fed the data from the
computer to the wire . . . Voilà! After several thousand years,
Kilgour had reinvented the wire recorder.

Finally the big moment had come. Sten and Alex hovered
over Sorensen and Kraulshavn as they got ready to fire up the
computer. Sorensen wagged his fingers for Kraulshavn to
start. The being shook its head. *No.* Finger wagging came
back.

"What's the problem?" Sten asked.

"He says it needs a name." Sorensen laughed. "Otherwise
it won't know who we're talking to."

Sten buried a groan of impatience. It was obviously impor-

tant to Kraulshavn. The last thing he needed was a big pouting
bird for a programmer.

"How about Brainerd?" Sten suggested. "Wasn't he the
guy way back when who got us all into this computer mess?"

Sorensen ran it through for Kraulshavn. No problem.
Brainerd it was. Feathered appendages manipulated the key.
Tiny sparks began rhythmically leaping between the gap. Sten
imagined the dot-dash symbols flowing along the wire. Un-
consciously he found himself leaning over the small speaker,
waiting for the crackling response of the computer.

Nothing. More flying fingers. More sparks.

"Come on, you little clot," Sten breathed. "Wake the hell
up . . . Come on . . . Come on . . . Speak to us . . ."

There was a crackling stutter. Then silence.

"Clot! What the hell's wrong with it?"

"Patience, young Horrie," Alex said. "Maybe the wee
beastie is afeared to wake up."

After all the time and energy invested, Sten failed to see
any humor in the situation. He was all for putting the boot into
it—and he did not mean the electronic variety. A big, heavy
leather boot was more along his line of thinking.

The one-sided conversation continued for many more long
minutes. Finally, Kraulshavn leaned back. There was some
finger wagging, silent quizzing from Sorensen, then more
finger wagging.

"What's he saying?" Sten asked.

"It doesn't like its name," Sorensen said. "He says we
should try something else."

"I don't clotting care what we clotting call it," Sten gritted
out.

The big washing machine/wire recorder *gaaronk*ed its
agreement in the background.

"Call it anything you like. Call it gaaronk-gaaronk for all I
give a clot!"

Sorensen nodded quite seriously. Fingers translated. Kraulshavn responded.

"Well?" Sten finally asked.

"Kraulshavn thinks one Gaaronk will be sufficient," Sorensen said.

And before Sten could kill someone, the sparking started

again. Almost instantly there was a return crackle. It was hesitant at first, and then there was one long stream of crackling. Kraulshavn bent his head to the speaker, listening. Then his fingers flashed at Sorensen. The big farm boy turned his innocent face to Sten.

"It's awake," he said. "It likes Gaaronk just fine!"

CHAPTER TWENTY

CRISTATA HAD PASSED the word that he wished to see Big X after the last roll call—which meant after all prisoners were securely locked into their cells.

Sten pulled on the tatters of a dark coverall and picked the lock on his cell. By that time, the lock tumblers were so used to being picked that a sharp smack on the doorjamb probably would have sprung the lock. He ran down the corridors and stairs toward the ground without worrying about guards—the few patrols that the Tahn ran inside Koldyeze's wings at night were large and noisy.

He picked the lock that led out into the courtyard and waited. He was following instructions.

Cristata's emissary had told him to wait until the large search beam—the one that was slightly blue—swept across the courtyard. He was to count six, because there was an amplified light beam behind it. "Then walk—do not run—*walk* twenty-six paces toward 1430 hours, assuming that the search beam is at twelve."

He paced the requisite number of paces, then stood, slightly hidden behind a ruined column, feeling stupid and waiting for the search beam to pick him up on its next sweep. Instead, the paving stones next to his feet slid away, and Cristata's tendrils probed out.

"If you wish," he said, "you could jump down beside me."

Sten wished—and jumped.

He found himself in a narrow pit next to the furry being. The paving stones—Sten realized they were a very clever trapdoor—slid noiselessly closed above him.

After a moment there was a spark, and then there was light. The lamp Cristata held was a small pannier with what looked a great deal like one of the prisoners' standard rations floating in its center, surrounded by liquid.

Cristata explained that the lamp was just what Sten thought it to be—they had boiled extra rationpaks until they yielded fat, then used the fat for fuel and the packs themselves as wicks.

"But that is not what I wished to show you. Come with me."

Cristata, without waiting for a response, dropped down into a narrower pit that Sten had not noticed and disappeared.

Sten followed.

The pit dropped about two meters and then, Sten could see, opened into a tunnel. The tunnel was completely boarded and reinforced, top, bottom, and sides.

Crawling through it was hardly claustrophobic—it was more like moving down a small but perfectly engineered corridor that led slowly but certainly downward.

At what Sten estimated were twenty-five-meter intervals, the passageway opened up into small but equally well built way stations.

It was, Sten thought, something that would take humans five years to engineer—or longer. But there was no one in the tunnel except the flailing fur-covered rump of Cristata moving ahead of him. Then the lay reader's rump wiggled and then vanished.

Sten crawled on and found himself at the lip of a larger, rocky chamber.

In it were Cristata and three humans. Sten vaguely recognized them as fellow prisoners. He levered himself over the edge and settled onto a granite boulder. There was complete silence except for the hissing of the fat lamp.

"Well, sir? What do you think?"

The question was asked by a woman wearing the stripes of

a lance bombardier—Markiewicz, Sten remembered. He answered honestly.

"I've dug some tunnels," he said. "But this is the best one I've ever seen. You've done a clot—sorry. An excellent job."

"In the spirit of the Great One," Cristata intoned. "By his leave only."

"In the spirit of the Great One," the other three said. What the hell, Sten thought. So Cristata was converting the masses. If believing in whatever Cristata did could produce a tunnel like that, Sten was ready to be baptized himself.

"I'm impressed, as I said," Sten said. "But I've already said that you people can have any help we can give. Why'd you decide to show it to me?"

Cristata's facial tendrils wiggled. "Because," he said, "we appear to have a problem." His tendrils indicated. Sten looked: The large rocky chamber, he realized, was composed on three sides of roughly cemented chunks of rock—what must have been the cathedral's foundations. But directly in front was one very large, very solid piece of stone, like unto a wall.

Sten figured out why Cristata had brought him down there. It was not pride. They needed help.

If Sten had not been Big X, he might have been more cooperative. But he had several thousand other people to consider, and so he put on his blandest face.

"You need help in getting through that clotting—beg pardon—rock?"

"We do," Markewiecz said.

"I could have more diggers come in," Sten said. "But it'd still take about a thousand years to chisel through that beast. And blasting, I'm thinking, is contraindicated."

The humans slumped. But Cristata had no reaction.

"But I think we might be able to help," Sten went on.

Cristata's tendrils wriggled once more. "When a more senior reader offered to deliver what might be considered the less interesting—forgive me, Great One—portions of the lesson, portions which were my duty under normal circumstances, normally there were what I have heard called tradesies involved."

"There are," Sten said.

"We are listening."

We, Sten wondered, far underground. *We* meaning Cristata and his converts, or we and his Great One? Sten considered the tons of rock, earth, and stone above his head and decided this was not the place to be terribly agnostic.

Sten was not offering a pigless poke.

Kraulshavn and Sorensen's computer had already begun *gaaronk*ing through the surveyors' figures. And yes, indeed, there were big missing spaces between what the measurements produced and what Koldyeze looked like.

Most interesting were the cheapjack echosondes the surveyors had run. Some of Avrenti's supersensitive antitunneling microphones had somehow ended up in the hands of Kilgour's thieves. Those had then been implanted in the stone courtyard, and an impulse had been introduced. The impulse was generally a somewhat unconnected chunk of stone atop the cathedral's battlements. When said chunk of stone came crashing down, of course as a result of natural causes, the crash was recorded at various points and fed through Gaaronk.

The crashes did not match—and showed that, mysteriously, there was a lot of unknown there underneath Koldyeze. Empty unknown there.

Cellars.

That was Sten's oinker in the sack.

"If," he began, "I can show you a way around or through this rock, your tunnel is no longer going to be exclusive."

The three humans growled.

"Continue," Cristata said.

"I would like to use the tunnel to take more escapers out."

"How many?"

"I don't know. But you four would be the first. And you would have all the assistance my organization could provide."

"We have all the aid we need from the Great One," Cristata said. His converts nodded in agreement.

Sten felt slightly sorry for what he was doing, but as yet there was no other viable escape plan in motion. And Sten remembered once again that warrant officer crying over his parcel.

"We'll give you more diggers. Diggers working under your

direction. And nothing will be done without your knowledge and approval."

"Do we have any choice?"

Sten did not bother to answer.

Markiewicz glanced at Cristata and answered for the four of them. "It appears as if the Great One wishes this."

It was unanimous.

Sten sort of hated to give them what looked to be the answer, because it was simple.

Dig down.

Disbelieving—except for Cristata, who reasoned that somehow the Great One was speaking through Sten—they did.

Many days later, they broke through into the cellars of Koldyeze.

And that, for Cristata, created an even larger problem.

Once again Sten went out and down late at night, then shinnied down from that small rocky chamber into caverns. High stone-ceilinged caverns that led on into darkness. Caverns that were flagstone-floored, with pillars stretching up. Caverns that, Cristata pointed out, held all the temptations of Xanadu.

Sten took a quick torchlight inventory, whistled, and agreed. Evidently the simple, monotheistic agrarian communards who had originally built Koldyeze had planned for some very rainy days. And they had planned on spending those rainy days in more than ascetic meditation. There were chambers with large barrels. Sten thumped them, and they appeared to still have liquid in them. He ran his finger along the barrel staves and tasted alcohol.

Other chambers held foodpaks; still others, clothing.

"And we have not fully explored these chambers," Cristata went on gloomily. "But it would appear that whoever stored these substances enjoyed life."

Sten eyed the foodpaks hungrily—and stopped thinking about what a meal composed of real food could do for him. Instead, he made plans.

Cristata—personally—would make a full survey of the cellars. What was in them would be told to Colonel Virunga and Mr. Hernandes only. The last thing Sten needed was for that tunnel, which looked to be their only salvation, to get blown because a bunch of tunnelers started looking fat, well dressed, and—worst case—drunk. The assigned tunnelers from the X organization would be conducted into the rocky chamber blindfolded and then taken through the cellars to the working face. Only Cristata and his converts would know what those cellars of plenty held. They would be kept secret for emergency rations and to help the escapers get into shape.

And Sten hoped most sincerely that none of Cristata's true believers would suffer a lapse of faith and a subsequent big mouth.

CHAPTER TWENTY-ONE

SENIOR CAPTAIN LO PREK sat nervously on the edge of his bunk, trying to decipher the radio chatter between the freighter captain and traffic control. The mysteries of naval patter were beyond him, but he could tell from the tone of the captain's voice that all did not bode well.

Prek had wrangled passage on a ship carrying low-priority materials for the Tahn factories. Already the ship's flight had been interrupted or rerouted half a dozen times since he had started his journey many cycles before. And from the captain's whining, he was sure it was about to happen again.

He squirmed impatiently on the bunk, almost welcoming the bite of the metal edge into his skinny haunches. He felt helpless. There was nothing he could do or say to hurry the journey. He had already called in the few favors that were owed him to get the short amount of leave that had been approved. And he had almost begged to get permission to travel on the puny freighter. Permission had been granted grudgingly—possibly out of guilt.

Prek knew that he was not a man anyone liked. He was

superefficient. Superobedient. Single-minded at his work. Never asking for any rewards for a job well done. Being noncompetitive, he had also never harmed anyone in his life. Still, he was not liked. There was something about him... and Prek knew and accepted it, just as he accepted the guilt that caused in his fellow officers. For a change, he had used that guilt. Acting completely out of character, he had molded it to his own advantage. Normally, even the thought of something like that would have disgusted Prek.

But not this time. Because this time he was sure he had found Sten—or, at least, where Sten was hiding.

There was a new prisoner-of-war camp. For troublemakers. For survivors. It was on Heath at a place called Koldyeze.

Prek listened to the resignation in the freighter captain's voice. There would be another delay. Another reprieve for his enemy.

CHAPTER TWENTY-TWO

THE PRISONER WORK detail, surrounded by their Tahn guards, clattered back toward Koldyeze. Just in front of them the cobbled street wound upward toward the prison.

"I'm waiting," Sten said.

"Shut up. You'll see," St. Clair whispered.

"Deee-tail... halt," Chetwynd bellowed.

The prisoners clumped to a stop. On either side of the road rose abandoned slum apartments.

"Five minutes. Rest. Be grateful."

Sten goggled as all the guards, including Chetwynd, ostentatiously turned their backs and the detail dissolved, scampering into the buildings like so many rodents.

"What in the—"

"Come on," St. Clair urged, nearly dragging Sten into a doorway.

"Didn't I say I had a surprise?" she went on.

"GA, Captain. And quick."

"Don't give me orders. Look. You know how to search a room?"

"I do," Sten said.

"Okay. We're going upstairs. You look for things. I'll talk."

They went up the rickety stairs, and Sten followed her instructions.

"What am I looking for?"

"Anything we can use. And anything the Tahn can sell. We got ourselves a business going, Big X."

Indeed they did.

The slum quarters had never been that well populated—the apartments were entirely too close to Koldyeze. And the periodic draft sweeps the Tahn made for their military started, of course, in the poor sections of Heath.

St. Clair had followed orders—if she was to be the scrounger, she would be a clotting good one. And the way to get things was, of course, on the outside. In spite of her total loathing for anything resembling manual labor, she had volunteered for every work gang going. She did not know exactly what to look for, but she knew there was something out there.

What was out there were the guards. And St. Clair knew that any being who was willing to batten on the miseries of others was corruptible. She had tested her theory—and her teeth—when she had found a jeweled tunic pin in some trash.

She had offered it to the nearest and—by estimate from body weight—greediest guard. He had snatched and examined it.

"Are there others?" he had asked.

"I guess so," St. Clair said innocently, waving a hand around at the multistory buildings. "It'd be interesting to look.

"Wouldn't it?"

The guard grinned. "Whyn't you an' the others go have a look?"

Within minutes, Captain St. Clair had the rest of the detail worming through the nearest apartment. That looked as if it could develop into something. Within two days she felt less like a corrupter and more like the corrupted. The "looting break" became an instant ritual for most of the work details on their way back to Koldyeze.

St. Clair stopped her explanation and marveled at Sten. He was listening intently while quartering the room like a bloodhound. He started at the far wall and quartered outward. Each piece of broken furniture was picked up or tapped for hidden compartments. The rags that had been clothes were swiftly patted down, then held up to see if they still could be used. The ripped mattress was kneaded for any interesting lumps. There were two pictures lying on the floor in their broken frames. Both of them were torn apart. Then Sten set to work knuckle rapping on the walls.

"I said to look for things," she said.

"That's what I'm doing."

"Pretty clottin' thorough, mister. What were you when you were a civilian? Some kind of burglar?"

"No," Sten said. He certainly had no intention of explaining to anyone, least of all to St. Clair, whom he trusted about as much as a Tahn, that his search was the product of thorough Mantis training. "Here we go," he said.

St. Clair stared—it looked as if Sten had pulled a sliver of metal from his arm and then knifed through a wall switch. The sliver disappeared, and Sten's fingers emerged with a wad of credits. St. Clair inhaled sharply.

"Money. Tahn money."

"Right. Now, go on out, Captain."

"What are you—"

"That's an order! Move!"

St. Clair found herself outside the broken door. A moment later, Sten stepped out beside her.

"Very good, Captain," he said. "Now. Here's the drill. Anything the guards want—play-pretties, alk, drugs—give it to them."

"Give?"

"Give. Money goes to me."

"Nice racket," St. Clair said cynically.

Sten paused. "You know, troop—you got a bad attitude.

You keep a log. Report what you bring in to Colonel Virunga. Or don't you trust him, either?"

"I trust him," St. Clair said grudgingly.

"Fine. I also want civilian clothes. Anything electronic. Wire. Tape. If you find any weapons—" Sten stopped and thought. A prisoner found with a weapon on him would be for the high jump—as would, most likely, the entire work detail. "Weapons—you stash them. Report to me, and we'll arrange to get them in the gate."

"Detail! Reassemble!"

"Let's go."

Sten clattered back down the steps. St. Clair followed, looking at his back and wondering several things.

Chetwynd was waiting in the street outside.

"You!"

Sten snapped to attention. "Sir!"

"What was your name again?"

"Horatio, sir."

"You sure you don't remember me?"

"Nossir!"

"Before the war, I worked the ports," Chetwynd went on. "Maybe you used to be a merchant sailor?"

"Nossir! I was never offworld before I joined up, sir."

Chetwynd scratched his chin. "Clot. I dunno. Maybe you got a twin brother somewhere. You two got anything?"

St. Clair felt Sten's fingers touch her hand. As an experienced gambler, she palmed the object, then held it out.

"Credits," Chetwynd said. "Very good. Very good, indeed. Maybe next time I'm in charge of the detail, and you two want to go off and . . ." He snickered. "I can make it a long enough rest break."

St. Clair thought fondly of how she could thank Chetwynd as she smiled and ran back toward the detail. Drawing and quartering, she decided, was far too easy. Bed Sten? She would rather make love to a mark.

CHAPTER TWENTY-THREE

THE SUPERSECRET OF the Prisoner's Aid parcels was that they were neither quite wholly altruistic nor neutral.

Mercury Corps—Intelligence—field operatives, which of course included Mantis, flag officers, and skippers of long-range penetration units or ships were given the secret orally when a mission suggested they might be captured.

A few items in each crate were loaded. For instance:

One key item to look for was any foodstuff that supposedly had been produced by a paternally named firm, such as Grandfather's Caff, Dronemaster's R'lrx, Packguru's Scented Tofu, and so forth. All the firms were quite legitimate, but the foodstuffs packaged were designed to be as close to inedible as the Emperor's most devious chemists could make them. Even a prison guard should have had little interest in them.

There was nothing out of the ordinary in their contents, but each of those cans contained something potentially useful for an escaper. Microwire saws were buried in the rim of the pak. Needle-size engraving tools were in others. Still other paks had miniature printed circuit boards sealed in the double layer that made up the pak's base. It would take a cursing prisoner two days to break the seal apart—but that might also prevent discovery even with a thorough inspection. There were other interesting devices in other cans. All the materials used would never show up on detectors.

All metals—such as the pins and needles in the archaic sewing kits—were magnetized and could be used in compasses.

The clothes themselves were indelibly marked with a black-white X on the front and rear. There was no reason for a prison official to object to issuing them—they certainly could never be used for any kind of escape. The X's were actually *almost* indelible. Each parcel contained small single-use artificial sweetener packs, artificial sweetener that was in fact tasteless. The sweetener was intended to be dissolved in water, and the clothing soaked in it. Four hours later, the X's would vanish and the POW would be left with a garment that, given enough tailoring skill, might be converted into an acceptable civilian-looking garment for his escape.

No one outside Imperial Intelligence knew about that— certainly not the gentle Manabi. It was a violation of every POW convention and any civilized ethos. And, of course, it had been the personal scheme of Fleet Marshal Ian Mahoney in the days when he had headed Imperial Intelligence.

Even the legitimate items in the aid parcels had their own, nonlegitimate purposes.

For one thing, the foodpaks were very useful for one of Kilgour's intelligence schemes.

This one he had mentally dubbed "Seduction of the Innocent/Reward for the Wicked (Wee Free Division)."

By that point he had selected the agents for the operation, choosing the friendliest and most open prisoners he could find. Each of them was ordered to choose a guard or two, then try to make friends with that screw.

To accomplish that, the "seducers" were given access to anything any of the prisoners had. If a guard fancied a ring, somehow he would be given it. If a guard needed someone to talk to, there would always be a sympathetic ear or auditory apparatus the seducer could provide. The only limit was sexual involvement—not because Kilgour had any particular moral qualms but because he was an experienced enough spymaster to realize that pillow talk usually was not significant and that there was the constant danger of the seducer eventually becoming the seducee. There were five primary goals:

1. Can this guard be corrupted?
2. Can this guard be blackmailed?
3. Discover everything about camp security, from the personalities of the guards to the location of sensors to shift assignments.

4. Find out everything and anything about Heath, from what can be ordered in a restaurant (escapers, unaware of civilian shortages, have been blown ordering a nonexistent item) through travel restrictions and requirements to current slang and civilian dress.

5. Are there ways to get offplanet? If so, what are they, and what are the problems?

There were also other requirements.

There was a tap on the door to Alex and Sten's cell. Kilgour beamed and bellowed, "Thae's noo need t' beat, sir. We're a' home."

The door opened, and Mr. N'chlos peered in.

Sten and Alex shot to attention, as prison orders required.

"No, no," the young man said shyly. "You don't have to do that around me."

"Just showin' a wee note ae respect, sir."

Kilgour was most proud of his work so far.

The heavy-worlder had noticed N'chlos watching him when he was on a work party. Kilgour was fairly sure the interest was not romantic. He was more sure after he had single-lifted a chunk of concrete rubble away after three other prisoners had struggled unsuccessfully to move it. He had also seen that the guard was undermuscled, even for a man trying to grow on the Tahn guard rations. Alex was absolutely sure after hearing a couple of guards make sarcastic comments about N'chlos and his weakness.

Alex had waited until he and N'chlos were away from the rest of the detail, then heaved a monstrous beam out of the roadway the crew was clearing. Apropos of nothing and seemingly talking to thin air, he had said, "Thae's a bit ae a' trick there."

The guard had asked, and Kilgour had shown him just a bit about body leverage: lifting from the legs, not the back, putting the entire force of one's shoulders into an effort, and so forth. N'chlos had never learned any of that.

Kilgour had generously offered to show him some other tricks yet had never suggested that N'chlos was anything other than a fine figure of a Tahn. N'chlos fell into the habit of dropping by Kilgour's cell when he was on walking patrol inside the prisoners' quarters.

The young man had quite a taste for caff, heavily sweetened with Earth sugar. Kilgour then had an unlimited draw from the aid parcels.

Sten had never before been permitted in the cell when N'chlos visited. There was a reason, Kilgour had told him. He said he might need a distraction.

"A brew, lad," Alex said, lighting a small fat stove and putting on the blackened, hammered-out tin they used to cook with. N'chlos sat down on one of the stools Alex had constructed.

" 'N how goes th' war?" Alex asked.

"They just cut the ration points again," N'chlos gloomed. "Even for us."

"Shameful," Kilgour said. "An' curious t' boot."

"Something about those who fight the hardest deserve the most."

"Speakin't frank, Ah considers tha' a bit of ae error. Meanin' no criticism. Dinnae th lords ken th' folks on th' home front be fightin't thae own way ae war?"

N'chlos shifted and unbuttoned the top button of his tunic. Damned right, Sten thought. He, too, was sweltering. In the cell below theirs three men were stoking a plas-fed jerry-rigged furnace.

"Bleedin't hot," Kilgour said sympathetically. "Canne y' take off thae tunic?"

"It's against orders."

"Clot," Alex swore. "A wee soldier should know whae orders are to be followed an' when. Mak't comfortable, sir. I' thae lead-booted sergeant comes, we'll hear his clumpin't in time."

N'chlos took off his combat belt and holstered his stun rod and his tunic-jacket after looking doubtfully at Sten, who was carefully positioned across the room. He looked for someplace to hang the jacket and spotted a peg—the only peg—driven into the cell wall very close to the door.

"C'mon, lad, Ah mean, sir. Caff's on."

N'chlos hung up the tunic and reseated himself.

"Y' were sayin't afore Ah interrupted?"

"Oh. Yes. Sometimes I think I should put in for a transfer. To a line unit."

"Sir, once't Ah thought th' same, an ne'ever harked t' m' poor crippl't brother. War dinnae be bonnie, sir. Lookit th' spot Ah'm in noo."

"*I* wouldn't want to be a POW," N'chlos said frankly.

"True. An' thae's nae th' worst thae can happen." Kilgour paused. "E'en when y'hae no fightin't, thae's little joy. F'r instance, dinnae Ah tell you ae the spotted snakes?"

"I don't think so."

Kilgour spared a minismile for Sten, and Sten glowered back. The clot had trapped him, well and truly.

"*I*' was ae Earth. Ae a wee isle called Borneo."

"You've been to *Earth*!" N'chlos was astonished.

"Aye, lad. Th' service broadin't thae background. At any rate, an' t' go on, Ah'd jus' taken' o'er a wee detachment ae troops."

"I didn't know Imperial warrant officers did that."

"Special circumstances," Alex went on. "An' so Ah calls th' sarn't major in, an Ah asks, 'Sarn't Major, whae's thae worst problem?'

"An' he say't, 'Spotted snakes!'

"An' Ah says, 'Spotted snakes?'

"An' he says, 'Spotted snakes, sir.'"

At that point the cell door opened silently, and an arm—St. Clair's arm—snaked in. Her hand lifted N'chlos's tunic off the peg, and tunic and arm vanished.

"Here's th' caff, sir. Anyhoot, Ah'm looki't ae th' fiche on m' new unit, an' it's awful. Thae's desertion, thae's a crime sheet thae long, thae's social diseases up th' gumpstump—m' command's a wreck!

"So, Ah call't th' unit t'gether an' questions m' men on whae's th' problem.

"An' they chorus, 'Ae's th' spotted snakes, sir.'

"'Spotted snakes?' Ah asks.

"'Aye, sir. Spotted snakes,' they chorus.

"An' thae explain't thae's all these spotted snakes in th' jungle. Ah did say th' detachment wae in th' center ae a braw jungle, dinnae Ah?"

Outside, Sten hoped, N'chlos's tunic was being searched. His soldier book and any other papers were tossed to the prison's fastest runner, who darted downstairs to a cell where L'n waited.

His papers were scrutinized and memorized by her artistically eidetic memory, to be reproduced later.

The tunic was measured, and all uniform buttons had wax impressions made, also for reproduction. The stun rod's measurements were taken just in case someone needed to build a phony weapon.

Within minutes the escape committee would have all the essentials on the off chance that an escaper might want or need to look like a guard. Or maybe to use N'chlos as a cover identity.

Unless, of course, N'chlos turned around, realized his uniform was missing, and shouted an alert.

But in the meantime Sten squirmed under Alex's story.

"An' aye," Kilgour went on. "Thae wee spotted snakes. All over th' place. Wee fierce lads w' a braw deadly poison. Crawl in th' fightin' positions an' bites, crawl in th' tents an' bites, crawl in the mess an' bites. Awful creatures. Som'at hae be done.

"So Ah considers an' then orders up aye formation. An' comit out, an th' men gasp, seein't Ah'm holdin' a spotted snake.

"An' Ah say, 'Listen't up, men. Ah hae here a spotted snake, aye?'

"An' th' men chorus back, 'Aye sir, ae spotted snake.'

"'Now, Ah'm goin't t' show you th' solution to thae spotted snakes. Ae's by th' numbers. Wi' th' count ae one, y' securit th' snake wi' your right hand. Wi' th' count ae two, y' secure th' snake wi' your left hand as well. Wi' th' count ae three, y' slid't y'r right hand up t' its wee head, an *pop*, on th' count ae four, y' snappit th' snake's head off wi' y'r thumb!'

"An' th' men's eyes goggle, an then they go t' war.

"F'r th' next two weeks, thae's all y' hear around th' detachment. *Pop . . . pop . . . pop . . . pop.* Thae's wee snake heads lyin't all around.

"An th' morale picks up, an' thae's noo more deserters, an' thae's nae crime sheet, an' e'en the pox rate drops a notch.

"M' problem's solved. An' then, one day, Ah'm visitin' th' dispensary.

"An' thae's one puir lad lying't thae, an' he's swathed in bandages. Head t' foot. Bandages.

"An' Ah ask't 'Whae happen?'

"An' he croakit, 'Spotted snakes, sir!'

"'Spotted snakes,' Ah says.

"'Aye, sir. Spotted snakes.'

"'G'on lad,' Ah says."

Alex was looking a little worried—then the door opened again, and the same silent arm replaced the tunic and weapons belt. Alex hesitated, then put his story—if that was what it was—back on track. Sten was trying to remember just what the most painful and slowest method of execution he knew of was and was determined to apply it to his warrant officer.

"'Sir,' th' lad in bandages goes on. 'Y' know how y' told us how t' deal wi' th' spotted snakes?'

"'Aye, spotted snakes. But Ah dinnae ken—'

"'Ah'm tryin't t' tell you. Ah'm in m' fightin' position ae stand-to th' other night. An' thae wee furrit object wi' spots slides in m' hole. An' just like y' ordered, Mr. Kilgour, on th' count ae one Ah grabs it wi' m' right hand, on th' count ae two Ah grabs it wi' m' left hand, on th' count ae three Ah slides m' hand up, an' on th' count ae four Ah *pop* . . . an' sir, can y' fancy m' sittin' thae wi' m' thumb up a tiger's arse?'"

There was dead, complete silence.

Finally N'chlos spoke. "That is the worst clotting joke I have ever heard."

And for the first and only time, Sten found himself in complete agreement with a Tahn.

St. Clair peered into the gloom, watching her strange roommate begin sketching—working from memory only— the Tahn identification card directly onto a photosensitive plate. She had wanted to object when Sten had ordered her to pair up with the shy Kerr, but she had swallowed her protest. She did not want to give the clot the satisfaction of knowing her objections. It had nothing to do with the fact that L'n was not human. St. Clair just preferred to be alone. She had always been solo, had always depended on her own wits, with never the thought of responsibility for another being to hold her back. St. Clair survived by taking chances, by not hesitating. And L'n was the kind of being that made those cold feelings difficult.

Also, there was some logic to the pairing. As the main scrounger, it was better for her to deal directly with the little Kerr artist. But it took some getting used to. L'n needed darkness to be comfortable, and outside the cell she was almost helpless in the bright Tahn sun. Gradually St. Clair had found herself automatically helping L'n with little things: guiding her to mess; finding tools lost in the glare of the late afternoon sun; pulling her back to reality when she became hypnotized by some freak manifestation of light.

In short, St. Clair found herself liking another living being. L'n was becoming that strangest of all animals—a friend.

It took some work, especially the way L'n went on about that bastard Horatio, who was so full of his own authority. The way L'n talked, the man was practically a saint. And then St. Clair heard the story about Lance Corporal Hansen, and she understood Hansen and Sten had become one person—an interchangeable hero. It was all L'n could do to hold on to her sanity living in the squalor and dense crowding of the prison camp. She yearned for the peaceful forests of her homeworld. L'n spent longer and longer periods of time lost in those memories. And the hard reality of the camp was becoming more and more difficult. Without Sten—or at least the idea of Sten —L'n would eventually cross over into silent madness.

St. Clair had made herself a promise to change that. If it was the last thing she did before she escaped, she would coax L'n into standing on her own.

"Tell me, L'n," she said. "You're interested in light. Have you ever seen that famous light tower on Prime World?"

L'n stopped in midsketch. "You mean the one built by those two Milchens? Marr and Senn, I think they're called."

"Yeah."

"Just pictures," she said. "Not in person."

"Oh. You've never been to Prime World. When this is over, maybe we can go see it together."

"Oh, I've been to Prime World before. In fact, when I was there, I heard there was going to be a big party at the tower. Now, *that* would have been something to see!"

"Why didn't you go?" St. Clair asked.

"I wasn't invited."

St. Clair was incredulous. "Why the clot not? You coulda crashed it easy. I did it a couple of times! At a Marr and Senn party, nobody could possibly know if you're legit or not."

L'n sighed, a little hopeless, a tinge jealous. "Crash a party . . . I've dreamed of doing something like that. You know, the new L'n. Bold. Determined. Daring. Sweeping into a party like I owned it. Making everybody think I've just got to be somebody famous because of the way I carry myself. But afraid to ask and show their ignorance." She shook her head. "Not a chance. They'd take one look at these big ugly eyes of mine and know right off I'm a nobody."

St. Clair was stunned. "What are you talking about? Ugly eyes?"

L'n shrugged. It was a shrug of someone resigned to an uncomfortable truth.

"I'm telling you, girl," St. Clair finally said. "You and I have got a lot of work to do. And we're going to start with your notions of ugly and work right up to party crashing."

L'n giggled as if St. Clair had just made a joke. But St. Clair knew better. She had just made a promise. And St. Clair was a woman of her word.

CHAPTER TWENTY-FOUR

"COUNT COMPLETE," VIRUNGA announced, echoing Isby's report. Then he pivoted, saluted Genrikh, and bellowed, "All prisoners present." He paused just a beat. "Sir."

Even Genrikh could not find a reason to prolong the afternoon roll call. He nodded and stalked toward the administration area. Virunga saluted his absence, about-faced and shouted again: "Unit . . . dis-missed!"

The semirabble became a babble of conversation, and the

prisoners headed toward their quarters, mess kits, and the evening meal.

Sten, who had more important plans, slid toward the stairs and Virunga's chambers—and, head in a tunnel, he nearly walked into Chetwynd, who was waiting and smiling down at him.

"Prisoner Horatio."

"Sir!"

"That's not your name."

"Pardon, sir. My mother would be surprised."

"Not too bad. I just remembered where I saw you before. Dru."

"Bless you."

"Knock off the drakh. I don't have a lot of time. Dru. Prison world. I was running a happy knot of villains, harvesting mollusks. And you and that tub Kilgour showed up in screwsuits. To harvest some weasel named . . . hell, what was it? Dunstan . . . no. Dyntsman."

Chetwynd's memory was excellent. Good enough to kill him.

"Sir. No offense, sir. But how could I—"

"How could you be a Tahn screw then and a POW now? Try this. You're Imperial Intelligence. When the war started, you got caught up in the net. Maybe your cover was firecontrolman. Maybe you grabbed it out of the hat when the drakh came down. Hell if I know."

Sten calculated. Could he kill Chetwynd now? Here? Negative. He could disappear before the body was found, but there would be reprisals. Second question: Could he stall Chetwynd from reporting this interesting piece of information to Avrenti long enough to arrange some species of fatal accident, preferably outside Koldyeze's walls? Possibly.

"Speak up, prisoner."

"I can't, sir. Anything I say'd get me tossed into solitary."

"Very good," Chetwynd said approvingly. "If you'd started burbling that I was a flip case, I would've had to smash you a few times and toss you in the cells. And might've started wondering about whether my mind's finally going. But . . ." Chetwynd smiled. "Now all I have to do is figure how to play the card. Or whether to play it at all."

"The prisoner does not understand."

"The prisoner surer'n hell *does* understand. I'm a screw right now. But my sentence's still on remand. These clottin' Tahn can yank my privileges and have me back on Dru—or off to one of the deathworlds—for any reason or no reason at all.

"So I got to figure this some more.

"And, just so you don't start trying to arrange some kinda incident that'd go and change my lovely body, I'll give you a further piece of my thinking. I like to back winners."

Chetwynd was a far more subtle man than he appeared, Sten realized.

"The war isn't going well?"

"The war's goin' just fine. So far." Chetwynd said. "We—clot. I'm even startin' to talk like a screw. The Tahn are poundin' you Imperials like you're drums. Question I got is how long. I go out the gate an' I see gravsleds grounded 'cause fuel's rationed. I see us scroungin' through the rubble for recyclables. I got to figure if the drakh's like this here on Heath, what's it like on the other worlds?

"You like my figuring? Maybe I shoulda been an analyst, huh? My thinkin' goes on—if the Tahn don't win some kinda flat-out battle real quick, the grinder's gonna go on. And there's more of you than there is of us.

"So maybe the war don't go like the lords and ladies want it. And maybe—sooprise—Heath's got a little different system of government. Like maybe we're payin' our taxes to Prime World.

"I'm thinkin'—in a case like that—Mr. Chetwynd might not get a little gold star by havin' set up some hero intelligence type to get his brain scanned and then burned. Might end up bein' some kind of war criminal.

"Wouldn't like that at all.

"Like I said, I back winners. So . . . least till things change, and I can get a better idea on what game we're playin', and with whose deck . . . I'm planning on doing just what I been doing about you. Nothing.

"That's all, prisoner."

*   *   *

Sten was about to make a decision he hated.

Even in escaping, there was strategy and there was tactics. Tactics—find possible escape route, build possible escape route, equip escapers—was very easy.

The strategy was the agony.

A POW's duties did not end with his or her capture. He or she was still a combatant. The war still had to be fought— even inside a POW camp. Everyone in Koldyeze not only had been hypno-conditioned during training but had accepted that with his continued resistance.

Part of that resistance was escape.

Escape did far more than get the poor sorry prisoner to home base and, hopefully, returned to war—it continued the war while it was being carried out. Each prisoner who was a pain in the butt to his captors took one or more potential enemy soldiers away from the lines and made them into guards. The bigger the pain in the butt, the more he or she decreased the available fighting strength. The fine line to walk, of course, was gauging at what point the enemy would decide that a bullet was more economically feasible.

Thus far, the prisoners of Koldyeze had done an excellent job of continuing the war and their own lives.

Cristata's tunnel might change all that.

That was Sten's decision, one that Colonel Virunga gave his opinion on and then qualified it.

Once the tunnel punched out beyond the walls, there were two choices for escape—mass or planned.

A mass attempt would mean that everyone who could fit down that hole would burst out onto Heath.

The end result?

Certainly all troops and auxiliaries on Heath would be yanked from their normal duties to hunt down the escapers. Other units, headed for battle, could well be diverted onto Heath. The end result would be that most, if not all, of the escapers would be rounded up.

And then murdered.

It was also very likely that the entire POW complement of Koldyeze would be slaughtered in reprisal.

That was Virunga's recommended option. Go for broke. We are all soldiers—and we all accept the risks.

Sten chose the second option, even though at best he was condemning people who had worked long hours on the tunnel to staying in captivity, denying them even the slightest possibility of making it to freedom.

The second option was to filter out a handful of completely prepared escapers, given every bit of kit the X organization could provide, from forged papers to money.

Sten did not reach his decision for any humanitarian reasons. Or, at least, so he told himself.

There had been almost no successful escapes by prisoners of the Tahn—at least very few that he had heard of. If Koldyeze broke out en masse—and the escapers were captured, given a show trial, and executed—that would effectively dampen any resistance, let alone further escape attempts from any of the other camps scattered through the Tahn worlds.

Better that one escaper make his or her home run all the way from the heart of the Tahn Empire—and the success be promoted.

Virunga grunted in displeasure. "I delegated . . . your decision. Now. Who goes?"

Painful strategy turned into more painful tactics. Sten would have to play God.

It was easier to start with the exclusions. Virunga, of course. He could not—and would not consider—abandon the beings in his charge.

Sten and Alex—Big X was banned.

Other beings who could not blend into the essentially human population of Heath. The crippled.

Who *could* make an attempt—and probably get killed in the process? Sten had only the original thousand prisoners, plus the various additions, to choose among.

Cristata and his three converts. It was their plan. Sten hoped to force the four into accepting some assistance and a plan more rational than flinging themselves on the mercy of country peasants.

Ibn Bakr and his partner.

Sten grimaced. St. Clair. He liked her about as much as she reciprocated. But if there was to be one solo attempt, he thought she probably had the best chance of anyone.

Hernandes. If anybody deserved to go out, it was he. Also,

Sten figured that Hernandes's continuing sabotage operations were due to get blown, and Hernandes due for the high jump.

Completely unsure whether he had made the right decision, or even if he had made the correct choices, Sten left Virunga's room to begin the laying on of hands.

Naturally enough, nothing worked out as Sten had thought.

"My friend," Hernandes said slowly. "Thank you. But . . . I shall not be going out through the tunnel. I dislike enclosed spaces."

Sten, having more than a bit of a tendency toward claustrophobia, understood that. But Hernandes continued.

"Probably what you've said is correct. Probably I've run the game about as far as I can. But I don't *know* that. Do you understand?"

No. Sten did not.

"I'll try it another way. Assume that I manage to wiggle down that tunnel without making an exhibition of myself. Further assume that I am able to disappear into the unwashed of Heath and, using your—I am sure—most clever plan, return to the Empire. That is all very well and good.

"But what then would happen to me? I assume that I would be pridefully exhibited across the Empire as someone who managed to—capital letters please—Find Freedom.

"I would be far too valuable to ever get assigned to combat once more. Isn't that probably correct?"

"You assume a helluva lot in how far you'd get," Sten said. "But you're right."

"My granddaughter died. As I told you. And I am not convinced that a full repayment has been made.

"Now do you understand?"

Sten did. There had been more than a couple of times when Imperial orders and duty had fallen second to personal vengeance.

And so he made apologies to CWO Hernandes—and made mental allowances that when Hernandes was caught by the Tahn, none of Koldyeze's secrets would be exposed.

Similarly, Sten went zero for zero with Lay Reader Cristata.

He had come up with—he thought—a severely clever plan for the three humans and one nonhumanoid. Rather than vanish into a guaranteed-hostile countryside, they should, Sten proposed, stay inside the capital city of Heath. Cristata should present himself as an absolute convert to the cause of the Tahn. He should become a street preacher, loudly espousing how, in seeing the way his own world had been "liberated," he had come to know the true evil of the Empire.

It would take a long time, Sten knew, for people to question a true believer if that true believer was telling them that everything they did was correct.

"But that would be a lie," Cristata pointed out, and his acolytes nodded.

Sten practiced jaw clenching and unclenching as a substitute for answering.

"The Great One would withdraw his support if we taught such a lie," Cristata went on. Also, I do not see what good we could do by remaining within this city, within this place of regimentation and uniforms."

"You could stay alive," Sten offered.

"Life is given and taken away by the Great One. It matters little which is the gift."

More jaw clenching.

"Also, you have failed to understand the teachings of the Great One. Only those who live close to the earth, who have avoided false mammon-professions and have realized that the duty of us all is to feed and help others, could understand and give us shelter."

Sten, remembering a long-ago time when he and his Mantis Team had been chased cross-country for several days by some supposedly uninvolved peasants, did not respond.

"I had hopes, Horatio," Cristata finished sadly, "that you were understanding my message and would become one of us. You did not.

"But we can still pray that those who will take advantage of what the Great One has given us will find truth within their own hearts and, once they return to freedom, will preach the light."

The best that Sten could hope for as he excused himself was that Cristata and his three friends would be sufficiently obvious to take the heat off the real escapers and find an easy and clean death.

St. Clair waited until the door closed behind Sten before she looked at L'n. Even in the dimness, she could see L'n's "hands" twitching.

"But you must go," L'n started without preamble.

Yes, St. Clair thought. I must go. I'm starting to go mad here. This would be escape number twenty-two? Or was it twenty-four? She had set the previous attempts at twenty-one but really did not want to know if she had tried more and failed in more.

This one had to succeed.

Because otherwise St. Clair could see herself, quite coldly and calmly, doing a run at the wire during assembly and getting killed.

Thus far she had avoided forcing herself to play in a rigged game because it was the only one in town. But the odds on staying cold and waiting until the numbers were right were becoming more and more slender.

And L'n?

At least she would have Sten to fall back on. She would survive, St. Clair told herself.

Besides, she was not an orphan. She was the Eel. A lone survivor and gambler. She needed no one and nothing.

Didn't she?

CHAPTER TWENTY-FIVE

THE BRILLIANCE OF Lady Atago was the same as that of the Tahn—and that of their failure.

In war, their plans were carefully worked out down to the last detail. If those plans went awry in midbattle, the Tahn were also geniuses at improvisation. They could—and did—cobble together units made up of the most disparate elements, pitch them into the front lines, and win.

The culturally programmed willingness of their warriors to die in place rather than yield did not hurt, of course. But what the Tahn lacked was the ability to modify a plan once the seal of approval was on it.

And so Lady Atago paced a battle chamber, her bootheels clicking against the emptiness.

She should have been busy briefing the twelve battlefleet commanders, giving final and full details for the attack on Durer, step by step. The battle chamber was fully equipped to show, on its hemispheric domed screen, any detail from the overall strategic advance to the disposition of the lowliest patrol craft.

Instead Atago had been informed, in the highest code, to postpone that meeting and stand by.

Further orders—EYES ONLY—said that the head of the Tahn Council, Lord Fehrle, requested the privilege of conferring with the commander of the fleets at her convenience.

Atago did not bother sending anything other than a routine confirmation. Nor did she arrange to be waiting when Fehrle's battleship broke out of AM2 drive and warped alongside.

The side people and staff officers could provide the panoply. Atago was worried. Something was about to go very, very wrong.

She was very correct.

Fehrle entered the chamber, greeted Atago with all the formality her office required, and then dismissed his aides.

Lady Atago, maintaining propriety, asked if Lord Fehrle wished the honor of seeing her plans for the upcoming engagement.

"No," Fehrle said. "I am well aware, and certainly approve of them."

Then why are you here? Atago thought.

"The council has met, and is committed to the grand plan. In fact, they wish to increase its strategic impact."

Atago smelled a—no, several reeks. Reflexively she palmed a switch, and the projection of the attack against the Durer System sprang across the night galaxy simulation of the chamber above them. But neither Tahn looked at it.

"Perhaps I don't understand," Lady Atago said flatly.

"We have realized, through your brilliant planning and analysis," Fehrle went on, "that your attack should be implemented massively."

He turned to the screen and picked up the control.

"Here," he said. "Twelve battlefleets shall attack through emptiness toward the Durer System. Over here, the feint against the Al-Sufi System will engage the Imperial Forces in the cluster until far too late."

Atago did not even bother responding.

"The strike, as we have all agreed, is for the heart of the Empire. Therefore, after full analysis and discussion, we of the council have agreed that we should expand this plan, both because of its brilliance and because of its perfection to the Tahn ideal."

"Which means?"

"We feel that those fleets which have been kept in reserve could be better committed to the full battle. We shall not worry about our flanks but rather practice a policy of leapfrogging ahead. Any ship, unit, or fleet which becomes engaged shall drop out of the main thrust. Other units will drive through or around them, toward the main goal."

"The main goal, Lord," Atago said, "was to secure the Durer systems and use them as a springboard for the final assault."

"An easily achieved objective," Lord Fehrle said. "One which could conceivably require us to slow and regroup. The council has decided to leapfrog Durer and make the final assault."

Go for broke.

"Suppose," Atago said, looking at the display overhead, "that the Imperial Forces that will flank us, in and around Al-Sufi, succeed in breaking free? And then attacking the main thrust toward Prime World?"

"That will not happen," Fehrle said with a note of impatience. "We are confident that your plan of deception will make them defend the nongoal until far, far too late. Also—" He paused. "We have a further reinforcement of that deception."

"Go on."

"There is another reason," Fehrle said. "Lady Atago, this war has gone on far beyond our most pessimistic projections. We simply do not have the AM2 resources to luxuriate in any battle pause."

Lady Atago, at that moment in time, could conceivably have provided reasons why Fehrle's battle plan—she knew better than to think it was the creation of the council—was an ill-conceived one, a roll of the dice when the dice could very well be loaded toward the house.

But she was a Tahn—and kept silent.

"There are two other modifications to your plan," Fehrle said. "The diversion which you have cleverly created against Al-Sufi. There is only one thing lacking. That force must be commanded by someone that the Empire feels to be our absolute best. Our most feared strategist."

Lady Atago felt her cheeks redden, her hand move toward her personal weapon, and fought to keep herself under control.

"I am honored," she managed, and was surprised that her voice was not shaking. "But if I am to command the diversionary attack—who then will take charge of my twelve fleets—correction, my twelve, and those additional elements the council has decided to add to the attack?"

"Since this is an all-out effort," Lord Fehrle said, "we that command the attack should seamlessly represent the force of our Empire."

Lady Atago managed the formal bow to the Will of the Tahn, the formal salute to her replacement, Lord Fehrle, and then she broke.

Somehow she was out of the battle chamber and in her own quarters before she exploded into rage and words that even a Tahn dockwalloper would have admired.

She calmed.

She took out her personal weapon.

Yes, her honor was besmirched. But not, she realized, by her own doing. Injustice had been done. That was the way. Such things had happened. She had risen above many wrongs. Just as her race had. Beyond those was victory. Very well, she would accept orders. She would command that deception fleet. She would do more, far more, than any timeserver would have accomplished. And she would stand by, ready to assist.

Because she knew that her plan would work—even with the idiot modifications of Lord Fehrle. But after Durer was obliterated, as the combined Tahn fleets struck toward Prime, Lord Fehrle would discover just how hard it was to truly lead rather than merely replace the battle leader and become a last-minute figurehead.

For the final victory, she knew Fehrle would need her help.

And she planned to make him pay most dearly for that, after the defeat of the Empire.

CHAPTER TWENTY-SIX

ONE-THIRD OF a meter to go. Sten could almost feel the cold blackness of the Tahn night just beyond the skim of earth on the other side of the tunnel. It pulled at him relentlessly, like an immense moon at the high tide of freedom. All he had to do was scrape away a little more dirt and he would be out. His long years as a Tahn prisoner would be over—leaving only his own survival to worry about.

He turned back, choking on the acrid air thick with fat-lamp smoke. It bit into his eyes, making them tear. He wiped the tears away with a sleeve and surveyed his troops, the men, women, and beings he had handpicked for the escape.

"Motley" was a distinct compliment. Some, like Cristata and his three converts, were dressed in the rough pale green and brown of Tahn peasants. Ibn Bakr had put all his sewing talents into his uniform and that of his partner, a tiny woman whose name Sten vaguely recalled as Alis. Bakr was dressed in what appeared to be the glitter of a full admiral. Alis's uniform was just slightly less so.

Actually, they were posing as the stationmaster of a grav-train and his assistant. They had identification and papers showing that they were on an inspection tour of all the main hub stations of Heath. Sten had laughed when Ibn Bakr had first shown him the sketches of what he and Alis would wear. He was instantly sorry when he saw Ibn Bakr's hangdog expression—there was nothing so mournful as a giant with his chops dragging on the ground. And then Ibn Bakr had explained about the Tahn love of uniforms and how the lowliest office tended to have some of the most glittering clothes.

"You should see the head garbage collector," Ibn Bakr said.

Sten closed his eyes against the glare and decided that was something he would just as soon skip.

The other members of the escape team were dressed somewhere in between Cristata and Ibn Bakr, ranging from farmers to shopkeepers to grunts to medium-and low-level Tahn officers.

One other standout was St. Clair. She was dressed in boots and a camo cloth jumpsuit so form-fitting that Sten found himself waver between lust and dislike. She had a small matching bag slung over her shoulder. Tucked into it were a change of clothing and the superlightweight camping gear favored by wealthy Tahn sportsmen and women. What St. Clair was relying on was that twice a year a very rare and very tasty tuber appeared in the ground on Heath. The tubers were so prized that only the nobility and the very rich were permitted to gather them. So twice a year the sports world turned out to comb the forests and meadows of Heath for those tubers. The locations where they could be found were as jealously guarded as the trout streams the Eternal Emperor had restocked on Earth.

St. Clair was posing as one of those hunters. She was convinced she could go to ground with ease and wait for just the right opportunity to get off Heath. Sten was not too sure. Still, he had turned down St. Clair's bet—even though the odds she offered were fairly juicy.

Sten observed it all in semisilence, waiting for the lay reader and his followers to finish their prayers for "the Great One" to look with favor on their efforts. The only words Sten could make out were the "ahhhmens" sighed by the three each time Cristata paused. Finally he finished and waddled over to Sten, plucking at the dirt clogging his fur. Every centimeter of his squat form was purposeful and somber. Only the sensitive tendrils ringing his nose squirmed with what Sten was sure was excitement.

"The spirit of the Great One is with us," Cristata said. "He told us it was nearly time to go."

Sten buried any sarcastic remarks that came to mind. After many thousands of tons of digging and shoring, who was he to criticize another being's beliefs? Besides, maybe it was some kind of "Great One" who had given Sten a nutball like Cristata in the first place. Would he have ever found the cellars that honeycomb Koldyeze otherwise? As far as Sten was concerned, it the Great One wanted the credit, he could clottin' have it.

So, instead, Sten grinned a weak grin and said, "Fine. Uh ... Next time you talk ... uh, tell him, or it, or whatever, I said thanks."

Cristata took no offense at all. He understood that Sten meant none.

There was a rumbling sound from the far end, and everyone pressed up against either side of the tunnel as Alex came around a corner hauling an enormous load of supplies on three trained-together carts, the same carts that had been used to move rubble back from the tunnel's face. The heavy-worlder moved with ease, as if he were pulling a few tots in a wagon. When a wooden wheel stuck in a rut, he simply lifted the front end of the train up and shifted it to an easier path. He was hauling at least a ton and a half of gear.

"Thae be the last of it, Horrie, lad," he said, stepping away as a few of the others began unloading his cargo and stacking the supplies at one point of the hollowed-out eye that was the tunnel's face. He glanced around at the faces in the small crowd, nodding pleasantly—a man without a nervous bone in his body. Then he casually moved over to Sten and leaned close to whisper.

"Ah dinnae like this, lad," he said. "Thae all appear dead t' me. Noo, ae we could only teach a few Mantis tricks ... Aye. Thae they'd hae a hope."

Sten shook his head. "This dress rehearsal went as smooth

as anyone could want," he said. "And as for teaching them any tricks...All they'd do is learn enough to be confident amateurs. Clot! Might as well kill them all right there, save the Tahn the pleasure."

"Still, lad. Ah'd feel bonnier ae they kenned a few more wee tricks ae th' craft."

"Believe me, Alex," Sten said. "They're better off this way. It's sort of like a style of fighting I read about. A few thousand years ago, they used to pile troops into these big clumsy aircraft. They'd load 'em down with maybe fifty kilos of gear, strap this big silk bag around them, and kick 'em out the door when they were maybe two three klicks up."

Alex looked at Sten in shocked disbelief. "Th' puir wee lads. Musta had Campbells f'r officers. Atrocity committin' Huns! Pushin't boys oot t' squash 'em ae thae be't bloody bugs."

"Weellll... That wasn't their intention. See, the silk bags were supposed to open, and the soldiers were supposed to float gently to the ground.

"Anyway, they used to train these airborne troopers for the jumps. Some of the toughest training of that era."

"Ah should hope so," Alex said, still a little shocked.

"Funny thing is," Sten pressed on, "when the drakh really hit the fan, sometimes they used to just grab any old grunt, put a sack on him, and toss him out just like the fully trained types. And you know what? There was no difference in the casualty rate. Just as many trained troopies ate it as the grunts who were still wet behind the ears."

"Ah dinnae believe it," Alex said.

Sten surveyed the nervous beings jammed into the tunnel and thought about what terrible things surely awaited them once they crawled out of the safety of Koldyeze.

"I *want* to," he said. "They go out in two nights."

Virunga put the word out during the morning mess. He wanted to see Sten. Urgently. Sten moved casually across the crowded central yard, weaving his way through small garden plots and exercising prisoners. He stopped here and there to chat, to laugh at the right moments, and to scowl and shake his head in disbelief at others.

It was an elaborate and constantly changing ritual he had to perform, else a Tahn stoolie might start taking note of how often a lowly firecontrolman visited the camp CO.

All the while, his mind churned with possibilities. Some news of how the war was going? Badly for the Tahn, he hoped. With a great stretch of luck, Virunga might be calling him in to report the greatest success in Koldyeze so far. Maybe, just maybe, they had managed to plant what Alex called "the Golden Worm."

They had spent an enormous amount of time and effort figuring out a way to suborn a petty bureaucrat named Fahstr. She was the middle-aged chief clerk in charge of pay vouchers. Every Tahn feared her. Even Derzhin, the camp commandant, walked softly around her. At the slightest insult, a pay voucher could be lost forever. And it would take another three small forevers to get it back. What was worse, if she felt particularly nasty, she would misinterpret the coding, and a Tahn victim might find himself docked a whopping chunk for back taxes—whether he owed any or not.

The problem was that Fahstr was seemingly incorruptible. No matter how hard they leaned on N'chlos and their other tame guards, they could not find a single weakness. The woman was fat—but did not particularly favor any type of food. She was obviously sexless, which Alex had remarked was a good thing, because he did not want to be the man who asked for volunteers. She seemed to revel in living a Spartan life, so money was out. How to get to her? It was important, because Fahstr was the key to planting the Golden Worm.

St. Clair stumbled onto the answer. She had gotten herself assigned to a janitorial shift at the payroll office, figuring that a woman of her experience certainly ought to be able to spot another's weaknesses. If nothing else, she might be able to scrounge a few cleaning fluids that might be put to more interesting use.

St. Clair had bumped around the office for half a day before she saw it. As the other clerks kept their eyes glued to their duties, afraid even to lift their heads and be seen not working, Fahstr had spent the entire morning enjoying herself.

It was an emotion that was difficult to recognize right off. Because to Fahstr, enjoyment seemed to be slamming away at

her computer board and gritting out a long string of obscenities that almost made St. Clair blush, interspersed with occasional screams of what seemed to be victory. St. Clair finally
sidled over to the computer to see what was going on. A
bewildering stream of figures swirled on the screen, then
firmed. Shouts of disgust came from Fahstr to be followed by
more hammering at the keyboard. More figures. More cursing. Then it slowly dawned on St. Clair. The figures on the
screen were algorithms. There was a game going on. And the
game was bridge.

St. Clair had not just found a weakness. She had found a
gaping wound.

"Typical bridge freak," she had told Sten later. "Including
her charming disposition. There isn't a thing in this universe
the woman cares for except bridge. She hates people. But to
enjoy bridge, you gotta have people."

"She's got her computer," Sten said. "It can give her any
kind of game she wants. At any level."

"You sure aren't a cardplayer," St. Clair had said. "To
enjoy cards you have to see your opponent squirm. Especially
bridge-type cardplayers. You can't see blood when you beat
the bejesus out of a computer."

"So you hinted broadly that you might know something
about this—uh, what was it called?"

"Bridge. And as for hinting broadly, clot that. I told her
right off that I had been watching her. Couldn't help myself, I
said."

"And she didn't get ticked? I would have figured she'd
have cut you off at the knees for even daring to talk to her."

"No way," St. Clair said. "Bridge players can't help themselves. She understood right off. Especially when I told her I
was fleet champ."

"Fleet what? Of what? There's no such thing!"

"So? She doesn't know that. Or care. Especially since I
allowed that although she might be good, I could wipe the
ground with her."

Grudgingly, Sten had to admire that. From what he could
gather, there was no way the type of fanatic St. Clair was
describing could turn down such a challenge.

"Okay, you get tight with her. Win a few games. Lose a

few to keep her interested. Then you find out what it takes to get her over on our side."

"Don't need to." St. Clair sniffed. "We're programming the computer to partner up with each of us. I got complete access to that thing any time you want."

Sten had instantly put Kraulshavn and Sorensen to work on the Golden Worm. They had completed it a week before and, with St. Clair's expertise, had coded it into a cutthroat north-south pair of hands.

All St. Clair had been waiting for was the chance to plant it. The problem was that time was running out. She was going out the next night. If she did not succeed in planting it immediately, they would have to start all over again. But after the escape, the bloody reprisals might make the whole thing pointless. Because the Golden Worm was their only hope to keep the Tahn from cutting all their throats.

Sten walked into Virunga's cell. There was only the old man to greet him. From the dark, solemn look on his face, Sten knew there was something very wrong. He assumed it had to do with failure. And that failure involved the Golden Worm.

"They caught her," he said flatly, meaning St. Clair.

"No," Virunga said. "She . . . was successful. But . . . there is another . . . matter."

Sten decided to quit guessing and let Virunga tell it.

"As you know . . . St. Clair has complete . . . access. To the computer."

Sten nodded. Fahstr pretty much let St. Clair noodle at will on the Tahn computer in her spare time. To have an opponent of any worth, St. Clair needed time to toy with new bridge strategies. But that had not seemed important to Sten.

The only records in there were the mundane details of Koldyeze life: Tahn payroll and personnel and the basic files of the prisoner. Sten could see little value in snooping and pooping in that area.

"St. Clair has . . . noticed something," Virunga said, interrupting Sten's thoughts.

He went on to explain: As St. Clair logged in and out of the computer, using Fahstr's code name, she had become familiar with the other people who used the same system and

with how frequently they used it. Then another code name had
popped up recently. It not only did not seem to belong to
anyone in the camp, it was searching through the records with
a regular one-plus-one-plus-one pattern that was slower than
clot but guaranteed not to miss a single detail.

St. Clair had become curious about who that person was
and what he or she was looking for.

"And did she find out?" Sten finally asked.

"Not the . . . seeker," Virunga said. "Only what was . . .
sought."

"Okay. So what was the person looking for?"

"You," Virunga said.

That rocked Sten back. "But how . . ."

Virunga told him the rest of it. The unknown person was
searching the records for someone matching Sten's description. It was a methodical search designed to see through any
disguise or assumed identity. It was only a matter of time
before Sten's file popped up.

Virunga assumed—with very good reason—that whoever
was looking for Sten did not plan on throwing his or her arms
around him and greeting him with a shower of gifts and
kisses.

Bottom line:

"You . . . and Kilgour must . . . go!"

There was no argument from Sten. He and Alex would go
out with the others. All he had to do was get his escape team
together one last time and fill them in on what he hoped was
the final hitch in their plans.

The news was greeted with silence by the others. They
took a quick look into the roles they were supposed to play,
checked to see how Alex and Sten would affect them, saw
there was no problem, and just shrugged. The more, the mer-
rier.

Then St. Clair stood up and announced there would be one
other change in plans. She was no longer going out solo. She
was taking L'n with her.

"That's the stupidest idea I ever heard of," Sten blurted out
before Alex could dig an elbow into his ribs and suggest a
more diplomatic way of dealing with St. Clair. Later on, Alex

explained that Sten should have hesitated first—then told the woman she was around the bend.

"Just the same," St. Clair responded. "That's the way it's going to be."

Before Sten could do something so foolish as try to forbid St. Clair, she played her ace.

"Don't bother trying to stop me. We're both going out tomorrow night—one way or another. Through the tunnel with the rest of you. Or under the wire."

Sten had no choice but to give in. If St. Clair did another cowboy run, she would blow whatever chance the tunnelers had—and Sten was pretty sure that nothing he could come up with short of murder would stop her. But he always wondered why St. Clair had decided on that course of action. As far as he was concerned, it was way out of character—because with L'n along, St. Clair would certainly get caught. He wondered what St. Clair thought she would get out of it—because personal gain could be her only reason.

He was wrong on both counts. For once in her life St. Clair was not being selfish. She knew what the news of Sten's escape would do to L'n. Without the crutch of her ideal, L'n was doomed. Second, although St. Clair could not know it, L'n's presence would save both their lives.

Sten curled his fingers, and the knife leapt into his hand. He smoothly cut through the dirt, carefully easing it away at first and then clawing at it with growing impatience. Then the night air bit through, chilling them all to the bone, drying the sweat, and clearing the smoke-laden air.

Sten found himself tumbling through. He came to his feet —numb and a little in shock. Below Koldyeze he could see the dim outline of the city with the blackout lights gleaming here and there. And then he felt Alex come out from behind him, grabbing him around the shoulders and pushing him on.

They were free.

CHAPTER TWENTY-SEVEN

DURER WAS A major victory.

The general history fiche, to which all Imperial worlds subscribing to the Imperial education scheme subjected their secondary-level students, portrayed the battle in a few, sweeping arrow strokes.

At this time, the attack was made . . . here. A red arrow, moving across systems. It was backed by a secondary attack . . . here. It was met . . . here. A blue arrow.

The results were . . . this.

The more curious might acquire a specialty fiche and, given access to a battle chamber, project more details of the battle.

At that point, the bewilderment would begin.

First, Durer was variously called the Durer–Al-Sufi Battles, the First Imperial Counterattack, the Second Tahn Offensive, Fleet Encounters of the Midstages of the Tahn War, and so forth, into degenerative and confusing accounts of the ships involved.

Still more confusing for the eager student were the accounts of anyone and everyone involved in that battle.

The battle(s) became a favorite study of both amateurs and professionals, all of them seeking a perspective that would enable them to understand what had happened during those weeks and, possibly more important to historians, to see some grandness in what otherwise appeared to be a bloody, blindfolded brawl in which several million people had died.

They would look for that understanding and perspective in vain.

Because that perspective never existed.

* * *

A Mantis Section captain named Bet sat in a spacesuit, watching what looked like the entire Tahn Navy float toward her, and wished that Vulcan had given her a god or six to pray for.

The Emperor had coppered his bets. Yes, he believed that the real attack would be made on Durer. Al-Sufi would be nothing more than a feint. He had so allocated his forces under Fleet Marshal Ian Mahoney.

But still . . .

Light-years beyond Durer drifted what appeared to be the ruined hulks of some Tahn destroyers. A complete flotilla thereof.

They were just exactly that.

What the Tahn did not know was that the flotilla had been ambushed many, many months earlier in an entirely different galaxy by an Imperial battlefleet. Their screams for help had been blanketed and had never been received on any Tahn world. To the Tahn, the flotilla had simply disappeared, probably doing something or other terribly heroic.

The hulks had been recovered, and strong-stomached salvors had cleaned out the ship interiors. Then those destroyers had been given shielded power sources, sophisticated sensors, and shielded com beams and positioned in place, beyond Durer.

They had been crewed with Mantis teams and given orders to sit and wait.

Bet and her team, and other teams, had done just that, fighting against boredom and the feeling that they were being stuck in nowhere for a meaningless mission.

All the teams viewed the assignment as a glory run and swore at the head of Mantis Section for the medal- and obituary-winning idea. Why hadn't far more sophisticated and unmanned sensors been used?

The head of Mantis was not to blame. The idea was completely that of the Eternal Emperor and Fleet Marshal Ian Mahoney. Certainly those zoot capri sensors could have been scattered in front of where they felt the Tahn forces would make their real attack. But suppose one of those sensors was found? Would the Tahn not conceivably guess that the Imperial Forces were waiting?

Instead, it appeared far less logical for the Empire to have some dumb troops inhabiting hulks. Plus, cynically, Mahoney pointed out that it would be very unlikely for any Mantis troopie to surrender and be deprogrammable, unlike the average machine.

Cursing, smelling, and sweating, the teams waited.

And then the sensors lit.

More Tahn fleets than even Bet's high-level briefing had suggested swam through space toward her hulks.

Bet burst-transmitted the information, then shut down. Her view of the battle—if there was going to be one—was complete. All she had to do was hope that none of the Tahn battleships or destroyers passing—almost within visual range —bothered to investigate her wreck for survivors.

The Eternal Emperor sat aboard the *Normandie*, his personal yacht/command ship. The ship was as far forward—and three more light-years—as he could logically go without potentially becoming involved in his own battle. His battle chamber was set to give full and complete reports of any and all intelligence forthcoming.

The Emperor figured that Mahoney would very rapidly become involved in the grind of the battle. The Emperor hoped to be able to stand off and help if Mahoney lost track of the grand strategy.

He was earnestly lying to himself when he said that he had no intention of stepping in. He had done everything possible.

The Tahn were moving into his trap quite nicely, the preliminary intelligence reports said—although he was astonished that somehow, somewhere, the anticipated twelve attacking fleets had become more than twenty. He had them cold. On toast. This, he thought to himself, is the beginning of the end. Or, his nonlinear alter ego whispered, the end of the beginning at least.

Bet me, Engineer H. E. Raschid thought. Suppose it's the end of the end?

And so he stood ready to save Mahoney's—and his own —cookies.

Unfortunately robot Tahn ships, intended only to blank off transmissions between the Al-Sufi and Durer systems, slipped through the Imperial perimeter, and the Eternal Emperor found himself sitting in the most sophisticated war analysis room ever installed on a spaceship, listening to static and watching pixels of misinformation interspersed with scattered bursts that showed either the Tahn or the Empire victorious and advancing or defeated and retreating on all fronts.

Durer, for the handful of Imperial tacships and destroyers assigned to hold and defend the system, was a very short battle.

There would be seven survivors of the eighty-nine ships that moved against the attacking Tahn fleets. Their orders were to stop the Tahn attack, to prevent landings on Durer, and finally to exert the maximum number of casualties possible.

They were, unknowingly, a suicide force.

The ships that had been assigned to Durer had been mainline attack units—neither obsolete nor state of the art. The Empire planned to maintain as long as possible the deception that Durer was underguarded and not expecting an attack.

The Emperor had therefore made the correct assignments, knowing he was sending people to their deaths.

"The Price of Empire," it might have been called if the Eternal Emperor had not been several centuries beyond believing such grandiose statements. Those were for the rubes, not the rulers. Besides, this was not the first time, the most murderous time, or certainly the last . . .

The Durer units' tactics were well-planned. One flotilla of destroyers came in on the same plane as the incoming Tahn. Two other flotillas waited above the system ecliptic until the forward elements of the Tahn were engaged. Then they dived "down" for the heart of the enemy. Shortly afterward, six wings of tacships came up from "below," each tacship under independent command with orders to find targets of opportunity.

All the sailors had done a fast head count of the enemy, realized they were doomed, and—at least for the most part—determined to make their dying quite expensive.

Very noble.

Unfortunately, such noble determination worked very seldom, and mostly in livies.

When the enemy had total numerical superiority, all the tactics in the world would not let the attacker get within killing range.

So it was with the ships from Durer.

The obvious flotilla vanished in long-range missile blasts from the incoming Tahn cruisers long out of their engagement range.

The two high flotillas got in among the fold—but for only seconds. Those thirty-two destroyers barely had time to acquire targets and make first launches before they, too, vanished. Results: Destroyed, four Tahn destroyers, five Tahn logistical support craft. Damaged: two Tahn cruisers, three Tahn logships.

On a battle chamber, or from a grand fleet projection, that left the space beyond Durer cluttered with trash, which the deadly little tacships whould have been able to swim through unobserved and deal death.

Battle chambers and grand projections crunched light-years into centimeters. The reality was that the destruction of the Durer ships left whirling wreckage across some twenty lightyears. A destroyer's screen, particularly one that was programmed to ignore destroyed targets, showed something different.

A raider, a guerrilla, a pirate—and that was what the tacships were—could not exist on a battlefield.

Perhaps the tacship commanders were overeager. Perhaps the Tahn were expecting an attack from "below." Perhaps they had bad luck.

No one would ever know.

There were no survivors from those ships.

The Imperial propaganda made much of their doomed attack and made several posthumous awards of the highest degree. Propaganda also said how effective they were: Two Tahn battleships had been destroyed, and one crippled. One Tahn cruiser destroyed, two crippled. Four Tahn destroyers crippled.

Postwar analysis: One destroyer smashed. One cruiser lightly damaged.

But by then no one wanted to be reminded of the war, let alone the fact that some of their dead heroes had died *trying* to be heroic instead of succeeding.

Lady Atago's original strategy had been for one fleet to bombard Durer, a second to invade, and a third to be kept in reserve.

Command on Durer expected something similar.

Ready for the last grand stand, they were surprised when the Tahn fleets swept through the system, well outside engagement range.

And maybe they were a little disappointed, at least at first. After all, when someone screwed his courage to the sticking point only to find it not needed, it took awhile for the stupidity and the adrenaline to subside.

But the disappointment did not last very long as the Imperial Forces on Durer realized that they were alive, that they were likely to stay alive for a while, that the battle was being fought without them, and that they were in ringside seats for it.

That was perhaps why so many of the personal memoirs of the Durer–Al-Sufi battle(s) were done by Imperial troops on Durer.

They lived to dictate them.

Lord Fehrle admired perfection on the bridge of his command ship as the first four fleets swept, almost unopposed, out of the Durer System. Ahead of them were rich industrial worlds and then the heart of the Empire. And thus far, the Tahn casualties had been insignificant.

Once again he pointed out to himself the necessity for an overseer. No matter how inspired, the man or woman who was in charge of a task needed someone over him or her, someone who could step back, uninvolved, and see whether that task was destined to be a success, a failure, or, Fehrle thought, able to be taken beyond its humbler goals.

Lady Atago is most brilliant, he thought. But thanks to our system, there will always be someone beyond those brilliant leaders in the field, those who can think, those who can say: Here. Here is the grandness you have overlooked.

Fehrle was basking in that grandness when the Kali missile blew his command ship in half.

Fleet Marshal Ian Mahoney was not at all surprised when the robot Tahn ships sent his big picture communications into la-la land. He had sort of expected something like that to happen.

In spite of the frownings and suggestions from his highly trained and educated specialists, Mahoney had insisted on setting up a series of links—locked and tight—with specific ships in each of the fleets under his command. Each broadcast came into a separate receiver, manned by an individual tech who was trained to report, not to interpret.

Probably, Mahoney thought, he was being an imbecile and trying to maintain the illusion that he was still a hands-on field officer. Probably all this drakh was going to confuse the hell out of him, make him get obsessed with trivia and lose whatever half-assed strategy he had to fight their battle.

On first contact, that was exactly what was going on.

And then the battle chamber became a kaleidoscope, all his computers started recycling previous information, and his interpreters found themselves with nothing to interpret.

Mahoney told them to keep interpreting, shut off the com links, and started listening to the field reports.

It was a stupid way to try to win.

The Tahn had opened the battle believing that they were masters of deception, without allowing themselves much of a margin for error. That was the single biggest error.

But there were many other mistakes that they made.

One of the largest—uncredited by historians because there were no visible heroes—was the failure of the Tahn automatic mine fields.

The Tahn, unlike the Empire, had spent many, many mancenturies developing those unglamorous objects that just sat and lurked until something made them explode. But once they had developed mines that could not only be rapidly deployed but had the sophistication to distinguish friendly from enemy targets and maneuver en masse by command, they had relaxed.

Some years earlier, a young tacship commander named Sten had discovered a fairly nasty way to subvert those mines. The Tahn, who were in the middle of other worries, never realized that. Sten had routinely sent a report through on his discovery.

That discovery, made by someone who was slowly crawling down the intermittently floodlit slope of a Tahn prison camp, was critical.

The Tahn had liberally sowed their mines between Al-Sufi and Durer, expecting them to serve not only as a block against the inevitable counterattack but as an early warning system.

Imperial destroyers, part of the fleets lurking in emptiness between and beyond the Al-Sufi and Durer systems, had long ago seen the minelayers seeding their deadliness, registered the mine fields, and then rendered them completely harmless, one by one. The effort was massive and successful. Any specialists who had made a small mistake defusing the devices would not be recognized until after the battle.

To the Tahn, the Imperial fleets lanced out of nowhere. Their battle computers, however, quickly analyzed the attack. Conventional. Tacships were screening the attack, with cruiser antiship killers in the forward screen. Behind them came destroyers and then a conventional structure—destroyers, cruisers, battleships, and tacship carriers.

The computers provided the proper response, and the Tahn admirals complied.

The Imperial Forces, however, were not what they had expected.

Mahoney knew good and well that he was a little untrained for grand strategy. Maybe he could have come up with some kind of superplan. He had done a little private research before leaving Prime on what kinds of things grand strategists did to make their living.

The record was kind of grim.

The one-roll-of-the-dice generals had as great a failure rate as success, from Darius to Phillip to von Schlieffen to Giap to M'Khee to P'ra T'ong. Mahoney, figuring he was not even in their class, decided to run war the way he knew how—which was to keep it simple and keep it unexpected.

The tacships were what they appeared onscreen. Mahoney figured that with the confusion he planned behind them, they would have a good chance not only of survival but of wreaking some damage.

Those cruisers were in fact lumbering, unmanned transports with false electronic signatures. Their missiles were set up on a launch-and-forget basis—and were so primitive that they had best be forgotten unless some complete incompetent stumbled into their trajectory.

The destroyers were also false. They were phony-signatured Kali missiles, modified for long range.

After them came the real warriors.

The battle opened.

The tacships swarmed.

The "cruisers" were quickly converted into gas clouds, and the Tahn felt reinforced as to their superiority. Their acquisition gear turned to the destroyers just as those "destroyers" went to full drive and homed on capital ships.

Warriors generally made an assumption: Someone who was attacking behaved in a certain manner. When a dangerous swordsman turned into a berserker, or a bomber into a kamikaze, it took a while to readjust.

The readjustment cost the Tahn most of their cover destroyers and threw the lead three fleets' battle array into disorder.

That was not a disaster. Admiral P'riser, who had automatically assumed overall command of the battle when Lord Fehrle's ship fell out of communication, ordered the three stalled fleets to engage and the banked fleets behind them to attack through.

The arrow sped onward.

Lord Fehrle glummed inside his suit helmet as technicians swarmed around the control chamber of the crippled command ship.

Go here and do this, he thought. He could order, he realized, any of the people around him to breathe space on general principles. Or he could program commands for the fleets he commanded.

Neither of those options would change his situation—the

battle was out of his hands, he was getting absolutely no information as to what was going on, and his ship was spinning in emptiness far behind the lines of battle.

The fact that there was a good possibility that the ship would explode in hours or become a vanished derelict was hardly important to his thinking.

Lady Atago's ships dove in against the Al-Sufi worlds almost unopposed.

Six outbound convoys loaded with AM2 were cut out and seized. Their escorts were quickly smashed.

Lady Atago, following orders, had determined that the feint against Al-Sufi would be as deadly and determined as she could make it.

Her attack ships swept destruction across storage worlds, creating havoc and hell that would take generations to rebuild.

Then, in the midst of a battle of triumph, Lady Atago realized what had happened.

She was wreaking havoc not because of her brilliance but because Al-Sufi was nearly undefended. Her success was merely that the Imperials had made no plans for *any* Tahn attack against the systems.

Which could only mean that her grand plan against Durer had been found out. The Tahn fleets were advancing into a trap.

Lady Atago had no hesitations at all. Less of a person, less of a Tahn, would have let Lord Fehrle and the never-to-be-sufficiently-damned civilians take the blame as they would have taken the credit.

Instead, she diverted and drove her swiftest battleships toward the Durer systems, broadcasting an alarm on all frequencies.

It was, by then, quite too late.

The man's name was Mason. And, from his no-rank-tabbed flight coverall to the scar seaming his face, he looked to be a killer.

He had been that—a highly decorated tacship commander, seconded after a crippling injury to flight school, and more recently Sten's nemesis. His injuries prevented him from ever

skippering a tacship again. But the war had promoted Mason. He was a one-star admiral, commanding a fast light-destroyer squadron.

He ran it as he had run his tacship flotilla. His crews hated him. He insisted on obedience, dedication, and originality. An error of omission or oversight produced a very rapid court-martial.

The story was that one of his destroyers had bounced a Tahn ship that turned out to be filled with Imperial prisoners. One of Mason's bosuns had seen the cheering rescued ex-prisoners streaming through the air lock and then bellowed "Get back, clots! Don't you know when you're well off?"

Mason was permitted to be in command for only one reason. His flotilla had the highest kill ratio of any equivalent unit in *any* of the Imperial fleets.

Now he led his destroyers, scattered in fingers-four formation, into the rear of the Tahn fleets.

Eleven Imperial fleets had been hidden far beyond Durer, with orders to attack only after the Tahn were initially engaged.

A surprise.

More of a surprise was their makeup. Sullamora's shipyards in the Cairenes, supposedly shattered with labor problems, had done very well. The Emperor had expected twelve more battleships to be ready.

Instead, thirty heavies attacked the Tahn—ships that were not leaky botch jobs but supersophisticated engines of destruction, completely unknown to the Tahn.

The slaughter began.

Even if, somehow, an all-bands receiver could have listened in on the battles, coherency would have been a joke:

"Samsun, Samsun . . . I have a target . . . damage report as . . . incoming observed . . . six Tahn ships now without power and . . . launch, you clottin' bastard . . . Samsun, are you receiving . . . units, stand by for . . . change orbit, Eight, you're acquired . . . I have a launch from . . . Samsun, this is Whitway. Do you receive this station . . . this is an all-stations broadcast . . . Nostrand units, redeploy to Sectors one by thirteen . . . *squaawk* . . . Allah give us strength . . . Samsun,

Samsun . . . Kee-rist, did you see that one go up? . . . All units, this is . . . Samsun, Samsun . . . do you receive . . ."

Four broadcasts, all set en clair:

To Fleet Marshal Ian Mahoney:

"Comm One, Comm One, this is Liberty Seven. There ain't nothin' left to shoot at . . ."

To Lady Atago:

"Unknown approaching units . . . this is the Tahn battleship *H'rama*. We have you ID'd as friendly. Do not continue your present orbit, over. Request you stand by for recovery assistance."

To Lord Fehrle—unreceived:

"Command . . . Command . . . this is P'riser. Plan Heartstrike canceled. Plan W'mon activated."

To all Tahn ships:

"All units. All units. Begin retirement. Support, if possible, friendly units under drive."

In eyes-only code, Fleet Marshal Ian Mahoney to the Eternal Emperor:

"Tahn seared. Repeat, all Tahn seared. Question—how to serve? Second question—what wine?"

Confused though it might have been from its name to its step-by-step execution, there were some completely obvious conclusions from the battle(s) of Durer–Al-Sufi:

The Tahn had been smashed.

Their major war-winning offensive had been blunted and turned back.

The nearly-total destruction of the Tahn's finest units meant that it would be years before they could mount another such offensive.

The Emperor hoped—and knew he was full of hops—that those conclusions were equally evident to the Tahn.

It might have been the beginning of the end—but getting there was still going to be a long, bloody, and certainly not foreordained process.

And the Eternal Emperor could afford to make no other mistakes.

BOOK THREE

KOBO-ICHI

CHAPTER TWENTY-EIGHT

THE TAHN REELED back from the awful blow of Durer like a man struck in the stomach with a lead-weighted bat. They were left doubled over, mouth gaping, lungs emptied of air and blood hammering at the temples, threatening to hemorrhage at the ears.

They were caught in that long, frozen moment in history that even casual students would point at eons later and say, "Here was the turning point. Here was where priorities needed to be reexamined, strategy revamped, scenarios rethought."

Because, as an ancient philosopher once said, "It ain't over till it's over." Or as the Eternal Emperor might have put it; stealing from one of his favorite political thinkers, "Winning isn't everything. But losing isn't anything."

Durer–Al-Sufi was lost. That was a tired fact almost as soon as it was over. But not the war. Another tired fact, viscerally understood by the Tahn. The trick was to make the mind understand what the gut was thinking without ripping open the gut and spreading out the entrails. History was a blackened landscape of great kingdoms that murdered the oracle to seek the message. That was a mistake the Tahn could not and did not make.

They turned inward, fighting every instinct to find fault, to point the blame. They turned inward to find strength but were confronted with the frozen poles of their culture: a north where defeat could not even be contemplated, and a south where every facet of Tahn life had to be controlled and molded to official will—all spinning on an axis of hatred for anything un-Tahn. And they had no Shackleton or Perry to lead the way. Only Lord Fehrle—the man who had presided over the second greatest defeat of their history.

147

Fehrle was no coward. After the defeat, he did not commit ritual suicide. Instead, he returned to Heath, fully expecting to be stripped of all honors, executed, his name excised from Tahn history. If his people needed to work out their rage on his quivering corpse, then so be it.

Instead, he was seen in his usual position of prominence—with the other members of the Tahn High Council lined up exactly around him as before—during a news broadcast covering the appointment of a governor-general to a newly won Tahn territory. It was an event noted with interest by every skilled Tahn watcher who knew about Durer. The Eternal Emperor—the most skilled of them all—grunted to himself when he reviewed the fiche. Fehrle's survival was not something he had expected.

When he had learned that the Tahn lord had personally led the expedition, he had thought the man's political destruction would be an added bonus to all that twisted metal and those blasted bodies. Still, there was an advantage to press for there and the Eternal Emperor went all out for it.

When the Emperor struck out and connected with that loaded bat, the only thought his enemy had as he reeled back from the blow, was that no one could know about Durer. Even that old cynic, Pastour, realized that it was not the time for recriminations or political infighting. When he had heard the news, he had vomited, wiped his lips, then hurried to the emergency High Council meeting, determined to keep his colleagues from removing Fehrle and then committing bureaucracide in the resultant fight over who would lead the council.

Even in normal times there were too many factions with too many self-serving interests to declare a clear winner. Given time, a consensus might be hammered out the way a cooper formed the hoops of an enormous barrel whose contents could not be contained under the normal laws of volume.

Pastour had a glimmering, even at that moment, that the only conceivable choice would have to be Lady Atago, as much as he disliked the woman. When the day came to replace Fehrle, she would be the only knight in white armor left. Because although Durer had permanently blackened Fehrle, it would have the opposite effect on Atago. To survive as a coherent people, the Tahn needed their heroes—like the ancient Persians needed the myth of Jamshid. Pastour went to the meeting armed with every diplomatic and political skill he could command.

Surprisingly, it did not take much argument. The others were as stunned and gasping as he was. All of them knew, without coaxing, that if news of Durer leaked out to the populace, the war with the Empire was lost. The first order issued was for a total clampdown on anything and anyone involved with Durer.

Even in a society where news was not just controlled but rationed, the order was carried out on an unprecedented scale. An enormous amount of credits, energy, and manpower was hurled at the task. It was a gag order with no journalistic equivalent. Scholars, looking for descriptive comparisons, would have to turn to human-wave assault battles—like Thermopylae, the Russian Summer offensive of 1943, the Yalu, or the Imperial disaster of Saragossa during the Mueller Wars.

The destroyed ships and personnel were removed from all files and logs. All survivors were seized and incarcerated, as were the friends and families of the dead and wounded. Behind-the-lines suppliers found themselves mysteriously reassigned to barren regions. Even minor officials were visited at night and grilled for any speck of information that might be damaging. Then the interrogators themselves were grilled. On and on it went as the Tahn searched out and purged every kink and crook in the line of the vast plumbing system that was the Tahn bureaucracy.

The Tahn even launched a crash Manhattan-style program to develop and fix in place the greatest jamming system ever conceived. And even that leaked as the Eternal Emperor turned up the volume of propaganda.

If the Tahn blackout effort had no known historical precedent, neither did the Emperor's effort to broadcast it. With his right hand, the Emperor directed his fleets and armies to take instant advantage of the vacuum left by the Tahn. With his left, he orchestrated a massive propaganda machine. He turned the equivalent of small suns into radio beacons, heralding to the many galaxies the news of the great Tahn defeat.

The Emperor attacked with information as if it were the spearhead of an invasion force of thousands of ships and millions of troops. And the more he turned up the volume, the more desperately the Tahn fought to shut it out. He pushed them to the point that, even for their barren souls, so many civil liberties were suspended that life was nearly intolerable.

The grim, bitter mood spread downward from the High Council to the lowest subaltern and petty official. No one knew what had happened, but everyone feared for himself. Even the simplest of decisions was left unmade in case it might disturb a superior. In actual fact, that was a wise way of behaving. Because the smallest change *would* upset a superior, who was equally in fear for his own hide. Added to that were increasing shortages. All the empty warehouses seemed even emptier after Durer. And as for AM2, there just was none available for any purpose other than military, and even there, each use was carefully judged and the proper forms filed with the appropriate signatures willing to take the blame in case of error.

Yes, the Tahn had turned inward after Durer. And it was the Eternal Emperor's official policy to shove their heads up until "they gag on the hair at the back of their throats."

CHAPTER TWENTY-NINE

POLICE MAJOR GENRIKH'S heart jumped when he heard the hunters hooting in the woods. Their quarry had been flushed. He whisper/prayed to himself that it would not be a false alarm. Ever since the escape, Genrikh and his men had been rushed from one tiny rut in the road to another, responding to even vague rumors that a POW had been spotted. As far as Genrikh was concerned, the entire effort to bring the prisoners to ground had been hamstrung by his superiors' insistence on a total blackout of the news of the escape.

Normally, any matter requiring secrecy would be second

nature to Genrikh. But he and the other teams of hunters had been handed the messiest end of the stick. The blackout meant that it was nearly impossible to pick any *real* locus to start from and then connect the dots until the quarry could be found, circled, and then flushed into waiting Tahn guns. There had been a few successes, but not nearly enough.

The only part of his orders that he liked was that any prisoner found was to be killed on the spot. There was to be no sizing up or interrogation, just a heavy-caliber projectile in the back of the head. That this shut down the possibility of one find leading to another did not bother Genrikh at all. He was not a man who enjoyed the confusion of many flavors.

The hooting from his tracking team grew louder. Genrikh took a deep breath, loosening his grip on his weapon. He did not have to turn to see if his men were in place. He could feel the tension drawing them tighter to him. Genrikh prepared himself for disappointment.

The odds were that when the quarry broke the treeline, it would turn out to just be some lost farm animal, walleyed with fear. Then all they would be left with to satisfy their frustration was to gun the animal into a bloody pulp.

His weapon came up at the same time he saw motion just inside the trees. Around him he could hear the others doing the same, sounding like a rustle in a dry wind. There! Over there!

Two figures shadowed away from the brush, hesitated, then started shambling runs across the meadow for the other side. In two heartbeats his mind registered that they were (a) human, (b) one tall, one short, (c) prisoners. He squeezed the trigger, and then all hell erupted as his men also opened up. The combined fire caught the prisoners only five or six steps from the trees. They gave massive, loose-limbed jolts and then were hurled aside as if swept away by a fire hose. There was echoing silence and then another swift *brrrp* of fire, and the bodies jerked and jumped on the ground.

There was a clash of magazines changing, and then Genrikh and his men were on their feet, sprinting for the large splash of red and white gore. He almost lost his footing in blood-slick grass as he skidded up to the first body. It was the big man. He kicked the corpse over. The features were twisted but clear—Ibn Bakr. Then the smaller prisoner—Alis.

Genrikh turned to congratulate his team of killers. He was greeted by beaming faces with shy, almost childlike grins. Except for one.

Lo Prek looked down at Ibn Bakr's face and cursed his soul for not being the man he wanted to see lying there. Once again Sten had slipped the net.

Virunga sat in a slatted metal chair designed for discomfort. Every aching joint in his crippled legs told him that he had been kept waiting outside the commandant's office for days. From the sounds of the prisoners shuffling through the courtyard outside, he knew it could have been no more than four hours. Virunga had spent too many years as a prisoner of the Tahn not to know the game Derzhin was playing. The wait was a routine softening-up process. Still, being familiar with the game did not make it any easier to play.

From the moment he had been summoned, the old self-doubts had come rushing in. Could he stand up to torture? He had before, hadn't he? Yes. But could he do it again? All right. Let's get past the torture part. (I can't. Please, I can't. Shut up! You have to.) What about the mind gaming? He had never gone one on one with Avrenti, Derzhin's expert in black work. But he had measured him. The man would be good. Virunga thought he was better. (Clot! There you go with a negative again! Eliminate "thought." Substitute "knew." Yes. That's better.) Try a new tack. A course with fresher breezes.

You have questions, Virunga. Put it on them. Make them answer. Don't give them time to gain the upper ground. Hit them with your questions. Questions, like . . . After the escape . . . why were there no reprisals?

Virunga and Sten had factored reprisals into the escape equation. There was nothing they could do about the immediate actions of the Tahn. In the first red flash of anger, there were sure to be victims, beatings, rations cut off, and personal belongings ripped to shreds in the search for the escape hatch. There was nothing they could do about that. But a moment later, when cooler heads prevailed, the planning would pay off. There were too many careers at stake in Koldyeze. Too many questions would trigger a hunt for scapegoats—careless guards, officers with questionable loyalties. The Tahn would be cautious, knowing that it would give enemies an opening to pin blame on the blameless. And there would be the ultimate threat that the crisis would spill over, flooding out the gates and catching the politicians who had put all the rotten eggs in the rickety basket that was Koldyeze.

Just to make sure, Sten and Virunga had stacked the deck, slipped a fifth ace in the cards. The fifth ace was the Golden Worm St. Clair had planted in the Koldyeze computer. It was a virus that day by day would monkey with the production figures. A decimal point slipped. A minus turned to a plus. And, voilà! Koldyeze would be able to boast far higher successes than even the most optimistic Tahn could dream of. Derzhin would have absolute proof that the POW camp was an experiment that was working.

There were too many lists of failures on the Tahn Empire's slate to ignore such a glowing success. The virus had a second function built into it. As time went by, it was eating away key areas of memory in the computer. In time, no Tahn would know up from down at Koldyeze—just that everything looked really good as long as one did not look that hard.

The expected first rash of reprisals came the instant the Tahn realized there were POWs suddenly among the missing. They had shut down the camp with a mailed glove. There were interrogations, beatings, and a few deaths. But the Tahn never found the secret of the catacombs and the tunnel that led to the hill outside. And then, almost as quickly as it had begun, the interrogations came to a halt.

It was just as well. Virunga was at the point of breaking out the ancient weapons he and Sten had found in one of the catacomb vaults. Such an action would have been suicidal. But briefly satisfying.

Virunga's goons reported the comings and goings of the camp hierarchy. There were many hushed meetings and whisperings to other, faceless Tahn over com lines. Virunga could feel some kind of crisis mounting. And then it stopped, just at the moment when he expected the pustule to burst. A sudden gloom engulfed the camp, affecting every Tahn from the top on down. The prisoners were surprised by a loosening up of attitudes. It was if they were all being handled a little gingerly, with just a hint of fearful respect. Something had happened, of that Virunga was certain. Some huge event that he would read about in the history books—assuming he survived. But no one had the slightest idea what it was. Especially the Tahn.

Virunga started to attention as the door to the commandant's office swung open. A cold-faced guard nodded to his two fellows standing on either side of the prisoner. A hard object jammed into his side, and Virunga caught his breath from the pain. He pushed the annoyance from his mind, positioned his crutches, and creaked up on his haunches. He shifted position, jammed the crutches forward, and leaned into them with his massive weight. He swung his body at the door as if the guard were not there. If was not physical strength but the sheer force of Virunga's immense dignity that made the guard step aside.

The atmosphere in the room was forcedly mild. Avrenti was slumped in a chair in a corner, seemingly riffling through some minor papers. The commandant, Derzhin, was standing at the window, his back to Virunga, gazing outside as if witnessing something of mild interest. Virunga came to a halt in the middle of the room. He did not look left or right or hint for a chair to hold his crippled body. He just stood there, leaning into his crutches, waiting silently for the game to begin.

After a very long time, Derzhin turned away from the window. He seemed to note Virunga's presence for the first time.

"Ah, Colonel. Thank you for coming."

Virunga did not give him the pleasure of responding. But Derzhin did not seem to notice. He crossed to his desk and sat down. He picked up a printout, studied it, then replaced it. He tapped his fingers on his desk as if trying to remember why he had called Virunga.

"I have some information about the . . . uh . . . shall we say lost members of your command."

Despite himself, Virunga stiffened. It was as if an arctic wind had suddenly cut through the thick fur guarding his spine. "Yes?"

He did not trust himself to say more.

"Forgive me, Colonel, but I am forced to bear grim news. From your point of view, that is. They've been caught. Every single one."

Virunga sighed, a little relieved. It was over, then. Okay,

they were captured. Now he would have to make sure of their treatment.

"I . . . wish to . . . see them. At once. To assure . . . they are . . . treated in accordance . . . with the laws . . . of wartime."

Out of the corner of his eye, he saw Avrenti sneer.

"I'm afraid that will be impossible, Colonel," Derzhin said.

"You . . . refuse?"

"No. I wouldn't be so rude. The fact of the matter is, there is little to see. All of them are dead."

Virunga found himself gasping. His twin hearts thundered. His ears rang from the sudden pressure. "What? Dead? How could—"

Shouts came from the courtyard outside. At first it was just a few voices. Then it grew in size and panic and anger. Derzhin smiled at him and waved him forward. Somehow, Virunga found himself leaning on his crutches, staring out the window. At first all he saw was a crowd of prisoners swarming around something in the center of the courtyard. Then he saw an old flatbed truck with a team of horses hitched to the front. On the truck was a contingent of Tahn guards. And Genrikh. They seemed to be unloading something—or somethings—pulling whatever it was from dripping gunnysacks and hurling it to the ground.

And then it was as if Virunga had suddenly acquired telescopic sight. He saw what they were unloading. Arms . . . and legs . . . and heads. The butchered bodies of Ibn Bakr and Alis.

CHAPTER THIRTY

CHETWYND, SPACEPORT/WATERFRONT thug, labor organizer, convicted felon, political prisoner, and now somewhere between a trusty and a pardoned guard at Koldyeze, contemplated the angles as he bulldozed his way down the dockside toward a needed and, he felt, richly deserved double quill.

Chetwynd had matured beyond the hustler who knew he knew what was going on—which was what had put him on a prison planet in the first place—into a hustler who knew he did not know what was happening.

Not that the change had produced much difference in Chetwynd's behavior.

What should have happened after the mass break from Koldyeze was suitable retributions. Derzhin should have been lowered by a head, Avrenti should have been transferred to a penal battalion, Genrikh should have been given command of the prison, and draconian measures should have been meted out. Chetwynd had already sounded out connections for another assignment—anything to avoid being sent back to Dru and being chased by gurions. Instead, nothing happened.

Nothing much, at any rate.

Two escapees had been nailed, dragged back, and blasted. But the others?

Nothing. Even through the guards' rumor mill.

More important than those vanished POWs was the fact that little had changed at Koldyeze. Things and people continued in their measured course. Chetwynd cursed in an aside at his wasted credits supplying that worm Genrikh's seemingly inexhaustible pit with alk to create a note of sympathy when the drakh came down.

Another angle that he had not figured out was what had happened to his richly beloved government, out there beyond somewhere. Chetwynd had been thinking aloud when he had told Sten that the Tahn needed a fast, vast victory. But, he realized later, it was so.

Something, out there in the far beyond—and Chetwynd was not sure where or what—had happened. Something that the Tahn were not pleased with.

His union might have been smashed when Chetwynd was convicted and sentenced to a prison world, but his contacts were not. There were still friends around. Friends . . . acquaintances . . . enemies . . . people he had knocked over gravsleds with as a boy. The labels did not matter—growing up on the wrong side of the power structure of Heath created a lifelong alliance. Us against Them. At least so long as it was profitable.

Heath was suddenly the transshipment point for strange cargoes—materials, tools, and shipwrights—to the previously unheard of Erebus System, and medical supplies and personnel by the kiloton to other worlds where Tahn hospitals were not based.

The far beyond, which meant the Empire, had not been kind to the Tahn, Chetwynd reasoned. That was another card he did not know how to play yet.

He stopped just outside the entrance to the Khag, the prime bar on Heath if one wanted anything illegal, immoral, unavailable, or beyond priorities—and his headquarters. Filled with his cronies.

Chetwynd put on a brave leader face and entered.

He bought a round for his boyos.

He sipped the shot he wanted to slug down.

He held court, awarded and withheld approval, granted or withheld favors—and told the latest joke:

"A mister finally gets the vid. He's on the list. Through priorities. His gravsled is fin'ly available.

"He goes bug. 'Bout time. Paid for it six years ago. When is he gonna get it?

"Salesclot says four years down. Whitsl-cycle. Fourth day.

"Mister asks that be in the morning or afternoon?

"Salesman says, 'Mister, that be four years away! Why do you care if it's morning or night?'

"'Cause I got the plumber coming in the morning . . .'"

During the laughter he blasted down the rest of the shot and waved for another.

Court business over with, his cronies drifted away to let the great man be alone with his thoughts. Chetwynd, rerunning the angles, was not pleased to have his concentration broken by two boiler-suited, drakh-reeking dock scrapers sliding into his booth. He was about to summon ancillary thugs for the slaughter when he recognized them and sprayed his mouthful of quill across the booth.

Alex smiled at him in sympathy. "Dinnae be wastin' thae lifewater, lad. Tha'll come ae time when y' regret it."

Sten was motioning for the barmaid. "Chien," he said, "you look like you need a carafe."

Chetwynd did. "I thought all of you'd be heading for the

woods," he managed, proud of not having asked any of the usual boring questions or made any of the expected responses.

"Can't speak for the others," Sten said. "But I'm a city boy. Scared of the dark, out there in the bushes."

"The bully patrols check in here regular," Chetwynd said.

"Ah hae nae problem," Kilgour said. "We're sittin' wi' our respect'd friend. Kickin't thae gong around."

Chetwynd grudged defeat. He could shout and scream—and the two escapees would be taken. He would be eligible for some kind of reward. However, he thought, if the official word is that all these clots were shot attempting to escape, how would my masters explain two suddenly alive Imperials?

"Besides," Sten said, reading Chetwynd's thinking, "we'd both be up for brain scan—and both of us have been spending five minutes a day thinking about how much we love you."

Chetwynd did not believe that—he did not figure that anyone, even these obviously talented Imperial Intelligence types, could precondition themselves to provide false information to the Tahn torturers. The problem was, his belly rumbled, he did not think the Tahn believed that.

"Excellent, cheenas. There are back rooms. There are 'freshers. You two stink. But first—what are you looking for?"

Sten explained. They had slid out the prison and gone to ground with no escape route or anything other than the most superficial false ID. They wanted identification—not false. They wanted to become real citizens of Heath. Sten—correctly—assumed that as the manpower barrel drained, the Tahn were drafting the young, the out of work, the criminal, and the dissident—all of which sounded as if they could be friends of Chetwynd.

Sten and Alex planned to replace any two of Chetwynd's cronies who were up for the high jump. They then would volunteer for the Tahn military. Certainly no one would look for two Imperials in the service. Chetwynd's cohorts could then go on about their business. "Ah'm assumin't," Alex added, "thae y' noo hae problems gie'in a bein' another name."

Once in the military Sten and Alex knew they could go through training easily, volunteer for a combat assignment, and then slither through the lines, ground or spatial, to make their home run.

At that point, Chetwynd started gurgling. Not in protest, Sten realized, but in laughter.

"Cheenas, cheenas," he finally said. "Now I see why you Imperials ended up in this war in the first place."

He stood waving—and Sten's knife slid out of his arm. Two barmaids bounced up.

"My friends," Chetwynd said, "need almost everything. They want a quiet room. Baths. Two baths. Each. Food. From my private supplies. Any alk they order. And someone to rub their backs." He turned back to Sten and Alex. "Women satisfactory?"

There was no dissent—Kilgour and Sten were gaping.

"Clean ones. And another pitcher now."

Chetwynd sat back down. For the first time in days, his angles coincided, and he knew what to do next.

"You want me to do all that, in the vague hopes that you two orphans can get home? Cheenas, let me tell you. All of my people are so safe from this war, it is disgusting. Your deal is the worst I've heard of late.

"Correction. The only worse one I can think of is if I recaptured you two clots.

"Now. Shall I tell you what is going to happen?

"There are chambers below this hellhole. You will disappear into them. You will be fattened and battened, dighted and knighted until a certain date.

"When I order, you shall be moved quietly through the streets to a certain place, where I shall introduce you to a charming man named Wild. Jon Wild."

Chetwynd was most surprised when first Sten and then Alex started laughing. Jon Wild was the urbane smuggler they had carefully cultivated years ago, before the beginning of the war. Sten had promised Wild to leave his operation alone provided that Wild smuggled no war goods into the Tahn Empire and was willing to provide intelligence. When the war had started, Wild's home base of Romney had been destroyed, and Sten assumed that Wild and his people had stuck around a little too long even though the warehouses were empty and there were no baddies in the ruins.

Maybe he had spent too long being one of the emperor's café society toughs in Mantis Section—but Sten was privately delighted that Wild and his operation were surviving comfortably.

"We know him," Sten said. "Go ahead."

Sails somewhat sagging, Chetwynd finished. Wild would take them out of the Tahn systems and deliver them to a neutral world. They would be provided with whatever money and identity they needed to get to an Imperial world from there.

"I'll finish," Sten broke in. "Since you obviously assume that we are connected, you would like a little gold carat in your fiche, so that when the Empire lands on Heath you don't get stuck in my old cell on Koldyeze."

"Of course."

And Chetwynd never realized how much that response meant to men who had spent years hearing of defeat and death.

CHAPTER THIRTY-ONE

TANZ SULLAMORA HAD constructed his fishing retreat in a time when he not only still believed in heroes but imagined the Eternal Emperor as the leader of any laughing band of handsome devils. It was built out of his desire to emulate the Emperor in every way.

The Emperor loved cooking, so Sullamora slavishly copied his recipes and presented them at elaborate banquets for his friends. Except that everything tasted like drakh—which Sullamora, having no palate, did not know, and he was too rich and powerful a businessman for his friends to tell him.

Then there was fishing. The Emperor loved fishing to such a point that he had invested over 300 years of effort and a large fortune to re-create a fishing camp on the banks of the

Umpqua River in the ancient region of Oregon on the planet Earth. Sullamora built his own camp—on a vastly smaller scale—many kilometers upstream from the Emperor. He threw himself into fishing with great enthusiasm and no talent at all.

For several years he would celebrate the end of any difficult business negotiations by taking off—with great fanfare —to the wilds of Oregon to relax on the banks of his retreat. After a suitable period he would return, boasting to everyone within hearing distance about how relaxed he was and about how a being could not really know his own inner nature until he had tested himself against a canny salmon fighting to escape his hook. What he did not admit to anyone, much less himself, was that he hated everything to do with fishing. After his first trip he hired gillies to catch the salmon for him, and after another trip he even refused to eat his catch and fed the fish to his servants and aides instead.

Not only that, he found himself going quietly mad in the silence of the Oregon forest. He began hating every minute he spent at his rustic retreat—which, like the Emperor's, at first consisted of only a few rough-board buildings that blended into the environment. There was nothing to see but green, nothing to hear but the bubbling of the river. And to him the air was disgusting, with its smells of ripe river mud, decaying plants, and too-virile pollen. Sullamora missed the bustle of the deal and the sharp smells of adrenaline and fear.

But the fishing retreat was not something he could just let go of. He could not just sell or abandon it. Somehow, he was sure, there would be a great deal of whispering, secret smiles, and a loss of face. Sullamora compensated by inviting more and more of his friends and business acquaintances to his camp by the banks of the Umpqua.

The rough-board structures were replaced by larger and larger gleaming metal buildings filled with humming machinery. The small landing pad became a large private port that could handle nearly a hundred vehicles. And the quiet times in between deals took on a loud, festive air, with more and more elaborate entertainments.

The final step took Sullamora and the retreat full circle. As his hero worship of the Emperor diminished and disenchantment set in, the camp became once again a quiet place. A place where odd alliances could be made and deals could be struck in secret. A place where the art of fishing took on a whole different meaning.

Sullamora used the excuse of a loose boot tab to stop and let his five companions stroll on through the trees. He glanced up at them, listening, measuring. The conversation was quiet and light. But Sullamora could sense the underlying tension, as if each being were waiting for someone to declare himself, to speak first about matters that concerned them all—and their solution. And the longer it took, the more wary each became.

Sullamora swallowed at the knot of fear in his throat. It was becoming increasingly apparent that it might be Sullamora who had to speak up first. And if he did so, and he was wrong about his companions, he would be very quickly humiliated, crushed, and then ...

The Emperor's privy council was like a man who suffered from obesity: bloated with all the rich meals but terrified that the next banquet was about to be canceled.

For most beings in the Empire, the war with the Tahn had created hardships of historic proportions. But for the six members of the council, it had been a time of historic profits and opportunity. And after the stunning Imperial victory at Durer they were faced with not only an end to the enormous profits but huge losses as the Emperor looked about for the means to pay the butcher's bill.

And at the moment, it appeared the first place the Emperor would look was at his six lords of industry: Volmer—mass media; Malperin—agriculture, chemicals, and pharmaceuticals; Lovett—banking; the Kraa twins—mines, mills, and foundries; Kyes—artificial intelligence; and finally, Sullamora—ships and trade.

Sullamora had approached his duties as a member of the Emperor's private cabinet with a great deal of reluctance and cynicism. Until the moment the Emperor had appointed him to the council—in a chilling and, for Sullamora, revealing conversation—he had not even been aware of its existence. And the appointment had been made in a halfhearted way when Sullamora had questioned the Emperor's strategy in dealing with the Tahn if and when they were defeated.

The Emperor was planning to remove the government and eliminate all vestiges of the Tahn culture, then to follow up with a massive rebuilding program. Sullamora saw that as pure weakness and foolishness. All Tahn should have to suffer for what they had wrought. Besides, the beings who had loyally supported the Emperor from the very beginning would therefore have to forgo vast potential profits. That did not make sense, and Sullamora said so—although he put it as a carefully worded suggestion, not a criticism.

When he had first met with his colleagues of the privy council, Sullamora had kept all that to himself. Groping for direction, he had bided his time until he had taken each member's pulse a hundred times and had their profiles drawn and redrawn as many times more by key people in his psych division.

Looked at from afar—something Tanz was not capable of doing—the privy council presented a strange but accurate portrait of the Empire itself: an odd kind of blend of vigorous entrepreneurism and dynastic capitalism. Seen up close, it was a confusing puzzle of wildly different interests and goals. Little by little, however, Sullamora gradually uncovered a common note.

Volmer was the most vocal of the group. Usually, when the others danced about a point, it was Volmer who tended to be openly and harshly critical of the latest Imperial policy they were deploring. That did not mean that anyone—much less Sullamora—trusted him.

As head of one of the oldest family dynasties in the Empire as well as the chieftain of the largest news-gathering, polit-prop, and advertising companies in the many systems that made up the Empire, Volmer was the least vulnerable of the six. He also had a private reputation among the various companies that made up his barony as a bit of a waffler, a man who would encourage his underlings to take hard stands when it suited him and then leave them hanging if the wind switched direction. Still, as the war dragged on and when even an idiot could see what a hollow shell the privy council in fact was, Sullamora was sure Volmer was moving out of the swamp of his own indecision onto the firmer ground shared by his colleagues.

It was the raw, open greed of the Kraa twins that made Sullamora put them in his potential allies column. They had a deserved reputation as the most corrupt, vicious, self-serving beings in the brutal world of high-stakes business. The two women were second-generation megarich. Their father had been a wildcat miner who had parlayed a minor fortune in Imperium X into a virtual empire consisting of minerals, exotic and common, and whole systems whose sole occupation was the milling and smelting of the same. Their father had been a canny man whose word had been his religion.

Upon his death, the twins had instantly dissolved the religion and sent his high priests howling into the wilderness, where they then had their economic assassins hunt them down one by one. The Kraa twins delighted in nasty plots and wild schemes that took their fortunes on wild roller coaster rides from treble profits to near bankruptcy and back again. Although they had been born identical twins, fifty years of indulgent living had stamped out two entirely different-looking beings. One was gross and banded with bulge after bulge of greasy fat. The other could best be described as anorexic— bones jutting nearly through pasty, unhealthy flesh. But appearance was the only difference. In everything else they thought and acted as one, seemingly taking turns as the dominant twin. Sullamora noted with minor interest their first names and then wisely forgot them. To think of them as anything but one was a fatal mistake too many others had made.

It was to Sullamora's credit that he saw the Kraa twins as the easiest members of the council to manipulate. With the Kraas, one only had to hoist the carrot and they would follow. If they did not, they had more than enough vulnerable spots to probe. And one did not have to be subtle about it.

Malperin, on the other hand, had only one area of vulnerability. She was a woman with an exterior *and* interior of ten-point steel. She was the ultimate chief operating officer, armed with academic degrees and hands-on management experience that stretched for three small forevers. It did not matter what kind of company she was called upon to manage, be it toy widgets or sophisticated electronics. In her case, it was an ability that was a two-headed coin. Because her viewpoint was necessarily fixed on the upper level, she had no feeling or gut instincts about specifics. That almost meant she had no loyalties to things, only to procedures.

It was for that reason that the Emperor had tapped her to head up ACP, one of the most bizarre but vital megacorporations going. Even an industrial historian's eyes would glaze over tracing the hydra head back to its beginnings. Suffice it to say that in a bewildering series of small fish somehow swallowing big fish swallowing whole schools of other fish actions, ACP came tentatively into being. It was a tacked-together conglomerate that operated millions upon millions of kilometers of farms and ranches, oversaw massive vats of brewing chemicals and gases of every nature, and also produced most of the basic important drugs and medicines in the Empire. It was a company born of business warfare, and it never got better after that. Each division was bred and educated to hate and distrust the others. The situation had been threatening to spin out of control when the Tahn war broke out. At any other time the Eternal Emperor would have let matters take their course. ACP was a dinosaur doomed to extinction. But there was no way that he could allow evolution to take its course while fighting a war. The only solution was to suggest strongly—read "you'd clottin' better or die"—that the various boards of directors go outside ACP for a chief operating officer.

After a great deal of squabbling and threatening, Malperin was picked. To firm up her position, the Emperor also named her to his private cabinet. That would give her temporary prestige. But as the war seemed to be winding down, Malperin was beginning to realize that her overlong honeymoon at ACP was as good as over. She would also have to be stupid not to realize that at any moment the Emperor could and *would* withdraw his support and let economic gravity settle the rest. Malperin was not stupid. She did not look upon her future gladly.

The next to last member of the privy council was the money man, Lovett. Like Volmer, he was from a great family dynasty. There were Lovetts who had acted as financial go-betweens in some of the Eternal Emperor's earliest business dealings. The newest Lovett scion was handsome, dashing, and daring.

Tragically, through a series of misfortunes, he was the last member of his clan, and he had taken over the helm of the banking empire upon his mother's death. He was also the wildest of wild cards, who refused to listen to his advisers and had a habit of taking large and unnecessary risks. Some said it was out of remembered gratitude to the Lovetts that the Emperor had stepped in. Others said that it was because the Lovett banks were too integral to the Emperor's plans to be allowed to collapse and that it had been purely in self-interest that the Emperor had reacted. Both were right. And so history would someday record that on such and such a date Lovett became the youngest being ever to head up the Imperial Monetary Foundation, a nonprofit organization whose charter was to play banker to the poorest systems in the Empire. In short, it was a position of extreme glitter and no substance at all. Sullamora grinned to himself, knowing that Lovett had *just* figured that out. Tanz Sullamora saw Lovett as the easiest one of all to manipulate.

If Lovett was paper, Kyes was stone. Kyes was a Grb'chev, one of the saddest creations of the gods of madness. He was a tall, slender, vaguely humanoid being of immense dignity, just entering his 121st year. His coloring was silver leaning toward white, except for a triangular slash of scarlet that rode across his bony skull. When he spoke, his limbs were animated and his eyes flashed with impatient intelligence. But in repose, the face slackened, the eyes went blank, and the great splash of red pulsed like an infection that had reached crisis. Kyes was two separate beings with one dominant will and a weaker, genetically suicidal other. The Grb'chev were the result of an odd form of symbiotic bonding. Before the bonding, when the Grb'chev were merely tall and slender and very white, with no red "birthmark" on their skulls, there was nothing to distinguish the race except for their great stupidity and even greater genetic luck. They had brains that were no more than a large pimple on the end of a spinal stalk. They favored a particular type of fruit that was edible only when the pollen was most active. The pollen was deadly poison to anything, including the Grb'chev. The Grb'chev developed an exotic system of nasal filters topped by superefficient sinuses that gradually bulged out their heads until they were oversize.

They also developed an immune system that was impenetrable to any form of virus and bacteria on their homeworld. Left on their own, the Grb'chev would have spun out their destinies of exceedingly stupid, exceedingly lucky beings who spent most of their waking hours gaping, scratching, and eating fruit. But although stupid did not bother nature one bit, happy seemed to give it problems. Enter, stage right, a lowly virus looking for a home. It was a virus that had only one ability to brag about: It could mutate its protein sheath to pierce any genetic structure, no matter how invulnerable. Usually that meant the instant infection and almost as instant extinction of any living forms it encountered. It was a closed-end deal, so that although the virus could giggle on into virus paradise, it could never be anything more than what it was, a wolf with changeable clothing.

It encountered something different in the Grb'chev. As quickly as it cast off its sheath and fitted on another, the Grb'chev's immune system threw up another shield. The virus finally found its home in the sinuses, the most recent addition to what made a Grb'chev a Grb'chev. The mutating virus met cells in the middle of their own transition. They met and formed an entity consisting entirely of brain cells, nerves, and nerve receptors, an entity operating with—but separately from—the bodily parts and functions. The brain cells were also far stronger and more durable than any main body cells. The closest cells one could compare them with were cancer cells. In short, they were immortal.

Next came awareness. And after that, despair. Because the Grb'chev came complete: an efficient fuel and waste-disposal system. Smooth locomotion. An ability to easily duplicate the Grb'chev structure as many times as necessary. And a perfect time clock that spelled out beginning, middle, a long senility, and an end. When Kyes entered his 121st year, he knew he had no more than five more years of awareness before the agonizingly slow deterioration of intelligence led to his ending up as a vegetable that gaped, bubbled, and then died.

In his hundred-plus years of adult-active life, Kyes believed that he had eliminated all the seven deadly sins from his system one by one. Ninety years before, he had rolled out of a prestigious institution armed with a degree in artificial intelligence, a sheaf of job offers, and a double sheaf of ideas. He ignored the job offers and struck out on his own. Twenty-five years later he was richer than any being's wildest dreams. He was also famous for the hundreds of vital patents he personally owned and the lean-mean company he had created that could identify and exploit any fad in the most faddish of fields years before his competitors. Kyes was good. And he was arrogant—as he had every right to be.

Then the big boys got together, kicked sand in his face, and took his company, wealth, and arrogance away from him. Kyes disappeared for fifteen years. But when he returned, he was a remade being. He had spent every second of every waking day studying his old foes. As he learned their weaknesses, he eliminated weaknesses of his own. He came on stage again quietly. He was still creative and inventive, but he buried his inventions in masses of partnerships and cutout companies. Just before his hundredth birthday, Kyes found himself the master of the greatest computer, robotic, and artificial intelligence conglomerate ever known. He was famous again, sought after for his views and insights. He even met the Eternal Emperor and had reason to believe that he had met him on as nearly an èqual level as possible. Had not Kyes been one of the first beings the Emperor had come to for advice in his dealings with the mechanics of the Tahn conflict? And was he not one of the first appointees to the privy council?

And then, little by little, Kyes began to believe that he was being used. After that, he began noticing that his firm was becoming more and more dependent on the Emperor's contracts. He had enjoyed enormous expansion in the past few years, but he was beginning to realize just how delicate the expansion was. A frown from the emperor would mean starting all over again. Except that with only five years left, to start again would be impossible.

Kyes became obsessed with newly realized vulnerability. He could see no way of stopping it. It seemed as inevitable as the winding down of his biological clock. Then he began thinking about the Emperor. The *Eternal* Emperor. And he realized there was nothing empty about either word in the title.

Kyes met envy face-to-face. And it was just about then that Tanz Sullamora began whispering in his ear.

After Durer, the whispering was replaced by louder and louder mutterings of discontent. At first, Sullamora just complained about how the Emperor's busy schedule prevented him from consulting his privy council for their thoughts on how to deal with the depression that was sure to follow after the war. The others not only agreed but became encouraged to complain that the few times they *had* been consulted, their advice had been ignored.

"Take me, for instance," Volmer had said. "The last time I spoke with the Emperor I strongly suggested that we had to start planning for the future right now. A good propaganda campaign isn't created overnight.

"We've got to come up with our message. Target our audience. Tailor the message for the various target groups. And then deliver it in a carefully orchestrated way."

The message, as Volmer saw it, was: "Hope through sacrifice. Each of us is going to be called upon to sacrifice for the good of the Empire. And of our children. And our children's children."

"I like it," Lovett had said, immediately thinking about some ideas he had concerning interest rates pegged to inflation, with a high floor to take care of any unexpected deflation. "What did he say?"

Volmer frowned. "He asked me what *I* was planning to sacrifice. He said for a message like that to work, people would want to see their leaders do a little suffering... Suffering, what a negative word! Sacrifice is much easier to sell... Anyway, I told him flat out that was an insane idea. Why, if people see us hurting"—he waved, including his colleagues in—"what would they have to hope for? Destroys the whole concept."

He found no disagreement in that.

Each of the other members had similar horror stories. Malperin wanted wage controls but no ceiling on prices. The Kraas wanted "more enlightened" pollution and safety laws.

Sullamora wanted a one-sided tariff arrangement to shield his merchant empire. And as for Kyes, well, Kyes did not say anything for some time. The others wondered at that for a while, disturbed that the Grb'chev was not reaching in for his share of the pie. What they did not know was that Kyes, with one huge exception, already had all that he wanted. And he figured that if he ever thought of anything else, he was quite capable of getting it on his own, without the benefit of Imperial intervention. Still, there was *the* exception . . .

Several meetings went by before he moved his first pawn. He opened on the king's bishop side. And when he spoke, everyone was respectfully silent, waiting for him to finally declare himself. They were not disappointed.

"Perhaps we are doing our Emperor a disservice," he said slowly, as if he were thinking out loud. Every member of the council knew better. "From his point of view, perhaps we are firing ideas at him from all directions. He has *so* much on his mind now. How can he pick here and there when he can see no whole?"

His colleagues nodded wisely, merely to mark time until Kyes got the rest of it out.

"Let's make things simpler for him," Kyes said. "We need to speak as one. To present a coherent view. And then have the authority to enact the needed reforms. With the Emperor's concurrence, of course," he added quickly.

"Emperor's concurrence . . . of course," everyone muttered.

What Kyes proposed was deceptively simple. The privy council would call upon the Parliament and then the Emperor to create a quasi-public agency—consisting of members of the sitting council, to start with—that could act independently of the whims and fads and pressure of any special-interest group.

Said agency would take the long view of the economy, carefully managing the AM2 pump to control the strength of the Imperial credit, keep a close eye on vital industrial and agricultural supplies, make sure that the government always spoke with one voice, and serve as a much needed check and balance between the competing views of business and the public good.

There was no disagreement. Sullamora, the man with the

most direct clout with Parliament, would take point. The first step would be approached cautiously. The skeleton of the proposed agency would be buried in a "sense of Parliament" resolution which, once enacted, would be difficult for the Emperor to shoot down without causing a very loud fuss. The trick was to keep anyone—especially the Emperor's back-bench toadies—from even guessing that something was up. The privy council decided to praise Caesar rather than to damn him. The praise took the form of a lengthy document profusely congratulating the Emperor for his victory over the Tahn at Durer and calling for Empirewide support of the Emperor to carry the victory forward to a final surrender and then beyond. Even on the surface, it was not an empty document. It was worded in such a way to make even the fence sitters who had been the bane of the emperor for some time to back his act. If approved, and Sullamora's people went out and twisted every arm and tentacle available to assure its passage, the resolution would break the back of the neutrals.

Sullamora knew that would ensure the Emperor's support. He also had his experts put together a swampland section that committed Parliament to "render every assistance" to the Emperor in his "brave and lonely struggle." The independent agency was the gator hiding in the swamp.

Sullamora's analysts pored over the document and finally agreed that there was no way anyone could ever spot the gator amid obfuscations no one would bother to read. As one patriarch of the Parliament once put it, "If everyone knew what they're voting on, we'd never get out of here." When the big moment came, Sullamora personally planned to present the resolution in a speech punched up to the nth degree by a team provided by Volmer. It was pure-dee guaranteed to be welcomed with thunderous applause.

Sullamora paced back and forth in the small anteroom, waiting to be called to the speaker's rostrum. As he paced, he rehearsed the speech in his head, punching out at the air with his right hand to mark the rhythms. A door hissed open behind him, and Sullamora turned, mildly surprised. The call was five minutes early. But instead of seeing the huge jolly figure of the Parliament's sergeant at arms, he found himself gaping down at a small, dark man with a large curved knife hanging from his uniform belt. It was a Gurkha, one of the Emperor's personal bodyguards. The Gurkha gave him a small, barely polite bow and handed him a message. It was a summons. The Eternal Emperor had spotted the gator.

The Emperor was a study in casualness, feet propped up on his antique desk, a drink before him, another in front of Tanz Sullamora, and a bottle between them. He even picked up his drink frequently as he talked, seeming to take a sip and then replace the glass on the desk. Sullamora noted that the level never went down.

". . . I appreciate your good intentions, Tanz," the Emperor was saying. "And I plan to personally thank each member of my cabinet for going to all this thought and effort. But . . ."

He let the word sit there for a moment while he took another sip of his drink. From that moment on, Sullamora knew the conversation would be one he would take to his grave— or, at least, to his memoirs.

"I don't go for this independent agency concept," the Emperor finally said. He raised a polite hand as if Sullamora would protest—not that he would ever *dare* to. "I know you may think I'm being shortsighted, but these kinds of things have a way of taking on a life of their own. The fact of the matter is, I'm a one-man show. Always have been. Hope to always be. You fellows are talking about taking the long view. Well, I have to tell you, from where I sit, there is no way your view can be long enough."

He waited, encouraging comment from Sullamora.

"There was no disrespect intended," Sullamora said. "But we just can't see how one person—no matter how good—can handle everything himself. What we're offering here, sir, is a chance for you to take advantage of the experience of some of the best minds under your rule."

The Emperor pretended to think about that for a moment. Then he nodded to Sullamora.

"Okay. Let's run through this and see if maybe I'm wrong. I suppose we all agree on what we're facing once this is over. Once the Tahn agree to my terms, we turn off the war machine. And then we immediately face one holy mother of a depression. I doubt there has ever been a depression the potential size of what we're talking about.

"All your shipbuilding factories, for instance. They'll come to a halt. We've got enough ships of the line now for ten long lifetimes. The same goes for every other area of the economy. The torque will be tremendous. A whole lot of great big axles churning away, with no place to go."

"We've got ideas that specifically—"

"I've heard of them," the Emperor snapped. "And they don't wash. You want me to raise the AM2 tax from two mills to three or maybe four. But what you can't seem to get through your heads is that if you take money out of people's pockets, there's no way they can buy what little you'll be able to produce.

"It's not war that has destroyed the great empires of history. It's money, or the mishandling of same. When the soldiers' job is over, you've got this big whopping bill. And you've got interest running on that big mother of a bill. And you better not make the mistake of not paying it off. Otherwise, next time you need to fight, the money people will drag their feet and jack up the interest on what little they will lend you. Same with the little guy whose life we put on the line. If he comes home to misery, he's not gonna be too thrilled about fighting for you next time out, no matter how worthy you tell him the cause is.

"Personally, I'm thinking about pulling in my horns. Reducing the tax to peacetime levels. One mill. No more. And maybe after a while a temporary decrease to two-thirds of a mill. That way the local governments can pop on a quarter-mill tax of their own to pay back their share of what this stupid war cost."

Sullamora gasped at that idea. "At least we can increase the AM2 output," he said. "That'll bring in more taxes. Besides making it cheaper for us all to operate."

"Sure it will," the Eternal Emperor said. "It will also kick hell out of the value of the credit. People will be walking around with wheelbarrows of the stuff to buy a glass of beer."

Sullamora did not know what a wheelbarrow was, but he got the general drift. "You mentioned beer," he said. "Now, there's a way to make money nobody can object to. A tax on beer. A tax on narcotics. A tax on joy—"

"Used to be called a sin tax," the Emperor said dryly. "Another dumb idea. Between me and the Tahn, we have killed and mutilated more beings than I like to think about. What we're left with is a pretty miserable group.

"Now, the beings in this group may not agree on a lot. But if we let them, misery will be the first hammer they'll pick up. And they'll hit us with it, Tanz. I guarantee you that.

"No. This is a time to start encouraging a little *more* sin, if anything. Lots of spectacle. And as close to free as dammit."

That made no sense at all to Sullamora. The Emperor pretended not to notice and moved on.

"And speaking of keeping people happy," he said. "You realize that we're all talking about some major increases in wages, don't you? And if you want to sell anything, a major *decrease* in prices.

"In fact, since a lot of my fellow capitalists are usually pretty slow to get the drift of these kinds of things, I'm considering some pretty heavy-duty legislation on the subject."

"How—how can you possibly see that?" Sullamora sputtered out.

"Simple. Fewer people to work equals higher wages. Lower prices means more productivity providing things those people can now afford. And lots of cheap material to build those things from. For anyone with vision, that is. Take all those ships of yours, Tanz," the Emperor said, slipping the dirk between Sullamora's ribs. Sullamora realized that the Emperor planned on sticking him with a lot of those soon-to-be-useless warships. "With a little creative retooling, you'll have plenty of scrap of just about any kind of material going to build some useful products."

"Like what?" Sullamora asked in a bare whisper.

The Eternal Emperor shrugged. "Beats the clot out of me. You've got R&D geniuses. Put 'em to work making some new things to cook food with instead of frying people. Should be easy.

"Hell, Tanz. The more I think about it, we're talking about *real* opportunity here. Almost makes me wish I didn't have this stupid job. A guy with a little brains, a bit of money, and a lot energy could make himself a great big pile out of all this."

Sullamora had to ask the question. "Do you really believe that?"

"Sure I do," the Emperor said. "At least I know *I* could, although you probably think that's just big talk. Fact is, most emperors think the same way. There was a queen, way back when, who used to say pretty much the same thing to her advisers.

"She used to tell them that if somehow she were plucked from her throne and dropped in nothing but her petticoats on any desolate coast, it wouldn't take her long to be running things again. Some of her advisers used to laugh about that behind her back.

"Her name was Elizabeth. Elizabeth the First. Ever hear of her?"

Tanz Sullamora shook his head, knowing his audience was coming to a close.

"She must have been really something," the Emperor mused on. "Some historians think she was the greatest ruler ever. Maybe they're right."

A small wild thought crossed Sullamora's mind. He wondered what had happened to the advisers. The ones who laughed. Had they ever thought about . . .

"Of course, she was pretty quick with the ax," the Eternal Emperor said, and it was almost as if he were reading Sullamora's mind. The ship baron rose quickly to his feet, nearly knocking over his drink.

"Excuse me, sir," he stammered. "But I think . . ."

"Are you all right?" the Emperor asked, giving Sullamora a strange, puzzled look. But maybe Tanz was just imagining that. He made an excuse about feeling slightly ill and, after being dismissed, hurried for the door. Just as it hissed open, the Emperor called his name. Sullamora forced himself to turn back.

"Yes, sir?"

"No more surprises, okay, Tanz?" the Emperor said. "I don't like surprises."

Tanz Sullamora gasped out a promise and hurried away, vowing to break that promise the first chance he had.

He spoke uninterrupted for a full hour. The members of the privy council listened in cold silence as he related in complete detail his conversation with the Emperor. Sullamora did not color his account in any way or attempt to paint himself as being larger or bolder than he had in fact been. These were businessbeings who had no patience for hyperbole. Just the facts was what they wanted, and just the facts was what they got.

The silence went on after he had finished. It seemed like an eternity as each one filled in the blanks and thought over the personal consequences of what the Eternal Emperor was planning to do.

Volmer was the first to break. "But—but—we're looking at disaster here. Doesn't he understand . . . My God! We've got to stop him!"

And then the impact of what he had just said hit him like a padded club, and he flushed and stuttered back into silence. After an appropriate pause, Tanz Sullamora made a suggestion. He said that maybe they could all benefit from a walk in the woods.

"A walk in the woods" was an ancient political phrase that had originally meant "to seek a meeting of the minds," for a representative of one camp to convince another that both had to swallow some very evil-tasting medicine. It meant a method of reaching a difficult decision without the pressures of the outside world.

Tanz Sullamora meant something similar when he proposed the walk. Except, in his case, there was obviously already a meeting of the minds. He was sure they all knew what had to be done but were afraid to be the first to suggest it. Sullamora was ninety percent correct.

The members of the council walked many kilometers, weaving through the trees and pausing here and there to sniff the air or listen to a bird's song. Pretending interest. Pretending pleasure in the simple things. Inside, each being's guts roiled with acid. Finally, it was Kyes who broached the subject.

"Volmer was right," he said. "I see no other solution. Perhaps it's just as well. The man is obviously out of touch with reality."

Everyone nodded, relieved that it had finally been said. Everyone except Volmer. The man was shocked, frightened. To him, his blurted remark was being twisted and turned into something he was not willing to deal with. Volmer might have thought regicide, might even have blurted regicide. But it was being tossed back at him as bloody-handed treason.

"What are you saying? My God, I don't want any... Look, we're all under a lot of pressure. We're not thinking clearly. Let's all just take our lumps like beings and get back to it. Okay? It's time to go home, right? Get back to business?"

Sullamora came in like a snake. He draped a soothing arm over Volmer's shoulder. He patted his back, ruffled his hair, and steered him slightly away from the others. "A misunderstanding... not what he meant... Speaking metaphorically..." And on and on. Volmer was grabbing at his phrases like a drowning man, agreeing, subsiding, and becoming calm again.

As Sullamora ushered the man through the door of the main building, he looked back at the others. They were all staring after him. The bargain had been struck, the deal made.

Sullamora laughed at some weak joke Volmer had made and pounded his back in manly appreciation—thinking, as he did it, that that was the first place the knife would have to fall.

CHAPTER THIRTY-TWO

THE REST OF Sten and Alex's escape was not the stuff livies were made from. True to his word, Chetwynd tucked the pair away in the lap of luxury, which consisted of an oversize bed with sheets and unlimited time to spend in it—alone and asleep.

It also meant being vermin-free for the first time in years. Being able to bathe in clean water any time they wanted. And there was food! Calories and glutinous calories of it! At first the foods were simple, so as not to stress their battered digestive systems. And finally there was the ecstasy of being able to walk away from a meal leaving food still on the plate.

The various joygirls and boys who offered other services might have been disappointed at the lack of response, but as Kilgour explained for the both of them, "Ah'd need a splint, but thanks f'r thinki't ah me."

Chetwynd left them alone. He knew how long it took for a prisoner to realize he was more than a stubborn survival machine.

Eventually the two were moved out of Heath, hidden below a ton and a half of metal scrap stacked on an ancient, bailing-wire-maintained gravsled onto, Sten guesssed, the private estate of some Tahn muckety. Chetwynd declined to provide information, of course.

The tiny smuggling ship hovered, Yukawa drive humming. Sten and Alex were bundled aboard, and the ship lifted off-world and vanished into AM2 drive.

Somewhere the ship rendezvoused with its mother transport, and Sr. Jon Wild greeted them.

He had, he told them, gotten off Romney just in time. The feeling that expert crooks get that the heat was breathing down

178

their necks had prickled his spine—and Wild had ordered an evacuation. He had lost seven ships and his base, but all of his people and, more importantly, his goods were saved. And anyone, he explained, rubbing his fingers together meaningfully, "can acquire a ship and a place to land it."

He was most delighted to be able to move them to safety, he explained. He owed Sten.

Some time before, a small convoy of his had gotten jumped inside the Imperial sector. The next stage would have been confiscation of ships and cargo and appropriate measures for the crew and Wild.

"There was some mention of prison planets," he went on. "Or for those of us considered rehabilitatable they offered some horror called penal battalions. I did not ask for details."

Sten had been Wild's ace. In honest bewilderment he wondered to his captors why they would interfere with an Imperial Intelligence operation. He had been met with loud laughter.

"I suggested they check with their own G, S, or whatever letter they use for the section. Shortly thereafter, to some surprise, the spyboys reported that I was a gentleman born to the colors.

"I am very grateful that you filed the proper paperwork, young man."

With grudging apologies, Wild and his people were freed and continued on about their own, quite profitable business providing Tahn luxuries for rich Imperials, and vice versa.

"I estimate that if this war continues another . . . oh, give it ten years, I should be able to go legitimate." Wild shuddered slightly at the concept. "So indeed, Commander, or whatever your rank is, you shall be treated, during this passage, as if you were the illegitimate son of the Emperor himself."

The remainder of the voyage was marked by a slow, steady increase in their waistbands, some occasional sweaty moments as patrols, either Tahn or Imperial, were evaded, and more sleep.

Sten figured they were returning to something close to normal after seeing Alex duck into a cabin with one of Wild's more shapely officers.

By the time they were landed on an Imperial base that coincidentally was in a system where Wild "had some interest-

ing people to meet," both ex-POWs would have made lousy
propaganda fodder. They should have been bearded. Haggard.
Emaciated. Scarred. Ready to testify to the monstrous inhu-
manity of the Tahn and the ability to tough it out that brave
Imperial soldiers had.

The propaganda mills were not even alerted.

Both men knew far too much to allow the public prints near
them. They were shuttled to Prime World, and the Empire's
most skilled debriefers worked them over using every skill and
technique they had short of mindprobe. Sten had been there
once, thank you, and would rather not repeat the experience.

By the time Intelligence grudgingly decided that whatever
else of value was inside their now-bruised and exhausted brain
cells, Sten and Kilgour felt as if they had been crucified by
Tahn torturers.

And then the real surprises began.

Both Sten and Alex expected various medals. Not because
they necessarily thought they had done anything particularly
heroic in captivity, except getting the clot out of it—for which
accomplishment they would have cheerfully accepted free alk
for the rest of their lifetime instead of a gong—but because
when any war got nasty, the survivors tended to collect bits of
tin as they survived.

Those they received.

Both of them expected promotions—and had theorized on
the long run back whether they would be kicked up one or
more grades.

Those they did not receive—yet.

Their orders were quite similar:

STEN (NI) (WITHHELD) Ordered to (WITHHELD) following (WITHHELD) leave time, authorized travel to (WITHHELD).
Upon return to duty, you will report to (WITHHELD) for further
orders. Conditions of reporting for further duty will be communicated to you by (WITHHELD) date.

KILGOUR, ALEX (WITHHELD) Ordered to (WITHHELD)
following (WITHHELD) leave time, authorized travel to planet of
EDINBURGH and other systems as desired. Upon return to duty,
you will report to (WITHHELD) for further orders. Conditions of
reporting for further duty will be communicated to you by
(WITHHELD) date.

Sten and Alex looked at each other. Somebody up there had plans for their future. Probability: unpleasant. But there was little that could be done about it short of deserting. And both of them had spent enough time on the run.

The second step was to collect their back pay, which would amount to a small fortune.

One of the few productive pastimes the Tahn POWs had was figuring out how much money they were due and how they would spend it.

The Empire paid its military somewhat differently than had governments of the past. A soldier's paycheck was either given to him in cash on pay period or banked in a civilian bank and allowed to draw whatever interest or noninterest it paid, bank to be determined by individual.

That was *not* done because of any particular kindness the Emperor felt toward each grunt. There were three very simple reasons that, one drunken evening eons before, the emperor had outlined for Mahoney:

1. This is a capitalist Empire. I think. Therefore, money in circulation is healthier than money sitting in anybody's vault.
2. I understand a lot of things. I can sketch you out, if you're interested, the mathematical correlation of the nine basic forces of the universe. I don't understand economics, and nobody else does, either. Therefore, I ain't gonna get involved.
3. Banks what get my troopies' money are very, very rational people. Which means they do what I clottin' tell them, when I tell them, or else suddenly they're on the "Not Recommended For Military Deposit" list.

And so, when Sten and Alex paraded into the Prime World bank that for years had been favored, for some lost reason, by Mercury Corps and Mantis Section operatives, they expected to be greeted politely, as if they were stockholders.

They did not expect to be ushered into the office of the bank president and informed they were now majority stockholders. And if it would please the gentlemen, now that they were . . . ahem, available, would they be interested in advising the current members of the board on future investment possibilities?

Sten gurgled.

Kilgour, however, rose to the occasion. He reached for a cheroot—real tobacco, it would appear—from a humidor, struck it on the president's desk, leaving scars across what looked like real wood, and inhaled. He managed to bury the subsequent coughing spasm and called for a printout on both of their accounts.

They were not just well-to-do.

They were rich.

Both of them had significant holdings in the most formidable corporations of the Empire. Plus a percentage in exotic metals. Plus a percentage in war bonds. Plus . . .

Sten goggled at about page thirty-six of the printout. He was most grateful that the bank president had excused himself.

"Uh . . . Kilgour. I own a world."

Kilgour was equally bemused. "Ah nae hae thae . . . but it appears Ah'll hae the richest estate ae Edinburgh. Ah can afford to r'store th' family castle."

"You have a castle?"

"Noo Ah do."

And both of them understood, just as the fawning banker returned with the contents of a certain safety deposit box, which, he said, was to be given to them personally and privately. Again, he withdrew.

They opened the box, found a fiche, and booted it up.

Gypsy Ida's less than conventionally lovely face appeared onscreen.

Ida was a former member of Sten and Alex's Mantis Team. She was a hustler, an investor, and one of the best pilots Sten had ever flown beside.

She had disappeared from the service years before but as she was leaving she had somehow tapped into her ex-teammates' bank accounts and invested, invested, invested—leaving them most comfortable.

The sound cut on: "Y'r clots, you know. Howinhell'd you two ever manage to get captured? Kilgour, you're as dumb as you are fat. Sten, why'd you listen to the clot?

"Anyway.

"I accessed your credits when I heard you were missing. Knew there weren't any Tahn smart enough to waste you on sight, and figured that you'd live.

"Hope now that you're listening to this and it ain't your heirs and assignees and the war's over.

"I started filtering all those credits you had sitting there and took care of you two clots.

"Near as I can figure, there ain't nothing that can go wrong, unless maybe the Emperor surrendered—an' by the way, you got holdings in the Tahn worlds if that happened—that can keep you from being richrich.

"Reason I'm putting this on fiche, instead of bein' there when you see how good care I took care of you, is ... aw, drakh, I went and listened to somebody, and, well, they want me to go do something out there somewhere.

"So that's the way it is.

"I guess 'cause I'm dumb I miss the old days."

Ida's image fell silent, and Sten was appalled to see what looked like a tear well up in her eye. Fortunately the image lasted only for a moment, as suddenly the Rom stood, turned, and hoisted her skirt. What looked like two oversize loaves of bread—pan point of view—went onscreen.

And the screen blanked.

"Th' lass still dinnae wear knickers," Alex managed.

Somehow they made the correct noises to the banker and, each clutching a full briefcase that proved, with full details, that he was richrich, went for the closest bar.

A day or so later, after sobering up, they made the correct noises at each other. Sorry to split up, mate, but that's the way the service works. Hell, it's a small world. Maybe we'll get lucky again and get paired.

Sten drank Kilgour aboard the ship headed for the world of Edinburgh and contemplated.

First he wanted a quiet place to figure out where he was going to spend his leave—whatever amount that WITHHELD figure was giving him before something else happened.

Not to mention that planet that he appeared to own. Planet? he thought. Nobody *owns* a planet. That's disgusting. But maybe he did. If so, he would like to see what his real estate looked like. Preferably with a friend.

He headed for a com and called the police.

Specifically, he called Prime World Homicide and asked for a Lisa Haines. Years earlier, she and Sten had been quite

seriously in love before Sten had been reassigned into the
maze that took him into the Tahn War and captivity. He sort of
hoped, just maybe, she was still solo and remembered him.
The copshop advised that yes, a Lisa Haines was still a police
person. And that they would accept a message for her. But she
was unfortunately not available at the moment.

"When do you expect her?"

"That information is not available," the synthesized voice
began, and then suddenly the screen blanked, and a second,
human voice came on. A very polite one.

"This is Message Center. You were trying to contact Captain Lisa Haines. We are prepared to relay a message ...
however, please stand by. We are experiencing difficulties
receiving you. Do not break the transmission. An operator
will be with you in moments when the signal is corrected."

Sten, out of sheer habit and training, never stood inside
camera range of any com. He was therefore unseen when the
red RECEIVING light glowed on. Shortly thereafter, he was
some meters away, appearing to be in the middle of a bargaining session with a shopkeeper when two heavyset men with
close-cropped hair thundered toward the com booth.

Security thugs, he made them for. He paid for whatever it
was he was bargaining for and slipped into the crowd.

Lisa had been caught up in the war. Obviously she was
somewhere in the bowels of Intelligence. Message Center, indeed. Sten grimaced. It looked as if he were about to spend a
solitary leave, at least until he ran across some local talent.
Speaking of which, he headed for a library to find out if his
real estate *included* local talent.

It did not—or so, at least, the various star fiches he consulted suggested.

The world's name was Smallbridge. About .87 E-size,
commensurate gravity, E-normal atmosphere, three AU from a
dying yellow star. Climate tropical to subarctic. Flora/
Fauna ...

The slender report from the Imperial Survey Mission that
said that there was nothing particularly interesting about the
world of Smallbridge—then called Survey World XM-Y-1134

and many other numerals and letters—other than extensive members of the Orchidae family, giant specimens of Polypodiosida... blur... blur... insect life... blur... blur ... nonmalevolent... water potable, with following blur blur presences... following water-dwelling species found edible, worthy of possible commercial exploration... fauna... nothing that would try to eat Sten, with the exception of a small, rather shy catlike creature that might try to nail him if he were passed out in front of its den—maybe. Nothing else of interest—which meant, to the survey crew, that nothing had tried to kill them. NO BEINGS OF HIGHER DEVELOPMENT OBSERVED.

Sten appeared to be owner of an eight-tenths-scale Eden, if one that seemed never to have progressed very far.

Now, what had man done to screw it up after discovery? After all, somebody had given Survey World Whatever-it-was a name. Sten fed in the fiche from his own files.

The answer was—nobody. It had been acquired by an entrepreneur who had made his fortune doing something that nobody had ever thought of and had then decided he had a corner on entrepreneuring. He had named the world, built himself and, Sten gathered, his paid companions in joy a rather wonderful mansion, added a state-of-the-art spaceport, and then gone bankrupt trying to make a second, third, and so on fortune.

Once again—an Eden.

Sten swore a rather surprised oath in Low Tahn, suggesting that the hearer's mother had private parts that could accommodate a battalion—and jerked away from the screen, hearing a giggle.

The giggle came from a very young, very tall, very blond woman sitting at the computer table next to him.

"You understood?" he asked.

"I understood."

Sten, all too aware that his somewhat limited social graces probably had not been improved by his time as a POW, made himself blush and apologized.

The woman, who introduced herself as Kim Lavransdotter, explained. She spoke High, Low, Medium, and War Tahn.

She was a researcher and historian, doctor of this in Tahn culture and that in Tahn history, and very pleased that her studies had been honored by a request to come to Prime World and work with Imperial Social Analysis.

"Maybe I shouldn't tell you this," she said, looking worried. "I guess we've got some kind of feed into Intelligence, even though they never say anything."

Sten reassured her.

He had clearances. Right up to and including "Eyes Only —Imperial Staff," although he did not tell her quite that much.

She was very beautiful.

And Sten was very lonely.

He offered to buy her a caff.

She stayed very beautiful.

Sten bought her dinner.

The next day, he took her with him to look up some old friends—Marr and Senn, in their crystal light tower.

She charmed them.

She continued to charm Sten.

And she *was* very beautiful, he noted the next morning as he studied her, lying naked beside him.

Perhaps . . .

Sten felt very lucky that it happened that Kim was well overdue for a vacation and thought that going with him to Smallbridge was perfect. She had never known anyone who owned his own planet, let alone the racing yacht that took them there.

He should have realized.

But he did not.

Perhaps Sten's perceptions were still dulled from the time in prison. Or perhaps it was Kim. Or perhaps it was Smallbridge itself.

Eden . . . from its arctic slopes to the long sandy beaches on its islands, with waves that curled in perfectly and endlessly. The fruit was delicious; the mansion was lavish, roboticized, and seemingly equipped with any liquor or food that could be conceived of.

Even that catlike predator turned out to be moderately

friendly and more interested in lifeboat emergency rations than a human arm.

As they lazed and explored, Sten was learning.

Lavransdotter, he realized, deserved however many degrees she had and then some. She was an expert on the Tahn. Even Sten, who thought he had learned, by the whip, everything there was to know about the warrior culture, learned. And his hatred subsided. He almost felt sorry for any single Tahn, crippled by his or her background and his or her culture.

Almost, but not quite.

After the last Tahn lord had been destroyed and their culture and works lay in ruins, he might be willing to concede that the Tahn would be eligible to join the civilized races.

Almost, but not quite.

And so the leave passed, dreaming days and nights.

Sten should have realized.

But he did not.

Not until the morning, when a remote from his spaceport buzzed and he came awake. Kim yawned, her head pillowed on his upper thigh, snorted, and went back to sleep.

Sten stretched and flipped a screen on.

He looked at the huge ship that sat on his tarmac, dwarfing the yacht, snarled, and was on his feet. He glowered at Kim as she woke again, stretched, and smiled.

"What's your rank?"

Kim's smile stayed in place. "Very good, Sten. Colonel."

"Mercury Corps?"

"Mercury Corps."

The huge ship sitting in the spaceport was the *Normandie*. The Eternal Emperor's personal yacht.

"Where," Sten wondered aloud, "did I ever get the idea that somehow, someway, I am so charming and clottin' attractive that, sitting in a library, the world's most beautiful woman just *happens* to fall in love with me?"

"You sell yourself short," Kim said.

"Thanks. But why you?"

"The Eternal Emperor said to tell you—when or if you

figured it out—that the best kind of dictionary is one you sleep with."

"Aw . . . clot!"

"It is a hell of a war," Kim sympathized. "Now . . . shall we get dressed and report?"

CHAPTER THIRTY-THREE

STEN GLOWERED HIS way up the ramp to the *Normandie*, saluted the OOD, snarled at Kim as she tried to say good-bye, and stomped off, following, as requested, a snappily uniformed aide.

He barely noticed the interesting fact that there were eight Gurkhas at the salute as he boarded, other than that they looked inordinately dumb wearing white gloves.

As the aide led him into a paneled conference room, the *Normandie*'s Yukawa drive hissed, and the ship lifted.

Sten was not all that surprised to find Warrant Officer Alex Kilgour in the room. Alex was grunting—loudly.

"Clottin' Emperor. Clottin' hae me, ae Ah'm supervisin't thae unloadin't ae cargo ae marble f'r my dinin't chambers. Clottin' lairds wi' nae clottin' understandin't ae naught.

"Clottin' chop m' leave wi'out clottin' sayin't ae word, an' next week wae the openin't ae shootin't season!"

He paused in his diatribe long enough to register Sten.

"Boss. Sorry the clottin' pismire scragged you, ae well. Clottin' Emperor. Whae w' need't here is ae some sanity an' nae a little anarchy."

That was a little much. Sten's fingers flashed in Mantis sign language: *Shaddup, clot. The room's bugged!*

Kilgour sneered. "Clot him, clot his snoops an aye th' Em-

pire! Ah'll speakit ae Ah wan'. Wha'es the clot t' do? Send us
back twa Heath?"

"That, in fact, is very much what I had in mind."

The dry voice, of course, came from the Eternal Emperor.

Fleet Marshal Ian Mahoney let the outrage from the babble
of politicians die into silence. He walked to the conference
room's window and looked pointedly overhead.

Twelve Imperial superbattleships hung over the capital city
of Gorj, their screens ringing the ships.

Mahoney turned back to the assembled rulers of Gorj.

"I shall reiterate the situation. Gorj determined to stand
neutral in this war. The Emperor respects that decision.

"However, under the original treaty signed between the
Emperor and Gorj, your world requested our support and aid
if, at any time in the future, Gorj was threatened with attack.

"You agreed in that treaty that Gorj would provide any
necessary logistical aid to that support.

"The Empire has determined that Gorj is imminently in
danger of being seized by the Tahn. This shall not be allowed
to happen.

"In exchange for our securing your independence, all we
are requesting is access to three of your primary spaceports
and the necessary real estate to develop basing for Imperial
maintenance crews."

"And if we don't willingly let you take over those ports?"

"There is," Mahoney went on, "recognized by Imperial
law, either the rights of force majeure or eminent domain. The
Empire will, of course, make proper restitution."

"The Tahn have made no signs of attacking us!"

"They are very subtle," Mahoney said. He was starting to
feel most diplomatic, even though he had wanted to start the
meeting with: Look, guys. You clowns are sitting here, right
on the edges of the Tahn Empire. You've gotten all the good-
ies from staying neutral. Too bad you've got the only populated and developed worlds handy for us to grab.

"We'll protest this!" another politician said.

"You have every right. The Imperial Court of Admiralty, I
might advise, has a case backload of some seventeen years."

"This is morally reprehensible! We'll have our military forces mobilized immediately."

Mahoney nodded politely, glanced again at the hovering fleet, and picked up his gold-braided hat from the table. "You have six hours to reach a decision. Good day, gentleman."

The war had gone on long enough for fine moral principles to become quite corroded.

At the moment all the wallscreens in the huge auditorium showed what appeared to be a rather obese walrus sloshing in a powered swimming tank.

The "walrus" was Rykor, easily the Empire's most skilled psychologist.

The auditorium was filled with her top advisers and the elite of the Empire's propaganda machine.

Rykor sprayed foam from her whiskers—the speakers around the auditorium squealed—and made her summation. "I am hardly equipped to specifically tell any of you gentle-beings how to do the job. All the various suggestions and proposals you saw onscreen will be made available to you. If you choose to use any of them, we would be flattered and honored.

"And, of course, none of the possible gray or black operations can be discussed at this gathering.

"But, overall, your thrust should be twofold:

"One. The victory in the Durer worlds is the beginning of the end. Those who serve the Empire well in hastening victory will be well rewarded.

"Two. What life under the Tahn means, particularly to a non-Tahn, should be developed. Worlds recaptured from the Tahn will be instantly available for visit by any accredited livie crew or journalist. Accreditation policy, I have been advised, shall be most liberal.

"Thank you. In our seminars, we shall attempt to further develop some more cohesive strategies."

A woman stood in the middle of the audience. "What about the Tahn? What direction will Imperial propaganda take?"

"Again, I am not discussing gray or black areas. It shall be quite simple. Large 'cast units will be established on the fringes of the Tahn Empire and relocated forward as we continue recapturing systems. Information broadcast to the Tahn shall consist of exactly what is going on."

"Even if we lose another battle?"

"Even so. We are attempting to prove to the Tahn citizenry that their own leaders *never* tell the truth."

"What about subversion attempts?"

"Yes. I assume you mean atrocity leaflets, livies showing the corruption of the home front, and so forth. I have some exact orders from the Eternal Emperor. I might word them a little more politely, but . . . he said that we are not in the business of preventing the bum fodder shortage for the Tahn.

"Thank you."

"As I see it," the young man said, "our race has a single problem."

Sr. Ecu, senior diplomat of the Manabi, floated above the immaculate floor of the deserted factory, his three-meter-long tail snaking gently below him.

"Ah," he hummed in his most neutral tone.

"You would understand it, I hope." the young man said.

Ecu's wings waved what might have been taken as slight encouragement.

"We see our race as a single being. Stretching from the days of stone on a planet known as Earth, when we ruled by racial right, through the days when a stronger race invaded, defeated, and almost destroyed us. But for centuries, we endured.

"When we emigrated to our own system, we determined that never again would we be creatures of the moment. History and our racial memory would provide the answers.

"We determined to take the long-range view.

"That was our first error: We neglected to wonder how this day's bread could be provided.

"Secondarily, we forgot that those who sit upon the fence become targets for both sides.

"The end result? We built factories before the war, and then the war begins. We refuse to build war materials. And no one is interested in anything else.

"Except for those," the young man spit. "Those who wish us to work on speculation. With a ninety-ten split. Ninety for them, who are the smokedancers, ten for us, simply because we are willing to build and beat their drums.

"And then those others, the Tahn, who we have been assured time and again have no quarrel with us, insist on being able to port and supply their ships and satisfy the demands of their crewmen to confirm our neutrality; who levy a tax against us because they realize that we wish to support them; and so on and so forth.

"Such might be livable. We have resources enough to support our workers who have nothing to do. We have tolerance enough for those who sell their services and bodies to the Tahn.

"But what will come after?"

The Manabi were known and used throughout the Empire as diplomats. They were air-floating beings who were completely neutral—and were, therefore, ideal for the crafts of state. It was completely unknown that just after the Tahn War began, Sr. Ecu had declared the Manabi support for the Empire—not because they thought the Emperor was the epitome of civilization but because they saw the defeat of the Empire as a collapse into barbarism. That support was known to the Manabi collective intelligence, the Eternal Emperor, and no one else. To the Tahn, the neutral systems, and the Empire itself, they remained as they were—the perfect statesbeings.

"What will come after," Sr. Ecu began, "is an unknown. I can only wish that your use of the past and your belief in racial identity provide you the path. Also, I thank you for your confidences and sympathize with your problems.

"But the reason I am here has nothing to do with any of them. I was requested by a representative of the Eternal Emperor to deliver the following:

"'The Emperor has noted the plight of the Five Nations and is deeply distressed. He will therefore provide a doubling of the treaty-allocated amount of Anti-Matter Two to your worlds and deeply hopes that your problems thereby become alleviated.'"

Sr. Ecu was very impressed by the young man, whose expression changed only three times during his announcement. Possibly, he wondered, after some epochs, humans might become capable.

"What are the strings?"

"Pardon?"

"The attachments. The obligations."

"None."

"I do not believe that," the young man said.

"I was so instructed that you would not," Sr. Ecu went on. "I was finally instructed that your ports should prepare for the arrival of six Imperial energy ships within six E-days of my arrival in your system."

Sr. Ecu, having delivered his message and received no answer for the moment, lifted, and his huge black and red–tinted body floated away toward his ship.

He wondered just how long it would take the Five Nations to renounce their neutrality and declare for the Empire. It was a pity, he decided, that he did not understand what was called gambling and could not think of anyone to perform that activity with.

Sr. Ecu thought that he was becoming a bit degenerate— and worried because he was not worried about it.

Fire Team Leader Heebner was a happy man in what appeared to be a desperate situation.

Sometime earlier he had been very unhappy in everything. Drafted into the Tahn forces and sent into combat when he would have been much happier pruning in his family's orchards, he had been most unfortunate/fortunate.

His unit wiped out, he had stumbled into a stubborn Imperial stronghold—and back out. He had informed his superiors of that way in—and had not been required to participate in the following bloody assault.

Instead, he had been promoted and given a nice safe assignment.

Not, as he had imagined, on something like recruiting duty but, to justify his new and staggering rank, as noncommissioned officer in charge of an SAA site on the Tahn superfortress world of Etan. A decorated soldier, his missile site was high atop a mountain, a post of honor, where he would be the first to engage any Imperial units stupid enough to attack Etan.

Heebner, already experienced at being shot at, rapidly and correctly redefined his post of honor.

He was a target.

And targets got hit.

Heebner was not quite sure what to do about the situation. Nor did he know how to order his soldiers in a proper military manner so that he would not be relieved and sent back to a frontline assault unit.

More importantly, he had no idea where his own retreat route should lie if his missile site *should* be attacked.

Heebner, once again, was very lucky.

His troops were for the most part volunteers from one of the Tahn Troops of Eager Youth, who were determined to show their leader, a hero of the Battle of Cavite and the scout who showed the very heroic, very noble, very decorated, and very dead Assault Captain Santol the way to assault that Imperial stronghold, that they were worthy of his trust.

The translation was that they made their own rules, slightly stricter than the brutal Tahn regulations; made their own living conditions, most Spartan; and made their own schedule. Fire Team Leader Heebner had only to wander out of his quarters at some appropriate hour, make appropriate remarks, and then go about his business.

Heebner was also lucky that he had no particular interest in luxurious quarters, the perks of rank, or the indulgences of command. His Troops of Eager Youth admired his Spartan life. It was, truly, the Way of the Tahn.

The fact was that Heebner was just too stupid to realize what he could have taken advantage of.

Since it seemed that his command was self-running, Heebner spent his hours wandering below the crags, looking for a nice safe place to hide when the drakh came down. He was very interested to discover one day that below his missile site was what looked to be several long-untenanted hectares of fruit trees.

Heebner's smallish mind flickered interest. He mentioned that there did not seem to be any pruning tools in the site's armory. His befuddled assistant decided that somehow, someway, the hero of Cavite was planning to teach them something, perhaps to think in other categories.

Two shifts later, Fire Team Leader Heebner was provided with hooks, clips, lifts, and baskets. He happily disappeared downslope with them. His Eager Youth determined that when the time was right, they would learn what he was doing.

Another stroke of fortune:

Etan's commanding admiral, one Molk, happened to be interested in the art of fruit. He wondered why a certain strategically placed missile base had requested what appeared to be farming implements and decided to place a surprise visit to said base.

The Eager Youth, all prostrate in honor, sent Admiral Molk down the crags, together with his bodyguard, to see what their most honored commander was preparing.

Heebner was counting buds, his lips moving silently, trying to determine which branch should be pruned short and where, when he heard the crash of bootheels coming toward him.

Molk also was a very lucky Tahn.

Because it was approximately at that moment that six Imperial fleets hammered Etan.

Impregnable fortresses, like impregnable generals, got lazy. If the enemy would be insane to attack them, of course only the insane *would* attack. And so they rested on their ever-fattening behinds. Spit-scared attackers, on the other hand, did not.

The Imperial admiral in charge of the fleets was most disappointed that there were no Tahn capital ships on Etan. After the disaster of Durer, they had all been withdrawn to Heath for reassignment.

Nevertheless, major damage was done in the series of smashing attacks. Fire Team Leader Heebner's missile site was obliterated in the first strike; fortunately for him and for his fruit trees, a nonnuclear missile was used.

That hardly mattered for his Eager Youth. There were three survivors. And those, all terribly burned, lived for only minutes after the strike.

When the fire, smoke, and earthquake shakes died away, six Tahn cruisers, twelve destroyers, and many auxiliaries and transports were shattered on their landing grounds.

Etan was still impregnable.

But with no significant warships based on the world, and

with the Imperial-forces severing Etan's supply routes, it did not matter. Etan could do whatever it chose to do until the war came to an end.

Several hundred other Tahn citadels were isolated, rendered impotent, and ignored in the same operation.

Not that Fire Team Leader Heebner had nothing to do. He was very busy—instructing Commanding Admiral Molk on the proper way to grow fruit.

It was a very important task. All the Tahn isolated and forgotten on Etan had to eat.

After nine months of humble instruction, Admiral Molk requested that Heebner begin calling him Yuki.

Admiral Mason defined diplomacy as a word occuring somewhere in a dictionary between dildo and dissidence. That explained his response when the supposedly neutral convoy complained: *"Imperial units . . . Imperial units . . . do not understand your order to stand by for boarding. We are from the Umed systems. Repeat, Umed systems. We are allies of the Empire. Our cargo is necessary energy supplies. Please respond, over."*

Mason, were he polite, could have responded over the com or boarded and delivered the same information.

The Umed systems, allies of the Empire indeed—on paper—were provided with X quanity of AM2. According to information received from spies, the systems practiced severe rationing. Nearly twenty percent of their allocated AM2 was not utilized in any known way. It was instead very profitably sold to the Tahn.

Such would have been the response—from a polite man.

Mason, instead, responded: *"Umed ships. All Umed ships. You have seven minutes remaining. Stand by for boarding. Any resistance will be met with maximum force. All Umed ships. All Umed crewmen. Prepare to abandon ship. Your ships and their cargo have been seized. Imperial Strike Force Mason clear."*

It was to be hoped that Admiral Mason would not survive the war and thus require that the Emperor deal with his vagaries.

* * *

"Cut it," Haines ordered.

The soldier nodded, touched the button of his flamer, and seared through the main power cable that led into the shabby apartment building above them.

"Good. Go!" Haines shouted.

Burdened by a stun rod in one hand, a willygun in the other, plus two separate ranks, Major (Imperial Forces–Mercury Corps–Reserve–Temporary) and Captain (Imperial Police–Prime–Homicide–Permanent) Lisa Haines led the raid upstairs. Two Security mastodons sent the door crashing down, neatly timed so that Haines did not miss a step going into the apartment.

The gray-haired old woman sat up in bed, befuddled, grabbing the ruins of what once might have been a lace nightie around her skinny shoulders.

"Imperial Intelligence," Haines intoned, pro forma. "Andrea Hayyl. You are under arrest as a suspected agent of an enemy power. You are advised that you can be detained for as long as six cycles without benefit of court or attorney. You are also advised that you may be subjected to wartime interrogation techniques authorized by the proper conventions.

"You are also advised that any cooperation you extend voluntarily will be recorded, and be of extreme importance as evidence when you are brought to trial."

The thugs, without needing any orders, had the old woman out and down the stairs in seconds.

The search team came in.

As expected, the transmitter was found in seconds, amateurishly hidden in a false-drawered dresser that might have been the old woman's prized antique.

That was one more.

Haines left the evidence team shooting pictures and went down the stairs.

Six thus far. Two more to go.

More than 12,000 raids were made by Imperial Intelligence at nearly the same time. Years had been spent identifying deep-cover Tahn agents assigned to capital worlds. And then, nearly simultaneously, they were taken.

Haines was disgusted with herself and her job, even more than after the officially sanctioned "disappearences" she had been witness to after the failure of Hakone's conspiracy, the conspiracy that had begun the war.

The agents would be isolated and then given a simple choice: either be doubled or be executed. Wartime penalties for espionage never changed.

The ploy worked. Almost instantly, Tahn Intelligence began receiving completely false information. The few agents the Empire had missed, who continued to feed correct data, were siberiaed as having been doubled. Eventually they were trapped, tried, and executed, along with those agents who had decided to remain true patriots to their cause.

The end result was that the Tahn's own lovingly developed spy network became one of the most lethal weapons the Empire had.

CHAPTER THIRTY-FOUR

CHIEF WARRANT OFFICER Alex Kilgour went into something approaching battle shock when he realized that not only had he bad-mouthed the Eternal Emperor, his Eternal boss, and been overheard, but he actually was in the presence of said Emperor.

The Emperor allowed himself a wintery smile. "Thank you for your input, Mr. Kilgour. Perhaps you would be interested in stepping into the next chamber, where more information shall be provided."

Alex numbly saluted and stiff-legged through the indicated hatchway, which hissed open and then shut behind him.

"In times like these," the Emperor observed, "you tend to allow yourself cheap little shots as I just did. Pour the stregg, my friend."

Sten, equally obedient, went to a sideboard and decanted two shots of the probably hydrazine-based Bhor liquor he had introduced the Eternal Emperor to years earlier.

The Emperor was in an easy chair, his feet propped on a tabletop, when Sten delivered the drink.

"Chin-chin," he toasted. Sten just mumbled and drank.

"Yes, indeed," the Emperor began, "I want you two thugs back on Heath."

"Yessir," Sten said after the stregg had finished replumbing his plumbing. "However . . . when I left there were people that were real . . . interested in me."

"No longer," the Emperor said. "Somebody who must've been taken by the charm of your smile planted a virus in the Tahn central computer. Seems that neither someone named Sten nor someone called Firecontrolman Horatio ever existed. No ID, no prison record, no *nada*.

"Any idea who your unknown benefactor could be?"

Sten had less than none.

"Light a votive candle to the patron saint of computer programmers. Whoever that is.

"However. If such circumstances are correct, would you be willing to go back to Heath? That's an honest question. You've already figured out, I assume, what your next assignment would be if you tell me to clot off."

Sten had not so figured. "Uh," he hazarded, "in charge of some garbage scow somewhere."

"Admirals don't run drakhbuckets."

"Huh?" was all Sten could get out.

The Emperor smiled. "You're most unobservant, Sten. Think. How many of my Gurkhas, looking stupid and uncomfortable in white gloves, were on the ramp when you boarded?"

Eight, Sten suddenly remembered.

"Exactly," the Emperor said. "Four clots to pipe you aboard when you're a working slob. Eight when you put up your star."

Sten, uninvited, got up, poured himself another shot of stregg, drank it down, and refilled his shot glass while recovering.

"If you don't go back to Heath, you'll get a destroyer squadron, and you can go out there and be one more dashing leader who'll get some nice medals and whom I'll be publicly proud of in the livies.

"Sten, the one thing I don't have a shortage of is heroes. What I don't have is somebody who knows what's going on on the bad guys' home turf."

A destroyer squadron, Sten thought. And a star. That was a bit beyond Sten's dreams. Years ago, he had decided to be career military. At the end of the line, he had figured, was, if not a gravestone, some kind of honorable wound and retirement as colonel—maybe, with his naval training added, commodore.

The Emperor filled his own glass and stayed silent.

Sure, Sten's mind went on, I could do some serious ass kicking on the Tahn. I know how what passes for their mind works. I could turn any Tahn ship or formation under a battle-wagon every which way but loose. But like the Emperor just said, I'm not the only one who could do that.

"Why?" he asked, his face and tone as blank as it would have been to any Tahn guard.

"The agents I have on Heath are button counters. Maybe. The clotting nets I have are low-level and, I suspect, doubled by the Tahn. That's one problem. Your tubby cohort can shake them out, if he's willing to go back.

"I need someone in place on Heath as *my* agent. We've reached, like the man said, if not the beginning of the end, the end of the beginning. I'm looking for somebody who can be a spy—and who can sit and talk like he's a diplomat.

"I am not praising you, by the by. You're at least a century too young and several assignments too gory to be my dream square peg. Mahoney, back when you first met him on Vulcan—don't jump, I did a little refresher course—would be ideal. But he's a little long in the tooth and too clottin' good as a fleet marshal to waste on Heath.

"No offense.

"And I've wasted enough time jacking my jaws while you think about it. Decision time."

Sten had already made it. Not only could he probably do more good on Heath than as a bucko destroyer leader, but there were certain things there he wanted to deal with personally. Such as the prisoners in Koldyeze.

"Thank you, Admiral," the Emperor said without waiting for a verbalization. "My intelligence types will brief you and set up the insertion plan."

Sten got up. "I think I'd rather use my own way to get in."

"Your option. Like I said, the only boss you've got this time is me. All orders that you get will be mine. How you carry them out—and even if you do or not—is your option. You're the man in place. Oh, yeah, before I forget. Mahoney had something that might be of help. He said there was a POW at Koldyeze. I think his name was Sorensen. Is that right?"

Sten nodded, remembering the big, smiling face of the farmbeing. He and Alex had debated for hours whether Sorensen was a Mantis battle computer.

"Fine," the Emperor said. "Mahoney said to tell you that Sorensen's code word is 'Saider.' Whatever that's worth."

If the drakh came down at Koldyeze, it would be worth a lot. Sten smiled to himself, but the Emperor was not through yet.

"One favor?"

Sten waited.

"If you decide to overthrow the clottin' government, don't put some anthropoid who likes stregg and can't speak the same language I do in. Or if you do, let me know first. 'Kay?"

Sten found himself saluting a rapidly closing hatchway.

All he had to do was get the detailed briefing, listen to Kilgour tell him why it was a good idea to go back to Heath, and then track down Wild and let him know the time for fence-sitting neutral smugglers was over.

CHAPTER THIRTY-FIVE

VOLMER, PUBLISHING BARON and member of the Emperor's privy council, was very proud of his complex mind.

He could sit, completely invisible, at the far end of a roaring Barbary hell, one of the rowdiest of the rowdy dock bars in Prime World's port city of Soward, and do some serious thinking, undisturbed by the noise and unnoticed by the occupants.

On one level, he was contemplating what the evening might provide. Volmer had never heard the expression "polymorphously perverse" and would have been grandly irked if he had heard it applied—after, of course, he had looked up the meaning of "polymorphous."

But that was one level of Volmer. Rich beyond comprehension and able to pay for safe, clean, comfortable sex of whatever category, he found it more interesting to look for it in the gutter. Volmer found it fully as satisfying to end up jackrolled in a gutter, Murphied, or badgered as it was to wake up next to an incredibly beautiful and insatiable sex object. That was his secret life, which only the top two percent of his reporters knew and laughed about. He had once heard a rumor that the Eternal Emperor did the same—and canned six journalists for being unable to verify it. But regardless, at least once a month Volmer gave his bodyguards and staff two days off and slipped away, in the appropriate disguise, through a hidden exit of his mansion to slink, disguised as "one of the people," onto the wild side.

He thought that he was able to blend seamlessly into the sexual underworld and that he was accepted as nothing more than a mysterious man. Actually, he had been accepted as a sicko mark. But just recently another rumor had cropped up—a rumor that would be acted upon that very night.

The second layer of Volmer's mind was pondering the recent meeting on Earth with Sullamora and the others. He had reacted, he thought, perhaps a little too quickly. Perhaps Sullamora and the others had considered their future problems more carefully than he had. Perhaps he should have been silent, or perhaps expressed more interest—if, he suddenly realized, he had even heard them correctly. Perhaps he had jumped to some incorrect conclusions. Volmer rewarded himself for considering all possibilities, even one that might not be the most ego-rewarding.

That kind of thinking, he added, was what had made him as successful and respected a media baron as he was.

He never knew that his staff referred to him as "Old Ademony-Kademony," a term lost in journalism's prehistory meaning a waffler who can never make up his mind on anything.

But if he was correct in his understanding, he went on, would he be better off informing the Emperor of his suspicions? Well, not suspicions. Actually there was not that much to report to the Emperor. Suppose he had misunderstood what Sullamora and the others were saying. Would he not appear as a prize ass, some kind of hysteroid, if he *did* trouble his Emperor with what had gone on?

Perhaps, he concluded, he should do nothing. Perhaps he should reapproach Tanz and let the situation develop.

Yes. That was the way to behave.

Satisfied that once again he had reached the decision to juggle, he turned his primary focus to the pleasures of the evening.

He listened with interest to the handsome young man who appeared at the bar beside him, discussing some dizzying possibilities as to sex partners, not the least of which was the young man himself. Volmer thought that a possibility—but he was more intrigued with what the young man told him about certain most unusual events that were occurring among the staff of a certain hospital, centering on that hospital's cold room.

The handsome young man was available, indeed. But not as a whore. The young man's services were available, in fact, at a much higher price, specifically to take care of annoy-ances.

The rumor that had spread recently about the sicko mark was that he was more than what he appeared. He was, in fact, a deep-cover copper. Why else had some of Soward's more eminent sex hustlers been arrested, charged, and convicted sans deal in the last month?

The rumor—no one knew where it came from—made perfect sense.

And for that reason it was logical for the underworld bosses, each of whom thought he was much more lethal and in charge than he in fact was, to put out an open contract on the mark. The handsome young man proposed to fill that contract.

Two hours later, as Volmer listened drunkenly and fasci-natedly to the young man's descriptions of necro-pleasures, he was skillfully sandbagged below his left ear, his pockets ran-sacked, his jewels and half boots stolen; then the unconscious body was tipped over the railing to thud soddenly down four levels to the concrete below.

When the body was discovered and reported two days later, Tanz Sullamora expressed appropriate shock. He announced that he would, out of pocket, have his shipping security pa-trols widen their assignments beyond the yards themselves. That terrible incident had no doubt occurred because Volmer, a respected hands-on newsperson, was conducting his own investigation of the corruption sapping the war effort. Sulla-mora even posted a reward for the apprehension of the lethal muggers who had killed his friend.

CHAPTER THIRTY-SIX

THE FOUR TAHN officers glowered at St. Clair. Even in the glitter of their full-dress uniforms they were looming, ominous. Without even checking rank tabs, she knew from the cut of their tunics and the gleaming custom willyguns strapped to their waists that they were higher-ups. They almost filled the small anteroom with their presence, and St. Clair had to wrestle with the urge to bolt. Their faces were set in the automatic brutish threat mode that high Tahn officials wore to get their way.

Instead of running, St. Clair greeted them with her priciest smile.

"Gentlebeings," she said. "Check your guns and credit at the door." And with that, she waved them into the main lounge of the K'ton Klub, the most exclusive and successful gambling hell in the Chaboya District of Heath.

And it's mine, all mine, St. Clair gloated as she watched the smooth, muscular hunk she had hired as her head host go into his little bowing and scraping act that eliminated all the sting from what the Tahn officers would have to go through to enter her members-only club. In a matter of seconds their rank would be verified, ability to pay checked, and weapons and cloaks tagged and locked away. Then they would be putting their fingerprints to a membership contract that would put the K'ton Klub first in line of debtors if there was any hint of financial difficulties. All that was accomplished with smiles and jokes guaranteed to crack even the thick varnish of gloom that the Tahn seemed to prefer in public.

Moments later, the door leading to the ground-floor casino hushed open and the four laughing Tahn officers were plunging into the boisterous throng of marks anxious to eat, drink, and gamble their souls away to St. Clair, because the next day they might find themselves volunteered as targets for an Imperial cruiser.

There was a tinkling of old-fashioned mechanical bells, announcing more customers. St. Clair motioned for her host to take over. From that time of night on, the customers would mostly consist of regulars that St. Clair would not have to sus out.

St. Clair followed the Tahn into the casino. It was time to check out the action. Not that she had to go too far to check —the joint was jumping. By the time the night was over, St. Clair figured, she would have another record take in the till.

The K'ton Klub was one of many multistoried casinos that made up the Chaboya District's gambling strip. But there were two, no, three, big differences between her club and the others: (1) The percentages were honest. (2) The percentages were honest. (3) The percentages were honest. From long experience, St. Clair knew that the rake-in from the house's built-in edge was more than enough profit for any fool. Every time her competitors skinned a mark, they lost that same mark permanently to St. Clair.

It was dishonesty in fact that had brought the K'ton Klub into her hands. The previous owner, like most of the other casino operators in the district, had been unable to swim against the new economic tide created by the war. As shortages tightened the supply and power screws, the casinos, instead of finding new ways to keep the customers happy, racked up the gambling machines' percentages until it was nearly impossible to win, then pulled in their heads, cutting back hours until many of them finally just shut their doors and walked away.

If St. Clair had been looking at the situation purely from a business point of view, instead of trying to find a nice comfortable way of hiding out in plain view until she and L'n were rescued, she still would have sized up the situation the same.

War brought shortages, true. But looked at another way, the shortages meant that the price of things simply went up. More importantly, the sin business always boomed during war. That was an economic curve on a chart that St. Clair had memorized before she had any curves of her own.

St. Clair had plucked the club off the tree within weeks after she and L'n had made their escape.

They had spent very little time in the actual escape itself. St. Clair had abandoned her plan to be a rich-bitch tuber hunter as soon as she had decided that L'n's only chance of survival was as her escape partner. She would have to trust to luck and play the situation by ear. There was no forged ID card that might fit the number of situations St. Clair and L'n might meet—So she did not carry any.

Bluff would be her calling card.

As soon as they had exited the tunnel, she headed for the nearest gravtrain station. Acting imperious as all hell, she had browbeaten the ticket clerk into selling her an unauthorized first-class seat on a train heading directly into the center of town.

"Travel permit? Ration card? My good man, I explained to you that I lost them, didn't I? I suppose you expect me to grovel in my carelessness, now, don't you? Very well, then. If that gives you satisfaction, I am now groveling! See me grovel?" She put her hands together as if in prayer and gave him a slight bow. "There! I hope that makes you happy! Now sell me the damned tickets!"

Her nongroveling grovel act scared the holy bejesus out of the clerk. From her clothes, she was obviously richer than hell. Either that or joygirl to a Tahn officer whose rank he did not even want to guess at. He sold her the tickets, not even asking why she needed two of them. He supposed it had something to do with the strange pink little furry creature accompanying her. Maybe rich types always bought seats for their pets.

St. Clair and L'n were just taking deep, shuddering breaths of relief as the gravtrain's generators wound up to a high keen, when they heard the station speakers crackle into life. There was a series of sharp, barked orders. The keen died down to a low hum. Then they heard heavy footsteps. St. Clair swore she would not look up as she heard someone in obvious authority grilling the passenger just in front of her. She felt L'n quiver in fear. Absently she ran her fingers through L'n's smooth fur, trying to calm her, but it was hopeless.

Authority Figure shouted. Passenger wailed. L'n choked back a low moan. And St. Clair found herself looking up against her will—straight into the eyes of a black-uniformed Tahn thug.

She would never forget those eyes. They were the color of a bottom-feeding fish. They took her in. Then L'n. Then her again. Fish Eyes dropped the papers into the passenger's lap and walked straight back toward her. St. Clair forced out what she hoped was an in-character haughty smile. She prepared to reach into her jumper suit pockets and fumble for nonexistent papers.

The man stopped in front of her. He leaned forward. Then, surprise of all surprises, he grinned, exposing a horrible row of black and yellow stumps.

"Chook-um, chook-um," he said. "Chook-um, chook-um." And he began stroking and tickling L'n!

"I say! What a great pet! What is it? Some kind of cat? I love cats! The wife and I must own thirty or forty of the little buggers. Ha! I should say they own us."

And all the while he kept stroking and tickling L'n. St. Clair burbled something between a laugh and a sob, thinking all the while, Purr, clot, you purr, to L'n.

"Yes," she said. "A cat. A type of one, anyway. Very rare breed..."

At that moment L'n started purring, saving her life and St. Clair's in what was probably the only actual case of interspecies telepathy ever to occur in the Empire's history.

And once she started purring, she never stopped. She purred through the entire conversation. St. Clair lied. Fish Eyes bought. And a little while later, he waved her down when she tried to look for the papers that were not there and exited a happy Tahn with a great story to tell his nice Tahn wife.

"You can stop purring now," St. Clair finally whispered to L'n.

"Not on your life," L'n whispered back. "The kid plans to keep purring for at least the next fifty-sixty years. And you will, too, if you know what's good for you."

And St. Clair realized that L'n did not understand that she had been mistaken for a pet. Oh, well. She would wait awhile before she let her furry friend in on it. But, oh, God, was there going to be an explosion when she found out.

Later, after St. Clair had explained and then scraped her friend off the ceiling of the compartment, she just had to ask it. "Did you know how to purr before?"

"No," L'n had said. "I've never even *heard* of a cat, either!"

"Then how . . ."

L'n gave a shrug of a furry pink shoulder. "I don't know. I just reached down inside and . . . purred, dammit! Now, will you shut up about it, before I show you what I can do with teeth?"

It was the turning point in the life of the once-shy being called L'n. And there would be no going back.

As soon as they reached the center of the city, St. Clair instinctively gravitated toward Chaboya. In any area where sin was largely ignored and corruption was waist deep, cops tended to ignore most of the evildoers and their victims. The crackdowns usually came against well-known types who had not coughed up enough to stay in business. Credits changed hands, and then it was back to business as usual.

St. Clair found a dive for them to hole up in and then hit the streets. For the first day or two she fooled around with a few penny-ante shell games just to get warmed up and increase her stash of credits. Then she hit the casinos. Unnoticed, she filtered through them one by one, dropping a little here, picking up a little there, always keeping a low profile. She found what she was looking for at the K'ton Klub. From the thin crowds and the peeling plas walls, she knew it was close to folding. She played small-time dice machines for a while, watching the crowds.

She identified the owner right off. He was an older, handsome man who tended to dress a bit too flashily. She noticed that he spent little time on the floor, appearing only when another obviously high-stakes flash gambler occasionally showed up.

He would personally greet him, then they would disappear upstairs to what St. Clair just *knew* was a big-time game. It was time to strike. She invested a healthy chunk of her stake for the flashiest, sexiest outfit she could find, then reentered the club, looking for all the world like a bored professional anxious to find some action.

The owner spotted her right off. A little flirting followed, and teasing remarks were exchanged. Mild sexual innuendo was used on each side to check out the gambler in the other. An invitation was offered.

A little later she found herself being ushered into the owner's office. As soon as she entered the room, she knew she was home. In the center of the table was the pot. And it did not consist of the funny money the Tahn laughingly called credits. Instead, there were rare gems and exotic heavy mineral baubles. And there were also stacks of parchmentlike papers that could only be Imperial bonds and real estate deeds.

One week of around-the-clock playing later, she was bowing the owner out of his own office, holding *his* deed to the club. All the objects that made up the pot were also hers. She expected a bit of a strong-arm bluff from the man. And she was prepared for it—St. Clair had a minipistol hidden in the voluminous sleeve of her blouse. Oddly enough, the man did not seem to mind all that much. He said he had been thinking it was time to move on, and the cards that they all worshiped had confirmed that.

There was one other deed on the table that proved to be of far greater value than was obvious at first glance. It was for the seemingly worthless cargo of a freighter—a museum ship stranded by the war in midtour.

As soon as she and L'n had cracked the rusted hold and entered, St. Clair had smelled money. Inside was a traveling exhibit of ancient Earth-style casinos: mechanical gambling machines, crap tables, bingo machines, roulette wheels, decks of *real* paper playing cards. And vidbooks after stacks of vidbooks on how the old folks had lost their money thousands of years before.

St. Clair stripped the K'ton Klub down to the ground floor, then installed the machines. The lure of honest percentages and old-fashioned gambling drew customers like beasts to carrion. The marks were sure they could not be cheated because there was little electronics involved. Things that went *crank-crank, whirr* were considered far more trustworthy and ruled by the laws of a kind nature than were computers that talked to one, fooled with one, and toyed with reality livie-style, all the while gulping away at one's credits.

From the very beginning, St. Clair decided that the place would be as exclusive as possible. Instead of garish, lighted signs outside, she had only a small glowing plaque on the front door reading "The K'ton Klub. Members only."

St. Clair congratulated herself as she slinked through the more drably dressed customers who made up the crowds on the ground floor. She noted the things that were going right and, just as importantly, what was going wrong—if anything. The room was ringed with the one-armed bandits she had salvaged off the museum ship. On this floor they were one of the biggest money-makers, second only to the dice tables and followed by chuck-a-luck and the marathon bingo games that featured a pot that grew each day until no simpleminded blue-collar type mark could resist laying his credits down.

To keep a bit of class and social strata awe going, the center of the room was occupied by a raised, roped-off platform where there was always a high-stakes whist game going. To encourage a constant supply of whist players, St. Clair charged only a minimum fee per chair and took no house percentage at all.

Sexily uniformed servers constantly moved through the crowd, offering cocktails, narcotics, and snacks. In peacetime it would all have been free, but now the marks were so grateful that there was anything available at all that they gladly paid. There were two ways a customer could go from there. A mark could either exit to the street—after passing through a brothel where joyboys and joygirls hustled whatever credits remained—or he or she could climb the stairs to the next casino, where the price soared along with the class of the clientele.

The previous owner had had a somewhat similar setup, with three working casinos on each floor and a nightclub restaurant on top. However, he had used entrances and elevators to separate the poor marks from the middle class and the middle class from the rich. One of the first things St. Clair did when she took over was eliminate the elevators and the separate entrances. Everyone had to go the same way to get to the top, and without exception, money was left on each floor.

St. Clair climbed the stairs, making sure at each level that the bouncers were properly culling the credit-level chaff from the wheat. The second casino leaned toward roulette and higher-stakes card games and crap tables. The next floor was invitation-only straight card games, mostly poker, whist, t'rang, bezique, and bridge.

The nightclub was on the top floor. There was no cover, no minimum. It was St. Clair's idea. The prices she charged for food, drink, and sex with the entertainers who swung that way were astronomical, even for those inflationary times. Everything else about the nightclub was L'n's.

She had designed it so that the mark and his mate would be overwhelmed as soon as they entered. It hit St. Clair even though she had known what to expect.

She was overwhelmed by the multicolored lights that dipped, dodged, swirled, and smoked, grabbing the viewer's mind in a soft glove and delivering him or her into the arms of the entertainers who danced and sang and cavorted on three stages. The moment L'n had spotted the dusty room jammed with creaky, high-tech seats, she had known she was on the verge of discovering a new art form, a living art form that would call into play all the powerful talents she had spent so many years developing. She used light sources of all types but seemed to get the most out of the more natural effects of resistor-based vacuum bulbs, and especially candles and torches whose burning centers she captured on moveable mirrors, split with prisms, and then re-formed again to be cast any place she chose.

L'n controlled everything from a computer console in a dark corner of the club near the door that led to their private quarters and offices. At first she had curtained off the console area. But as she grew more confident, she had the curtain removed. If one looked in her direction, she could be seen playing at the board with all the flair and drama of a concert pianist.

St. Clair edged around the room so as not to disturb the audience. Spotting her, L'n toggled a few switches, spun a control wheel, then joysticked the lights to a higher crescendo. Then she motioned with her head to the door.

Someone was waiting in the office. St. Clair mimed a

"who is it?" but L'n merely smiled. It was all very mysterious.

She went through into the hallway and marched to the office door. She did not remember it opening. But it must have, because standing in the middle of the room was Horatio, an immense grin on his face. St. Clair shouted and sobbed and hurled herself across the room into his arms. And she was kissing his neck, and hair, and anything else she could find. And Horatio was doing the same until the sudden heat in her loins brought her back to reality. Of all the men she had ever met, this guy was way up there on her hatred list. The slimy so-and-so was probably there to . . .

St. Clair shoved him roughly away, eyes blazing, finger stabbing into his chest. "Listen here, you son of a bitch," she said. "I'm not in your clottin' military, remember? I'm a civilian. And you guys can't touch one mill of our hard-earned. Got it, buster?"

Sten gaped. What the clot did he care? Besides, he was as confused about what had just happened as she was. What was with this woman, anyway?

"Fine with me," he said.

"I suppose you think you're here to rescue me," St. Clair said. "Well, think again, bud! I've got transponders blaring out a coded SOS, here we are, on half the Tahn freighters in the merchant marine.

"Although I don't know what's taking those clots so long. I've got a sweet thing going here. And a hell of a deal to offer. Why, we've got customers who are generals and admirals, and—"

"I know," Sten said. "We got your message."

"Say clottin' what? What are you blabbering about? Who got what message? When?"

And then St. Clair got it. Sten smiled, admiring how lovely she still looked even with her jaw nearly brushing the floor in surprise.

"Let's start all over," he said. "First off, the introduction. If anyone calls me Horatio, or Horrie, or whatever starts with an H again, I'll kill them. My name is Sten. So much for boy meets girl. Now, where do you want to go from here?"

St. Clair started to say something terribly biting and terribly clever. She had about six well-tested ways to emasculate this insufferable little...Except that was somebody else, wasn't it? That was—

She bit off the remark. She just looked up at Sten, waiting.

It was a good thing the office desk was a museum relic. Because what happened next had probably happened to it many times before.

CHAPTER THIRTY-SEVEN

HIS NAME WAS Chapelle.

Until recently, he had been a landing controller at one of the Empire's busiest spaceports. Like most controllers, he was very young and very intense. The pressures of his career guaranteed burnout by the age of forty. Unlike most controllers, his entire life was spaceports. He spent all of his offshift times haunting the port. He had walked the hills around the port time and again. He had been through all the buildings around that port. He boasted—only to himself, since Chapelle was a neurotically shy man—that even if all radar, laser ranging, and the port's other artificial GCA systems went out, he could land a ship by mind and voice. He could visualize "his" spaceport from any angle, under any weather conditions.

Chapelle's proudest possessions were two holographs. One was of the Imperial yacht *Normandie* settling onto "his" field, and the other was an autographed portrait of the Eternal Emperor. His leader, whom he had brought safely to a landing. Of course, the portrait was machine-autographed and had been routinely provided by the Emperor's flack as part of another show-the-flag tour.

Chapelle had *known* he was being recognized for his abilities when he was unexpectedly promoted and transferred to the main port on Prime World.

Immediately he began the same self-education program he

had used before. Perhaps his superior did not understand what he was doing. Or perhaps Chapelle's obsession was becoming worse. It did not matter. The supervisor had mildly suggested that Chapelle might consider taking some time off, with no loss in status at all. But . . . he seemed so very intense. Perhaps he might consider consulting a specialist. Chapelle had barely kept himself from striking the man. Perhaps his supervisor was right—about being too dedicated. Of course he was not right about Chapelle needing psychological help. Yes, he would take the time off.

At that point, Tanz Sullamora's agents discovered Chapelle's lovely profile.

Chapelle, feeling rested, was ready to return to work when the fax in his high-stack apartment complex delivered a notice, placing Chapelle on extended unpaid leave. Chapelle found the guts to vid his department and ask why.

"The reason is sealed."

Sealed, Chapelle wondered. Why? Who could do such a thing? Who had the right? No one . . . except . . . and his eyes found the smiling portrait on the wall.

Why?

He was the Emperor's most dedicated subject. Had he not, after all, saved the *Normandie* from a possible crash?

Chapelle sat for hours in the tiny apartment, staring at that picture. He barely picked at the meager, welfare-provided rations that slid out of the dining slot. There had to be something wrong.

He determined to visit the library. Perhaps he needed to know more about his Emperor.

While he was away, his apartment was visited.

Several hours passed after he returned before he noticed. That portrait, the portrait he had always thought was smiling benevolently at him, had a cruel edge to it. The twinkle in the Emperor's eye was not that of a kindly leader, but that of someone who thought it humorous to play a meaningless practical joke on his most loyal subject. Yes. Perhaps he was wrong about his Emperor. The histories he had read suggested that the Emperor was more than the universe's paterfamilias.

He needed to learn more.

And again his apartment was visited. And again the picture of the Emperor was changed.

It was, Chapelle recognized, the face of all evil. He had been a fool. He would have served the Empire better if he had allowed the *Normandie* to crash.

That night, the voices began.

CHAPTER THIRTY-EIGHT

IT SHOULD HAVE been a routine meeting, Kilgour's third for the day. All he had to do was be sitting quietly in the dispatch clerk's efficiency apartment when the man returned. After the man recovered, Kilgour would apologize for letting the man, one of Tahn Counterintelligence's most valued agents, fall out of contact. But, he would explain, the man's control had been desperately needed in a fighting sector, and unfortunately, there was a bit of disarray. Now he, Senior Specialist Fohch, was reactivating the man.

Nothing would change. He should continue to report any anti-Tahn sentiments at his workplace and, most importantly, describe exactly how those affected the efficiency of his plant. There was no more important part of the war effort than the continued production of Imperium X, which was used for shielding Anti-Matter Two.

The only change, Kilgour would be delighted to inform the man, was that his superiors had authorized an increase in the small retainer paid to the dispatch clerk. And once final victory over the Empire had been achieved, appropriate medals would be awarded to men and women like him, who performed vital duties far from the fighting front but were as responsible for that soon-to-arrive victory as the most decorated hero.

Et cetera, et cetera, et cetera.

Certainly there was no need to confuse the poor man with reality. If he felt happy being a fink for Tahn CI on his fellow workers, Kilgour would offer nothing but support.

So it was up the emergency slide, pick the window's friction catch, and inside. Perhaps, he hoped, the man would have a bit of alk chilled. Spymasterin't, Kilgour thought, could get thirsty.

There was a half-empty container of something that tasted like soya wine. Kilgour gagged but continued sipping as he wandered around the apartment, gloved hands routinely lifting, moving, and checking.

He lifted a lamp and *tsk*ed sadly. Then he replaced the flask in the reefer and went back out the window, leaving no trace that he had ever been in the room.

Kilgour wandered back toward the nearest transit dump point, considering possibilities.

Most interestin', he thought. Thae's little if any safety here. An th' puir workers boil out frae th' tubes like salmon up a weir.

Pity should a wee dispatch clerk who just happens to hae a bug in his apartment which nae should be there happen to come a gainer in front ae the outgoing.

It was. He did.

And Kilgour headed for the next address. Nae two shabby. Thirty agents so far. Five gone, three lost nerve, and two doubled. The rest were all humming away, happily back in harness, reporting what they were told to, to whichever spy service Alex thought appropriate for them to be employed by.

Sten briefly admired his reflection in the large mirror. He looked rather dashing, he thought, in evening wear, even if it was a shade too flashy for his personal tastes. But big-time gangsters were never known for their subtlety. He minutely adjusted a shirt stud, sipped brandy, and leaned back, waiting for Connl to make the next move.

It appeared to be a straightforward deal. Connl had a warehouse, custom-sealed, full of the high-protein glop the Tahn military used to augment its ship rations.

Sten wished to purchase said glop.

A straightforward deal—on the black market.

How Connl had come into possession of the glop was not Sten's concern.

Sten had made his offer, calculated to be several units per kilo above what Connl could get from other black market commodity dealers and far above what the Tahn would be willing to pay.

He was also willing to pay in hard Imperial credits.

The details of Durer still were not known. But the entrepreneurs had heard bad things. Plus they were not particularly thrilled doing deals in the already inflationary and good-faith-based Tahn currency. Even if the Tahn managed to win, would Imperial credits be worthless? No one thought that would happen.

Plus Imperial credits were weatherproof. Buried under the gazebo in one's estate, they would be safe from wear, tear, and rodents. The fact that possession of those credits made the owner subject for the high jump worried no one. At worst, bribery would be called for.

Connl ran a fingertip around his snifter. "Interesting offer you've made. May I ask an intrusive question?"

"You may ask."

"There have been some interesting stories about your background."

"I've heard some of them."

"Connections straight into the Tahn Council itself, I've heard. A man with a private army, somebody told me. Very, very interesting."

"Perhaps one or two of them might be factual," Sten suggested.

"Perhaps." Connl did not press it; he had asked merely to gauge Sten's reaction. He had gotten, of course, none.

"To return to business. You don't have the reputation of being foolish. So I assume you have an idea of the actual market value of my hi-pro."

"I do. Quoted this morning, for delivery, of seventy-five units per kiloton."

"Yet you offer eighty. Interesting. If you are not a fool, then neither am I. Offer accepted."

Connl was paid within the hour and went on his way,

somewhat delighted. He had made a huge profit, and he had never had to put his hands on that slimy hi-pro to make it. He also had figured out what Sten's game was. The man was actually trying to corner the market. Once he had a sufficiency, he would turn the screws.

Connl determined to reinvest. His half-mill warehouse of hi-pro was, of course, worth nearly three-quarters. He would adjust his price accordingly.

The end result of Sten's maneuver: Even less high-protein additive was available to the Tahn at any price. Plus he had done his bit to destabilize the currency. Those credits, if not buried, would go back into circulation and further devaluate the Tahn unit.

L'n was curled up on a silken pillow, looking terminally cute and asleep. Her ear sonared on the conversation at the table next to her.

The four Tahn officers were playing an incredibly complex game with counters, multiple sets of dice, and variable rules, a game that could only have been invented, let alone played to the point of expertise, by military types trying to while away long, boring hours on patrol.

Such was the case.

And it made the game a status symbol—anyone who knew the rules, let alone how to win, was of course intelligent, part of the Tahn hierarchy, and probably noble to boot.

The game went on.

And the officers talked, paying no attention to St. Clair's pet napping beside them.

The conversation was most interesting. Such and so had been relieved through no fault of her own. X Unit would never be deployed to Y Sector on time, not with the shortage in medium weapons. And did you hear about poor Admiral Whoosis? His new flagship's the *Sabac*. That's the first of the Amtung class, y' know. What a pile! TA can't pick up more than six targets without going into program reject. Power room, he told me's got leaks from the drive. Good thing he's a hero sort.

There was laughter, and the game and conversation droned

on, L'n filing every bit of the hard intelligence for transmission to the Empire.

Kilgour dropped from the skylight onto the top crate in the huge stack. He looked around the deserted warehouse, laid out his tactics, and went into motion.

The warehouse was a ration outshipping point. Each crate contained fifty cases of rations. Each case held one day's rations for ten combatants.

Kilgour had in his overall pockets six cans. Each of them would be inserted into a different ration case, and the case and crate would be resealed without notice.

The poor sod getting that particular can would not be happy. Not that there was anything lethal in the cans. Each of them contained exactly what it was supposed to and was as edible as military food ever became. There was, however, a small addition to each can.

Puir, wee, slikit beastie, Alex thought sentimentally.

Not that the cans contained an entire mouse.

Just its tail.

Kilgour wondered how long the rumor would take to spread as to just what those war profiteerin' clots were feeding the poor frontline fighters.

Not long at all, he knew.

"A pint, cheena?" Sten suggested.

Chetwynd, feeling most proud, merely looked up and smiled. "I'm drinking brandy these days."

"Life's been good to you?"

"Life's been acceptable," Chetwynd said neutrally.

The two men stared at each other as the barmaid delivered drinks, was paid, smirked at the two, and wobbled back to the bar.

"So you made it," Chetwynd said then.

"So I made it," Sten agreed.

"Did my, uh, message get delivered?"

"It did. At the highest level."

"And?"

Sten answered by sliding a case across the table. Chetwynd

glanced to either side, snapped the case open a crack, and then, at light-speed, closed it.

"Someone," he said, "out there likes me."

Sten smiled. "We love you, Chetwynd."

The case was stuffed full of Tahn money.

"And what am I expected to do with this?"

"Whatever you want. An estate in the country, if that's what turns you over."

"Nah. I've learned."

Chetwynd *had* learned. He had spent time reestablishing contacts and making them very happy. He had a chubby finger in almost anything crooked that went on around Heath's spaceports. He had even begun making most vague noises about unions. But this time he was not messing with the longshoremen, having realized that someone with a size twenty-six neck and a size three hat who got political might be easily replaceable. Instead, he was listening with great sympathy to the dispatchers, ramp rats, controllers, and bookkeepers around the spaceports. Technicians were hard to retrain.

"That's nice," Sten said. "A suggestion. Are you still a loyal prison guard?"

"I've thought about—"

"Don't," Sten ordered. "That gives you a nice solid ID. Keeps you from getting sent back to Dru."

Chetwynd shuddered, then understood. "You want a pipeline into Koldyeze?"

"You have learned."

"Anything else. Mister?" Chetwynd spit.

"None. Just keep on keeping on. I'll be in touch every now and then. If you need more gelt, just ask."

Chetwynd considered. "How deep's your purse?"

"How wide is the Empire?"

That was a correct answer. Sten was prepared to give Chetwynd, or any other Tahn, a limitless amount of units— flawlessly counterfeited units that would further inflate the economy. Every five thousandth bill had its serial number duplicated. When two bills, perfect examples of Tahn currency, showed up at bank clearinghouses, there would be hell to pay

—further lessening the Tahn's willingness to trust their own monetary system.

Sten got up. "Oh. There was one other thing. Don't have me tailed. And don't show up at my nice safe home." He reached across and tweaked Chetwynd's cheek. "I want you to be my back-street girl. You'd look clottin' stupid with a tag around your toe."

And Sten was gone.

St. Clair systematically laid the markers, scrawled in various stages of desperation and sobriety, across her desk. The young woman on the settee sobbed convulsively.

"Come, now," St. Clair said. She crossed to the side bar, poured a drink, and waited while the woman choked it down.

"Are you all right?"

The woman nodded.

"Let's look at it from my point of view," St. Clair began. "Of course you didn't know what you were doing. Mayd, I've gotten myself into the same kind of problem. When I was young."

There were perhaps no more than three or four years between the two women. But St. Clair knew how to play the script.

"And you can't pay.

"And if you ask for units from your family, you'll be out in the cold. Your father doesn't sound like the understanding type.

"If this were the livies, I would be twisting my mustaches and—what would I be doing? Suggesting that you become available, since you are very young and very attractive, to some of my older guests? Or maybe stealing the family gems? No. I have it. You should deliver all your family secrets into my keeping. Blackmail, that's how the livies play it.

"No wonder I haven't seen a livie in years.

"I am certainly a loyal Tahn. And would do none of those sillinesses.

"Mayd, I like to think of you as my friend. I have always been honored that a woman of your caste honors my establishment with your presence. The fact that you have had unspeakable luck on the tables doesn't change that.

"But . . ." St. Clair sighed and swept the markers into a pile. "I am also a businesswoman. I frankly don't know what to do.

"I can tear these markers up—" She paused and Mayd looked at her hopefully. "But then I would be forced to bar you from being allowed here ever again.

"Still worse, I would be forced by my agreement to mention what happened to the Casino Owners' Security Block. That could be embarrassing if you were blacklisted in all of Heath's establishments."

St. Clair pretended deep thought. "Wait. I have an idea. I am a gambler. As you are. But, well, I like an edge. As you did."

The woman blushed, not wanting to remember the time that she had tried to introduce a set of shaved dice into a game.

"Your father's conglomerate produces rare metals. I have been interested in taking a plunge in business investments. Maybe you could tell me how your father's business is doing. Nothing specific, of course. But strange things that help an investor. For instance, I know that a lot of the metals go out-system. But where?"

Mayd looked at St. Clair's smiling, open face. "That won't work, Michele," she wailed. "I don't know anything about business. You just asked about where the metals go. I can't tell you. All I know is that Daddy keeps complaining about having to go somewhere called Aira . . . Airabus, where it's nasty and cold and Daddy says they don't treat a nobleman the way he deserves.

"You see? I'd like to cooperate, but I don't *know* anything."

Erebus. The long-secret shipyard system of the Tahn. That information was worth, to the Emperor, a year's income.

"Oh, well," St. Clair said. "We tried. Look. Here's what we'll do. I'll keep these markers. And I'll personally guarantee you an open line for, say, ten thousand more units. Your luck is due to change—and maybe next time I'll be asking *you* for markers. Mayd, this is on my personal guarantee.

"Do me a favor. One gambler to another? Stop doubling

the bet when you're losing. The way to come out on top is to double up when you're *winning*."

Mayd behaved as if St. Clair had presented the six lost commandments to her. St. Clair knew that it would not matter; all she had to figure out was how to keep the woman so confused that she never remembered when she had lost the next ten grand.

It was too good to be true.

"It's ta braw t' b't true," Kilgour muttered to himself as he glowered across into the park from his position under an abandoned gravsled—abandoned, he was realizing, because of a total hemorrhage in its lubrication system as the oil soaked through his rather becoming, he thought, suit.

The contact had come most skillfully, Alex admitted.

One of his agents—very trusted, at least until twelve minutes earlier—had asked if Kilgour would be interested in talking to a certain minor bureaucrat in the Tahn naval payroll department. The man was upset, the agent said, evidently because he had been passed over for a promotion. He was prepared to deliver—for hard Imperial credits—the payroll roster for any naval unit anywhere in the Tahn Empire.

The meet had been set up twice, and blown twice, supposedly because of the bureaucrat's paranoia. Third time lucky.

They were to meet in a certain park—which looked, to Alex's country eyes, more like a vacant lot—minutes before curfew. The money would be passed in exchange for a complete roster of Tahn Council operations personnel.

The bureaucrat had said that if anyone else was in the park at the time of the meet, he would vanish once again.

Too good, indeed.

Kilgour had shown up hours earlier and cased the park and surrounding buildings. He found it most interesting that the apartments surrounding the park appeared to be very interested in livie transmissions, and all of them could afford new 'cast antennas on their roofs.

He had then rented himself an alky. He had bought the man two bottles of cheap plonk and said there would be two more if the man drank them in the park.

Then Kilgour had crawled under the gravsled and waited.

An hour before the meet, a handful of very battered vehicles had settled around the square. They lacked anodizing or washing but were equipped with very shiny McLean generators.

Oh, well.

Kilgour wanted to stick around until the bureaucrat showed up, then see about seven zillion Tahn Counterintelligence thugs swoop on that poor alky, passed out on his bench, and attempt to grill him.

But the last act was usually anticlimactic. Kilgour slid—literally—out from under the gravsled and then low-crawled around the corner away from the scene.

Nice try, lads. But nae Oscar.

Kilgour wondered who clottin' Oscar was, anyway, then headed back to the K'ton Klub and degreasing.

It took three tries before Senior Captain (Intelligence) Lo Prek was received by Lord Wichman.

The first attempt had been rejected after he had scared holy clot out of Wichman. Wichman's adjutant—so he had dubbed his executive secretary—had informed his boss that a certain captain in Intelligence wished to see the lord.

Wichman, even though honest to the point of caricature, had still turned pale. Intelligence officers, so it was said, could find guilt in their mothers if so required—and make the bones confess on vid.

The captain did not, however, have an official sanction.

His request was ignored.

When the second request was made, Wichman ordered his secretary to check into the background of the officer.

He scanned the fiche with interest, admiring Lo Prek's commendations and obvious ability. But he still saw no reason why he should waste his valuable time.

The third time Lo Prek was lucky. Wichman was bored and not interested in viewing the latest industrial projections—down—or in why things would improve shortly.

Lo Prek might have been a monomaniac, but he also knew how to present his case.

Wichman listened in increasing fascination.

The captain was determined that one man, formerly a POW

in Pastour's vacation prison, was on the loose on Heath. He had already committed many depredations before being captured. Depredations, hell. Defeats.

Perhaps. A bit grandiose, but perhaps . . .

Now that individual—Sten—was loose and underground in Heath's society. He would strike again. Already, Lo Prek said, there were instances of sabotage, espionage, and generally antiwar sentiments abroad.

Wichman scanned the microfiche that Lo Prek had presented and marveled. This single Tahn officer, technically over leave from his assigned unit, had managed to collect this amount of data without any resources except what he could borrow.

Fascinating.

Wichman reached a decision. He thought Lo Prek to be a loon. The Imperial, whatever his name was, either had never existed or had gotten drowned in a ditch somewhere. But it could be very useful to have such a dedicated person around collecting evidence of anything that had gone wrong—what he had once heard the never-to-be-sufficiently-damned Emperor call a stonebucket.

Wichman looked up from the screen and smiled. "Captain, I think that I can definitely use a man of your caliber."

CHAPTER THIRTY-NINE

ADMIRAL MASON'S DESTROYER squadron made a full-power bounce on an entire planet. The planet was the Tahn homeworld of Heath. The ships' noses were already heat-glowing from the atmosphere by the time the first alarms went off.

Antiaircraft crews who were more accustomed to ceremonial posturings and polishing brass fittings scrambled for battle stations trying to remember real-world target acquisition and launch procedures. Several crews lost minutes tracking down the officer with the input code for the armed missile loaders.

Civilian block wardens dug into dresser drawers for their arm bands and hard hats, fumbling through their time-passed briefings to find out what exactly they were supposed to do.

The invasion alert hammered out on a thousand channels, then rescinded, then rescreamed. Heath's workers sheep-panicked to the shelters that had never been anything more than the subject of jokes, following drills that were considered one more way to get in trouble with the police if one did not instantly obey.

The three interceptor squadrons around the capital, more familiar with providing ceremonial escort to VIP ships, took fifteen full minutes to get into the air.

By the time the first missile came out of its tube and the first gun opened fire, the destroyers were outatmosphere and under full emergency AM2 drive.

The raid was a carefully designed one-time affair. Mason's flotilla, equipped with every known ECM and spoofer, bulging with additional supply containers, and using Tahn codes broken after the debacle around Durer, took weeks to slither through the Tahn Empire.

The Eternal Emperor was making two statements.

The first was made by Mason's DD, the *Burke*, as it launched a lovingly tailored monster missile.

The missile was a slim needle, set with offset fins front and rear. Its AM2 drive unit had come from a Kali shipkiller and nearly-instantaneously flashed the missile to full speed. The warhead, many tons of nonnuclear explosive, was buried far behind the nose cone, which was a solid mass of Imperium X.

Six separate guidance systems, using everything from inertial navigation to a prewar street map of the capital, made sure the missile would not miss.

It did not, impacting squarely in the center of the Tahn Council chambers. And nothing much happened.

The watch commander in charge of the palace's guards had time to pick himself up from the ground where the initial shock had dropped him, recover, and grin to his second.

"Clottin' Imperials. All that trouble to drop a dud that—"

That went off.

The missile had driven nearly 300 meters underground, its Imperium X nose cone crumpling, before the detonator went off.

The explosion, far underground, created a cavern.

The original design was eons old and had been set aside as a peculiar footnote when the age of nuclear overkill had arrived. Its original designer, one Barnes Wallis, had originally described it as an "earthquake bomb," an incorrect if impressive label. More exactly, the bomb was intended to "camouflet"—to dive deep below the earth without breaking the surface. And then to detonate.

A more exact description was a "hangman's drop."

That is exactly what happened. The entire Tahn Council palace fell through the "gallows trap."

All that remained was a stinking hole whose perimeter was littered with the stone ruins of the Tahn's proudest symbol of power.

The strike had been ordered for the early hours of the morning, and so only a handful of Than noblemen died, and those low-ranking. Not only was the palace communication system destroyed, but the standby relay stations below the palace vanished.

The Emperor had not intended the strike to kill the Tahn Council. He preferred them alive, worried, and having to explain to the Tahn just how the unthinkable—an Imperial strike on Heath itself—could not only have been thought but carried out. Also, he wanted them alive to consider that he had proved he could kill them any time he felt like it. Even fanatics like those who ruled the Tahn Empire might think about that.

The second statement was made by the rest of Mason's destroyers as they contour-flew over the city, launch bays spewing thousands of tiny incendiaries.

Carpet bombing.

The Emperor might have told Sullamora he would try not to win by mass slaughter. But his histrionic speech one cycle after the war had begun might have been more accurate, when he promised the Tahn that eventually their own skies would be flame.

The heart of Heath exploded in a firestorm. The city center—and everything in it—melted. People outside—who probably were already doomed from the radiation generated by the missile's impact—disappeared. The pavement ran like liquid. Oxygen was sucked out of even the filtered shelters. Ponds, fountains, and one lake boiled dry in an instant. The firestorm, reaching thousands of meters into the sky, created a tornado nearly a kilometer in diameter, swirling carnage and rubble at speeds over 200 kph.

Fire departments, disaster agencies, and hospitals were buried in a tidal wave of catastrophe—those which survived the fire itself.

The city center of Heath burned for nearly a week.

Half a million people were dead.

The Emperor's second statement was self-evident.

CHAPTER FORTY

PASTOUR FELT DIRTY, smelly, and just plain angry as he and his bodyguards exited the shelter. From the distance, he could hear the dying wail of all-clear sirens. Another clotting false alarm. In the three days since the bombing raid, at least two dozen false alarms had sent him, his bodyguards, and his entire household staff scurrying into the cramped bomb shelter about twenty meters under his garden. He was sick of feeling like a small rodent that bolted for a hole at even the hint of a predator's shadow. It was especially humiliating when the shadow turned out to be that of something innocuous, like a poor flying berry-eating creature.

He stopped just outside the steel door that covered the tunnel entrance to the shelter. Most of his staff headed straight for the comforts of the square-built structure he called home. As a man who had grown up in the greasy squalor that the Tahn called factories and had then fought his way to the executive suite, Pastour treasured his privacy over almost all else. He had constructed his home many years before on the edge of the industrial slum near the outskirts of Heath. Despite the grimness of the surroundings, Pastour believed it was important not to lose touch with his roots. That was definitely un-Tahnlike but was also probably the secret to his immense success.

A former factory slave himself, Pastour liked to believe that he knew how to get the most out of his workers. His industrial competitors used only the stick. Pastour had accepted that necessity. It had always been done that way. But he had also reinvented the carrot.

In a Pastour factory, the worker was treated with a comparative measure of respect, with healthy bonuses for the most ingenious or the hardest workers. It was not out of kindness. It was pure calculation—like his plan to put POWs to work for the Tahn cause at Koldyeze. His factories were far from being utopias. In most other systems the conditions would have been considered barbaric. Even Prime World capitalists would have been shamed into shutting them down. On other worlds the workers themselves would have gone after them with bombs and guns. Still, if there ever was going to be a Tahn future history, Pastour would someday be judged "enlightened."

Therefore, the house had been built, in his words, "right among 'em." Still, he had a need for privacy. So he had his architect design a multistoried home that presented four blank walls to its neighbors. It was constructed around a sprawling courtyard, complete with paths, fountains, and, right in the center, a small-domed structure containing his garden.

He had almost lost the garden when he had become a full member of the High Council. A minus side of the perks and influence he had gained was the insistence that each council member "shall cause to be constructed or personally construct a facility which shall be capable of withstanding . . ." mumblemumblemumble and other legal jargon that bottom-lined out that he had to tear out his garden and put in a bomb shelter capable of standing up to a nearly direct nuke hit.

Pastour had actually been toying with telling Lord Fehrle where he could put the great honor he was about to bestow upon his proud Tahn brow, when he came up with a solution.

Armed with his pet architect, a great wad of credits, and a lot of heavy string pulling, Pastour had weaseled the military out of its heaviest-duty laser cutters and gravjacks. It still took months of cutting and burrowing to lift out the entire courtyard, ground and all. Then the shelter was constructed to the meanest standards possible—Pastour had no intention of wasting any credits on such foolishness. And the courtyard and his treasured greenhouse were lowered over it and sealed in place.

He glanced around, still noting the accomplishment with a bit of pride. True, there were a few flaws. Drainage had proved to be a problem, but he had tacked together a barely adequate system that dumped into the neighborhood sewer system. There was a tendency for it to flood the street, but Pastour did not mind taking on the burden of the pumping and the cleanups that followed a heavy storm.

He acknowledged the salute from his chief guard, who reported that the shelter had been secured and that they were ready to escort him inside the house. Pastour impatiently waved them away. Over the past three days of scares, the situation had become routine—something that did nothing to make it easier on Pastour. They would insist that he go inside while they doubled-checked with Security Central—a process that could take hours. Pastour would refuse, sending them all reluctantly away while he instead retired to the solitude of his greenhouse. There were purposely no means of communication once inside, and Pastour sometimes spent many hours roaming the aisles of hydroponic pans, where all he had to listen to was the soft hum of the recycling pumps and the buzz of the sunlamps.

That day was no different. The exchange had almost become formal. Once again Pastour won, and once again the guards went sullenly away, and once again Pastour stormed through the door of his greenhouse and peace.

But once inside, the scowl faded and the wrinkles of anger softened into the permanent grin lines that wreathed Pastour's face. Today, however, it was quieter than usual inside. He shrugged. It was probably because his machines did not have to work nearly so hard to maintain the false atmosphere inside. The same bombs that had killed and maimed so many of his fellow Tahn had also briefly left behind a more accommodating world for his beloved plants.

He moved along a row of legume vines, picking off dead leaves, replacing flailing tendrils on their support nets, and generally taking note of the small differences that only a careful gardener saw in his progeny.

Pastour was just turning the far corner of the center aisle when he realized that it was not the hum of pumps that he was missing. It was the whine of the supersensitive pollen-carrying insects that he had imported across vast distances at no small expense.

The insects darted for cover the moment they sensed an alien presence. They knew Pastour; he was no longer considered a threat. Ergo . . . someone else . . .

"Be very careful, Colonel," the man said. "You would be advised to rethink anything you're planning to do next."

It was better than good advice. Because as soon as Pastour saw Sten and the deadly weapon aimed at his gut, his first reaction was to throw himself on the man, pummeling and shrieking for help as hard and as loud as he could. He rethought. After murder, kidnapping seemed the next most obvious fate. Pastour relaxed. If kidnapping was the intent, then talk and negotiations must follow. Pastour was good at both. Therefore, outward calm was in order.

Sten watched the thinking process carefully. A moment before Pastour knew that he had reached a decision, Sten allowed the weapon to droop. He leaned against a tool bench and motioned for Pastour to perch on a gardening sledge. Pastour obeyed. He looked about curiously, wondering how Sten could possibly have penetrated his elaborate human and electronic security system. Then he spotted the grate lying beside the halfmeter-wide mouth of the greenhouse main drain. Pastour could not help laughing.

"I knew that clottin' bomb shelter was a rotten idea," he chortled.

Sten did not see what was so funny, but Pastour just said never mind. It would take too long to explain.

"How do you plan getting us both out of here?" he asked instead. "I'm much too old to crawl through that thing." He pointed at the drain.

"Don't worry," Sten said. "You're staying right here."

Pastour frowned. Was it assassination, after all? Was the man a maniac? Did he plan to toy with him first and then kill him? No. There was nothing maniacal about the young man.

"So what do you have in mind?"

"Talk. That's all. It was my boss's idea."

Pastour raised an eyebrow. Boss?

"You know him as the Eternal Emperor. Anyway, he suggested we chat. See if we can come to some sort of understanding."

Pastour was beginning to doubt himself. Maybe the man *was* nuts. How to handle this? He warned himself that whatever he said next, he must be sure not to condescend. Before he could form his thoughts into words, Sten casually reached into a tunic pocket, pulled something out, and tossed it on the floor next to Pastour. The Tahn picked it up, glanced at it, and was jolted back. It bore the Emperor's personal seal! Pastour did not need to have it checked to know the seal was genuine.

Sten was exactly who he had said he was, an emissary of the Eternal Emperor. Questions flooded into Pastour's mind. Then one huge, glaring one wiped the others away: Why me? And he became very, very angry. Did the Eternal Emperor see some supposed flaw in his character? Did the man think he was a traitor?

"All my boss wants," Sten said, as if sensing what was going on in Pastour's mind, "is to let you know that he is aware of you. He said to consider this nothing more than the opening of a dialogue."

"And just what does he expect me to do or say?" The words were etched in heavy frost.

"Nothing right now," Sten said.

"Is anyone else being contacted?" By "anyone else" he meant other members of the High Council.

"Just you."

Sten allowed a long silence to follow. He wanted Pastour firm in his anger. He wanted hatred to build. Because when the shift came, confusion would follow. And then he set the hook.

"How did you like the little party my boss threw the other night?"

Pastour squirmed, knowing that Sten was referring to the bombing raid. To him the raid had been a sign that the Emperor could strike at will. And Sten's presence in his private garden only underscored that fact. Still . . .

"If the Emperor believes his cowardly attack on innocent people will in any way weaken our resolve . . ."

"You're sounding like a politician, Colonel," Sten said. "I hope that's not what you really think. Because if it is, you might as well kiss a lot more of your innocents good-bye."

"You didn't answer my first question," Pastour came back. "Or, if you were, you were just being glib. I don't like glib. Once again, what does he expect from me?"

"If you think my boss wants you to turn traitor," Sten said, "you're dead wrong. If you were a traitor, you'd be no use to him at all."

"And what use does he see in me?"

"At some point in time," Sten went on, "you people are going to realize that this thing is over. That you've lost. And when that happens, the Emperor would like to have someone sensible to deal with."

Pastour knew that Sten was talking about surrender. How odd, he thought. The word doesn't make me angry. The lack of feeling disturbed him. What kind of a Tahn was he? Surrender? It should have been unthinkable. Instead, it seemed . . . inevitable. "Go on," he said.

And by those two words, Sten knew he had struck pay dirt.

"There's not that much more. Except to say that a great deal of grief can be avoided if some sort of Tahn government survives. The Emperor is betting that it will be you."

Pastour nodded. Survival was something he knew a great deal about—unlike most of his brothers and sisters on the council.

"What else?"

Sten hesitated. What he was going to say next had nothing to do with his instructions. Then he plunged headfirst. "Koldyeze."

"What about it?" Pastour was puzzled.

"The Emperor is worried about the prisoners there," he said, lying, lying, lying. "He hopes that no matter what happens, they'll be treated humanely. And since the place was your idea to start with . . ."

Now it made sense to Pastour. He had heard that the Eternal Emperor had some strange ideas about the treatment of the lower classes. Even prisoners of war. Why the man bothered with the plight of cowards, he had no idea. Still, what would it cost him?

"Tell your Emperor that he need not concern himself about their fates. I'll do my best for them. As long as he doesn't interpret this as some kind of concession. Or acknowledgment from me that anything but his final defeat and humiliation is—"

Sten laughed and raised a weak hand, calling for surrender. Pastour could not help laughing with him. There he was, sounding like a politico again. Sten straightened up and headed for the mouth of the drain.

"Are you just going to leave me here?" Pastour asked. "How do you know I won't instantly call the guard?"

"There's a lot more lives at stake here than mine" was all Sten said. And then he dropped out of sight.

Pastour only had to think about that for a second. The man was right. He kicked the grate back in place and returned to tending his garden.

CHAPTER FORTY-ONE

A HISTORICAL ATLAS fiche, equipped with a time tick, would show the Imperial assault on the Tahn Empire as if the war were a liquid projector. The red—or whatever color—representing the Tahn conquests would ebb back as the color assigned to the Empire and its allies flowed smoothly forward, excepting, of course, those blotches representing fortress worlds like Etan that had been isolated and left to rot.

That would suggest that the average Imperial grunt also had an idea of how the war was going.

He, she, or whatever did not.

The sailors loaded supplies and ammunition, boarded ship, and transited in minor fear and major boredom to a certain point, where they off-loaded supplies on a ramp and off-loaded ammunition through launching tubes.

The soldiers trained, boarded ship, transited in major fear to a drop or landing point, and attacked. When the last Tahn lay dead, they returned to their base or were moved to a new location where they built a new base, trained, and tried to find ways to burn off the sickening realization that the only end to it all was death, wounding, madness, or victory.

Seeing the next sunrise became the only major victory.

It took twenty years, fortunately, for a statistician to come up with the cheery news that during the war against the Tahn, a combat troop could expect to survive no more than thirty personal days in battle.

Also fortunately, very few Imperials experienced those thirty days back to back.

But there were exceptions, just as, contrary to what that "liquid projector" showed, there were disasters.

One was the landing on Pel/e.

The Pel/e systems were priority one to the Emperor's strategists. They were at the midpoint of a galactic arm that was a longtime part of the Tahn Empire. Once the systems were taken, the Empire would have a base, a striking point to search and find the long-sought secret Tahn shipbuilding system.

The always hard-luck Eighth Guards were chosen for the "honor" of the assault. After two weeks of prior bombardment, the Imperial Navy advised that all Tahn resistance was battered bloody. The assault transports went in. The first wave was shattered in-atmosphere. The second made it to the ground—and then the Tahn opened fire.

Imperial strategists and psychologists had blundered. Because the Tahn used a rigid military and social structure, it was assumed that once the command elements were destroyed or out of contact, the soldiers themselves would stop fighting, commit suicide, or at the worst fight ineffectually.

The ignored statistic, known to the Empire before the war began, was that the Tahn used far fewer officers and noncoms per serving soldier than did *any* of the regular Imperial units. And so the Tahn regrouped, by squads, by fire teams, by pickup combat elements, and fought back.

Conquering the Pel/e systems was supposed to have taken two E-months and required only the Eighth Guards to accomplish. Final victory took two *E-years* before the last Tahn element was killed. Six divisions were used in the process, and it became SOP for a new division to spend time on one of the Pel/e worlds getting final live-fire training before being committed to a frontal assault.

The Eighth Guards was shattered. Two commanding generals were relieved, and the unit took eighty-three percent casualties before being pulled from combat. Its colors were cased, the guardsmen were reassigned to other units, and the unit was rebuilt from scratch.

That was disaster enough. What made it worse was that the assaults on Pel/e were made before St. Clair discovered that the secret shipyards were in the Erebus System—half an empire away from Pel/e.

Seventy-five thousand Imperial deaths. One and a quarter million Tahn corpses. In a completely meaningless battle.

Six battlefleets hit Erebus under the flag of Fleet Marshal Ian Mahoney.

So-called panacea targets—hit here and the war's gonna come to an end the day before yesterday—were normally a joke, useful only when a space force was arguing for larger appropriations that would probably bankrupt every other service if made.

Also, those glamour targets usually got hit once and once only. If the factory was trashed, they would not have to worry about it ever, ever, ever producing nasty widgets anymore.

The fact was always ignored that after a war, when the bean counters went in to figure out how effective the bombs had been, they learned that said factory probably was not trashed that badly and that concerted effort brought it back online within a few months.

Erebus looked to be such a panacea target.

Mahoney, coming from a more realistic background than most of the skyjocks serving under him, approached things differently.

The Erebus System was a bastard target, defended by every onworld weapon and heavily armed spacecraft the Tahn could afford to divert from mainline combat. And the pilots and missile crews fought to the death.

Mahoney made sure it was a real death.

His first strike took thirty percent casualties. There were splintered destroyers and tacships broken on the ground of Fundy, the Erebus System's main world, and more hulks spewing debris out in space.

He sent his ships in again the next day.

Twenty-eight percent casualties.

There were ship crews who broke and refused the attack order. Mahoney calmly ordered their courts-martial and relieved any skipper who hesitated at his orders.

Then he threw his guts up in his cabin, washed his face, and sent more men and women to their deaths.

After six days of hammering, the Tahn had nothing left to fight back with.

Mahoney sent in his battleships, monitors, and cruisers.

Three battlewagons and two of the ponderous cruisers went down—but the Erebus shipworks appeared to be permanently out of business.

Mahoney ordered the strike repeated the next day.

He had to relieve a fleet admiral for objecting.

But the attack ships went in again. And still a third time.

The worlds of Erebus looked to be suitable parking lots.

But just to make sure, against all conventions of war, Mahoney had the worlds dusted.

The factories of Erebus might go back to work—but every worker assigned to them would glow in the dark.

The First Guards, Mahoney's old command—now led by Major General Galkin—spearheaded the landing on Naha.

By that point they knew how to fight the Tahn:

Don't shoot at the civilians—they've got their own set of problems. Get them to the rear. Don't believe that *anything* isn't booby-trapped, from the ceremonial flag to the ugly plas casting of Lord Fehrle that'd make a great souvenir.

A Tahn can be anywhere. In a crater beside the road. Tied into a tree. Sited in a weapons position in the base of a statue. Waiting for days inside a burnt-out track, waiting for the chance to kill any Imperial within range, whether fighting man or woman, clerk, or civilian. And very competent at his or her trade of slaughter.

Eventually, Naha fell, in spite of the fact that the final days of the resistance were personally commanded by Lady Atago. The casualty rate was twice what had been expected, and the battle lasted three times longer than expected—expected that was, by staff people. The line grunts thought themselves damn lucky and damn good to have gotten off that lightly.

Naha gave the Empire the long-needed major base inside the Tahn worlds.

Now the real hammering would begin.

CHAPTER FORTY-TWO

EVEN AN EXPERIENCED Tahn watcher might have drawn some wrong conclusions if he had observed the meeting between Lord Fehrle and the leaders of the two major factions on the High Council, Wichman and Pastour. If a hidden camera had captured them sitting at ease in Fehrle's darkened study, the Tahn watcher would have been most interested in who was *not* present. Meaning Lady Atago, Fehrle's heir apparent. The expert would make the instant assumption that new alliances were being struck and that Atago was on the way out, obviously because Fehrle perceived her new hero status as a threat.

The expert would have been wrong on both counts. Yes, it was true that Fehrle had thought of her when he had issued the invitation to Wichman and Pastour. It was because of her "white knight" image that he pointedly ignored her.

He did not want what he was about to propose to tarnish her image in any way. If he fell, he wanted her to be able to pick up his sword wearing armor that was mirror-bright. Fehrle was about to suggest a plan that assumed and depended upon the corruption and disloyalty of his own people. Atago would be enraged at his even suggesting that such a thing existed. It was a fact that Atago's simple soldier's mind could not accept.

Wichman would argue, it was true, but he could eventually be convinced. With the help of Pastour, the realist, Fehrle would have no difficulty at all.

Lord Fehrle served his guests with his own hands, helping them with their choice of delicacies on the tray and building them drinks. And as they ate and drank, he talked, setting the background: There were traitors everywhere, spies at every level, and fools who leaked vital information to enemy agents. To make his point, he vastly overstated the situation.

As expected, Wichman was shocked and immediately called for a heroic medicine-style purge to remove the poisons of disloyalty. What he had not expected was Pastour's reaction. The man sat in silence, his face growing bleaker with every word. Had Fehrle misguessed? Instead of support, would Pastour take on the role of an Atago and back Wichman's call for a bloodletting? If so, Fehrle would have to do some fast reanalysis of the situation or his plan would never get off the ground.

What he did not realize was that Pastour was suffering from a nearly terminal case of guilty conscience. Did Fehrle suspect him? Were there guards waiting with drawn guns just behind the door? If so, why did the man keep looking over at him, as if he were looking for help? Gradually, he realized that was exactly what Fehrle wanted. But help doing what? What the clot! He already had his genitalia on the table. Maybe it was time to dare the knife.

"Forgive me, my lord," he said. "Along with you, and my Lord Wichman, I certainly deplore the situation you are out-lining. We should take drastic action. But . . ."

"Go on," Fehrle said a little sharply, trying to prod the man into giving him an opening.

"But . . . perhaps there is some way we can make use of some of these people first."

Wichman almost exploded at that. He came halfway to his feet. "How dare—"

"Exactly my thinking," Fehrle said.

Wichman thumped back down. "What? Oh, yeah! Good idea. Uh . . . right!" Then the poor bewildered man could not help himself any longer. "Clot! What am I saying? What's a good idea?"

Fehrle and Pastour laughed, and Wichman, after a mo-ment, had the good grace to laugh with them. They had more drinks while Fehrle laid it out for them.

He did have a way of making use of the leakers, but in a contorted way that even the Eternal Emperor would have ad-mired. In fact, he had taken the whole plan right out of the Emperor's book.

Fehrle planned to pull hope out of the ashes of the ruins of the High Council's palace. They had all been puzzled at the Emperor's behavior after they had launched their own sneak attack on his headquarters in the opening blow of the war. The Emperor had immediately flooded the airways with an endless series of propaganda portraits showing him shaking his fist at the Tahn in defiance. At first it had seemed like empty gestur-ing. What did that accomplish? Immediately after that, they were surprised at how many of his straying allies returned to the Emperor's camp. There was nothing empty about the cam-paign at all. It brought in badly needed ships and troops in a swell of public opinion.

Fehrle was proposing the same thing, but on a much larger scale. He wanted to launch a grand tour of twenty-two sys-tems in which he would personally appear with the leaders of said systems, giving the Emperor the finger at every opportu-nity.

The lonely Tahn, fighting on despite the odds against the warmongering running dog Imperialist giant. Vowing to win against all odds. That sort of thing. Privately, he would use a heavy cudgel to stiffen the spine of their allies. He would convince them all to dig into the trenches and fight to the last being. If it worked, any victory the Emperor hoped for would come at an exceedingly high price that Fehrle doubted he would be willing to pay.

Wichman loved it. Pastour, grudgingly, admitted there might be some wisdom in it. Still, he remembered the blood-bath of the bombing raid on the city and the strange appearance of Sten in his heavily guarded domain. If the Emperor could do all that at will . . .

"I fear for your life, my lord," he finally said. "What is to prevent the Emperor from learning of your plan and then attacking when you least expect it? If you were assassinated, I'm not sure how the people would behave."

"I *want* the Emperor to learn about it," Fehrle said.

Once again, Wichman was surprised. Pastour, however, got it right away. Fehrle would have his staff plan two itineraries. The first would show the tour commencing on Arbroath. On the surface, that would seem like a logical choice, since the Arbroath were totally loyal to the Tahn. They would grovel at Fehrle's knees and praise him, making for wonderful propaganda. That itinerary would be leaked. In reality, Arbroath was a rotten jumping-off point. The people were so stupidly and blindly loyal that they would fight on anyway until they were all dead.

The real stepping-off point would be Cormarthen. Pastour saw the wisdom in that right off. The people there were wild rebels—a semi-Celtic splinter cult whose sole motivation for aiding the Tahn was their unreasoning hatred of the Empire. When the war was over—assuming the Tahn won—they were sure to instantly turn on their allies. In fact, after the string of recent defeats they were already wavering. Fehrle planned to put a stop to that immediately. On day one of the twenty-two system tour he would be able to present his people with a diplomatic victory.

The rest of the tour would be plotted the same way. False clues would be planted with the Imperialists while Fehrle maddeningly popped up at the least expected places to flip off the Eternal Emperor.

Pastour and Wichman pledged enthusiastic support. They would work on their own people as well as lobby the other factions. Fehrle was guaranteed unanimous acceptance when the proposal was formally presented to the High Council.

While Fehrle and Wichman were congratulating each other on the yet-to-be success, Pastour remembered Sten. And Koldyeze. He had thought about the young man's odd request. He had recently seen a way not only to make good his promise but to bump the value of the pot 1,000 percent.

During the course of the conflict the Tahn had taken millions of prisoners of all kinds. But a very few of those prisoners presented special difficulties.

They were the important diplomats, politicians, and high-ranking officers who had fallen into Tahn hands. Even the instinctive Tahn disdain for prisoners did not allow them to treat those beings with anything other than kid gloves—relatively speaking. The problem had been finding the proper guards with at least a modicum of political reality.

At the moment, that was impossible. The prisoners were spread out in camps all over the Tahn Empire.

What Pastour wanted to do was to solve that problem at one stroke. He would place them all at Koldyeze. Then he would personally oversee their treatment through his emissaries. There was also an even greater advantage in putting all his rocks in one stonebucket. If and when the Tahn were defeated, Pastour would have heavy-duty trading stock to strike his bargain for peace with the Emperor.

Obviously he could not word any of that exactly the same way if he wanted to bring Fehrle and Wichman to his side. Instead, he appealed to their blood lust.

"If we had them all in one place," he said as he came to the end of his explanation, "we'd only need one gun to hold against their heads."

"And if the Emperor refuses us," Wichman broke in, "we kill them all. I like it!"

Fehrle also added his support.

When Pastour went home some time later, a little warm and tiddly from the drink and the companionship, he thought fondly about how well the Tahn system of government worked. A few well-chosen words—out of hearing from the squabble of conflicting viewpoints of the public—and the correct measures were taken to ensure the future of the race. It made him feel proud and patriotic.

The next day, when he was sober, he would plan his next moves at Koldyeze.

CHAPTER FORTY-THREE

STEN WAS FAIRLY disgusted with the Tahn. What, after all, was an evil empire without an internal conspiracy or six? The Tahn were short on dissidents. Those few enemies of the regime seemed to have gotten policed up years earlier, and their dissidence was mainly made up of the idea that maybe the Tahn Council ought to say please before conquering somebody. From the limited leaks he had been able to get from Tahn CI, the current treason seemed to consist of street gossips or poor sods who complained about having to work a double shift without getting a food break.

Sneakiness abhorred a vacuum, and so Sten and Kilgour went to work, building themselves a good list of traitorous swine. They decided, just to keep things interesting, that it would be a military conspiracy.

There were three requirements:

1. The conspiring officer had to have complained about how the war was going. Even a recorded mutter into a shaving mirror made the officer eligible. So, in that manner, Admiral Whoosis on the *Sabac* made the grade.
2. The conspiring officer had to be highly respected.
3. The conspiring officer had to have served in combat, on a frontline world, or, during peacetime, on a world where there was an Imperial presence.

It was not necessary that the eager conspirator actually be anything other than a rabid believer in the Tahn right to grab anything around from anyone weaker. As a matter of fact, Sten did not want anyone like that. People with real politics made him nervous—even if he had been able to find any.

Once Sten and Kilgour had the list, they put it up on a computer screen and started cross-connecting the conspiracy. The officers chosen for links needed no particular qualifications, except that their absence would not improve Tahn efficiency. That was, for instance, how the third assistant paymaster general, the Tahn Counterintelligence number two, and the chief of the chaplain's acolyte division became dangerous threats.

Once Kilgour had the list all neat and tidy, it went out on a burst transmission to the Imperial base station located somewhere they never knew for appropriate usage.

Most of the conspiracy list was handled by Alex. Sten had another problem: Lord Fehrle's "show the flag" tour. It did not make any sense. Not that the tour made no sense—but everybody seemed to know about it. Either Tahn Security was composed of numbwits—which Sten did not dare let himself believe—or else everyone connected with the tour was suffering from terminal oral diarrhea.

He sent through the reports of when Fehrle was going, where Fehrle was going from the Arbroath worlds onward, what he would eat and drink, where he would be banqueted, and whom he would meet straight on to the Empire. All graded Category Two or lower, ranging from reliable source, personally received, down to outhouse rumor. But none of it was Category One: accepted by this station as truth.

Then one afternoon Chetwynd sent word, through the cutouts, that he wanted a meet.

They fenced recreationally for a couple of drinks. Wasn't it about time that Chetwynd's credit allowance was increased? Couldn't he be more helpful to the cause if Sten gave him some idea as to what was happening next? Had he heard anything about a new offensive failing? Then he got down to it.

"One a' my longtime cheenas hit on somethin' you might find interesting. He's one of my best agents, y' know."

"A thief, in other words."

Chetwynd looked ponderously injured. "Clot, Sten, don't be so suspicious. The clot's a hard-core freedom fighter."

"I stand corrected. A *good* thief."

"He was out last night. Around the 23YXL area of the port. Y' know, that's where most of the bonded warehouses are. He was looking for good intelligence and—" Chetwynd chuckled and drank. "—anything else that wasn't riveted down.

"Came on this warehouse. Security up the yahoo. Which was interestin'. He got up on the rooftop and snaked in. All of a sudden couple Tahn plainclothes come out from behind a vent. Damn near popped him.

"He come off that roof and said the place was crawlin' with rozzers. Funny—he said he knew a couple of 'em. CI, they was.

"Dunno what's in that warehouse. But thought you might want to be tipped the wink."

Chetwynd waited. Sten dug out a wad of credits and passed them across. They were not given with any pretense on either side that they were intended for Chetwynd's organization. Maybe Chetwynd's tier ranger, if he was indeed a longtime cheena, might see a little of it. But probably not.

Kilgour swept the warehouse with a palm-size set of available-light binocs and hissed through his teeth. "Thae tub's wae bein't conservative. Thae's more screws around yon warehouse thae a Campbell hae fleas."

There were other interesting things happening. A ship had landed about half a kilometer beyond the warehouse. Sten IDd it as being a standard armed transport—but with very nonstandard security around it. The ship sat on an absolutely bare stretch of tarmac. There were three, no, four rings of guards around it, uniformed soldiery, each bashing his beat in a military manner. Between the rings, searchlights mounted on portable towers on the field's edges swept the darkness.

"The ship's bein't loaded," Kilgour whispered. "An' by a braw crew ae stevedores."

He passed the binocs to Sten, who looked and nodded.

"The only civilian thing about them is they ain't in step."

Fascinating. Not only did the warehouse obviously hold

something enormously valuable—which made it enormously interesting for Imperial Intelligence—it was being loaded by soldiers in the dead of night. Sten rather wanted to pry open one or another of those unmarked crates. They were being loaded very carefully, he noted, as if they contained delicate merchandise.

Kilgour, mumbling, had a tiny multifunction computer dug out of his boot and was tapping keys and staring intently at the ship. Sten concentrated on the warehouse and put his Mantis joint-casing skills to work.

Can we sneak in? Not unless somebody happens to come up with an invisibility suit. Can we go in over the roof? We've got to be sneakier than Chetwynd's boyo. Unlikely. Under? No time to play caver—at the rate they're moving, the ship will be loaded by dawn. What about a simple walk-up? Pretending to be some kind of warehouse inspector? A superior officer? Negative on both. Not that we can't get out if we're blown—but I have this feeling I'm not going to want anybody to know we were here. Join the loading party? Nope. Ten-man teams. Even the Tahn noncoms would notice if there were more spear-carriers than the number of fingers on each hand.

"Ah think w' kin do it, boss," Kilgour broke in. "Ah've been runnin't a timer on thae guards. There are lapses. An' thae searchlights dinnae cross-sweep like thae should."

Sten stared at the completely bare expanse between the building they crouched next to and the ship and gulped in a cowardly manner. "Choreograph it, Mr. Kilgour."

Five minutes later:

"On thae count . . . be followin't mah twinkli't toes . . . three . . . two . . . now!"

And the two black-clad men trotted out toward the ship.

"Sixteen . . . seventeen . . . down, boss! One, two, three, four, five . . . up. Twenty paces . . . down!"

They became part of the tarmac as the searchlight beam passed very close to them.

"Eleven, twelve, now! Three, four, five . . . six and freeze!"

The only music they "danced" to as they crossed the field was their own hoarse breathing.

"The skid, boss. Straight for it an' look like a shock absorber. Two, one, on th' way, lad!"

Sten flattened himself next to the huge, grease-stained landing skid, wondering if he actually did look like an oleo strut.

"Na," Alex growled in his ear, "if Ah'm right, we'll be doublin' up thae gangplank shortly. Y' ken thae ramp watch is posted behin' an' under thae ramp. Lookit like he nae like thae glare when the beams hit him. So be goin't up softly, wee Sten. W' dinnae want thae thunder ae y' hooves alertin' him."

"And if there's a watch *inside* the ship?"

"We'll say we're solicitin' frae the home f'r wayward banshee bairns an' scoot wi' a smile. Three . . . two . . . hit it!"

Running on tiptoe up a ramp—even a cleated ramp—was interesting. *Pointe*, uphill, was straining.

They made it through the port. Kilgour was lucky—there was no interior boarding watch posted.

Sten extended his hands, palm up. *Well?* Kilgour shrugged, then spotted an order board and grabbed it. Assuming a worried expression, he waved them forward into the heart of the ship.

Actually, it was more of a private joke—nobody ever interfered with a man who looked upset and was carrying a clipboard—than a practical disguise. Both of them knew full well that no sailor worthy of his hangover would board until three blasts after the final call. The passageways were deserted. There was clattering from what probably was a galley and some drunken snores from a berthing compartment, but nothing else.

Sten noted that the ship was very, very clean—freshly refinished. Either it was run by a bully captain, or high-level passengers were expected.

They found the hatchways leading down to the hold and slid down the ladders. The hold was a little over half-full. The loadmaster and his assistants were bellowing instructions to the laden soldiers as to what went where and why the clot was doing it wrong.

Sten and Kilgour found a pile of not yet secured crates near the forward area of the hold, and Sten deployed a pry bar quietly

The first crate held dinnerware—expensive dinnerwear

with the Tahn Council crest embossed on it. Sten thoughtfully opened more crates.

The sixth was the tip-off. It contained ceremonial robes made of a material that no Tahn would have seen for years and years. And each robe's left breast area was embroidered in gold and silver with a small three-headed dragon. Kilgour's eyes widened, and he applauded silently.

The crate's top was replaced, and Sten and Alex went back the way they came, dancing a pas de deux past the searchlights and guards.

Neither of them needed a short course in heraldry to know what that triple-headed dragon was. The natives of Cormarthen were too well known for carrying that emblem wherever their intransigence led them and for putting that emblem on everything, including, some theorized, their toilet paper.

So, as Sten had predicted, Fehrle was not going anywhere near Arbroath or the other supposed systems. But he—or some other muckety on the council—*was* making a grand tour. And Sten thought the Emperor might be vaguely interested in knowing what Fehrle's *real* itinerary appeared to be.

CHAPTER FORTY-FOUR

THE ETERNAL EMPEROR *was* interested.

He just was not quite sure what to do about having the facts on Lord Fehrle's wanderings. Actually, he corrected himself, he knew quite well what to do about it. The problem was *how* to do it.

Damn, but he missed Mahoney. If the flaky Mick were still head of his Intelligence—Mercury Corps—the Emperor would merely have had to hint heavily. But his current intelligence chief happened to be a tolerably straightforward man.

Which meant too moral to be a good spy. Clot, he swore. Why'd I promote Mahoney?

The Eternal Emperor's fingers were on the decanter of stregg. They hesitated, then went to the concoction he called Scotch. He needed a bit of brainpower, not blind instinct.

Icing a fellow ruler was acceptable only in fiction—historical fiction. And even then it had better be hand to hand, the Emperor thought glumly. If Hank Doo had personally clunked Beckett with the nearest mace instead of sniveling about things to his clotpole court, he might have gotten a better press.

It was not that any politician found assassination *morally* abhorrent. But it made them nervous to think that the fellow across the negotiating table might actually take things personally. Killing millions of citizens was one thing—but wasting one of his own class? The boss class? Shameful, indeed.

After thought, the Emperor put the operation in motion. It never had a name nor any permanent fiche, even in the most classified files of the war.

The Emperor requested the specifications, to include the signature in all ranges from visual to output drive, of the most current Tahn battleships. Since Fehrle's profile showed that he liked to travel in style, he would use the newest, most modern class available—regardless of whether that ship would be better deployed in combat instead of being used for transportation.

Intelligence showed that the Tahn were building three new superbattleships. One was—?—in commission, one was in shakedown, and the third was nearing completion.

Mercury Corps technicians were given instructions to prepare a detonator that would explode the charge only when the active signature of that particular class of ship was within range. They had only days to build that detonator—Lord Fehrle's tour was almost ready to begin.

There was no problem. The technicians were—self-described—so used to doing the impossible with the improbable under circumstances that were preposterous that they felt capable of doing everything with nothing.

Explosive charges were prepared. Sixteen of them. The requirement was to provide a cased, nondeteriorating, small amount of explosive with the given CLASSIFIED detonator, capable of destroying a large object, such as a Tahn battleship, when it came within close range.

Sixteen was not an arbitrary choice. Cormarthen's capital port had sixteen pilot ships.

Mantis operatives were given those sixteen charges and inserted on Cormarthen.

All the pilot boats were booby-trapped, and the Mantis people withdrew without contact. They would have felt shamed if anything else had happened. They expressed no curiosity as to what was in the casing or what it was supposed to do and to whom at what date. They would find out—if the operation worked—in the privacy of their own bars or barracks. Very conceivably not until after the war ended.

The entire amount of "paperwork" on the operation against the ruler of the Tahn occupied one fiche. That fiche was hand delivered to the Eternal Emperor and destroyed. He then sent his Mercury computer experts back through the system, ensuring that there were no backup, ghost, or FYI copies of the fiche.

Satisfied, he poured himself a stregg and waited.

Lord Fehrle's battleship, the *Conemaugh*, cut AM2 drive power and, under Yukawa drive, closed on Cormarthen. The ship's commander felt proud that his navigators had been able to pinpoint within 0.10 AU. Six ships were reported coming out-atmosphere: the pilot boat and appropriate escorts.

The commander so notified Lord Fehrle, who was in his cabin making final adjustments on one of the dragon-breasted robes he would wear.

While Fehrle's staff diplomats were on the com with the escort ships, the pilot craft closed to a forward lock without ceremony. On contact, the bomb went off.

Mercury demolition experts had planned for the blast to remove the entire nose section of the Tahn battleship. But because the *Conemaugh* was new, its fire-control circuits were still under test. Backup systems were not what they should have been. And so the blast ravened through the hull and then down into the drive system.

The AM2 fuel detonated.

The *Conemaugh* no longer existed—nor did the pilot boat, two of the approaching Cormarthen ships, and six of the Tahn warships escorting Lord Fehrle.

The Emperor, as he had promised some years earlier, was getting very personal about things.

BOOK FOUR

ZANSHIN

CHAPTER FORTY-FIVE

IT WAS THE Rangers versus the Blues in what every sports commentator in the Empire agreed was the gravball match of the decade. One hundred thousand beings were packed defecating organ to elbow in Lovett Arena to see if the homeplanet Rangers would revenge themselves on the dreaded Blues, who had whipped the Rangers for the gravball championship three E-years in a row. Despite the war, billions upon billions more —including, it was said, the Eternal Emperor himself—were watching the match on their home livie screens.

So far, the game had lived up to expectations. At the bottom of the fifth and final period, the score was fifty-three all after a series of seesaw duels that had marked the four hours of play. In the last period, Naismith, the big red-uniformed Ranger center, had fought his way four times through and around the Blues' heavy-gravity hotspots until he was within scoring distance. And each time the Blues had rallied, blocking the light-gravity lanes and driving the Rangers back onto their own territory. The game had been so fiercely contested that every hotspot on either side had been racked up to a full penalty three gees.

Rabbaj, the Blues' center, took the ball. Forwards veed out from him, hunting for a weakness in the Rangers' defense. Blue guards took up position near the light-grav lanes in their own territory. Then it was Rabbaj! Shooting past his own forwards, feinting left at a hotspot, then driving through a hole in the line. Then he was in the clear. An undefended light-grav lane just ahead! And beyond that, the tantalizing splash of red that marked the Rangers' goal line! The home crowd groaned. They were looking into the maw of a fourth humiliating defeat. A heartbeat, and Rabbaj was into the light-grav lane and jumping . . . jumping . . . jumping—

Tanz Sullamora palmed the switch that chopped the sound and blacked out the big windows that overlooked the playing field. He shook an angry finger at his colleagues on the privy council.

"I'm the one taking all the risks," he said, his voice shaking in fury. "We all vote Volmer has to go. Fine. But then I'm the one who has to do it. We all agree on the plan. Wonderful. Except once again, it's good old Tanz who sticks his neck out with Chapelle."

"We're all behind you, my friend," Malperin murmured. "I don't see what the problem is. If you fall, we all fall. We agreed on that, didn't we?"

"Sure," one of the Kraa twins soothed. "Me 'n' my sister been with you from the start, Tanz. All the way in or not at all is our motto."

Sullamora snorted at this. There were few businessbeings who were more notorious than the Kraas when it came to backstabbing. He looked over at Kyes for support, but the silvery eminence did not seem to be paying attention. Instead, he was lolling in one of the huge, ornate overstuffed armchairs, staring at the blank window as if he were still watching the in-progress gravball match. Sullamora slumped down in frustration and choked back a fat drink. The other members of the council were silent, staring around the owner's suite in pretended curiosity at the baroque-upon-baroque setting.

One of Lovett's more eccentric ancestors had built the enormous all-weather arena. It had no equal on Prime World. It could be converted within a few days to play host to any event from agricultural fairs to high-speed boat races. The seating was designed so that even the poorest fan could see the action. And looming over all of it was the imposing dome that was the owner's suite. Several hundred "close friends" could easily be entertained in that suite, although the multitude of garish paintings, stuffed animal heads, rickety statuary, and oddly formed furniture tended to make even two people feel claustrophobic. It produced the kind of atmosphere that would bring out the violence in even the most committed pacifist.

Perhaps that was what was making Sullamora behave so

out of character, allowing his anger to be seen by his peers. Or maybe it was because he was suddenly feeling very vulnerable. The way things stood, if the plan failed, only Sullamora would take the blame. The others were clean. Nothing could be traced to them. Adding to the pressure was that this was most certainly the last time the members would be able to meet out of public view without arousing suspicion. The match between the Rangers and the Blues was likely to be their last excuse.

It was Kyes who finally broke the silence. He went right for the bottom line. "What do you require of us, Tanz?"

Sullamora acknowledged him with a nod and fished six cards out of his pocket. He skimmed them across the table like a dealer, one for each being at the table and one for himself. The cards were made of indestructible plas. Kyes was the first to slide his card into the viewing slot in front of him. A small port opened in front of him, and words lit up on a tiny screen. The others did the same with their cards.

WE, THE MEMBERS OF THE PRIVY COUNCIL, AFTER DUE CONSIDERATION, HAVE COME TO THE RELUCTANT CONCLUSION THAT THE ETERNAL EMPEROR HAS BECOME INCREASINGLY AND DANGEROUSLY UNSTABLE. THEREFORE, WE HAVE DETERMINED TO TAKE THE FOLLOWING ACTIONS . . .

It was the preamble to assassination. And at the bottom were six places for the signature prints of each being at the table. Once the marks were made, there would be no turning back. And each conspirator would be equally culpable.

There was a long moment. Once again it was Kyes who went first. He smiled and made his mark. One by one the others did the same.

Chapelle would be activated.

Out on the playing field, the home crowd happily rioted. The defeated Blue team was retreating behind a phalanx of armored cops. Naismith was being hoisted on his teammates' shoulders. And the celebrating fans poured out of the stadium for a glorious night of rapine, looting, drinking, and general head busting.

Honor had been restored.

CHAPTER FORTY-SIX

"GOT A QUESTION. Sir," Fleet Marshal Mahoney growled. "And a request. Sir."

"GA," the Eternal Emperor said.

"First. What's the official Imperial policy on torture?"

"Bad thing. Don't get caught doing it."

Mahoney nodded. "You mind if I brainburn this clot a little bit? Slow? Promise not to get caught doing it."

"Tsk. And she appears to have such a bright future."

"Future," Mahoney snarled. "Listen to this drakh."

He read aloud from the news dispatch on the video display. "'Suddenly the smile vanished, and I was reminded that this man is the Empire's fiercest fighter, a leader who sends millions of men and thousands of ships into battle, a strategist whose very presence in a sector has caused the Tahn to surrender in droves.'

"Droves," Mahoney said. "I got more POW interrogators than I do POWs."

"Yeah," the Emperor agreed. "I would've said hordes. Better word."

Mahoney went on. "'Now we're preparing for the grand offensive,'" Fleet Marshal Mahoney said in a steely voice. "'Against the Fringe Worlds. I got thrown the hell out of there and didn't like it. I promised that one day I would return.

"'Now we're going back.

"'We have the Tahn reeling in all sectors. This should be the death blow. It will be a long and a hard struggle. But this will put us within sight of the end.'

"Drakh, drakh, drakh, charming wife, Spartan but well-chosen quarters, idolized by aides, men hold him in awe, dedicated to the welfare of his grunts. Drakh.

258

"The hack that wrote that deserves torture."

"*Por que?*" the Emperor asked.

Mahoney started to snap, then caught himself. Okay. The Emperor's getting cute. Getting up, he went to the sideboard and reached for the Scotch. He changed his mind in midreach and poured a blast of stregg.

"Okay, boss," he said, reseating himself. "I'm the straight man. You aren't upset that this writer seems to have bashed security in talking about where we're gonna strike next.

"And this is the first time I've heard about this general offensive. Ignore that. Let's get into the small stuff. Like I never met this hack in my life. And where'd that charming wife come from?"

Mahoney cogitated—then swore. "Boss, you're not really gonna do this to me, are you?"

"Sure am," the Emperor said. "We need a real hero-type general, and your name came out of the hopper. By the way, you think that story's bad, you ought to see what the *real* credit-dreadfuls are doing. How about the fact that you're a real fighting leader—you still carry a hand weapon everywhere. And the story about when you were a young lieutenant in charge of some outpost somewhere and the ration ship was delayed and for six months you fed your troops out of your own pocket? Real admirable. Especially considering you came from a poor but honest family."

Mahoney's father and grandfather before him had first been fairly high ranking officers and then made comfortable second and third careers in civilian megacorporations.

"I say again my last. Why?"

"Maybe the twinkle in your Irish eyes," the Emperor suggested. "Or maybe because I've got the Tahn in a reactive situation and am grinding it in.

"By the way. That wasn't a breach of security. We—or rather you—*are* going against the Fringe Worlds. With every ship and troopie I can strip out of other sectors. And I want the Tahn to know about it.

"Their prestige isn't doing too good these days, what with Lord Fehrle happening to have gotten dead and their legions getting obliterated.

"The Tahn believe in symbols. I'm giving them one.

"Every clottin' 'cast that goes out is talking about how important those clottin' Fringe Worlds are to the Empire and to me personally. There is no way those imbeciles aren't going to take the bait."

The Emperor, having made one of his longer private statements, found it necessary to have a drink or two.

"So I'm part of the symbol?"

"Yep. You'll notice, if you do any reading besides Op orders, that I went and stole colorful bits from at least three old-time generals. And the hype is going to get worse.

"You see, Mahoney, we're going to win. Soon.

"Which brings up the question of what we're going to do with all these clottin' Tahn worlds. Rykor had a suggestion. Seems there's some types who respect the clot out of somebody who beats hell out of them."

Mahoney shook his head. "Don't understand that, sir. My dad always said the only people who fight and make up are tinkers and Englishmen. Whatever they are."

"Yeah. That's the way I've always operated, too," the Emperor agreed. "But we aren't Tahn.

"So you're going out to the Fringe Worlds. The Tahn are going to throw everything at you they can, and you're going to be my little Imperial meat grinder.

"Couple of side notes that might help you. We'll use Naha as a forward strike base into the Tahn worlds. So you'll be able to access a good left hook if you need it.

"Another thing. Seems there's this terrible conspiracy going on in the Tahn worlds."

Mahoney looked interested, if disbelieving.

"Said conspiracy is composed of a whole cluster of Tahn officers who maybe have been recorded as not being happy with the way the war's not being run.

"We can thank our friend Sten for discovering all these quote traitors endquote."

Both men grinned—unpleasantly.

"He built me a conspiracy and sent it forward. Now, some of my—pardon, the Tahn's—most trusted agents are leaking that conspiracy back. Category One intelligence and all that.

"Where were we?

"Oh, yeah. You've just finished slaughtering every Tahn

that shows up in the Fringe Worlds with a chip on her shoulder. So next, when we make the final assault into the Tahn worlds themselves, you'll be in charge.

"Don't plan on any long vacations after the war's over, either. Because I'm going to put you in as—hell, maybe I'll call it governor-general—for their whole stinkin' ex-empire. At which point you'll have ten years or so trying to teach the Tahn how to pretend they're human."

Mahoney meditated. Finally, he laughed. "Great stew, boss. Now all we have to do is catch the rabbit."

"Exactly," the Emperor agreed. "Do me a favor, Ian. Don't get your butt whipped out there in the Fringe Worlds. I don't want to have to start planning from day one all over."

CHAPTER FORTY-SEVEN

THE MEMBERS OF the Tahn High Council gloomed their way to order. The elder secretary drowned through the final draft of Lord Fehrle's official obituary. When he finished, the first order of business would be the vote for approval and then scheduling it for broadcast.

The second order of business would be the vote for Fehrle's successor. What would happen next was anybody's guess.

The king is dead, Pastour thought sourly. Long live the king.

He looked at the tight, guarded faces of his twenty-six colleagues. They were all holding their cards nipple-close to their chests. But Pastour already knew the outcome. He had counted the votes. Wichman's faction of nine was backing Atago. No surprise there. Wichman was in love with the trappings of war. And even among the military-minded Tahn, no single being shone more as a soldier than the Lady Atago.

The second faction—of equal size—favored a troika composed of various candidates but with Atago, Wichman, and Pastour mentioned most often. That left Pastour and his faction: another nine votes, nine swing votes to be played any way he chose. But there was no question in Pastour's mind on how to play the hand. All he had to do was wait through the endless droning of the late Lord Fehrle's accomplishments.

Sten had visited him again in his garden a few nights after Fehrle's death. Pastour did not know how he had gotten in— Sten had not used the drain again. The clot just seemed to appear out of the shadows of one of Pastour's most prized trees. As soon as he had spotted him, Pastour's Tahn emotions had jumped like a crown fire from frightened surprise to pure hating anger over Fehrle's assassination.

"Don't be stupid, Colonel," Sten had warned him. "The last thing your people need right now is a stupid man for a leader. A dead stupid man."

Pastour had pulled himself back. "What do you want this time?"

Sten had relaxed then. He had tucked his weapon away and hoisted himself up on his perch. It was a casual action, but Pastour realized that it was carefully calculated to eliminate any hint of threat from his body language.

"First of all, I heard about the changes at Koldyeze. I wanted to thank you for that."

Pastour shrugged. "There's nothing to thank me for. Nothing you said influenced me. It was the logical course."

"If that's how you want to think about it, Colonel, fine. We were just worried about some friends. Doesn't matter how they were taken care of. Just as long as it was done.

"Although I did notice some refinements from our discussion. A lot of new faces. Important new faces. I assume you're planning to use them as a hole card. If so, I've got to warn you. It won't work."

Pastour could not help showing his curiosity. "Are you telling me that if we held a gun to their heads, we couldn't win *some* concessions from your Emperor?"

"It'll just make him hit you harder," Sten said. "Believe me. I speak from long and very personal experience. The only thing you get out of the Emperor if you threaten him is a lot of bloody stumps."

Pastour understood. That was also the way of the Tahn. Perhaps that was where they had gone wrong years before. The public image of the Emperor was kindly, concerned, that of a vigorous and handsome young uncle with wisdom well beyond his visible age. But that was obviously a falsehood. Perhaps the Emperor was more Tahnlike than the Tahn themselves.

Pastour wondered how bloody the Emperor's vengeance would be if the prisoners—especially the important prisoners —of Koldyeze came to harm. Pastour shuddered for his people. He knew what *he* would do if he were in the Emperor's place.

He pulled himself back. Sten was studying him as if he were seeing Pastour's thoughts form and dissolve and re-form.

"Koldyeze is not why you're here," Pastour said flatly.

"No. That's only part of it."

Sten slid off his perch and started pacing up and down the aisle, casually peering at the plants in their hydroponic trays. "The Emperor is concerned about what's going to happen to you people next. Now that Fehrle is dead. Who's going to take over? Who will he have to deal with?"

"I imagine he would be," Pastour said, not bothering to hide his sarcasm. "I suppose he thinks we're just going to roll over and play dead. Like those old livies. The warrior chieftain is killed. The tribe loses its heart to fight. Another war won and over."

"If you think that," Sten said, "then you really don't know my boss. I imagine what's really on his mind is how many more of you he'll have to kill before you people finally realize you've lost.

"You do know you've lost, don't you?"

The question caught Pastour by surprise—mainly because he had been dodging it in his own mind for some time. And now he had to answer it. It was as if a great black storm cloud had been ripped open and he was standing under its emotional deluge. Defeat. Surrender. Humiliation. But, yes. They had lost. It was over, but there was nothing Pastour could do to stop the insanity. He could not bring himself to speak and only nodded.

"Then all you can do now is fight for what happens after the surrender," Sten said. "Peace with honor and all that diplomatic double-talk. What your people need very badly is a true leader who can deal with the Emperor and still guard the honor of the Tahn."

"And the Emperor thinks that person is me? Not a chance. I haven't the votes—assuming I was willing, of course."

"Assuming you were willing," Sten agreed. Both men realized that Pastour had just stepped over the line with that hedging phrase.

"Here's how the Emperor sees it," Sten continued. "The only clear leader anyone can hang a reputation on is Lady Atago. But she has too many enemies on the council to win the vote.

"Second is for there to be some kind of patched-together leadership group of compromise candidates. Say, Atago and one each from the major factions. I imagine your name would be on any such list."

Pastour knew it would. "And third?"

"There is no third," Sten said. "Only those two choices. And frankly, the way I personally see it, nothing ever came of group leadership. It tends to lead to costly blunders. No one is ever willing to take the blame, so nothing is ever done. Or you end up with political civil war, with no one in charge."

"I agree," Pastour said.

"Then the only logical choice," Sten said, "is Lady Atago."

Pastour could not believe what he was hearing. Sten was right, of course, but why would the Emperor back someone who had to be his greatest and most fervent enemy among the Tahn? Lady Atago was so single-minded that . . . And then he got it. That was just the quality—or weakness, depending on one's point of view—the Emperor needed.

It was like isolating a cancer that then could be simply and easily removed. Atago would lead the Tahn to final defeat. Someone else would hand over the sword. And the Eternal Emperor was betting that someone else would be Pastour.

"He *must* understand that I am no traitor," Pastour insisted, striking the bargain. "You must impress that on him."

"I will," Sten promised.

Then he turned away, moving toward the shadows. But just before he ducked out of sight, Sten turned back.

"Oh, I almost forgot. How's your health?"

"Excellent," Pastour said, wondering what the clot Sten was talking about.

"I wouldn't be too sure of that," Sten said. "If I were you, after the vote, I'd develop something lingering and nasty enough to warrant a long, well-deserved rest. Out of the line of fire."

Pastour had still been reacting to that mysterious bit of advice when he had realized that Sten was gone.

The elder secretary had finished reading and was calling for the first order of business. Atago and Wichman were glaring around at the other members of the council, sure they had a bitter fight on their hands. Pastour knew that all the private overtures they had made had been rebuffed and that they were resigned to a rare around-the-table battle. Pastour had carefully kept his people quietly neutral. The word was that they would vote for whoever the clear winner was. But there *could* be no clear winner. As soon as Atago lost the vote, the troika proposal would carry the day.

At least that was the conventional wisdom of the bean counters. The count began on Atago's side of the table. It would move through Pastour and his group, then the troika faction. The first nine "affirms" went swiftly. Then it was time for Pastour's vote.

"Abstain," the elder secretary said automatically. "Next?"

"Excuse me," Pastour said. "I haven't spoken yet."

The elder secretary peered at him, wondering what was going on.

"I don't want to abstain," Pastour said. "I want to vote affirmative."

His words were met by instant shock—and then excitement, as everyone realized what had just happened. There was a babble of voices and a plea for order, and then the vote flashed the rest of the way around the table.

In a moment it was unanimous, and Lady Atago was affirmed as the new leader of the Tahn High Council. The victory came so swiftly and so surprisingly that the gloom dropped from everyone's shoulders. Fehrle was forgotten, and the council members were pounding each other on the shoulders and generally congratulating themselves for their political wisdom.

They had a leader. It was time to face the enemy again.

"One question, my lady," one member of the council broke in. "The Imperial news reports are filled with stories about Imperial Fleet Marshal Ian Mahoney. He's sworn to return to the Fringe Worlds. Retake Cavite. How do you plan to deal with him? Or is it too early to say?"

Atago rose to her full, substantial height. Leadership glowed from her like a mythical aura—the stuff heroes were made of.

"I welcome him to try," Atago said. "I've beaten him before. Badly. In fact I took Cavite *and* the Fringe Worlds over his blasted and bleeding body. And this time I'd be glad to finish the job."

There were cheers all around, with one exception: Pastour. He poked up a finger for recognition. Atago could not help giving him a hate-edged glance. She did not know why he had backed her, but she expected that the price would be high. Then she caught herself, and the expression changed to a grim smile.

"Yes, Colonel?"

"Why is the Emperor putting so much importance on the Fringe Worlds? To me they no longer seem to be a particularly strategic target. Are we sure it's not just a ploy? To force us to commit?"

"Of course it is," Lady Atago said. "They're making it seem important so that any victory they win there will appear to take on greater meaning than it in fact would have."

"Then, if we react," Pastour said, "aren't we in danger of turning fiction into reality?"

"Only if they beat us," Atago said. "And I promise you that can't happen. I've proved it once, and I'll do it again. And we'll turn the Emperor's sword back on himself."

With that promise, Lady Atago double-thought her way into taking the Emperor's bait. And Pastour fully understood the Emperor's strategy. The only thing still puzzling him was Sten's odd comment about his health.

"Now for the next order of business," Lady Atago went on. "I have here a list. A very important list. It was stolen by our agents from Imperial files."

The council members looked at the printout she was holding in her hand. She was waving it at them like some kind of accusation.

"On it are seventy-two names. Tahn names. Traitors. And I ask full authority to purge them from our midst. And that's only the start. I want to follow their trail to wherever it might lead. No matter how high the traitor, no matter how. . ."

Pastour tried an experimental first cough.

CHAPTER FORTY-EIGHT

THE CAFETERIA HAD several advantages, but they were not visible to normal citizens. To them, the large converted storage building stank of grease and the unwashed, and it was up a side street in a very bad part of the port city of Soward. It looked like a very good place to get either ptomaine or a shank inserted between the third and fourth ribs.

That was an accurate summation.

But it did have very definite advantages: It was not automated. Instead, it was run by living beings who really did not care what happened so long as the blood was mopped up afterward. Caff was a tenth-credit, and alk a half-credit. The alk, of course, had never seen an Imperial tax stamp.

Anyone was welcome to hang out as long as he, she, or it wanted. A cup of caff could be nursed for half a day, and no one would object. It was an excellent place to make an illegal drug deal, plan a job, or just hang out, as an alternative to sitting in one's apartment, letting the four walls close in.

To Chapelle, the cafeteria had still other advantages.

He could stare for hours at the blank concrete building across the street and listen to the voices. Every day he learned of a new iniquity and injustice caused by the Emperor.

Sullamora's operating team had removed the subaudible projectors weeks earlier. Chapelle listened to voices of his own making, and the stories they told were fascinating.

A few days earlier, he had realized that he *had* to do something. Just what, he was not sure. The only possibility he could think of was the cafeteria's other advantage—its proximity to the Democratic Education Center.

Any war, no matter how "just," had opponents. Opposition ranged from true pacifism, through a quite logical reluctance to get one's ass shot off for any reason whatsoever, and on into less savory areas.

It was a constant battle for the Emperor to keep his intelligence organizations somewhat under control. Someone who merely thought—or even said—that the Eternal Emperor was full of drakh was not a danger to society, the Emperor had to remind his CI types.

It was a nice theory. At present, however, it was not widely practiced. Freedom of speech, like many other civil liberties, was not encouraged at that time. There were many thousand dissenters, who had merely mildly suggested that the Eternal Emperor did not have all the answers, and were spending the war in internment centers.

The Democratic Education Center was something else entirely. Its philosophy was very simple: that the Empire had overreacted to the Tahn and that more peaceful means could have been used. Before the war the center had lobbied for Imperial funding to establish other centers within the Tahn Empire. The good people of the society believed that truth would win out—once a Tahn, no matter what his class, was shown that his socieity was inhumane, that society would be changed. Fortunately, funding was not granted, and none of the theorists ended up as missionary stew.

The Tahn being what they were, they had loudly welcomed the existence of the Democratic Education Centers as long as they were all located on Imperial worlds. And they had promptly used the organization as a front.

All the active agents had been rounded up at that point, of course. But the center continued to exist—at the Emperor's teeth-gritted acceptance. The organization provided an excellent means of locating future dissidents and was riddled with Imperial Intelligence operatives. Imperial Intelligence did not realize that if it were not for their own agents, the center would have gone bankrupt years earlier. Even a front organization required regular dues paying, and very few of the center's members were considered politically employable at anything above the janitorial level.

Chapelle had known of the center for some time. How he had learned about it, he was not sure. The information, of course, had been planted in an early subaudible broadcast.

Not that Sullamora actually wanted Chapelle to join the organization. But once the man had reached that decision, the fourth stage of his education could begin.

The problem was that Chapelle appeared to be somewhat brighter than Sullamora's profile would have suggested. Even though Chapelle was a näif, he had somehow thought that the evil Emperor's agents might have penetrated the center. His walking through that door, Chapelle knew, would be his death. The Emperor would use that as an excuse to grab and torture Chapelle and then put him into a lethal chamber, just as the voices had told him had happened to millions of others.

But there appeared to be no alternative, Chapelle brooded.

Realizing there was somebody standing beside his table, Chapelle brought himself back and cowered. Not that he had ever been threatened in the cafeteria—the other patrons realized that it was very unlikely that Chapelle had anything worth stealing. Plus there was a certain sheen in his eye that suggested that even pushing the man around for sport could produce unpleasant ramifications.

The man did not belong in this dive, Chapelle thought; in fact, he belonged even less than Chapelle did. He was older. Gray-haired. Soberly and expensively dressed. Chapelle wondered why the man had not been instantly jackrolled, then eyed the bulging muscles and the barely visible scar on the man's neck. No. The man was not an easy target.

The man looked sternly at Chapelle. "You don't belong here," he said flatly.

Chapelle stammered—and the man suddenly smiled.

"I don't, either. But I seem to have a problem."

Somehow, unasked, he was sitting across from Chapelle.

"My problem is that I'm lost." He laughed—a rich bass laugh that showed a man who had learned the vagaries of the world and appreciated them. "I thought that just because I still had that built-in compass I could find my way around a city. Wrong again, Colonel General Suvorov."

Chapelle gaped. "You're a *general*?"

"Forty years. Pioneer Development Corps. Retired. Guess it's a courtesy title now. At least the clottin' Empire hasn't figured out a way to take *that* away from me, too. Or at least not yet.

"At any rate, I'm new here on Prime World. Thought I knew my way around. Got lost. Looked for somebody who might be able to help. Everybody I saw looked like the only help they'd give me is into a dark alley.

"Except you."

Chapelle was embarrassed.

"I'd be grateful," the man who called himself Suvorov said, "if I could get a guide back to the nearest pneumostation and out of this slum."

Chapelle was only too grateful to volunteer.

At the station Suvorov checked the schedule and muttered. "Typical. Very typical." He elaborated—the first pneumosubway run out to where he had rented quarters was an hour away. "Talk about your bureaucracies. Makes sense not to schedule runs out to where people who can pay live. But not when you've blocked all the gravcabs out of business.

"Wartime contingencies."

"You know, Sr. Chapelle, and I probably shouldn't be saying this to a stranger, but this is sure a good example of the way the Emperor thinks."

Chapelle nodded eagerly.

"Although," Suvorov went on, "you'd have to have been out on some of the Pioneer Sectors to see what it's really like. Out where there aren't any laws. Except the kind one person makes.

"And out there, you better not talk too loudly about things like that.

"Guess I was lucky. All that happened to me was I got requested to resign. And then the agrofarm I'd built up got requisitioned by the Imperial Quartermaster Corps.

"Why I'm here on Prime. Hoping I'd be able to get my toady rep to do something. Should've known better. He's been bought and sold so many times, he ought to have his soul in for a rebuild.

"Sorry. Man doesn't respect somebody whining."

During the wait, it was very natural for Suvorov to buy Chapelle a meal at a very expensive restaurant—and express amazement when he found out that Chapelle was an ex-landing controller.

"Did a lot of things. Have to, when you're out on the frontiers. But I could never handle all the things you people have to keep in your mind." He paused. "Not prying . . . but what the hell are you doing stuck down there in that slum? You don't have to answer."

Chapelle did, of course.

Suvorov was aghast. "Guess you feel sorry for yourself for not having shoes till you run across the man with prosthetics," he said. "You really got the shaft."

He ordered a second bottle of wine.

Chapelle, being a near-teetotaler even when he had credits, got a little drunk. And so did Suvorov.

"You know, Chapelle," he said over dessert. "One thing I'm sorry I never had was a son. Nothing left behind once I'm gone.

"Clotting Emperor—sorry for the language—is going to make sure of that."

They had brandies, and he called for the bill.

Outside the restaurant, Suvorov looked at Chapelle and apologized. He had gotten his guide and new friend drunk. It sure as hell would not be safe for the young man to go down those mean streets in his condition.

Chapelle should come stay with him. Hell, that clotting mansion he was leasing had room for a whole recon force.

Chapelle, stomach and mind full, found it easy to agree.

He also found it easy to agree the next day when Suvorov suggested that Chapelle might consider staying on. "Guess we both know I need a guide around this clotting planet. Besides, you're easy to talk to, son.

"I really like what you've been telling me about the Emperor. Learning a lot, I am."

Six weeks later Suvorov presented Chapelle with a willy-gun—and showed him the previously sealed shooting gallery below the mansion.

CHAPTER FORTY-NINE

LADY ATAGO'S HEADQUARTERS/HOME was as Spartan and single-purpose as her mind. The furnishings were sparse and deliberately uncomfortable. It was not a place for lounging but for quick decision making. Aides came with their reports, sat on hard nervous edges for her decision or comments, and then were quickly gone, to be replaced by others.

The only thing on her desk was a small, framed fading fax print of the Eternal Emperor. She kept it there to focus herself constantly on her enemy. Atago would have been mildly surprised to learn that her opponent had done something similar; her picture had recently gone up in place of Lord Fehrle's in the Eternal Emperor's office.

On the far black-glass wall was a constantly changing map of the disputed areas. The Imperial positions were in red, the Tahn in green. The green areas had been swiftly dwindling of late, pinching in from the sides, with a red spearhead driving toward the Fringe Worlds. Even Erebus, that distant system Lady Atago had single-handedly turned into one of the great war factories of history, was firmly in Imperial control.

In any age Lady Atago would have been considered a military genius. And since Fehrle's death she had been poring over the battle map, desperately searching for an unexpected blow that would reverse the tide.

Although she had never heard of the man, Atago would have known and approved of Napoleon's decision to land 35,000 troops in Egypt, seemingly far from the main contest. And she would have been dismayed at his failed attempts to flank Britain in Ireland. The reasoning was sound; it was only the application that had gone wrong. And, as happened to many great generals, it was the details that were overwhelming her. The only thing that was clear to her was that whatever the target, she had to set the stage first. She needed a victory, and she needed it badly.

The only place she could see such a victory coming was in the Fringe Worlds. The most frustrating thing about that was that she had to wait for the Emperor to play the card before she could attempt to trump him. And Lady Atago was too much of a Tahn to be good at playing a waiting game.

Adding to that frustration was the constant barking of her aides, calling her attention to this, bemoaning that, and continually demanding that she concentrate on the bottom line. Early that morning, for example, her financial advisers had descended, warning her of the empty treasury and waving demands for payments from allies and neutrals alike.

"Tell them to wait," she had said angrily. "I haven't heard of any Imperial bankers dunning the Emperor. And this war has to be costing him five or six times what it's costing us."

"That's different," one adviser had said. "The Emperor has a financial history. We don't. Besides, he's fighting on borrowed funds at three percent interest. We're fighting at upwards of fifty percent."

Lady Atago did not know whether to scream for the adviser's instant execution or to cry, although crying was something no Tahn did easily. It wounded her soldier's soul that this conflict could boil down to something so filthy as money. But the advisers assured her that all was not lost.

After the Fringe Worlds battle—assuming victory—they would be able to bargain for much better terms, and the money tap would be turned on again. But for the time being, the only thing she could do was order the seizure, stripping, and selling of everything of value.

Her advisers did not dare tell her that there was almost nothing left. Even the plas inner walls and insulation in the meanest of Tahn dwellings had already been carried away by the tax collectors and sold for scrap.

And so, blocked from action at every corner, Lady Atago turned inward. If she could not yet fight, she would put the Tahn house in order. At the top of her agenda was the leaked list of seventy-two traitors. She attacked the problem with cold glee. The Tahn military police were already sweeping them up.

Along with the seventy-two they were arresting anyone connected with those foul beings. Not only that, but more and more names were surfacing daily. Lady Atago realized that some of the victims were innocent—their names appeared merely because they had made the wrong enemies. But that was a fact she was willing to live with. Besides, she had a list of those who were providing the names. She was already ordering police visits to those homes. Filling the jails and military tribunals with suspects was providing an outlet for her frustrations. It was a new and different kind of body count, and she pursued it with relish.

And so it was a flushed and glowing Lady Atago who ushered Wichman into her office. If only the livies could capture this, he had thought as she greeted him. She was beautiful and sensuous and deadly—every millimeter of her tall, flowing form was that of a great Tahn hero. To see her, to be near her, was to realize that the current difficulties were momentary, that victory must eventually fall to the righteous.

The purpose of Lord Wichman's visit was to aid Atago in ferreting out wrong-thinkers. He came armed with Lo Prek's steadily mounting evidence of criminality and corruption on Heath.

Lo Prek had examined thousands of police and intelligence log entries and had sifted out evidence that Heath was in the grip of a wave of crime and dissidence. Moreover, he had tracked many of the crimes that appeared to be minor hooliganisms back to the bureaucracies and officials responsible. That many of the tarnished were in fact blameless did not matter, because Lo Prek had uncovered a pattern that led to the flawless conclusion that an Imperial conspiracy was behind the crime wave.

Lo Prek was correct in every detail, including the fact that

Sten was not only behind that conspiracy but directing it. That was the only point that Wichman disbelieved and for the moment withheld from Lady Atago. When Lo Prek had haltingly spelled out his findings, Wichman had only buried a smile at the man's obsession.

If the carrot of the mythical Sten produced such results, Wichman would only encourage him. Just because Lo Prek was insane, it did not necessarily follow that he was stupid.

As Lady Atago leafed through the printout with growing enthusiasm, Wichman congratulated himself on his foresight in roping Lo Prek into his organization.

"This is exactly what we need, my lord," Atago said. "I admire your dedication. If only a few others . . . I must confess, some of the members of the High Council are disappointing me.

"They only do what is absolutely necessary. They take nothing upon themselves. No extra effort. Sometimes I wonder if they expect me to fight this whole thing alone."

Wichman preened but quickly made halfhearted noises of support for his colleagues. Lady Atago waved him down.

"Take Pastour, for example," she said. "He's practically gone into retirement. I know he's ill, but . . . Oh, well. I suppose we should be grateful for his support. And at least he's continuing his work at Koldyeze. An amazingly successful program. Personally, I never held out much for it. Expecting prisoners—cowards and malcontents all—to perform that well. In fact, according to the latest data, all previous performance records have been broken."

The data she was referring to had all come from Sten and Virunga's Golden Worm. Mickied figures were hiding what was in reality a dismal performance that had only worsened as the Tahn shipped captured dignitaries to Koldyeze.

The thought of Koldyeze darkened Wichman's mood. It did not help that the people he had placed there grudgingly supported the data that so impressed Lady Atago. Still, he firmly believed that if he were in control at Koldyeze, he would be able to find far better uses for the prisoners. Especially now that it housed the best and the brightest of the Imperial prisoners. Sometimes he was awakened by dreams of what he would do to them. He never remembered the details of the dreams, only that they were pleasurable.

Lady Atago brought him back to his good mood and the business at hand. "I wonder if I could impose myself on you, my lord?"

Wichman made self-deprecating sounds. Atago ignored him. She tapped the report compiled by Lo Prek.

"I would like you to assume command of this program," she said. "I've not been pleased with the results of the sweeps so far. So many seem to be slipping through the net.

"I have been finding myself distrusting the officials responsible for carrying out my aims. And from the information you have gathered here, I may have good reason. There may be more than laziness and inefficiency behind their lack of performance."

Wichman did not know what to say. He was too overcome by emotion. To think that his efforts met favor with a hero the like of Lady Atago! He gladly accepted the new responsibilities. Also, not too far in the back of his mind was the realization of just how much power had been handed him.

Just as he was regaining his composure and was about to thank her, Atago broke in with a new thought.

"There seems to be one thing missing, however," she said as she folded up Lo Prek's study. "There is a clearly indicated trail here. But it seems to stop short. It's as if something, or someone, has been left out."

Lady Atago was right. The only part of the report Wichman had excised was the man Lo Prek believed responsible for the conspiracy: Sten. Wichman took a deep breath and then plunged in. He explained about Lo Prek and about the little being's belief that the person behind it all was also the being responsible for the murder of his brother. Lady Atago nodded as he talked. Lo Prek was clearly mad, but as a Tahn she could understand his obsession for revenge.

"Who is this man?" she finally asked.

Wichman told her.

Lady Atago frowned. The name was familiar. "Sten?" she asked. "Would that be a Commander Sten?"

Wichman said it was but wondered how she knew the rank. But he did not ask, because her face had suddenly gone blank. As if she was remembering something.

The Forez *was vomiting fire. Firing everything—anything
—to stop the* Swampscott. *Lady Atago leaned over Admiral
Deska, gaping in amazement at the damage the enemy ship
was taking. There seemed to be little left, and even as she
watched, huge hunks of the* Swampscott *were being hurled
away into space as Deska's guns and missiles hammered,
hammered, hammered. But still, the* Swampscott's *chainguns
kept firing. Wild communications, monitored by her probes,
told her that Commander Sten was the ship's CO. Over and
over, Deska killed the ship, but it kept coming in.*

*Then she heard the strangest voice mocking her. "Ah hae
y' noo, lass." She would never know that the voice was that of
Sten's second in command, Alex Kilgour. And then the chortle
became two Vydals spearing out from the oddness that was the*
Swampscott. *The* Forez *was racked by the explosion. The
blast tore a wall chart from a bulkhead and sent it spinning
into Admiral Deska. His eviscerated corpse slammed into her,
and she was falling back—back, back, into darkness. Later,
when she had resumed consciousness, she had fought off her
nurses and sent a boarding party to the* Swampscott. *She
wanted the names of everyone aboard the ship—living or
dead.*

*Atago personally checked through the ID discs until she
found the correct one. Sten. And then she carefully wiped the
blood away to make sure.*

"The man's insane, all right," Lady Atago finally said to
Wichman. "Sten is dead. I killed him myself."

Then she remembered something else.

"Twice." The word was a whisper.

"Pardon, my lady?"

"Twice. I killed him once before. And then he came back.
And I killed him again." She shuddered, pushing away the
ghosts.

A moment later, Wichman found himself being ushered
gently out the door. He left, his ardor for his heroine un-
cooled. Still, he could not help wondering at the demons, or
demon, who troubled Lady Atago's sleep.

CHAPTER FIFTY

STEN FORCED HIS body to fit the slight depression that was the only cover for 100 meters on either side of him. The prison searchlight swept across the barren landscape, methodically exploding deep shadows into light. To Sten, it seemed to hesitate a beat just before it crossed over his curled form. It was as if a living mind, rather than a computer, controlled it. Sten felt himself tense as insane thoughts flashed through his mind: Did someone know he was there? A gloating someone who was toying with him? Had there been a tip-off? Would the light suddenly stop on him, and then a dozen laughing Tahn guards jump out of the darkness to drag him into Koldyeze for a few years of solitary confinement, periodic torture, and then execution? Sten ran an old Mantis Section mantra through his mind and felt his pulse slow to normal and his breathing ease.

The light passed over him without incident.

Sten lifted his head and peered into the darkness. He pushed his senses up the series of gradual rises and then the steep hill that led to the rear of Koldyeze and his own private back entrance. Nothing.

Still, he could feel his hackles rise at the thought of pulling aside the camouflage that covered the entrance and reentering the tunnel. Then he would crawl into the catacombs beneath Koldyeze. And finally he would be back in prison!

Alex had protested when Sten announced his plan to personally touch base with Virunga. There was nothing to worry about, Sten had reassured his friend. He would be in and out before dawn.

"Y'r stir-crazy a' me, lad," Alex had said. "Ah nae hae kenned th' hae wee symptoms. When Ah wae but kilt-hem high, m' mum gie me three warnings: Nae play a' cards wi' ae

278

bonny lass—"At that he had shot St. Clair a grin full of Kilgour charm. "—nae eat ae a place called Campbell's, and nae
go inta a room wi' brawny bars ae its door!"

Clot! Sten thought. Kilgour's mum was right! What was he
thinking of? His body temperature dropped to zero at even the
prospect of another long stretch of forced confinement. It was
at that point, as he hesitated between going on and calling the
whole thing off, that he heard footsteps. And then humming.
It was a Tahn sentry. Freezing was no trouble at all.

Sten hugged the depression, turning his head just slightly
to the side so that he could see—a cautious hunter's peep he
had learned in Mantis basic. You never tested your quarry's
instincts by looking directly at him.

Only to the sides of him, young Sten, he warned himself,
and then only for a tick at a time. He saw that the sentry's path
would bisect his hiding place only a half meter or so from his
head. The sentry's steps were slow, ambling.

He or she was badly trained, lazy, or just plain vanilla
stupid. As the sentry approached, the humming grew louder.
Sten, recognizing it as a popular Tahn war-crossed lover's
ballad always in demand from the lower-class crowds at St.
Clair's club, chose a combination of all three.

Then he felt a heavy bootheel crush his fingers and resisted
the temptation to snatch his outstretched hand away. The
sentry paused, and agony smashed up Sten's arm as the Tahn
turned slightly to the side—grinding Sten's fingers even further—and stopped.

There was the fumbling of a heavy greatcoat and then
blinding pain as the sentry shifted most of the weight to the
foot, jamming Sten's hand into the ground. Sudden relief
flooded in as the Tahn stepped away, still fumbling with
clothing, then more pain as the blood forced itself through
crushed capillaries and veins.

Sten sensed that the sentry's back was turned to him. His
head rose slightly, and he saw something large and pale peering at him. It was the sentry's naked behind.

From the splashing sounds on the ground, it was pretty
obvious what she was doing. As she rose from the squatting
position, adjusting her uniform, Sten curled his fingers, and

his knife dropped from the surgical sheath in his arm. Its slim coldness in his palm comforted him.

Then he sensed startled motion. He had been discovered! Sten shot up like a great sea beast with a head full of glittering fangs rising above the surface of the water.

Numb fingers of one hand reached for her throat, and his knife hand drove at her abdomen. For one brief flash, Sten saw the sentry's face. She was young, no more than sixteen. And slender—no, skinny. So skinny that she looked like a poor, scrawny bird with flapping greatcoat wings. The eyes that widened just before death were filled with innocence and terror. A child, but a child who was about to die just the same.

It was prudence, not pity, that saved the girl's life. It was because there was no time to hide the body that Sten held back just before the knife plunged its needle length into her. Instead, he took a chance that his numbed fingers would work before she could scream.

He pinched the artery that cut off the flow of blood to her brain and then caught her in his arms as she collapsed. He lowered her carefully to the ground, fished in his pocket for a bester grenade, pulled the pin, covered, and blanked her memory.

There would be hell to pay when her sergeant found her on his next rounds. She would be cuddled up softly on the ground, sleeping the sleep of the blessed. The beating the sergeant would administer for sleeping on duty would be awful. But what were a few cracked ribs compared to a pile of pale guts glistening in the starlight?

Sten made sure the young sentry was comfortable, then slithered on up the hill, the ghost of her song humming softly in his head.

The chair groaned in protest as Virunga's 300-kilo-plus body rocked in mirth. Sten was catching him up on the war news. Although he tried not to paint a too-glowing picture of things, he could not help pumping up a morsel into a soufflé here and there for the hope-starved N'Ranya.

There was also a great deal of information about Sten's current activities on Heath that he was forced to censor on a need-to-know basis. And so, when he had the opportunity to embellish, he did, knowing that Virunga would do some censoring of his own when he filled in the others on Sten's visit. At the moment Sten was telling his old CO about St. Clair and L'n's adventures, exaggerating only a bit.

". . . and so, there they were, General Lunga, his two aides, and at least a dozen joys of both sexes, and a couple in between, when they get the call.

"Priority One. Ears only. And all that rot. So the general shoos the whole shebang out. Punches in a supersecure line on his porta-com, and half a belch later he's on a direct to some muckitymuck aide to Atago herself.

"The aide double-checks. Is everything A-okay? No keen little ears hiding in a closet? The general looks around, then gives the guy an all-clear. The general gets his orders. He's to get his big-brass Tahn butt to the Fringe Worlds not yesterday but the day before yesterday. Big things are coming down.

"The general does a little lightweight protesting. Already heavy duties and that sort of thing. Meaning brass or no, he expects to get his previously reported butt shot off out there.

"There's a big long discussion. Pros and cons of ship and troop movements. A small shouting match. The general loses and storms out, his two boot shiners in tow.

"Of course, what he doesn't realize is that we've taken the whole thing down. Heard every word!"

"The . . . room . . . bugged," Virunga said flatly, knowledgeably.

"Not a chance," Sten said. "That room is permanently leased for the general's pleasures. His people run a sweep through before he comes and after he leaves."

"So how—"

"L'n," Sten said. "She heard the whole thing. The entire time the general was talking, she was curled up in the corner. Right in plain sight. You see, the general thinks she's just a pet. A largish, pinkish, cattish-type pet."

Virunga laughed again. But then the laughter cut off in midchortle. "Are . . . you positive all . . . this is good for . . . her? L'n is so . . ." His words trailed off not out of linguistic patterns but because of a lack of vocabulary for what L'n had to be witnessing daily.

"Innocent? Sheltered? Sensitive?" Sten filled it in for him. Virunga nodded.

"Not anymore," Sten said. "You wouldn't believe the change. She made the jump from Koldyeze to freedom and landed on all four of her pretty little feet. Even Michele—I mean, St. Clair—is surprised how she's blossomed. She sounds like a dockworker now. Or a pro thief. It's cheena, and sus, and a pretty good use of drakh and clot when she needs them."

Virunga marveled at that. He was soaking up everything Sten said as if he were personally living each word. After his own years as a prisoner of war, Sten understood that, just as he knew that in a few days the euphoria would die and be replaced by deep depression. And the great walls of Koldyeze would press in even more. Then Virunga—along with the others whom he chose to tell about Sten—would start doubting if he would ever live to be free again. And the chances were, Sten thought, that the doubters would be right. He knew the war would end soon, but he could offer no guarantees on the fate of the Koldyeze prisoners in the melee that was sure to precede the Tahn's last fighting gasp.

But Sten had a plan—a plan that would do more than just relieve a little of the depression. It was a plan designed not only to save as many prisoners' lives as possible but also to hand any Imperial invasion force a small edge in the battle for Heath. It would not be a fifth ace. No, not that good. But it just might be a fifth face card of some kind. And there was a glimmer that it might even fill an inside straight.

You gotta quit thinking like Michele, Sten told himself. I mean, St. Clair. Like an imp, her lush form popped into his mind. Soft fingers. Even softer lips. Tingling whispers in his ear. Knock it off, Commander. Uh, Admiral, that is. Keep your mind on business. Remember, you're a high-ranking officer now.

Still, Admiral Sten had to bury a grin and cross one leg over the other. Thankfully, Virunga interrupted his thoughts.

"What . . . was . . . name of . . . Michele's—I mean . . . St. Clair's . . . casino again?"

Sten looked closer at Virunga. Had he guessed? The blank expression on the big, beetle-browed face gave no clue.

"The K'ton Klub," Sten said. "Why?"

"Oh . . . I just . . . didn't know . . . the young woman had
. . . knowledge of . . . music."

"I didn't know you did, either," Sten said, mildly surprised.

"Yes . . . Oh . . . yes. I do. Although I . . . cannot . . . enjoy
any longer." He tapped his ears. "Tone-deaf . . . now. An old
. . . artillerybeing's . . . complaint. The guns . . . deadened . . .
the ears. But when . . . I was . . . young. I very much . . .
enjoyed the . . . music. I even . . . played . . ." He fingered an
imaginary instrument. "A little . . . The saxophone. Not . . .
the synth-sax . . . But . . . with the . . . reed. A real . . . reed. It
sounded . . . so . . . Ah. I cannot . . . describe."

There was silence as Battery Commander (Lieutenant Colonel) Virunga briefly recalled a time before he gave up the
wail of the saxophone for the thunder of guns.

More clottin' music, Sten thought. There must have been
something catching at Koldyeze. Something in the air.

In a way he was correct. There was something in the air at
Koldyeze. A great deal had happened since his chat with Pastour. To begin with, the prison was quickly becoming jammed
with prisoners—of every variety, from high-ranking officers,
to diplomats, to even a few captured provincial governors.
The Tahn were heaping all their golden eggs in one big stone-
walled basket.

And Pastour had heeded Sten's words about their treatment. Along with the prisoners, he had filtered in a small
contingent of his own loyal officials. All of them had been
placed in key positions. A stern warning went out that all
inter-Empire laws involving prisoners of war must be adhered
to down to the finest point. The clampdown was so severe that
even Avrenti and Genrikh—especially Genrikh—were afraid
to move.

Pastour had also set up a personal office inside Koldyeze.
And he had made a habit of unannounced visits in which
shaking transgressors would be lined up outside his office and
called in one by one to be dealt with personally.

On top of all that, the awful losses the Tahn had suffered
made it increasingly difficult for Derzhin to keep the prisoner-
guard ratio at any kind of rational level. He was down to

recruiting the very young or the very old. Supply shortages had also undermined the guards' morale. At home, and even on the job, their rations were at starvation level. And the treasure trove of foodstuffs and other materials that Cristata and Sten had discovered in the catacombs not only kept the prisoners from suffering equally but left them plenty for generous bribes.

It was so bewildering to many of those untrained Tahn that they seemed puzzled about whose side they were really on. If there were two sides to a troubling incident, the new breed of guards instinctively sided with the prisoners. The prisoners fed them, didn't they? They even gave them a little for their families, didn't they?

Besides, even Lady Atago's thought police could not squash the rumors that the war would end soon—and not in the Tahn's favor. Like Chetwynd, many of the new guards had decided to copper their bets and look out for their own hides.

There was something in the wind, all right, but Sten was hoping it would not all turn to flying drakh when the Tahn hit the fan. And that was why Sten had slipped back into Koldyeze. He wanted to give Virunga something to throw back.

He had told Virunga that Sorensen was Mantis and a battle computer, plus given Virunga Sorensen's activating code word. Now Gaaronk would be a backup computer. As for what Sorensen could be used for:

"Do you ever get up on the walls to snoop around?"

"A few . . . times. It is . . . difficult . . . with my . . . injuries." Virunga gripped his cane tighter.

"When you look at the city, what do you see?"

Virunga laughed. ". . . Lately . . . some big . . . holes in . . . ground. Our bombers . . . did . . . well!"

"Too right," Sten agreed. "But that's not what I meant. I mean as an old artillerybeing. What do you see when you see the city?"

Virunga's giant brows furrowed, his eyes nearly bushing out of sight. Then he gave another laugh—more like a bark, really.

"Koldyeze . . . is the highest . . . point," he said. "If . . . I had my . . . guns . . ." He lapsed into a brief dream of shells falling on Heath. His shells. Then he snapped into alertness.

Sten could see coordinates flashing across his eyes. There were many targets of opportunity. He stirred in excitement, remembering the stored weapons hidden in the catacombs.

"I . . . can get . . . the guns," he said. "They're . . . much out of . . . date. But . . . I can . . . fix them."

He blinked out of his planning and stared at Sten. There were no ifs or hows or buts in his next question.

"When? Just . . . tell me . . . when?"

Sten came to his feet and walked over to the N'Ranya. He gave the big slab of furry muscle and bone that Virunga called a shoulder a hard squeeze. "I'll get word to you," he said. "You just be ready."

Virunga merely nodded. But Sten could tell that in his mind, Virunga was a battery commander again, and he was already moving up his guns.

CHAPTER FIFTY-ONE

STEN SLIPPED OUT of Koldyeze just before dawn. As planned, he hid in the rubble surrounding the ancient monastery and waited for the lines of sleepy workers to stagger out of the slums and join the long labor lines that were marched off to the factories each day. Sten skipped the first two formations.

He was much too clean-cut for the ragged bands of obvious textile dye workers. The third group was a little cleaner, a little better dressed. From the conversations he big-eared after he joined them, most of those Tahn workers toiled at pharmaceutical vats or were janitorial crews for the munitions works.

By the time anyone woke up enough to wonder who the new guy might be, they were already in the center of the city, and Sten broke off to mingle with a marketing crowd. He bought a string bag and a greasy blob of some kind of animal protein and elbowed his way into a lane of Tahn who were vaguely pressing toward the direction of Chaboya and the K'ton Klub. Two more turns, a dive down an alley, and he would be home with a nice cold brew.

There was a stirring in the crowd ahead of him, then puzzled muttering. Before Sten had a chance to figure out what was going on, the crowd moved around the corner—to be greeted by a long line of green-uniformed Tahn cops spread out across the street, blocking the way. Sten's heart jumped orbit, and he whirled, crushing toes and ignoring protests. And as he whirled, another long green line snaked across the street, barring the back door. He was trapped in a Tahn sweep!

The beefy cops pressed in, their stun rods held at port arms, their black faceshields jutting forward. The crowd was strangely—Sten thought—silent, the muttering turning to a puzzled lowing with a few barks of pain as someone ran afoul of a stun rod.

Then phalanxes broke off from the main cop lines and speared through the crowd. Sten noticed from the rank tabs that the phalanxes were composed entirely of sergeants. Their eyes had purposeful hunters' looks as they scanned faces in the crowd, picking individuals out with a shout. "You! You! You!" Before any of the unfortunates had a hope of reacting, they were muscled into the wedge and swept away.

Sten was trying to back off, to slip close to a wall and then tunnel out through the mass of Tahn around him. Just as his elbow dug back, expecting more soft flesh but finding the hardness of a wall, an enormous sergeant spotted him. The cop thrust his stun rod out like a bludgeon, screaming, "You!"

And before he knew it, Sten was being strong-armed into the wedge and carried off to clot knew where.

More than a million bodies were crammed into Heath's gigantic central square. The late-morning sun was turning hotter, and the crowd was packed so densely that the stink from their sweating bodies rose like fog from a primordial swamp.

Vidscreens many stories high had been set up on three sides. On the fourth was a towering porta-stage, behind it the blackened hole and ruins of all that was left of the Tahn High Council's palace after the Imperial bombing raid.

Sten's group was trotted around the edges of the crowd to

its front, and huge placards were thrust into their hands. Still waiting for the ax to fall, Sten glanced at the sign he held. "Down With Imperialist Hegemony!" it screamed in thick, blood-red letters.

A big sergeant threatened with a stun rod. "Wave the sign!" he screamed like a basic-training drill instructor.

"Oh. Okay," Sten said. And he waved the sign.

"Cheer for victory!" the sergeant advised him at the top of his lungs.

"Sure," Sten said.

And he began cheering for victory. Taking a clue from the others, he pumped his sign up and down vigorously. To begin with, he confined himself to bellows about nothing. Then, as the crowd's voice grew into an incomprehensible roar, Sten started relaxing. He was not in trouble at all. All he had to do was stand there and demonstrate for the Tahn livie camera crews, hear whatever speech he was supposed to listen to, and then go home when it was over. No problem. So he would be a couple of hours late.

Then he remembered the peculiar habit all totalitarian speakers had of railing on for half the day, and corrected that to maybe five or six hours late. It would be wearying, but he had undergone far worse on many other cesspools—such as the Lupus Cluster, where the phrase "papal bull" took on new meaning. So he decided to enjoy himself a little and mixed in a few obscenities with his bellows.

Five hours later Sten realized he had yet to cure himself of optimism. The crowd was still screaming—even louder than before—and any sign of weariness was quickly prodded out of them by roving cops with stun rods set on blister. And on the stage there was still no sign of activity.

Then from the distance he heard a howling sound that triggered his old infantryman's instincts, and he hunched his shoulders and pulled his neck in just before a black tacship squadron popped up over the horizon behind the ruined palace and thundered over the crowd so low that it gave the lie to the fact that there were no nerves in bone marrow.

It was all Sten could do to keep from flinging himself to the ground as that squadron was followed by another and then another, and then the whole sky became black as a thick fleet of battlewagons came between the sun and the ground in an awesome display of Tahn military might.

Even Sten was impressed at first, but then he began noticing things. There was something visibly and obviously out of kilter if one picked any single ship out of the mass. They were all creaky, battered, and old, with signs of hasty repairs, leaking fuel lines, and thick armor plate warted over gaping battle scars. But apparently only Sten noticed that, because the tone of the crowd changed from enforced duty to thrill.

A moment later, the sky cleared and Sten found his professional cynicism washing away, to be replaced by cold fear as he saw three of the biggest and most awesome battleships ever built parade into view. Their hulls were sleek and as black as a null star. The many artistically crafted ports hinted at firepower that would make the editors of *Jane's* weep in frustration at not having a picture and breakdown for their new fiche. Sten was only beginning to guess what those ports hid when the ships rumbled overhead and then passed from view.

The crowd's voice was momentarily stilled by pride and awe. Even the cops were quiet, their eyes glazed with patriotic fervor. It was like a religious experience, Sten thought. The Tahn's Great Spirit obviously loved things that went bang. Sten wondered wryly what Lay Reader Cristata would make of it.

A low hum broke off his thoughts, and Sten found himself craning back around along with the rest of the crowd to find its source. It came from the ashes of the palace.

He stared in fascination as something blazing white lifted from the ruins. It was shaped like an enormous spoked wheel, and it hovered just above the ruins for a few minutes, as if waiting for the last of the ashes to be repelled by the purity of the white and shower to the ground. Finally, it rose about half a kilometer above the ruins, then smoothly moved toward the stage.

Sten's head stalked back along with a million-plus others as a huge port slid open and a large black capsule appeared. The capsule broke away and settled silently down until it nearly touched the stage. There was a series of sharp cracks, and then red pods shot out and the capsule grounded, its legs taking up the weight.

Silence. Not a mutter or a whisper from the crowd. Then martial music trumpeted from giant vidscreen speakers. A portion of the capsule's smooth skin broke away, revealing a yawning arced doorway. Uniformed Tahn guardsmen marched swiftly out, their boots reaching knee level and then slamming down in unison.

They took positions around the stage. Sten noted swiftly that their weapons were not ceremonial and were kept at edgy ready. He saw officers among them—probably Intelligence—scanning the ground, looking for any hint of trouble. There was none. The crowd was firmly in the arms of its leaders. Music swelled louder, and first one and then another member of the Tahn High Council appeared.

As they spread out on stage, Sten automatically checked their positions against his small mental library of vidpics of the council, making what he could of who was in favor and who was not by where they stood.

Except for the absence of Pastour and Lord Wichman's spot directly to the right of the empty center place of honor, he could detect no difference. He quit trying as soon as he saw the first of the combat-clad Tahn soldiers wheel out of the doorway: The man towered well above the others on the stage. He was joined by another and then another, all equally tall. The squad formed up, and as Sten remembered where he had seen those troopers before, Lady Atago stepped out behind them. Her personal guardsmen were probably among the few Tahn in the empire who were taller than Atago.

The crowd erupted into a howl of greeting as the guardsmen marched her to the place of honor, then withdrew. But not very far, Sten saw. They were hovering right behind and on either side, ready to throw themselves around her as living shields if necessary.

Lady Atago stretched both arms over her head, and the cheers of the crowd became even louder—so loud that they echoplexed and howled as the vidscreen speakers picked up the reverb. For a moment, although he was surrounded by many times more than a million beings, Sten felt completely alone.

He remembered the last time he had seen Lady Atago. It had been back on Cavite in the early days of the war. She had worn a red cloak and green tunic, just as she did now. And she stood barely 150 meters away. He remembered that brief moment when he had shifted the willygun until the green tunic was centered in the cross hairs. He had inhaled, let out half that breath, and taken up the slack on the trigger. In a moment an AM2 round would blow a fist-sized hole in that tunic. And then Atago's bodyguards were moving like a corps de ballet, closing around their charge—and all Sten could see was the white of their uniforms instead of the red and the green.

To this day, Sten was not sure whether he had missed the shot out of cowardice or lost an opportunity. As he watched her, he cursed himself for both. It did not matter which side of the coin came down. Both were losers. And he could not help wondering what would have happened if he had succeeded. Who would be standing on the stage now? Wichman? Pastour? Anyone at all?

On the stage, Lady Atago had lowered her arms and let the cheers wash over her. Then she raised them again, asking for silence. She got it.

"Thank you, my fellow Tahn," she began, "for joining us in this celebration."

Sten saw not a flicker among the rapt faces around him. To the crowd there was no incongruity in the fact that they had not joined anything voluntarily. And what was there to celebrate?

"These are trying times for us, my people," Atago continued. "Our resolve is being tested more than in any other era after the Great Shame. And it is this resolve of ours—this dedication to victory basic to our Tahn way of life—that we celebrate today.

"But there is more than just resolve that makes up the Tahn genetic code. There is also the absolute willingness to sacrifice all to preserve—"

She waited, and then the final word snapped out of the speakers like a metal-tipped whip.

"Honor!"

"Honor!" the crowd screamed back. *"Honor!"*

"Yes, honor," Lady Atago said. "Let no outlander mistake the meaning of this word to the Tahn. To us it is not just a phrase requiring sacrifice for the future of our children and their children's children. Because we would sacrifice all for honor. And we are willing to die to the last Tahn lest our honor be fouled."

Again she held the moment, bowing her head.

"For without honor there can be no future," she went on. "Without honor the Tahn are extinct as a race. And if we all die to fulfill this unique and holy vision of ourselves, what does it matter? We may all be gone, but we still will have left our mark on history.

"And a thousand years from now—and a thousand after that—beings will read of us and marvel at the standard for honor we set. And they will curse themselves for their weaknesses and damn themselves as cowards because no living thing will ever achieve that mark again. But they all died, their children may protest. And their parents will nod, yes. But they died for . . . *honor!*"

It took a half hour for the crowd to calm down before Lady Atago could go on. They shouted and wept and hugged one another and passed children from shoulder to shoulder so they could reach out and touch history.

Lady Atago kept very still during that time, letting the wave of sound wash over her, seemingly unaffected. Her face was stern—and waiting.

"And so, my fellow Tahn," she continued when the time was right. "I have called you here to celebrate. To celebrate and to rededicate ourselves to honor.

"It will not be easy. We face a formidable foe. A foe who will not be satisfied until the last of us has been ground up for his bread and meat. We have won great victories against this foe, and we have suffered great losses.

"But it does not matter. I welcome this foe. As you all should. Because we are fortunate to live in a time of our ultimate test. This foe has forced us to confront our own weaknesses. And when it is over, we will be strong and pure and good. Or all of us will be dead . . .

". . . for honor." The last words came softly, like a prayer. The crowd was silent, as if sensing what was to come.

Lady Atago slowly raised her hands to the clear Tahn skies. The odd thought crossed Sten's mind that not once had Lady Atago mentioned the Eternal Emperor by name. It was a speechmaking tactic that he immediately mentally wrote down in his little Mantis book of propaganda tricks.

"I pledge to you this, my fellow Tahn. I will hurl at our foe every bolt you build me. I will track him to the Fringe Worlds. I will hunt him out of his coward's lair in Cavite. And then I will follow him wherever he flees to.

"I pledge you battle, my fellow Tahn. I pledge you victory. Swift and sweet. But I may not be up to your measure. Some weakness in me may make my aim go astray.

"And so . . . if in the end I fail you . . . If I cannot give you the victory you deserve . . ."

There was a long, last wait . . .

"I pledge you honor!"

Sten barely noticed the tumult around him. The crowd was insane, but that did not matter. Because he was witnessing a rare thing: a leader who was addressing her people—and believing every word she said.

Since Sten had set off for Koldyeze, the K'ton Klub had closed, reopened, and then closed again. In a few hours it would reopen once more, and Alex and St. Clair and L'n were waiting anxiously at a table in the empty nightclub.

To cover their anxiety, they were doing what soldiers have been doing ever since beings had picked up a rock and learned to throw it at others. In short, they were grousing and wondering what foolishness they would be asked to do next.

"Look, I don't mean to complain," St. Clair was saying. "Business is great, and I'm also enjoying beating the snake-snot out of the Tahn. But I'm a bottom-line kind of a person."

"True," L'n said. She said it a little too quickly but presented a guileless pink furry face to St. Clair's quick questioning look.

"Whae be y'r wee problem, lass?" Alex asked.

"Lately I don't feel like we're getting anywhere. We're wrecking their money. Fine and good. We're fouling up production. Messing with their morale. Stealing their secrets. And being a general pain in the tush. This is great. As it should be. We're hurting them bad."

"I don't see what your problem is," L'n said. "What more do you want?"

"I want to hear them yell ouch," St. Clair said. "I mean, how bad are we *really* hurting them?"

"Aye," Alex said, tapping the table thoughtfully. "Ah ken whae y' mean."

"You do?" asked the unsuspecting L'n, who still had a few innocent bits left in her.

Alex nodded wisely. " 'Tis ae old malady," he said. "How much hurt hurts. Aye. An old tale, lass. Let Kilgour tell y' how old."

And Alex settled back to tell a suspicious St. Clair and an intrigued L'n his story.

"Ae gran'sire ae mine wae trappin't. Ae Eart'. Bleakit an' cold an' a'. Been oot ae th' wilderness aye weeks an' months.

"An' one day, thae was a wee town. Nae, no e'en a town. A village. Thae see't thae great pourit ae snow comin't toward them. An' thae thinki't ae's a bear or some'at.

"M' grandsire, 'twere.

"Lookin't f'r ae dentist.

"Turns oot, thae's a diploma-mill quack ae thae village. An' m' gran'sire sits doon ae th' chair, an' thae dentist lookit ae' his teeth an' say, 'Aye, thae's got to coom oot. But ae nae hae anesthesia.'

"M' grandsire say, 'Dinnae fash. Pull it.'

"An so, wi' great gruntin' ae groanin't, thae dentist yankit thae tooth. An' he's sweatin', an m' grandsire's sweatin't.

"An' thae quack say't, 'Dinnae thae be th' greatest pain y've ever felt?'

"M' grandsire says, 'Nae. Thae's naught.'

"Wi' considerable astonishment, thae dentist say, 'Whae's worse?'

"M' grandsire, explain't. 'Last week, Ah come down wi' th' runs. S' bad, Ah canne mak't oot m' cabin t' thae back-house. So, Ah drap m' trews ae th' snowbank, right outside m' door. An' Ah forget Ah was cleanin't m' bear traps before thae snow fell, an' Ah left a wee trap set right where't Ah be crouchin't.

" 'Which Ah'm remindit aboot when thae trap closit.

" 'Snapit closit on m' balls.'

" 'Good Lord,' thae dentist sae. 'Y'r right. Thae's th' biggest pain ae all.'

" 'Nae, nae, lad,' m' grandsire say. 'Th' biggest pain ae all wae when Ah come to the *end* ae th' chain . . .' "

His punch line was greeted by the usual cold, stony silence. But only from St. Clair. L'n was on the floor with laughter. Alex gave her a huge, fond smile.

"I don't get it," St. Clair said flatly.

"You—you don't?" L'n gasped through laughter. "Why not? It's—so simple that it's—" She broke off to compose herself. "Look. A bear trap has this big long chain."

"I know that," St. Clair said, a little miffed.

"And one end of the chain is staked to the ground. And on the other end is—well, the bear trap. And, see, when the jaws snapped shut, they caught Alex's great-great-whatever-grandfather by the scrotum."

She erupted into laughter again. St. Clair just glared at her. Alex thought she was absolutely wonderful.

"But—see, that still wasn't what really hurt the most," L'n went on. "What really hurt was—"

"I don't want to hear it again," St. Clair said. "Please!"

Alex got to his feet and strode around the table to L'n. He patted her fondly on the shoulder. She was a being after his own heart. Kilgour had found himself a duck.

"Do you know any more like that?" L'n asked hopefully.

"A few, lass. Just a few. D'ya e'er ken thae one aboot th' spotted snake?"

"Nooo . . . I don't think so. Why don't you—"

"Don't get him started, L'n," Sten's voice boomed from across the room. "Or you'll wish you were back in a Koldyeze cooler."

The three turned to see their wandering boy. Poor Sten. His hair was wild, his eyes were glazed, and his clothes drooped from him like wet gunnysack material. And as he walked toward them, he moved with a footsore limp.

"What the clot happened?" St. Clair asked.

Sten sighed and shook his head. He slumped into a seat and made desperate pointing gestures at a gaping mouth. Alex handed him a throat-soothing brew. Sten gulped it straight down in less than four swallows. He slammed the mug on the table. Alex refilled it. Sten chugged only about half of it. Then he belched and took a tentative sip.

"Well?" St. Clair prompted.

"For a while there," Sten said, "I thought I was for the high jump. I got picked up in a Tahn sweep."

His three companions started. Sten waved them back down again.

"They just needed some clean-cut types to stand in front of a demonstration to wave signs at a livie crew. We all stood there in the sun for five hours or so, and then Lady Atago came out to make general nice and urged us to commit suicide. We all thought this over for a bit and said that was okay, but can we go home now?

"No such luck. Atago said stick around there's gonna be a show. And we were treated to eleven more hours of traitors confessing their sins on the big screen and then getting themselves geeked for our pleasure."

"Any traitors in particular? L'n asked.

"The ones we made up. Toward the end there, I almost felt sorry for them."

"Thae'll no be blame in pity, young Sten," Alex said, "so long a' y' dinnae make a habit ae it."

Sten did not comment. Instead he did a little gentle whining for food, and while he ate, he filled them in on his mission to Koldyeze.

"What do we do next?" St. Clair asked.

"Right now there's not much more we can do. We keep our agent network nit and tiddy. Feed the corruption meter whenever the flag pops up. And make general low-profile pains of ourselves."

"Clottin' borrring," L'n said. "Where's all the romance and pulse throbbing you promised? Intrigue! Danger! Clandestine action! I didn't sign on to be bored, cheena!"

Everybody laughed.

"I'm afraid that's what's in the cards for a little while," Sten said. "We've done all we can to this point. Now we have to wait for events to catch up to us. Big events. That we have no control over. Like in the Fringe Worlds. And Cavite."

He got up and refilled everyone's glass with brew.

"Although I hate to confess this, it's sorta like Alex's

story," he went on. "We've got the Tahn by the scrotum in the jaws of a big steel trap. But they still don't know they're hurting yet.

"So we gotta wait until they reach the end of the chain."

CHAPTER FIFTY-TWO

THE EMPIRE HAD learned—at least slightly—from the slaughter in the Pel/e systems.

Fleet Marshal Ian Mahoney looked at the preinvasion bombardment plans for the Fringe Worlds and snarled, "Double it."

"Double what, sir?"

"Everything."

His staff looked at the overheads and followed orders. Twice the conceivable amount of ordnance was scheduled for delivery on the Fringe Worlds, and then, once more, Mahoney told them to double *that*.

He doubted that it would work—but then, Mahoney had never been convinced that putting a man where a bomb or a bullet might go necessarily worked.

But he would do the best he could.

He would have liked to have leveled the worlds as he had done to the Erebus System—but there were civilians resident. Mahoney wondered how many of them had survived not just the Tahn conquest but the subsequent occupation.

Had he his druthers—but he did not.

Finally there came a day when there was no return fire taken on any of the Fringe Worlds selected for invasion.

Mahoney ordered the assault.

He acted knowing that the Tahn defenders would come out of the rubble as if all the firepower expended had been so many fireworks.

He was quite correct—which was why Mahoney chose to disobey orders.

According to the Eternal Emperor and his psych staff, Mahoney's return to the Fringe Worlds was what the Emperor insisted on calling, using jargon unknown to anyone around him, a "photo opportunity." Whatever the clot a photo was did not matter—his propagandists went into motion.

Before Mahoney's battlewagon lifted with the fleets toward the Fringe Worlds, several chaingun galleries had been stripped of weaponry and converted into press suites. As many livie crews and journalists as could fit were packed in.

The battleship was supposed to land on Cavite, center of the Fringe Worlds, in the fourth wave. Assumption: First wave gets slaughtered, second wave takes casualties but holds, third wave consolidates, and we can land some camerabeings in the fourth wave. Bangs will still be banging, but nobody's going to get killed.

Least of all Ian Mahoney as he strode nobly down the ramps of his battleship and made a noble statement that he had returned or declared this world open or whatever noble statement he chose. Noble statement-type propagandists were assigned to his staff.

Unfortunately, on L-Day, H-hour, Mahoney was nowhere near his command ship.

He was strapped into a troop capsule on an assault transport next to the First Guards' command sergeant major, a noncom whose body, guardsmen thought, had been replaced sixteen times, bit by bit over the decades, but whose brain had never been modified after the CSM had been declared clinically dead a century or so before.

Mahoney had forgotten how much it hurt when the transport, just in-atmosphere, blew its twenty assault capsules down toward the surface below. He had also forgotten just how many times "down" changed places as the capsule dived toward the robot homer below.

Just before impact, he and the sergeant major forced grins at each other: See, we're used to this drakh. Neither of them realized how much his own smile resembled the rictus of a corpse or thought about it as the capsule slammed down in the usual semicontrolled crash. Semicontrolled was defined as less than fifteen percent incapacitating injuries on landing.

The minicharges exploded and the capsule's walls blew off. The straps came free, and Mahoney grabbed his willygun and stumbled out into the rubble of Cavite.

There were various reports as to what noble pronunciations on the order of "I have returned" or *"Lafayette nous arrivons"* Mahoney made as his boots crashed down. They were all tissues of lies.

His first observation: "I forgot how much this clottin' armpit world smells like an open—incoming!"

And Mahoney chewed gravel as the missile smashed down bare meters away.

The First Guards had been singled out for the "honor" of being the first to land on Cavite by Mahoney. Years before, the division had been wiped out holding Cavite in the opening of the Tahn War. Only a handful of noncoms, officers, and technicians had been evacked during the retreat at the Eternal Emperor's personal orders. They had been used as a cadre to reform the unit with fresh blood and then sent back into combat.

Mahoney thought they deserved the "privilege" of revenge. He might have been a little battle-happy in his thinking. There were no more than a dozen guardsmen who had been on Cavite—the grinding down of the Tahn had ground the division, as well. In addition, they still had not finished training the replacements after the Naha.

The "honor" that all the combat-experienced troops would have liked was a return to Prime, a nice parade, and the next half century spent garrisoning some R&R world. Two beats after the first *Wheep-Crack* past his or her ear, even the most gung-ho replacement agreed with that idea.

But the Guards pushed on, day by bloody day, across the planet and into Cavite City. The battle was a reversal of their bitter defeat—now they had complete air and space superiority and an unlimited amount of weaponry and ammunition.

Not that the Tahn defenders surrendered. *K'akomit'r*, in their language, meant both "I give up" and "I do not exist."

Most of them chose just that—fighting to the last round,

then suiciding with a grenade or charging armor with an improvised spear. Mahoney saw one stubby Tahn private, surrounded, tap-arm a grenade on the ground and then tuck it under his combat helmet. By that time he and the other battered guardsmen around him thought the subsequent explosion the best joke of the day.

Less than an hour later, one of Mahoney's aides, one who *had* landed on the battleship, found the fleet marshal and handed him a message.

EYES ONLY, from the Eternal Emperor. The message was in an old Mantis code that Mahoney could decipher blindfolded and in a typhoon. It read:

QUIT PLAYING GAMES AND GET BACK TO WORK.

Mahoney growled, stripped his combat vest of grenades and magazines, threw them to a nearby guardsman, and headed back to maps, computers, and projections.

Lady Atago fulfilled her vow.

Every Tahn fleet that was combatworthy was grouped and launched at the Fringe Worlds. She ruthlessly stripped reserve and home defense squadrons of all warships and sent them into battle.

The slogans were chanted, and the livies were ominous with takeoff after takeoff.

The Empire's defeat was certain.

It was very *un*certain to a nameless Tahn supply officer who sat in the cramped cubicle of his obsolete battle cruiser. Finally he shut off the com that was still broadcasting inspirational messages from the council and stared at his screens.

He keyed to the bottom line of all of them.

CREW: 50% of mandated personnel. 11% rated "Trained." 4% "Station-trained."

SUPPLIES: 71% required for mission accomplishment including return to base.

ARMAMENT: 11% bunker capacity chainguns; 34% tube capacity missiles.

SYSTEMS: 61% functional.

As he watched, the "sixty-one percent" hesitated, then changed to "fifty-eight percent" as, somewhere in the guts of the ship, another weapons system succumbed to cumulative wear.

The livies that showed the Tahn going off into the final battle were supposedly broadcast live. Atago, no fool, was not about to allow that.

Accidents, after all, could happen. And accidents were most demoralizing even to the thoroughly conditioned Tahn populace—which was why the livies showing the takeoff of those three brand new superbattleships that had chilled Sten were never seen.

One of them—the replacement for Atago's obsolescent and battered *Forez*—was not scheduled for the assault.

But the other two were.

One, the *Panipat*, lifted up to twenty meters away from its massive docking cradle before losing two Yukawa drive units and almost crashing. Only skillful pilotage brought it back down, seemingly undamaged. Immediate system analysis showed, however, that not only were the two drive units out, but *all* other units would be failure-prone. Also, the AM2 drive would produce no more than fifty percent capacity.

There were no explanations—except that all three ships had been slammed together, even more hastily built than were the usual Tahn warships. Plus, in a time when all strategic materials were in critical shortage, compromises had been made.

The new *Forez*-class ships might have looked awesome. But there was not a lot of them there.

The third ship, the *Gogra*, lifted successfully. Out-atmosphere from Heath, the ship's commander ordered the ship and its four escorting cruisers into AM2 drive.

Someone blundered.

The *Gogra* and one cruiser managed to collide. Collisions, in the macrodistances of space, never happened.

This one did.

There were no survivors from either ship, so no explanations as to exactly what had gone wrong were ever available.

Just beyond detection range of the Fringe Worlds, the Tahn fleets three-pronged for the assault, becoming the first, second, and third attack forces. The formations, timing, and deployment would have produced, from any prewar Tahn admiral, relief of at least half of the ships' captains and probably a tenth reminded of their "honor" and given one projectile round.

But there were not very many prewar Tahn admirals, let alone ship captains, left. Their bodies were desiccated in space, filmed across the bulkheads of shattered ships, or were simply a no-longer-visible contribution to entropy.

But war was the fine art of making do with what one had.

Plus the Tahn knew that destiny was on their side.

Destiny, of course, was generally on the same side as God.

And so the Tahn fleets attacked the big battalions.

The Tahn second attack force never made it to the Fringe Worlds.

Admiral Mason, commanding six destroyer squadrons from the bridge of a brand-new cruiser, was waiting. His ships were lying doggo, barely within detector range of each other, as the Tahn came in. The first DD making contact linked up, and Mason sent all in ships in carefully and endlessly rehearsed attack formations.

They broke the Tahn on the first sweep, then went independent. Mason's skippers might have been drilled to the point of brainburn, but secretly each of them was proud to serve under a killer like Mason—even if he was a complete clot, he still put them "in harm's way."

The Tahn battleship that was flagship for the second force center was killed by at least three launches from three separate ships, and all command of the ragtag fleets was gone.

At that point Mason grudgingly reported to his superior— and nine full Imperial fleets came in to finish the job.

One Tahn cruiser, eleven destroyers, and a handful of auxiliaries, all damaged, survived to break off and limp back to Heath.

Admiral Mason had to admit that his ships had performed adequately.

A full sector away, Fleet Admiral Ferrari fought his battle almost perfectly.

He had had more than enough time, since Intelligence had alerted him that the Tahn fleets had launched, to prepare himself.

He had run endless progs on several screens as to what exactly the oncoming first attack force would do. He even had an Imperial Intelligence strategic/tactical bio-fiche on the Tahn admiral in command. Some clot named Hsi, Ferrari thought, who's been piloting a bureaucracy for most of the war. Now, what did he do to get himself beached? He consulted another bio-fiche—one that, although Ferrari never knew it, had come from Sten and St. Clair's intelligence.

"The gentleman," Ferrari thought aloud, "appears to have managed to lurk up on four Imperial fleets way back when and make them unhappy. That should not mean that . . . mmh. Perhaps he has well-connected friends? No. Ah. Here is the tiny malfeasance. Appears to have lost control of his units during the midpoint of the battle. Incurred casualties. Mercy."

Ferrari smiled to himself. So the clot did not know his midgame.

Ferrari blanked all the progs. They were all incorrect. He *knew* where Hsi would attack.

Admiral Hsi had planned to use the "clutter" of the Sulu systems to mask his approach on the Caltor System and Cavite itself. There was no way that even the sophisticated Imperial detectors could pick up his fleets before they attacked.

Hsi had not calculated that the reverse was also true—the Tahn detectors showed the Sulu systems as a blur of asteroids.

They did not pick out Ferrari's waiting fleets until the last few seconds. Ferrari was slightly disappointed; he had hoped that the Tahn would come in even closer before he began the battle.

But it was enough—and he ordered action.

Looked at from "above," two-dimensionally, Ferrari's fleets came laterally across the spearhead of the Tahn force— what had been known as "crossing the tee." All Imperial weapons could acquire targets, but the Tahn weapons systems were "masked" by their own formation.

Ferrari hammered in on them. The battle, at that point,

went from chess to the greater subtlety of battle-axes at one meter as the Imperial fleets slaughtered Hsi.

Hsi ordered his force to break off battle, retire, and regroup.

Ferrari sent his units after them, and the battle continued, a blind melee in the emptiness between systems.

Ferrari won, quite handily. Again, only a few Tahn ships survived.

But he had made one mistake.

When he had decided to go after Hsi, he had neglected to inform Mahoney, who was trying to coordinate the battle from Cavite, of his decision. He had left a large, undefended hole in the perimeter around the Fringe Worlds. And through that hole, three E-days later, poured the Tahn's third attack force.

There were no Imperial combat fleets between it and Cavite.

Someone once said that most heroes could be explained simply as sane people deciding to do something that was completely insane.

William Bishop the Forty-third would have defined the action that won him the Galactic Cross and his second star as something that only a nut who had managed to convince himself he was not a nut would have even begun.

So far, Bishop had not had that bad a war.

He had originally been a guardsman, an infantry sergeant who had gotten his share of gongs for ducking at the appropriate moment in the appropriate place. Realizing that if he went into places where people were shooting at him, eventually they were going to connect, he had volunteered for flight training.

His intentions were to graduate and then push big ugly clot transports around the sky until his time came up, then work quietly on his own abstruse mathematical figures. The only other medal he wanted was some kind of long service without getting caught doing anything too terrible award.

He was a natural pilot.

When he had graduated as part of Sten's flight training class, he had gotten the assignment he had wanted.

But things had caught up with him.

Perhaps it was that no one could believe that a man with that many medals, who looked like that much of a commando, had no interest in seeing any more combat. Or perhaps someone with a sense of history had looked up who William Bishop the First was.

But in any event, Bishop not only had been forcibly transferred from his REMF supply wagon to an assault transport but had been given more and more promotions.

Currently he was a one-star admiral in charge of two divisions of assault craft. Worse yet, he had been hand selected to be in charge of the Cavite landings.

A man could get dead doing things like that, he had thought. Going in.

But so far, not much had happened—not much, at least to Bishop's mind. The air-to-space missiles, the Tahn tacships, and the occasional suicide attack had been discounted.

Bishop was determined that it was not that bad a war. Survive this, he thought, and all I have to make it through is the final landing on Heath.

That produced a wince and another train of thought. It was more important to wonder whether Fermat was not right, after all. In the meantime, his assault ships went in on Cavite, their support transports cross-loaded, and the handful of combat craft kept the Tahn mosquitoes away.

At that point, the alarms shrilled.

Bishop found himself on the bridge of his assault command ship, looking at the incoming reports that input and then blanked as the oncoming Tahn third attack force came in.

Bishop then realized that he was a psychopath.

His orders were most clear. "Com . . . close beam to Com-Escort. Commander, stand by for orders."

"Admiral, we're getting—"

"We're getting hit by the whole clottin' Tahn spaceforce. I know. I noticed. Orders, I said. I want your ships out of orbit and headed out. Now."

"Toward what?"

Bishop groaned to himself. "Do you have a breakdown on the incoming Tahn?"

"Uh . . . that's an affirm. We have seven BBs, several tacship launchers, twenty-eight cruisers ... you want more, Billy?"

"Negative. That's about what I show. Orders . . ." He motioned to his nav officer. "Stand by for relay. Contact orbit will be for the third—no, fourth battleship in line. Relay—"

His paling navigator nodded.

"—on transmit. Activate on a ten-second tick—from now."

"Further orders. Sir?"

Bishop stared into the screen at his escort commander. "Hell, no. You need any more?"

"Guess not. You know any good prayers, Billy?"

Bishop shook his head.

And the attack began.

One armored assault command ship. One cruiser. Twelve destroyers. Eleven escort ships. And seventeen tacships.

Attacking four Tahn combat fleets.

It was insane.

It *was* insane.

The Tahn admiral in charge of the third attack force saw the handful of ships incoming on a collision orbit and realized that he had fallen into a trap.

No one would attack like that. Not unless, behind those absurd attackers, was the full force of the Empire.

The admiral admired the temerity of the attackers. They could, truly, be Tahn. To be willing to die merely to pin down the Tahn fleets for a few moments, moments enough for the yet-to-be-detected Imperial battleships to strike.

The admiral issued a string of orders.

Break contact and re-form. Go back, beyond the Sulu systems. We shall let the Empire strike against emptiness, then come in again from the flank.

Four Tahn fleets fled back into emptiness. For the most logical of reasons.

The admiral in question never had a chance to realize what had happened and what had not happened, because his reassembly point happened to be only light-minutes from the orbital path of Ferrari's fleets, returning from the destruction of Hsi.

There were no surviving Tahn ships.

Bishop looked at the receding Tahn fleets, retracted all those last words he had been muttering, and, reflexively, looked over his shoulder.

There was nothing "over his shoulder" or "behind" him on the screens.

William Bishop the Forty-third, not believing in bluffs, in what had happened, or, more importantly, in what had *not* happened, returned to his orbit off Cavite, seriously thinking about the virtues of early retirement and then perhaps joining an intensely religious monastery.

Lady Atago stood in the litter of disaster and read the on-screen message, sent en clair from General Lunga's command post on Cavite:

> Imperial units have broken through. Contact lost with fighting elements. Last reports say all positions resisting to last man. This post now three combatants, no remaining ammunition. Will attack. Repeat. Will attack. My apologies to the council and to my race for failure.
>
> Lunga

Atago turned away. She had her own honor—and her own pledge—to fulfill.

CHAPTER FIFTY-THREE

WITHOUT CEREMONY, THE new *Forez* hurtled into space.

Lady Atago might have been the ultimate Tahn, but she had been more than grudgingly acquiescent to the Tahn's cultural love of ceremonies.

There were rituals for warriors choosing to go into battle, seeking the final victory of death: the touching of the home-world's earth to one's temple. A last sip of pure water. An oath over one's personal weapon, preferably one that had been in the family for generations. Exact instructions as to how the memory of the about-to-fall hero(ine) was to be honored.

Lady Atago chose to die in her own fashion.

The livie crews could cobble together some kind of scene from stock footage. In fact, she imagined, they probably were already hard at work doing just that.

Atago did not care.

After lift, the *Forez*'s second officer had turned to her, eyes glistening, and stammered something about it all being a dream. The old and the new, culminating in a moment of history.

Atago puzzled at him for a second. Old and new? Oh. Yes. She remembered. The officer had been something or other on the old *Forez*, which was now probably being cut apart and recast into something or other. Atago did not know or care. A ship, like a weapon, was a tool and noth-ing more.

But she managed a frosty smile and a nod of agreement to the officer. If those were the thoughts he chose to carry into emptiness, so be it.

Atago was busy with her final plans—such as they were.

Any culture that managed to admire the slaughter of other beings also lionized the fighter who went to war in a hopeless cause. But to qualify for legend, that fighter also had to accomplish something by his death, even if it was nothing more than keeping the bad guys out of a pass for an hour or so.

That had been true even on ancient Earth. For instance, before Roland was an acceptable hero, his pigheadedness at Roncesvalles had to be changed from a minor ambush by irked Basques to a grand last stand against several million Saracens. Custer and his people *had* to be doing something worthwhile instead of what they actually were to get to Little Big Horn—drunk, untrained, ignoring intelligence, and having less than no idea of what they would do when they got wherever they were going.

There was an exception: the kamikazes—Second Global War—who went out to die with only the forlorn illogic that somehow their deaths would work magic and change history. Other cultures had tried to explain by claiming they were psycho cases, drunk, or using drugs. Only their home culture had made them into heroes.

The Tahn would have understood the kamikazes quite thoroughly.

Lady Atago's "battle plan" was to drive directly for Cavite. Somehow the *Forez* would battle through the surrounding Imperial fleets and somehow attack Cavite itself. Of course they would all die.

But somehow that would turn the war.

The crew believed. Perhaps a bit of Lady Atago's own emotions did as well.

But more important to Atago was her honor and her expiation of failure. She had done something—and had no idea what—wrong. The war should have been over already. And the Tahn victorious. To consider anything else was impossible.

"Impossible" was also the word for her plan.

The never-to-lift-again *Panipat* was stripped of its missiles, armaments, supplies, and the few crew members who were properly trained.

But even so, the *Forez* launched with only eighty percent of full complement. They had, however, almost 175 percent more than the specified systems basic load for all weapons systems—weapons systems that had seen, at best, a single test firing during the ship's trial passage from shipyard to Heath.

A battleship was normally escorted by a fairly largish fleet —cruisers, destroyers, ECM ships, tacship carriers, and half a horde of auxiliaries.

The *Forez* attacked the Empire with one cruiser and seventeen destroyers.

Ensign Gilmer thought himself a clever man.
He came from a family that had served in the Empire's

military for generations. Such service was obligatory for any Gilmer's first career. Ensign Gilmer had groaned into adulthood with the knowledge that he was sooner or later going to have to go out there and play with people who probably had evil intentions. But it was either that or disinheritance, a far worse fate.

He had hoped, without success, that at the very least the war with the clotting Tahn would end before his tender pink body saw its majority. No luck.

Gilmer joined up.

But he had a plan that would not only make his somewhat suspicious elders realize that Gilmer was true to the tradition but keep said pink body unscathed.

He volunteered for picket ships.

His fellow graduates at the academy were in awe—they had never expected the flaky Gilmer to become a firebrand. Picket ships, after all. Out in front of the rest of the fleet. Waiting for the enemy to come at them, *in force*.

Picket ships were even more suicidal than tacships.

A being could get killed doing that.

Gilmer took their admiration badly—the same way he had handled their earlier polite contempt—and gloated to himself.

Gilmer had been sent to hack one day in his first year at the academy and spent it doing some interesting research: looking for a future home. He discovered that picket ships indeed were in front of everyone. But unlike the tacships, intended to shoot and scoot, picket ships just scooted. He ran a stat analysis on their casualties, all the way back to the Mueller Wars. Most interesting: less than two percent. Lower, even, than a transport. So much for cadet wisdom. And most of the losses, he discovered by wading through endless fiches on accident boards, had been due to inept pilotage.

Gilmer was a superb spacepilot. Everyone agreed on that.

And so he went off to war.

His picket ship was not a happy one. The twelve beings in his crew hated Gilmer's guts—not that there was anything concrete they could dislike him for. The ship was tautly run. Promotions and punishments were handed down promptly and according to regs. But there was something wrong.

Gilmer had not been pleased when his picket ship had been

attached to a flotilla assigned to the Pioneer Sectors invasion. But thus far he had kept well out of danger. He had flashed first contact reports, in fact, on several Tahn ships trying lone-wolf runs against the Empire, which should have gotten him a respectable gong or two to take into civilian life and his planned new career as a livie producer.

And he could see that the Empire was winning.

A few more weeks, and then it would be over. He planned for his ship to need a massive quarterly that would keep it out of the final battle against Heath.

Therefore, Gilmer, that clever man, was not pleased when a screen lit, showing a single incoming blip at full drive.

He enlarged the scope, cutting to a sensor he had planted several light-years away, and then gurgled as the monstrous bulk of the *Forez* swam at him. It was, a second screen told him, not an illusion. The *Forez*'s orbit, indeed, would pass less than one light-minute away!

His com team was already yammering its close-beam report back to the fleet. Gilmer slammed full power, programmed a random evasion pattern, and looked for something else to do. Frantically he ordered a weapons panel up and then blind-launched two missiles.

The four missiles with which the picket boat was armed were about as useless as a weapon could be. They were single-lobe homers less than a meter long. In theory, they were to be used to stop an enemy picket boat or maybe even a tacship from sucking up a defenseless ship. In fact, they were intended to give the picket boat crewmen something to do before death if they were inept enough to be caught.

Gilmer gnawed his knuckles, waiting to stupidly fulfill one of the family's *other* traditions: death in battle.

But nothing happened.

None of the Tahn ships bothered to launch against his ship, let alone go in pursuit.

Gilmer then knew he was not only a superb pilot but a master tactician as well. For a moment he even considered staying on in the military after the war. No, he caught himself. Don't be arrogant. Take the big medal they're going to give you and be content.

He did at least receive the medal. And it was a very large one.

The picket boat survived for one reason: Lady Atago *wanted* the Empire to know she was attacking—and to come out to face her. Perhaps that picket boat had given the alert a little earlier than she would have liked, but no battle was ever fought exactly to plan.

She did not even notice when one of the picket ship's missiles actually hit the *Forez*.

A junior damage-control officer saw a screen report a hit somewhere near the ship's stern. Damage was through the outer skin of the ship, and an unknown object had lodged in the baffling just next to the second skin before exploding. The damage-control officer tapped keys, dumping fire retardant into the baffling area, ordered the evacuation of the storeroom next to the impact area, and also filled that compartment with retardant.

He wondered what had hit them, then concentrated on other screens.

Mahoney paced his command center.

He was angry.

Again, he looked at the screen. Great, he thought. So some Tahn clot in some kind of new battlewagon wants to count coup before we put him away. Real noble, he thought. Nobody ever told him, Mahoney's thoughts ran, that ain't the way modern war gets fought. All that happens is they wait for you to ride out and then open up with the machine guns.

Pity some people who don't want to be heroes generally get killed in the process. Clotting clot, he thought, as his mouth routined moving entire fleets out against the doomed ship. Maybe part of his anger, he thought with a flicker of humor, was that way down deep he thought counting coup *was* a better way of making war than machine slaughter.

A tech shouted at him, and Mahoney whirled.

"Who the hell trained you to report like—"

And Mahoney gaped, staring at the screen the tech sat in front of.

On it was Lady Atago.

"What the hell is that?"

"Broadcast on all channels from that incoming Tahn ship. It's a still. No audio, no other vid."

"Holy Kee-rist," Mahoney swore. "Com link. Immediate. Sealed beam to Prime. X-ray code."

That code would put the cast straight through to the Eternal Emperor.

Not only had his carefully planned trap of the Fringe Worlds attack nailed the kits, but now the mother dire wolf was on her way.

Two tacship flotillas made the first attack. The first bored in, straight on, hoping that their angle of attack would, roughly, keep some of the weaponry masked. Their orders were simple: Kill the battleship.

That was incorrect—the *Forez*'s target acquisition systems had been designed to pick up attackers from any angle, and the weapons systems to have the same launch capabilities.

The tacships should have been obliterated light-years beyond even the screening destroyers.

The ships were hit—and hard. Five out of twenty-five survived the battle. But they were not obliterated, and it took a while for the twenty to go out.

The first disaster should have been a nasty little surprise. For the first time, the Tahn had built a battleship fitted with four internal hangars, housing sixteen tacships.

Ports slid open, and the tacships struck.

But the war had been hard on Tahn pilots; it had been especially lethal for the young beings who chose to strap themselves into the semiguided missiles called tacships. The sixteen pilots had, combined, less than 8,000 real E-hours' experience. Before the war, that would have qualified a Tahn as graduate trainee and nothing more.

The Tahn tacship pilots scorned such niceties as evasive tactics and spoofs—not that they would have been capable of running them, especially against the highly experienced Imperial officers they faced, all of whom had thousand-thousand-mission stares and steel teeth.

The tacships lived for only seconds before ceasing to exist. They made only one hit—and that was on one of their own destroyers. But the clutter of missiles fired served nicely to fragment the already nearly chaotic Tahn battle formation.

Atago, standing on the bridge, kept her face immobile. She had not expected much from the tacships—but this was absurd. But it *was*. She issued further orders.

The chief weapons officer had already decided on the system. He ordered a massive Nach'kal launch—self-homing ship-to-ship missiles, medium range.

The second disaster was the inept, un- or undertrained Tahn weaponeers. Computer simulation did not equal combat reality.

Acquisition techs misreported targets, and aimers "lost" aim points or, worse, missiles themselves after launch. Gunners fumbled through firing sequences that should have been genetically imprinted by then. Loaders hit the wrong buttons and sent missiles back into storage bays or made them jam half-loaded.

The third disaster was the new untried weapons systems themselves. The Nach'kal launch should have been 100 percent. In fact, less than seventy-one percent of the tubes fired.

Others refused to admit that they had been loaded or had acquirable targets or simply sat there. One entire bank of launchers went on automatic—but did not order the missile's drive systems to activate after launch. Several dozen Nach'kals were jettisoned into space before a volunteer short-circuited the bank's computer—electrocuting himself in the process.

But the tacships took hits even as they launched their Kali shipkillers.

One hit the *Forez*, exploding in a now-empty tacship hangar bay. Damage-control crews fought their way into the roaring fire and managed to damp the flames in minutes.

And then the first flotilla was trying to get out.

Five made it.

But the Tahn's attention was taken up by the second flotilla. Their orders were to kill the escorts.

They mostly did.

The Tahn destroyers maneuvered frantically under individual control. After the disaster of the Nach'kal launch, the *Forez*'s weapons officer was reluctant to give them support.

Nine destroyers incandesced before the officer ordered the launch.

Twenty operator-guided long-range shipkillers spit out from the *Forez* and went looking for targets.

The flotilla, under tight control, spewed Fox countermissiles and Goblins keyed to home on the large Tahn shipkilling missiles. The operators, confused, lost targets and control. The missiles, told they were no longer in contact, obediently self-destructed.

The Imperial tacships came in again. Four of them struck for the cruiser.

Three of them hit the old ship, and it shuddered and broke in half. The halves, orbiting aimlessly but still moving at their initial velocity, were next sighted three E-years later by a survey ship. By then, it was of course far too late for the handful of Tahn who had survived the initial explosion.

The tacships broke once more and headed for home.

They had done enough.

Waiting in the wings were the heavies.

Atago ordered the first launch against the incoming Imperial ships at extreme long range.

Twelve self-guiding monsters floated out of their ports, and then their AM2 drives cut in. Each of them had multiple guided warheads with enough KT to kill a city the size of Heath's capital. The missiles, so new that they had not even been given a code name by Imperial Intelligence, worked superbly.

They ignored, as per last-minute instructions, any of the destroyers screening the larger Imperial ships, homed, and exploded. Their warheads had been instructed to *not* split on final acquisition. They disobeyed.

But the effect was still grim enough:

Two Imperial battleships destroyed.

One put out of action and later scrapped.

One cruiser destroyed.

One cruiser badly damaged.

Four cruisers forced out of battle.

Mahoney had been correct in anticipating the damage potential of the berserker.

Seconds later, in-range, the Imperial ships launched.

More than 30 Kalis, each operator-guided, homed on the *Forez*.

It was a confusion—Kalis were homed on each other, were operator-lost, and were even lost in sympathetic explosions after nearby missiles went off.

But the huge area of space occupied by the *Forez* and its escorts was a hell of explosions.

The remaining Tahn destroyers were dead or smashed out of battle.

The *Forez* itself took two hits.

But it was still coming in, still under full drive—and still firing.

The weapons officer was slightly pleased.

Recognizing the incompetence of his weapons crews, he had come up with a plan. The Nach'kal missiles were aimed for the incoming Imperial ships, but with little expectation of success. Also, they were set on rapid fire.

More effective were the close-range weapons: the ballistically aimed Don rockets and the volley-fired Mirkas. Even the chainguns were yammering at the Kalis when they got in range. The explosions were wreaking havoc with his electronics and sensors—but his ship was still alive.

The three hits were acceptable. One had taken out a combat information center near the stern—but there was a secondary center. Another had blasted the Nach'kal's main computer. No loss there. The third shattered the crew living spaces. No one should have been in them, anyway. The fires would soon be brought under control, he assumed. Besides, that was a task for damage control.

The fourth Kali, from the Imperial second launch, smashed into the Forez at that moment. A quarter of the Leviathan died in seconds as the nuclear blast ravened.

The bridge's lights died. Atago heard a suppressed shriek in the blackness. Then the secondary lights went on. She scanned faces. Who was the weakling?

There was no clue.

"Admiral," she snapped to the *Forez*'s CO. "Damage?"

It took a long moment. Half the bridge's screens were out or blinking nonsense. But eventually she had her information:

Engine Room: Capable of fifty percent drive. Yukawa drive units defunct.

Weapons: Percentages . . . percentages . . . Atago scanned on. Not good. The long-range missile system was dead. But she still had most of the shipkillers and even some of the Nach'kal systems left. The close-range systems had about twenty percent capability.

Casualties . . . Atago turned away. That was meaningless. She could still fight.

Another screen showed that the *Forez* would be within the heart of the Imperial fleet in minutes.

Atago's honor would be redeemed.

One of the more pointless and trivial pastimes military historians always had was trying to discover the specific person who got credit/blame for killing a great warrior/tyrant. Arguments as to whether von Richtofen was shot down by a fellow in-atmosphere pilot named Brown or potted out of the sky by a nameless Australian grunt were endlessly boring. Another Earth example: Which atmo-pilot had actually assassinated an admiral named Yamamoto—Lanphier or Barber?

More recently: Was Mordechi, battle leader of the Mueller, really killed in hand-to-hand combat by the mortally wounded Colonel Meinertzhagen, or did he in fact stumble on top of an antipersonnel mine?

So it was with Lady Atago and the *Forez*.

There were two main claimants.

One was a destroyer weapons officer named Bryennius. She had launched her Kali and then let it go "dead" in space, directly in the orbital trajectory she had calculated for the oncoming *Forez*. At the right second she brought the missile alive and aimed it at the heart of the Tahn battleship.

The other was a particularly skilled tacship commander named Alexis. He had decided to fight his mosquito battle at the same time as the big boys and had tracked the *Forez*. When he assumed that the Tahn had other things on their minds, such as the recent three hits, he had launched his own Kali. He had screened it against the close-range rocket and chaingun fire by punting all eight of his Goblin XII missiles in front of the shipkiller.

Neither one of them was the hero, even though both Kalis were hits.

The historians, not for the first time, were wrong.

Lady Atago and the *Forez* were killed by Ensign Gilmer.

Or maybe the *Forez* killed herself.

The tiny hit on the *Forez*, hours before the battle had begun, had come from the tiny missile launched from Gilmer's picket ship.

It had, as the damage control computer said, only punctured the ship's outer skin. But it had not just lodged in the baffling. A small rip was made in the inner skin.

The compartment having been evacuated, no one noticed.

It was also not noticed that:

The fire retardant system between the ship's skins failed to operate.

The storage compartment's retardant system had never been filled.

The fire alarm itself was out of circuit, as was the alarm system for that entire subsector.

And there was a fire.

It was quite a small one, glowing, barely a spark. If the hole in the center skin had been larger, the fire would have gone out in the resultant vacuum. But the ship's atmosphere system kept pumping air into the compartment.

That was enough to feed the spark.

The spark grew. Flickered.

The compartment walls should have been treated with retardant. They were not. They were also made of a relatively low-temp synthetic. The compartment itself had nonmanifested crates of waste rags.

The compartment walls melted—but not into the other corridor, where the fire could have been seen. Instead, it spread down the ship's side, toward the stern.

The damage-control computer still reported that nothing was wrong.

Finally the fire ravened, gutting through compartments. Crew members died before they could scream. Maybe, at that point, one of the computers made a report. If so, it went unnoticed in the heat of battle.

Eventually the blaze hit a firebreak. Two huge chambers ringed the ship, one above and one below the AM2 fuel storage. The chambers not only were filled with a completely inert and nonflammable material but were given multiple antiblast, antiradiation, antianything drop shields.

They did not drop when the outer wall went down.

Nor was the nonflammable substance perfection.

The *Forez* exploded microseconds before the two Kali's struck what had once been matter and now was energy.

Lady Atago might not have been that disappointed with her death. She had not reached the heart of the enemy, but she was firmly in command of her ship and about to issue an order— still in complete control.

But nearly instantaneously, she ceased to exist.

Along with more than 5,000 other crew members.

There were worse ways to die in a war.

Lady Atago had been responsible for many millions of people discovering almost all of them.

CHAPTER FIFTY-FOUR

LADY ATAGO DIED with her honor intact. The living paid with their own. Her symbolic act of heroism backblasted all down the line, exploding every joint in the pipe of authority. Leadership collapsed in shame and despair, and the mob took to the streets, looking for someone to blame. The mob declared the season open on anyone wearing a uniform or even the lowliest badge of officialdom.

Sailors were dragged out of port bars and beaten to death. Thousands upon thousands gathered outside military posts to wail and grieve and tear their hair and then hurl themselves against the wire until they broke through. The soldiers fired on them, but only halfheartedly. Hundreds died, but still the crowds kept attacking. Many soldiers stripped off their uniforms and joined the mobs, leading the hunt for their officers. Police stations were set on fire, and the fleeing cops were pursued and hammered into gel with fists and feet. Postal workers were stoned to death on their rounds. Conductors were hauled out of their trains and hanged from light stanchions, then their bodies set ablaze to scream and struggle as living effigies. Many members of the Tahn High Council hid in their homes, beating their breasts in self-blame and remorse, not lifting a finger or even considering calling for help as their furious fellow citizens killed first their guards, then their servants, then their families, and finally them.

When the mob could find no one in authority left to slaughter, they turned on the merchants—most of whom had used their capitalist good sense to flee—looting the stores and shops, smashing open warehouses, and destroying everything they could not carry away. Huge columns of smoke and angry flames erupted across Heath, as if the planet had been thrown back in time to the volcanic age.

Only Chaboya—and the K'ton Klub—was left strangely alone. Sten and Alex had planned well. Each time a mob was tempted to invade the sin district, their agents steered the crowd away with shouted promises of softer and more deserving victims. Backed up by St. Clair and L'n, the two of them monitored the rioting from the rooftop nightclub. The big com unit they had smuggled into the club was alive with the back-and-forth chatter of their agents as first one target and then another fell. Heath was being prepped for invasion.

The rioting had raged for two weeks before Mahoney finally breached the last of the Tahn defenses. Sten and Alex got the word at midday. Suddenly all the radio chatter was swept away under the weight of Mahoney's wide-banded broadcast. He and Sten had decided before that there would be no time for a series of scrambled hide-and-seek broadcasts.

Mahoney figured that a big planetwide bellow was sufficient cover.

"At that point," he had said, "I couldn't give a clot who knows I'm coming. And if I yell loud enough, the Tahn should have enough drakh in their shorts that they won't have the foggiest idea who I'm talking to. So. Soon as I say the word, you trigger the operation."

"What'll we call it?" Sten asked.

"Oh, I dunno. How about Operation Black Cat?"

"Isn't that supposed to be bad luck?"

Mahoney had given him a wolfish grin. "I was thinkin' more of the dead kind. That you drag across a grave."

Sten did not have to ask whose grave Mahoney had in mind.

Alex and Sten had tumbled to their feet as soon as the com unit fell silent. They waited for agonizing seconds. Then the message came through. "Institute Black Cat. Repeat. Institute Operation Black Cat. Are ya listenin', lad? Repeat. Institute Black . . ."

Sten bleated a fast "I hear you," and the signal cutoff in midmessage. He turned to his staff of three. They stood there, gaping, not believing that after all that time the end was finally there. They were all staring at him—even Alex—waiting for him to speak. Sten searched for something historical-sounding, something that an admiral would say. And right then and there Sten decided he would not be that kind of admiral. Clot history!

"You know what to do, people" was all he said. And his staff of three jumped into motion.

St. Clair and L'n would immediately put the word out to their key agents. Alex would notify Chetwynd to get his big crook's behind to Koldyeze and stand by.

Sten would take care of Pastour himself. He dialed in the code, toggled the broadcaster timer to peep and out, peep and out, and then punched the button that would send the message to Pastour.

The chief bodyguard, Lemay, found Pastour working peacefully in his garden. The man's hands were shaking as he handed his superior the coded message. Lemay had no idea what it said, but he had been told to keep a twenty-four-hour watch on the basement com. Anything that came across was to be brought instantly to Pastour's attention. The man had failed in his duty. Lemay was the most loyal member of Pastour's personal staff and had spent the last two weeks in terror for his boss. Oddly, the mob never came to Pastour's door, so the terror was for nothing. Still, it had exhausted him, and he had fallen asleep on shift. The message came and went unnoticed, for how long, he did not know. For that slipup he firmly believed he should have died if Pastour chose it. That the message was finally brought to his attention by a new member of the guard made his crime seem even worse. For that he should have died twice. The fact that the new guard was in Lemay's professional opinion a weasel and a worm did not help the matter.

He anxiously explained all that to Pastour, making no excuses and fully expecting the ultimate punishment. Then he realized that his colonel was not paying attention. Pastour read the message for the fourth time. His face was pale, his body cold. All the mental bracing for that moment was no help. Pastour was to make his way to Koldyeze as quickly as possible. There he and the most trusted members of his staff were to hold in position. They were to make sure that no prisoner was harmed as they waited for the Imperials to land. And then Pastour was to surrender for his people. For a moment Pastour thought he would prefer death over what was to come. Then he remembered Lady Atago and what her death had brought on. The moment passed, and Pastour gave Lemay his orders.

Sergeant Major Schour had the honor of being the first member of the Imperial invasion force to address a Tahn peasant. Schour's transport was part of the rear perimeter of the First Guards landing fleet that touched down just outside Heath.

Her lieutenant had chosen a nice soft green field. Sergeant Major Schour was the first trooper off. She lumbered down the ramp on short, muscular legs, willygun at the ready, eyes searching for some sign of enemy activity.

"Get out of my tubers!" a voice rasped out.

The sergeant major spun, fingers tightening on her trigger. Then her mouth fell open. Standing in front of her was a small, brawny figure dressed in the rough pale green and brown of a Tahn peasant. Pink tendrils wriggled angrily from what Schour imagined was the being's nose. The peasant in question was heatedly waving a hoe at the bewildered noncom. Schour noticed that the being was fur-bearing and had enormous forearms that ended in strong, stubby claws.

"What the clot did you say?" was all Schour could get out.

"Don't swear in my presence," Lay Reader Cristata said. "The Great One does not tolerate swearing!"

"I'm s-s-sorry," Schour stuttered. "But what—"

She broke off in bewilderment as more "peasants" appeared. Three of them, all wearing the same pale green and brown, were obviously Imperials. The others were Tahn. Peaceful Tahn. Sten would have been at first massively surprised and then equally massively amused that everything had gone according to plan for Cristata. The lay reader not only had successfully escaped but had converted an entire Tahn peasant village.

"Are you going to remove yourself from our tubers, or are you going to force me to complain to your superiors?" Cristata asked.

All the amazed Schour could do was blurt, "Don't you know there's a war on?"

Cristata sniffed, unconcerned. "War—like governments— is for the lower orders," he said. "Both are forbidden. We who bask in the glory of the Great One do not participate in these mundane matters."

The other peasants muttered in agreement, waving their hoes for emphasis. All Schour could do was gape and sweat and stutter. Cristata took pity on her. He put down his hoe and walked to Schour's side.

"You look very tired," he sympathized. "Perhaps this humble follower of the Great One could help you lift this burden from your spirit."

And Cristata set about adding Sergeant Major Schour of the First Imperial Guards to his flock of converts.

* * *

Wichman had always been suspicious of Pastour's sudden illness and decision to reduce his public duties. The reports of Pastour's increased profile at Koldyeze had only added to his suspicions. And so, when the young, fresh-faced guard he had planted on Pastour's staff came to him with the news of the mysterious message and the sudden saddling up of the colonel and his staff to head for the monastery, it did not test his reasoning powers to add one and one and get the obvious two: Pastour was planning to protect the prisoners of Koldyeze. But for what purpose? What did Pastour expect to gain?

As the next piece of the puzzle fell into place, Wichman was filled with loathing. Pastour was a traitor. And he intended to use the prisoners as trading stock to assure his future as a toady for the Emperor.

But what could he, Wichman, do about it? Lady Atago, the last Tahn hero, had fallen. At that moment Wichman imagined Atago beckoning to him. And in his mind, the hero's mantle was passed on. Wichman would pick up her sword. And he pledged that before he died, there would not be one prisoner left alive at Koldyeze.

Senior Captain (Intelligence) Lo Prek ducked into the ruined tenement that lay just below the approach to Koldyeze. He had an assault rifle slung over his shoulder. At his belt was a rationpak. He tugged with all his puny strength at the door that hung from sprung hinges, jamming the entrance to the stairway that led up to the second floor. It finally gave way with a loud shriek that almost stopped his heart.

Lo Prek waited for a moment, breathing in deeply, until his heartbeat returned to normal and the fear was gone. Then he padded up the stairs. On the top floor, he found a gaping hole in the wall where a window once had been. From there he had a clear view of the front entrance of Koldyeze and the narrow cobblestone street that wound up the hill to the old cathedral.

Lo Prek cleared a space and settled in to wait.

That it was probably going to be a long wait did not trouble him at all. It was patience that had allowed him to track his brother's murderer across many years and millions of miles, and now he was sure his moment was near. Lo Prek had added one more factor to Wichman's logic. If there was to be a final fight for Koldyeze, Sten was sure to be there.

Lo Prek would be waiting.

He loaded his weapon and made final adjustments to the sights.

CHAPTER FIFTY-FIVE

THE SURVIVAL OF Koldyeze—and the lives of the many hundreds of VIP internees and POWs inside the walls—was perhaps attributable to the fact that Lieutenant Colonel Virunga had been a bit more of a musician than he had admitted to Sten.

When the young Virunga had become fascinated with reed instruments, to the point that his parents grudgingly paid for the astronomical cost of importing—from Earth—an archaic instrument called the saxophone, he had become part of a rebellion. The N'ranya's music at the time was formalized into a thirty-nine-tone structure, with each musical composition in two parts. Part one began with a certain number of notes, which were then repeated in varying patterns, with the section ending in a different key. Part two rang changes on those notes to finish eventually in the beginning key.

The N'ranya delighted in descending from their trees, gathering in great glades, and listening to those pieces. Virunga's generation found that boring, boring, boring and created other forms of music—music in which not only might a key never be repeated but each musician was permitted endless individual variations as he or she saw fit. They called it y'zz and gathered secretly in small clearings to perform the banned music.

Virunga, loving improvisation, was in no trouble when

Sten's sonata in the key of freedom, for unaccompanied soloists, went badly awry.

The first movement opened in the cellars below Koldyeze. Combat-experienced prisoners unsealed the long-forgotten weapons in the crypts and trained those who were still sane and healthy enough to use them.

Grudgingly, Virunga let Kraulshavn and Sorensen prepare azimuth cards and range sketches for his soon-to-be-used artillery. He himself spent hours closeted with Derzhin and Avrenti, discussing what was inevitably going to happen—and what must occur. Avrenti, ever the professional, had no trouble realizing that he almost certainly would be serving new masters in short order. And Lord Pastour's increasing presence inside the prison made it easy for Derzhin to give in. The problem was Genrikh and the handful of uncorrupted Tahn guards he had as followers. But it was still not a problem, Virunga thought. His armed prisoners, plus Chetwynd's now-enlightened—translation: corrupted or scared—guards, would be capable of dealing with them.

The first movement closed, as expected, as Imperial ships blasted overhead. The landing was under way. Minutes later, sirens shrilled for an emergency formation and to open the second movement. The prisoners formed up slowly in spite of the screams of the guards. Virunga took the count. His formation leaders reported all prisoners accounted for. An alert Tahn was about to bellow in anger at the huge gaps in the formation. Instead, he found himself trying to shout through the ruins of a windpipe and then collapsed.

The killing had been done by Sorensen. Mahoney's giving Sten Sorensen's code word had done more than merely grant access to his mental battle computer—it also freed Sorensen to exercise some of his other Mantis Team skills.

Police Major Genrikh was standing at the head of the guards' formation, facing the prisoners, when he saw that guard die. He could see other prisoners—armed prisoners—suddenly appearing on battlements and on balconies. He was shouting a command, gun coming up and aiming across the courtyard at Sorensen when Chetwynd moved. Initially, Chetwynd had growled at Sten's orders. By rights, he should have been out on the streets running his teams. He considered further. Suppose things did not go exactly right in the beginning? A being could get killed being the first to fight. Koldyeze seemed a fairly good place to wait until the Empire stabilized things. And there was something else to take care of.

The something else was Genrikh—Genrikh and all the clotting Tahn guards and cops who had bashed Chetwynd around from the time he had first jackrolled a drunk sailor to the present day.

Genrikh took aim—and two anchor cables smashed around him. Then he was kicking, lifted into the air in Chetwynd's bear hug. His shout became a gurgle of blood as Chetwynd's arms tightened, smashing ribs and caving Genrikh's chest in.

Chetwynd pitched Genrikh's body aside and went for the other "loyal" guards. He dived for the cobblestones as projectile weapons cracked and men went down. The POW marksmen practiced some restraint, killing the rest of Genrikh's bullies no more than two or three times apiece.

Virunga stood motionless, waiting for the slaughter to end. Then he turned his attention to Derzhin and Avrenti. The remainder of the guards fingered their weapons, unsure of what to do.

"It . . . begun. Lay down . . . arms. Return to quarters. Wait further orders. Follow orders . . . no one harmed."

And so, when Lord Pastour and his escorts arrived, Koldyeze was already in Imperial hands. He was greeted politely and shown to very safe quarters deep in the castle cellars.

That was the end of the second movement.

The third movement should have been nearly pastoral. Imperial ex-prisoners manned Koldyeze's gun towers, the guns turned outward.

All the prisoners had to do was wait inside their prison for eventual relief by the Empire. Any still-fighting Tahn should have been easily discouraged by a few accurate rounds and convinced to go elsewhere to find more meaningful death.

Instead, the third movement opened with the grating of tracks as four heavy tanks rumbled up the cobblestone street toward Koldyeze.

Lord Wichman. And friends.

Those friends consisted of the squadron of heavy tracks,

one squadron of recon tracks, a scout company of gravsleds, and nearly a battalion of soldiers. The prisoners of Koldyeze could be very grateful that Wichman had not been able to acquire any tacnukes.

A prisoner team manning one of the watchtowers ran a burst from its chaingun across the bow of the lead track—and the tank's cannon blew the watchtower apart.

The new arrivals were not there for a casual investigation.

Virunga got on the com to Sten.

The rest of the symphony would be y'zz.

Sten, even though he had gone through the long, drawn-out defeat in the Fringe Worlds, still had not realized there were so many ways of being told he was clotted.

He stood in the middle of what had formerly been the K'ton Klub's main lounge and was now his com center. Koldyeze was up against it. There was no way that Virunga and the rest of the POWs could hold out against an armored attack. And there appeared to be nothing that could be done. His link with the Imperial Forces around Heath told him their attacks were stalled. They had three days minimum until they broke through. Negative on tacair. There were still enough AA missiles sited to make any air support run nearly suicidal. And Wichman's units were too close to hazard even an operator-guided missile attack.

He glanced out a window and winced. He did not need a weatherman to tell him that a storm front was closing in. He saw drizzle and fog. Across the room, Kilgour was already at a computer terminal. A wallscreen cleared, and a map appeared. The map showed Heath's capital with five-meter contour lines. The map shifted, and Koldyeze was suddenly at the map's center.

Sten crossed to the map and studied it. The contour lines grouped very close together around Koldyeze, and Sten's leg muscles memory-ached, remembering the number of times he had groaned up that steep cobblestone street when he was a prisoner. Oh-ho.

"Turn that sucker and animate it," he ordered.

The map changed, and Sten was staring at a lateral projection of Koldyeze showing that outlined, ruined cathedral atop the rise.

"Alex," he wondered aloud, "you got any read on what kinda crunchies Wichman's got?"

"Negative, boss. But Ah'll bet it's nae th' Tahn's finest."

Probably not, Sten thought. "Spin it again."

Once more Sten stared "straight down" at Koldyeze.

He had an idea—of sorts. But he needed one thing.

He asked Kilgour.

"Ah lack exact whae y' need, but Ah hae a wee ersatz."

"Nobody's looted it?"

"Ah gie m' word, wee Sten. Nae e'en a desperate Tahn'd go near it."

"You got two gravsleds running?"

"Ah hae."

And Kilgour was out the door.

Sten, who had planned to spend the last few days of the war sitting in his web being big daddy spider, grabbed the waiting combat harness from the wall and tugged it on.

He looked across the room at St. Clair. She shook her head in disbelief, and he shrugged, then went down the stairs.

Kilgour, already in fighting gear, was waiting outside at the controls of the gravsled. Behind him were two of Chetwynd's agents at the controls of a cargo sled. Both vehicles were battered and battle-damaged but still lift-capable. Sten clambered in, and Alex took off.

"How do you know the stuff's still there?"

"D' ye ken," Alex went on, "thae quadrped we noted, aye back th' day we arrived ae Heath?"

Sten thought back—and recalled that four-legged creature ridden by a Tahn officer. "A hearse?"

"Close, lad. At any rate, dinnae y' wonder whae happens to horses when they die?"

Sten had not.

"The term is renderin't. An' stinkit. Th' recyclin't center's still there an' reekin't. We'll hae our social lubricant."

Kilgour did not have an order of battle for Wichman's assault unit, but his guess had been correct.

The recon squadron was a recently activated reserve unit

made up of soldiers previously invalided out of combat; the gravsled unit had been formed by cadets from one of the Tahn military secondary schools; and the infantrymen had been grabbed from the walking wounded, replacement centers, and transport depots.

The heavy tracks were factory-fresh and intended to be driven directly to the front lines and sent into combat. They were so new that they lacked even a coat of camouflage anodizing. Their crews were civilian—final line inspectors who had been grabbed and given orders by Wichman's people. Only one inspector had objected—and been promptly shot by H'nrich, Wichman's chief of security. The others did what they were told.

They attacked Koldyeze.

The first tank made Sten's plan possible.

The first watchtower destroyed, the tank ground into motion up the cobbled street, its cannon finger probing for a new target. The gunner's sights swept across the second watchtower on the other side of Koldyeze's gates. There was no sign of motion. The gunner looked for a better target.

Very slowly, the chaingun in that second watchtower swiveled. The skinny man crouching in the gunner's seat turned to the equally emaciated man kneeling beside him. "Is it loaded?"

"I think so. You figure out how to shoot it?"

"Hell if I know."

"You know that popgun ain't gonna punch through that tin can down there, don't you?"

"Shaddup. I live a clean life."

The ex-POW loading the chaingun would have been correct—under normal circumstances. The antipersonnel rounds in the chaingun should have spattered off the heavy tank like raindrops. But the tank's designers had assumed that no clotting driver would ever be dumb enough to take that track over a pile of rubble and expose its belly and extremely vulnerable escape hatch.

The scared civilian behind the tank's controls was that dumb.

And the Imperial soldier behind the chaingun's triggers was a very good shot.

Ten rounds blew the hatch off its locks—*into* the tank's crew compartment—and then ricocheted. Heavy armor could keep things in as well as out.

There were two survivors, and they were shot down by riflemen as they scrambled out the rear hatch for safety.

"Not bad," the loader said.

"Not bad at all," the gunner said.

Ten seconds later smoke wisped out of the tank's atmosphere exhausts, and the track "brewed up" in flames.

The easy way to take Koldyeze had been cut.

Virunga wondered what his still-unknown attacker would try next.

Probably an infantry assault.

That indeed was what Wichman had in mind. But his cobbled-together assault unit was still getting itself organized, and most of the improvised platoons were nowhere near the line of departure when whistles shrilled.

About a company of grunts started up the hill. They were quickly shot down or into shelter. There was no second wave. Instead, they started building barricades across the streets and creating fighting positions inside the tenements.

Perfectly fine, Virunga thought. We have no intention of counterattacking, and if they turn this into a siege, perhaps we can hold on until the Imperial Forces arrive.

Perhaps. He went to prepare what he was trying to convince himself was his artillery.

At twilight, Sten and Alex were crouched on the roof of one of the tenements, looking for a way in.

Below them, hidden in wreckage, was the larger gravsled, its cargo slooping and stinking, just as Kilgour had promised.

Sten saw an opportunity to create some chaos.

The cadets manning the gravsleds were evidently trying to attack Koldyeze as if they were Scythians bashing out a Roman legion. Their sleds darted back and forth up and down, the sleds' gunners occasionally blasting off a burst or two. Good shots. They hit Koldyeze almost every other time.

Sten waited until dark, then flipped on the light-enhancing sights of his sniper rifle. It was a fairly nasty weapon that fired a tiny, shielded AM2 round that on impact would blow a hole in a man's chest that a gravsled could be driven through. But unlike the issue willygun, the heavy sniper rifle used a modified linear accelerator to propel the round. The scope was used not merely to give a precise range and fix on the target but could be turned if the target happened to go behind a wall. On firing, the accelerator would spin the round at the appropriate time—and the gun was quite capable of shooting around a corner.

Sten did not need that much trickery.

He put the scope's cross hairs on a gravsled pilot and blew him out of his seat. When the gunner jumped for the controls, he died, too.

A few seconds later, five gravsleds were orbiting around the ruined streets below Koldyeze aimlessly.

That would provide the necessary chaos.

Kilgour and Sten dropped down the shattered tenement steps and into their own sled and moved slowly forward. Their advance went seemingly unobserved—at least none of the rounds that slammed into the ground nearby seemed particularly aimed.

They reached the still-smoldering tank, and Kilgour steered the sled around it. He turned, free hand questionmarked, then pointed down. *Here?* Sten signed: *Ten meters more.* Kilgour obeyed and then grounded the gravsled.

And they almost got themselves killed.

In spite of Virunga's bellows and protests about losing his battle computer and fifty percent of Gaaronk's operators, Sorensen put together an ambush team. He was—at least as far as he knew—the only Mantis operative inside Koldyeze. But there were POWs from other hands-on lethal units who wanted a bit of close-in revenge. They slid out of the cathedral toward the destroyed track.

Sorensen knew that Wichman's forces had to remove that hulk before they could send in more armor. Figuring that combat engineers were few and far between those days, he intended to kill a few recovery specialists.

He saw the gravsled ground and crept toward the two Tahn —he thought—getting out of it. Eyes away, he reminded himself. His backup men flanked him. Sorensen readied the long ceremonial knife he was carrying. He would take the heavier one first. Then—

A flare bloomed on the horizon, and all five men became bushes. The flare sank down, and Sorensen's two targets were alive once more. The smaller man's hands moved to one side, then together, as if holding a package. Patrol sign language, Sorensen realized. Had the Tahn stolen that from the Imperials? He decided to take a chance and hissed sibilantly.

The two men crouch-spun, weapons coming up. But they did not fire.

"ID," Sorensen whispered.

Sten realized that the whisper was not in Tahn. He assumed that the ambushers must have come out of Koldyeze.

"Imperials."

"One forward."

Kilgour rumbled toward Sorensen.

Sorensen's night vision was almost gone—the vitamin-lousy diet the Tahn had fed them ensured that. Even with the added rations from the discovered stores, he still was looking at a blur when Alex recognized him.

"Wee Sorensen," he whispered.

The accent was enough.

Sorensen waved his team forward and hand question-marked. *Need help?* Sten nodded ostentatiously, then indicated. Two out as security. The rest—start pouring.

Sten lifted the gravsled's nose slightly, and the semiliquid cargo sloshed out. As Sten shoveled glop out onto the cobblestones, he wondered if it was a lum. Kilgour was always closing letters with some nonsense phrase about somebody's lum reeking. And dead hearse—horse, he corrected—did reek. Kilgour had been quite correct—no one had looted the rendering works. And the liquefied fat from the vats should work very well.

They finished and regrouped. Sten had planned on reentering Koldyeze with Alex through the still-undiscovered tunnel. But obviously Sorensen had a better way.

Sten sent the gravsled, at full power, back down the street. It ricocheted away, caroming off buildings and providing an excellent diversion. Then everyone doubled back toward Koldyeze. Sten had ordered Sorensen's run aborted; he figured that the demolished track would not be recovered by specialists. Wichman's people were more adept at brute force—and Sorensen would be more than a little outgunned.

Sten went through the half-opened main gate, hoping that Koldyeze's water supply was still turned on. He smelled. Smelled like . . . a dead horse.

A very dead horse.

Sten was correct. The ruined track was bulldozed out of the street and through a tenement wall early in the morning by a second heavy tank. Sorensen's ritual butcher knife would not have done much good.

Wichman attacked, predictably at dawn.

And Virunga unmasked his artillery.

It was not much.

The crypt had held four cannon. Real cannon, not lasers or masers: put shell and propellant in one end and yank a handle, and it works—maybe. Virunga thought the cannon were probably intended for some kind of ceremonial use, although that did not explain why they had sights, and ordered the barrels wire-wrapped for reinforcement. Virunga had marveled at the sights. They were primitive. It had been years since he had seen a laser ranging cannon, and then only in a museum.

Working parties had managed to hoist the cannon onto the battlements, and firing apertures had been bashed through the walls and then concealed. Virunga was pretty sure that the recoil mechanism of the cannon was rusted solid. Regardless, he did not plan on taking chances and had ringbolts spot-welded to the cannon and bolted to the cathedral walls themselves. Cables linked the guns to the wall bolts and, hopefully, would prevent the cannon from recoiling straight off the battlements when they were fired.

Virunga had found and trained cannoneers, then dubbed his four popguns "Battery A."

"Battery B" was eight multiple-tube rocket launchers, firing solid heads, powered by propellant picked from the projectile rounds stores in the crypts and then hard-packed into containers. At least there was more than enough propellant.

Aiming consisted of squinting through a V-sight atop the tubes until the target was more or less aligned and then getting the hell out of the way while someone hit an electrical firing connection. The launchers were crewed and then sited atop other battlements.

"Battery C" was even worse.

Observing that the castle's plumbing seemed built for all eternity, Virunga had ordered sections of pipe to be cut into meter-and-a-half sections and wire-reinforced. He was making mortars. Very, very big mortars.

Micrometers, small inspection telescopes, bubble levels, gears, and knobs had been stolen from the various workshops that the POWs slave-labored for and had been cobbled together to make sights for the mortars.

Virunga discovered that the propellant used in the rifle rounds could be liquefied and cast without harm. He decided to use that powder, cast into round increments, to fire his mortar rounds. The rounds themselves were smaller sections of pipe built up again with wire to approximate the interior dimensions of the mortar tubes. They were handgrooved so the pipe would shrapnel on impact, but not deeply enough that the round would explode on firing.

Maybe.

The rounds were packed with more propellant. Nitric acid, alk, and mercury were gingerly mixed by self-taught POW chemists to make the horribly dangerous mercury fulminate that would be used to detonate the rounds on impact.

Maybe.

Virunga readied firing positions in the courtyard for the mortars, with high-stacked stone around them in case the bad guys had mortars of their own.

The tiny com units that had been brought to Heath by Sten and smuggled into Koldyeze by Chetwynd were the only modern items Virunga had. They linked the observers to the batteries. In spite of the risk—the observers were located anywhere the streets around Koldyeze could be seen from— there was no shortage of volunteers.

Thirty seconds after the first tank popped into open, Virunga opened fire.

"Battery A. Armor in the open. Acquire targets visually. Fire on individual control."

The gun commander of the first cannon had one of the recon tracks in his sights. He held his breath and yanked the firing lever. The cannon cracked and slammed back against the cable restraints. The commander stared down at the streets below. The round slammed into a wall about five meters from the recon track.

"Come on down a little bit and right a skosh," the commander advised the gunner. He was not, needless to say, a trained artillerybeing.

The third round ventilated the thinly armored recon track, and its crew bailed out.

Virunga smiled in pleasure.

His other three guns were also firing and hitting.

Down below, the three heavy tracks ground up the street toward the cathedral. One of them took a direct hit from a cannon, but the solid round ricocheted off the track's armor plating.

Sten peered through a battlement's machicolations and swore. He had hoped that somehow Virunga's cannon would have enough power to punch holes in the heavy tracks. The only thing that could stop them, he realized, was his deceased horses.

The tank clattered slowly up the cobblestones toward Koldyeze, infantry moving forward in its shelter. Then the track hit the grease. Its tracks spun uselessly on the cobblestones. The huge tank slid sideways and back down the hill, slamming into the first hulk.

And then the defenders of Koldyeze got lucky.

Not, of course, that luck was ever mentioned by either Sergeant Major Isby, observing for Battery C, or by the mortar crew. Isby, even though he was a supply specialist, had been given infantry training, which at one time had included artillery/mortar observation. He remembered his lessons quite well.

"Charlie Two," he broadcast. "This is Observer Six. Fire Mission. Azimuth 5250 down 30. Distance 3200. Tanks and infantry in the open. Will adjust."

The sights of the mortar were adjusted, and two still-brawny women, VIP hostages, fitted firing charges onto the mortar bomb and hoisted it up over the mortar's mouth, let go, and ducked away.

The mortar thudded. Sten saw the wobbling pipe climb high into the sky, then turn and drop downward. The first round hit the stalled track directly on top of its engine exhaust plates and exploded. The tank itself blew up, sending its turrets cartwheeling away into the infantry around it.

Once again, the way was blocked.

Isby and the mortar crew, of course, said that the first-round hit proved how good they were. They bragged accordingly. They did not think it worthy of note to mention that they hit nothing else for the rest of that day.

And then the infantry began its assault.

They came in cautiously, keeping to the cover of the tenements and rubble. But they still had to come into the open eventually.

Sten methodically sniped down an entire squad of grunts who were hiding behind what they thought was solid stone. Other marksbeings, now familiar with the projectile sporter weapons they were equipped with, decimated the infantry.

But the siege of Koldyeze was still being lost by the ex-prisoners.

Slowly the ring of Wichman's troops closed on Koldyeze. There was just too many of them.

The single chaingun that survived atop the second watchtower was smashed by three accurate rounds from another heavy tank firing over the corpse of its brother. Tahn soldiers countersniped from positions on the roofs of tenements.

Sten saw a POW lying on the battlement not far from him slump, the top of her head suddenly missing.

"Dinnae y' hope, young Sten," Alex observed, "thae our wee Guardsmen aren't takin't long mess breaks?"

Sten hoped that very desperately.

Chief Warrant Officer Rinaldi Hernandes had wondered what would happen if he survived imprisonment long enough to get a weapon in his hands. Could he kill—even beings who had been responsible for his grandchild's death?

He could.

Somewhere Hernandes had found an enormous rifle—nearly as long as he was—that single-fired a round the size of the cheroots he missed desperately. It was an ancient rifle fitted with a museum-quality optical sight.

But it was a very effective antique.

Hernandes held his sights on the target—a Tahn in the gunner's seat of a gravsled. He breathed in deeply. Then he let out half the breath and held. His finger pulled the forward trigger, then moved back to the set trigger. It touched the metal, and the rifle slammed him.

Kilgour had taken one look at Hernandes's weapon and dubbed it a "dinosaur gun."

"Because it'd kill a dinosaur," Sten straight-manned.

"Na, clot. Because it takit a dinosaur to fire the beast."

It damn near did. The rifle kicked—hard. Hernandes was pretty sure that his shoulder was if not broken at least cracked a lot.

But it was far worse on the arrival end.

The gunner in the gravsled had time enough to notice that he lacked a pelvis before he died.

Hernandes carefully scratched a mark on the stone next to him. That made twenty-seven.

He looked for another target.

Downslope, a Tahn sergeant spotted the movement, sighted, and touched a trigger.

The three-round burst blew Hernandes's abdomen apart.

The decimation went on.

Virunga reflexively ducked when the explosion went off, the blast echoing seemingly endlessly around the courtyard walls.

And then the screams started.

The first of the mortars had exploded. Thirty-one people were dead or maimed around the shattered metal. Medics scurried to help.

Virunga kept his expression untroubled. At least the blast walls had provided an unexpected side benefit and kept the damage moderate. But Virunga knew that the three remaining mortars would be shot on a duck-and-fire principle. Koldyeze, he estimated, could hold no more than another day, at best.

And that night Wichman's forces mined the wall.

Wichman gave precise orders. Even though he was inexperienced at combat, he was learning rapidly.

I could have served better, he realized with resentment. *I should have resigned my post for a combat command when this war began. Perhaps . . .*

But he was not egotistic enough to think he could have changed things.

But this would be enough: a final revenge against the traitors and a final strike against the Imperials. Koldyeze was to be completely illuminated, both by flares and from six mobile searchlights that one of his aides had scrounged. Chainguns on the recon tracks were to sweep the walls. Any Imperial prisoner who stuck his head up would be slaughtered.

His plan worked.

When he was satisfied that all fire from the cathedral had been suppressed, he sent in the troops with demopacks. Nearly ten tons of high explosive was arranged at the foot of the wall. His next assault, which would occur an hour before dawn, was certain to succeed.

Unfortunately, Lord Wichman did not survive to see whether his tactics were successful.

Sten, outranking Sorensen, pulled the plug on the young man's commando operations. Virunga was right—they could not stand to lose him. Especially not now, with Virunga's cannon firing by calculation, calculation made possible only by Sorensen's mind functioning as a battle computer.

But those orders did not hold true for Sten.

After dusk, he and Alex went out looking for trouble. They went through the Tahn perimeter easily, all the old Mantis moves returning. Beyond the front lines, they split up and began their head-hunting.

Sten carried a miniwillygun with a single magazine of ammunition. If he was blown, he knew better than to imagine he would be able to shoot his way out. He carried four Mantis demolition packs with him, along with two grenades and a Gurkha kukri he had brought back to Heath.

The demopacks were the first to go. With a variable time set on the fuses, they were deposited, one on the deck of a recon track, one in the middle of four parked gravsleds, the third on one of the searchlight's generators, and the final one under what Sten thought was a com trailer.

Large cables led from that trailer into a well-guarded building. Sten found that interesting. He slipped into that building's neighbor and found an appropriate-length section of metal stair banister. On the roof, he positioned the banister across to the guarded building and hand-over-handed his way onto its roof, the rusty metal bending slightly as he went. He crept down the stairs, keeping low and close to the wall.

Lousy blackout, he thought, seeing a gleam of light from the curtained doorway of a room on the second floor. Then he saw the bulk next to it.

H'nrich might have been an excellent bodyguard against normal intruders.

Sten was not normal.

H'nrich'e eye registered a flash in the dimness as the kukri came up from below. That was all.

Sten yanked the kukri out of H'nrich's neck—he had pulled the slash so he would not have to worry about a head bouncing around the hallway—caught the sagging, blood-spouting body, and eased it down. He sheathed the kukri, wiped stickiness from his face, and took three deep breaths.

The question was not what was going to happen next but what would happen *next* next. Specifically, would Sten have time to get out with his vital signs vital before the reaction.

Possibly.

He took the two grenades from his webbing and rolled the timer until the X was under his fingers. Ten seconds.

Come on, son. Don't get cowardly now.

His hand blurred the pistol from its holster, and Sten went through the blackout curtain.

There were seven beings in the room. One of them, Sten's mind registered, was wearing a dress uniform, and then he

ID'd Lord Wichman as his finger pulled the trigger to its stop and the AM2 rounds spit around the room.

Four rounds tore Wichman's body apart. Sten's free hand lobbed the grenades at the com console, and then he was gone.

There were screams and shouts and somebody outside shooting at something.

Sten was back up the steps, three at a time, almost falling through a broken lift, then on the roof and across. Running. He hit the far edge, eyes telling him he could make the jump, mind saying you ain't no Kilgour, and then he was in the air.

He landed at least a meter on the other side of that third building's parapet. Getting cowardly, he thought once more, and then melted into the night toward Koldyeze.

Sten came back to awaiting catastrophe.

He had seen the searchlights blinding on the walls of Koldyeze, realized that he could not return the way he had come out, and went once more through the tunnel.

Virunga brought him quickly up to speed; they had heard, and seen, the demolition charges being planted. When the Tahn had pulled back, four brave men and women had tried to get to the charges. Their bodies lay only a few meters beyond the gate.

Not, Sten thought privately, that they could have accomplished much. He assumed that the demo charges were not only separately det-timed but booby-trapped as well. The romantic days of putting the fuse seconds before the bang banged were as ancient as Hernandes's rifle.

"Ordered," Virunga said, "all troops back from wall. If Koldyeze doesn't fall on our heads . . . will retake fighting positions after blast.

"Better suggestion?" he asked Sten hopefully.

Sten had none. Neither did Kilgour when he returned an hour later.

They looked for a big rock to hide behind.

Wichman might have been dead, but his troops soldiered on.

The blast went off—on schedule.

The shock wave blew down five entire rows of already-shattered tenements. The ground earthquake-shook, and in their still-separate battle two kilometers away, Imperial guardsmen ducked, sure that somebody had set off a nuke. The blast cloud rose more than three kilometers into the clouds despite the continuing drizzle.

The entire front wall of the cruciform-shaped cathedral crumbled, and slid down the hill.

But only six POWs died. Koldyeze had indeed been built to withstand almost anything.

The Tahn mounted what was to be the final attack—and ran instantly into trouble.

The ruins of that front wall made an excellent tank trap—far superior even to Sten's grease. Even the heavies could not grind through the building-high boulders.

Only the gravsleds could provide support for the infantry.

Somewhat surprised that they were still alive, the Imperial defenders boiled out of their holes and found fighting positions.

Gravsled pilots were hit, and the gravsleds orbited out of the battle. The first wave of the Tahn infantry was obliterated.

But the second wave found forward positions and laid down a base of fire.

The third wave attacked, and the gravsleds were able to move in.

The prisoners pulled back. Back and down.

Into the crypts.

"Clottin' convenient place to die," Kilgour observed, sourly looking around the cellar. "Thae'll be na need to dig a wee grave."

Virunga herded the last of the hostages down more stone steps deeper into the subbasements and limped back toward Sten.

Sten had hastily reorganized the surviving fighters into five-man squads and given each one a position to hold: a stairwell, a landing, a portion of the huge basement he himself was in. Anything bullet-resistant had been dragged up as a barricade.

He had not needed to tell his squads they were to hold till the last—none of the Imperial prisoners were stupid enough to believe the Tahn were interested in recapturing them.

Kilgour, three-gee muscles straining, had lifted a stone altar into position for his and Sten's personal last stand. He spread out his remaining grenades and ammunition in front of him.

Sten followed suit.

"Y' know, wee Sten," Kilgour observed. "If thae clottin' Tahn hae brain one, thae'll just filter gas down the steps an' be done wi' us. Thae's nae a filtermask t' be had."

At least, Sten thought, that would be relatively painless.

"Or p'raps," Kilgour went on relentlessly, "thae'll just seal us up alive. Thae'll be no bones f'r m' mum t' mourn over. An me a claustrophobe, too."

Sten showed his teeth in what he realized probably did not much resemble a smile and settled down to wait for death.

It was, surprisingly, a fairly long wait.

They dimly heard the sound of firing from above. Sten wondered. Had the Tahn found some other way down to them? The firing suddenly rose to a dull storm and died away. There was the crack of single shots then.

Sten looked at Kilgour.

"Na," Alex suggested. "Thae's too convenient."

But both of them replaced their grenades and ammo into their harnesses and moved slowly up the steps toward the courtyard. A burst of fire shattered down at them, and they ducked behind the turn in the stairwell.

"Clot," Alex swore. "Ah was right. Too convenient."

Sten waited for the requisite grenade to roll down on them. But instead there came a shout in very bad Tahn.

"Surrender. Weapons no. Hands air in."

Sten and Alex grinned. And Sten shouted back in Imperial.

"Friends. Imperial. Kiss to be kissed."

"One up," came the shout, in Imperial but still suspicious.

Sten shucked his combat harness and, moving very slowly, hands in plain sight, climbed the steps until he saw two battered guardsmen, their red, exhausted eyes glaring through filthy faces. And he kissed them both.

Out of common courtesy, the one with the beard got the first one.

They were rescued.

The relief force was commanded by a one-star general. Imperial forces had mounted a massive armor assault and driven a wedge through the Tahn lines.

They had not stopped to widen that perimeter but had kept on moving, their tracks slamming at full speed through the city of Heath. Gravsleds hovered above them. Gunners opened fire on any movement without checking to see whether the target was a scared civilian or a Tahn soldier. They had hit the remnants of Wichman's forces in the rear and scattered them.

Sten and Alex stood in the courtyard, listening to the general. He was very proud of himself and his men.

Why not? Sten thought in stupid fatigue. After I sleep for about six months, I'll buy him a beer, too. Come to think, I'll buy anybody in this unit as much alk as they can pour down. Or whatever else they take, he amended. He was turning to Kilgour to suggest they find somewhere to collapse—and suddenly the Scotsman's rifle was snapping to his shoulder.

Senior Captain Lo Prek was aiming very carefully. He had followed the assault wave into Koldyeze, and no one had bothered asking who the hell he was.

He had found a position inside Koldyeze itself and waited. Perhaps Sten was outside the walls, or perhaps inside. But he knew that he would have his chance.

He ignored the destruction of Wichman's soldiers and the victorious Imperials. That was not a part of his war.

And at that point he was rewarded, seeing below him the man who had murdered his brother.

As his sights found Sten, his heart thundered and he aimed, knowing he would get only a single shot.

Sten and the Guards general went down as Kilgour fired a long, chattered *snap-burst* that blew apart the cathedral window above them.

Kilgour lowered the rifle.

"What was—" Sten managed, and Alex waved the barrel.

A body slumped forward out of the window and hung, motionless.

"Clottin' sniper," Kilgour said.

Sten picked himself up. That was it. For him, the war was over.

The body of Senior Captain Lo Prek was eventually picked up by a press gang of Tahn civilians under the direction of an Imperial sanitation expert, loaded onto a gravsled, and taken outside the city. It was cremated, along with several thousand other, equally nameless bodies.

And the war was over.

CHAPTER FIFTY-SIX

THE SURRENDER DOCUMENT was a small off-white sheet of parchment. There were very few words penned on the document itself, because there were *no* terms. The surrender was unconditional.

From the moment the document was signed and then countersigned, the Tahn would have to depend on the charity and mercy of the Eternal Emperor.

The document sat upon a small linen-covered table. Behind the table sat Ian Mahoney, the Emperor's representative and newly appointed governor-general of what had once been the Tahn Empire. The table and chair were the only furnishings in the yawning main banquet room of the *Normandie*.

It was in that room that the incident that had triggered the war had taken place. On that day it had been crammed with tables laden with delicacies to be enjoyed by the cream of Tahn diplomacy. It was there that an entirely different sort of document was to have been signed: a declaration of peace.

And the Emperor himself had presided. But the incident had ended in murder and the betrayal of both camps.

Now the Emperor was nowhere in sight. His deliberate absence was a calculated act to add to the Tahn's humiliation. Instead, there was Mahoney, his two chief aides standing at full attention on either side of him, and, lined up along the walls of the room, the top officers of the Emperor's fleets and armies.

On the far side of the room, partially hidden by a hastily hung curtain, was a livie crew filming the event for Empire-wide broadcast.

The main portal hissed open, and Colonel Pastour stepped in. He was the sole surviving member of the Tahn High Council. In a moment he would be just citizen Pastour. The Emperor had decreed that once the surrender had been signed, there would be no ranks or titles permitted in the lands of the Tahn.

As Pastour started the long, slow march toward the table, two other Tahn trailed behind him. One was dressed in the ragged uniform of a customs officer. The other wore that of a postal official. They were the highest Tahn officials anyone could find. Pastour himself, at the demand of the Emperor, wore civilian clothes.

Pastour came to a stop just in front of the table. The only movement in the room was Mahoney's head as it lifted. Two eyes below bushy, forbidding eyebrows bored into him. Pastour hesitated, unsure what to do next. He thought of his people watching on the public-square screens that the Imperials had erected in every major city. He knew it was his duty to abase himself for them. But how much humiliation would be required?

Mahoney slid the document toward him.

"Sign!" was all he said.

Pastour fumbled for a pen and scratched his name. Mahoney flipped the document over and signed his name beneath Pastour's. He handed it to one of his aides. Then he looked up at Pastour, his eyes filled with hate. Oddly, the hate was comforting. *That* Pastour understood.

"That's all," Mahoney said.

And in total silence, citizen Pastour turned and stumbled away.

Admiral Sten paced back and forth in the passageway. A commentator's voice crackled from speakers mounted on either end of the corridor, analyzing the events that were unfolding for his audience. As Sten paced, he kept glancing at the door that led to the Emperor's stateroom. And any moment, he would be called into his commander in chief's presence. Sten was one of the few people who were aware that the Eternal Emperor *was* aboard the *Normandie*.

"He said it was his damned show," Mahoney had explained, "and he planned to have a ringside seat, even if he couldn't allow himself to be there in person."

Sten understood that, just as he admired the Emperor's willpower in staying away from the ceremony itself. If it were Sten, protocol be damned, he would want to see his enemy squirm close up. But that was not what he was thinking as he paced nervously.

His head was buzzing with questions, which mostly boiled down to, What did the boss want of him next? Sten was sick of anything vaguely involving official violence. He was sick of killing. Sick of manipulations. Sick of giving orders and sick of seeing his fellow beings dying carrying them out. He was wearing his new admiral's uniform for the first time, and he was already sick of that, as well. Sten was fuzzily imagining some kind of life that had nothing to do with the military. He was not sure what he would do with it, but he felt good just wondering.

St. Clair and L'n were in the process of selling the K'ton Club. Maybe he would join them in whatever venture they had in mind. Clot, after the bundle Ida had made for him, he could bankroll streets and streets of nightclubs. Sten in show biz? Nah. Wouldn't wash. Maybe he should talk to Kilgour. Maybe they could team up and do a little poking around some frontier systems. See what the Indians were up to.

He was casually considering the prospector's life and wondering if St. Clair or Haines might fit in, when the door *whoosh*ed open and a Gurkha beckoned him inside.

The Eternal Emperor palmed the switch that cut the vidscreen off as Sten entered and came to full attention.

"Knock it off, Admiral," the Emperor said impatiently, "I've had it with ceremony. And I hope it doesn't offend your military sensibilities when I inform you that soldiering of any kind is starting to give me a pain in my royal behind."

Sten laughed, not offended at all, and slumped into a chair. The Emperor got up, fetched a bottle of stregg and two shot glasses, and filled them both to the brim.

"We've got time for one of these and then one more before I chase you out of here," the Emperor said. "Soon as those clottin' Tahn clear the *Normandie*, I'm taking off."

"Going home, sir?" Sten asked.

"No such luck," the Emperor said. "I've got a lot of fence mending to do. You know the drill: shake hands, kiss babies, have my picture taken with people I've allowed to think are important, thank my allies for missing every time they tried to stab me in the back, and generally pump up my popularity polls.

"Hell, I won't see Prime World inside of six months. And I'm already fed up with the whole thing. Shows what a rotten attitude I've got."

He raised his glass in toast. "Here's to rotten attitudes."

Sten chinked his glass with his boss's, and the two of them choked back the raw stregg. The Emperor refilled the glasses. One more shot to go, and Sten's time was up. And he was . . . free?

"Look. When I get back is when the real work starts," the Emperor said, "and I'm gonna need some help."

Sten saw his freedom vanishing.

"I've had to rebuild this whole shebang more than once," the Emperor said, "but I don't think things have ever been this bad. Don't get me wrong. I know *what* to do. But after this war I'm short of talent to help out.

"Sullamora and his boyos won't do much more than get in my way. All they can see is bottom-line profits. Funny about those types. They have some minor money-making abilities— if you call pirating business savvy. The thing that bothers me is that they don't seem to have any fun doing it.

"Bunch of gloomy clots. And they don't help my mood at all. All right. Forget them. I bring in some young, spirited types like yourself. We bust our scrotums for just fifty or sixty years, and maybe we end up with something looking kind of nice. Something we can be proud of."

If Sten had been uneasy before, when the "we" crept into the conversation, he really started getting worried.

"Excuse me, sir," he broke in, "but I'm not sure how I can fit into all this."

The Emperor waved that away. "You're not to worry about it," he said. "I've got some pretty good ideas."

"It's not that," Sten said. "And I don't mean to sound ungrateful. But..." He hesitated, then took the plunge. "You see, I've got some pretty severe doubts about where I want to be in those next fifty or sixty years. And right now, the military doesn't feel like it. Like you said, it feels like a pain in the behind—although mine isn't royal."

The Emperor laughed. "So, what are you thinking?"

"I'm not sure," Sten said. "I've got leave coming to me. Probably a couple of years' worth if I totted it all up. I thought maybe I'd just kick back and see what happens."

The Emperor gave Sten a measuring look. Then he smiled and shook his head. He tilted his glass at Sten in a silent toast. The audience was over. Sten drained his glass and got up. He set down the glass and gave the Emperor what he hoped would be his last salute. The Emperor returned it, very formal.

"Within six months," he predicted, "you'll be bored out of your skull. I should be back home by then. Look me up."

Believing that the Emperor was wrong on all counts, Sten wheeled and was out the door.

CHAPTER FIFTY-SEVEN

THE ETERNAL EMPEROR clumped down the ramp of the *Normandie*, his Gurkha bodyguards pressed tightly around him. He paused at the bottom, then breathed a silent sigh of relief. As per his orders, there were no welcoming crowds at Soward, Prime World's main spaceport. Instead, a short distance away, there was only his personal gravcar and its escort to take him back to his dreary makeshift quarters beneath the ruins of Arundel.

He would have to do something about that, he reminded himself. Time to give the rebuilding program a boot in the butt. It was not the image of pomp and splendor he missed but the carefully built-in comforts and, above all, privacy. Just to be alone for a little while with one of his nutball projects—like reinventing the varnish used on a Strad violin—would be an immense relief.

At the moment he felt that if one more being asked him for a decision or brought some trouble to his attention, he would break down and sob. The problem was that emperors who sobbed publicly were never eternal. Still, that was exactly what he felt like doing. Just as his face felt as if it was going to fall off from smiling at vidcameras, and his fingers were bleeding from shaking the hands of so many grateful subjects. They were all anxious to tell him what a hero he was.

He thought of another hero and winced, with a small smile. After a decisive battle, one of the man's aides had told him what a great hero he had become. Sure, the new hero had observed. But if I had lost, I would be the greatest villain in our nation's history. What was the guy's name? Who knows. Probably something Prussian. So much for clottin' heroes.

The Eternal Emperor pulled himself together and headed for his gravcar. A few years earlier he would have slept the clock around three or four times, then donned his Raschid identity and gone on a long drunk at the Covenanter, with maybe a tumble with Janiz for old time's sake. But the Covenanter was gone because of treachery. As was Janiz. Both gone, and it was his fault, dammit! He had let it get away from him somehow.

The master of doublethink. Bah! Maybe that's your problem, Engineer Raschid. You overclottin' complicate every clottin' thing. Keep it stupid, simple, and a whole lot of folks might still be breathing—instead of dead or, worse, on their knees, praising your name.

The Eternal Emperor was feeling every year of his 3,000-plus span as he reached the car. Then he saw Tanz Sullamora's smiling face, and he groaned and almost groaned again as Tanz stuck out a hand to be shook. Instead, he took it—gingerly.

"Welcome back, Your Majesty," Sullamora gushed. "We're all very proud."

Sure you are, the Raschid side of him thought. You just can't wait to figure out how to intrigue me out of a few more warehouses full of credits. But the Eternal Emperor side of him made him merely smile and mutter a polite thanks.

"I have one small request," Sullamora said. "I know you're anxious to get home, but . . ."

The Emperor raised an eyebrow. He was about to be put out. He was too tired to speak, so he just motioned for Sullamora to continue.

"It's the spaceport employees," Sullamora said. "They've been waiting for hours and . . ."

He glanced over where Sullamora was pointing and saw a small mixed-uniform crowd near the main gate. Oh, no! More smiling. More hand shaking. More . . . Ahhh . . .

"I can't handle it, Tanz," the Emperor said. "Get Mahoney to do it. He's back on the *Normandie* taking care of some last-minute business. He'll be out in a sec." He stepped to the door of his gravcar.

"It won't be the same, sir," Sullamora insisted. "It's you they want to see. I know these beings aren't *real* fighters and all. But they have done their best in their own ways. So, won't you please . . ."

The Eternal Emperor resigned himself and changed direction for the gate. He wanted to get it over with, so he picked up speed until he had his Gurkhas trotting on their stumpy legs to keep up.

The little crowd broke into cheers as he approached them, and the Emperor, who was too professional to disappoint under such circumstances, painted on his most Imperial smile and started shaking hands. He made sure he asked each being's name as he took the outstretched hand with his right and clasped the elbow with his left. It was a handshake guaranteed to generate warm feelings, and at the same time he could use the elbow hold to move them gently to the side as he pulled back his shaking hand and stepped to the side to take another.

He was about a third of the way down the line when he came to the man with the pale face and too-bright eyes. The Emperor asked the man's name and went into his hand shaking act. He could not make out the nervous mutter he got back so that he could repeat it, so he just grinned more widely and started to withdraw his hand and pass on.

The hands stayed clasped.

The Eternal Emperor had only a heartbeat to puzzle at what was going wrong, and then he saw the pistol coming up in the man's other hand. And he was falling back, trying to get away, but he could not let go as the pistol went *crack-crack-crack-crack* and he knew he was hit but could not feel a thing except maybe that his stomach was bruised and—

The Gurkhas were on Chapelle, slashing with their deadly kukris, and the man was dead even as his trigger finger kept pulling in reflex and the gun was clicking empty. It happened so fast that only then the crowd began to get the idea that something awful was occurring. The first screams began.

Tanz Sullamora stood there for a frozen moment, shaken at being so close to violence, even though it was of his own making. Then he turned and started to drop to one knee before the Emperor's body.

There was only a small bloody splotch on the Emperor's dress uniform to mark where the bullets had penetrated, and for a moment Sullamora was not sure if he had even been hurt.

A minute later, the worry was over. The Eternal Emperor was dead.

Then the privy council turned up the joker in the Emperor's deck.

The bomb implanted in his body exploded. The size of the blast had been determined thousands of years before. Sullamora died. And the Gurkhas. And the sobbing crowd. And anyone and anything within a precise one-eighth of a kilometer.

Odd things happened in all explosions, and that one was no exception. A week later, a tech from the pathology lab found Chapelle's face. That was all—just his face. There was not a blemish or a mark on it.

Chapelle's face was smiling.

CHAPTER FIFTY-EIGHT

MAHONEY PRESSED HIS thumb against the print sensor, and the door to the Eternal Emperor's study hissed open. He hesitated before he entered. This would probably be his last time. There were only a very few beings the sensor would pass, and for an hour or two more Mahoney was one of them.

After that, the memory would be wiped and a new order of permitted presences would be installed. Mahoney knew there was no way his name would be on that exalted list, just as he had known there was something very wrong almost as soon as he had scattered his handful of dirt on the Eternal Emperor's coffin and stepped back to let the others pay their last respects.

The five surviving members of the privy council stood slightly apart from the other mourners on a small grassy knoll, just beyond the screen of rosebushes the gardeners had hastily planted to fulfill the Emperor's burial wishes.

But there was only one rose blossom on the entire span of bushes. It had no hidden meaning, but Mahoney found it strangely apt, and as it drew his attention, he made note of the presence of the Council of Five.

They stood together, but at an apparent measured distance, as if they were afraid to be too close. Not a word was whispered between them, and their faces were stony and guarded. It was as if they had something to feel guilty about, Mahoney thought; then he wiped away the thought as a product of Mick romanticism.

But the image nagged at him, and when he saw the news feed that night, he marked the announcement that an emergency session of Parliament had been called. Now, what could be odd about that, my friend? Mahoney thought. This is an emergency, isn't it?

Sure it is, Ian, but bless your sweet dumb Irish behind, don't you see it? The session was called by the privy council. Mahoney did not have to be a legal scholar to realize that such an action was well beyond their constitutional authority. All right. So why didn't any member of the Parliament complain? Or, better yet, refuse? Simple. Because it was wired, dear Ian, dear Ian, wired.

The Emperor had been murdered, and Mahoney knew who had done it, and it was not the poor mad fool the livies were going on about in their endlessly recycled analysis. It was not Chapelle.

Sure, Chapelle had pulled the trigger. But the real guilt rested with the five lone figures on the grassy knoll. And there was not a thing Mahoney could do about it because, even if he wanted to, he would not be part of the new order. Just as he knew that the hero of Cavite had better get on his horse and haul butt out of town before they came to *really* thank him.

Mahoney stepped into the clutter of the Eternal Emperor's study for the last time. He was not sure why he had come, except for the mad hope that there would be some clue about what to do next.

He was so used to his old boss having every base covered

that it had not quite sunk in yet that this was one contingency that had been impossible to plan for.

Mahoney looked in dismay at the many scattered books on the shelves, some lying open just as the Emperor had left them as he searched for some arcane fact or other.

The study was jammed with the idiosyncrasies of his old boss: from ancient windup toys that clattered about with no purpose but to amuse to experimental cooking tools, plas bags of spices he was considering, scattered notes and scrawls, and even music sheets crammed with marginalia. An entire division could not have found a clue there in half a thousand years.

So Mahoney decided to have a drink. What else could he do?

He walked to the Emperor's desk and slid out the drawer where the boss kept his Scotch. He noted that the seal on the bottle was unbroken. That was strange. The Emperor never put an unsealed bottle in his desk. He always took a snort first. Mahoney shrugged, pulled out a shot glass, and reached for the bottle.

As he picked it up, something small and white came unstuck from the bottom and fluttered to the floor. Mahoney stooped over to see what it was. When he saw the scrawling on it, he almost let it drop from his fingers in shock.

Mahoney dropped heavily into a chair. He held the piece of paper before his disbelieving eyes. His face was flushed, sweat leapt from his forehead, and his pulse rate jumped into triple time.

The message was for him. From the Eternal Emperor. And this was all it said:

"Stick around, Ian. I'll be right back."

About the Authors

CHRIS BUNCH is a Ranger—and Airborne—qualified Vietnam vet, who's written about phenomena as varied as the Hell's Angels, the Rolling Stones, and Ronald Reagan.

ALLAN COLE grew up in the CIA in odd spots like Okinawa, Cyprus, and Taiwan. He's been a professional chef, investigative reporter, and national news editor of a major West Coast daily newspaper. He's won half a dozen writing awards in the process.

BUNCH and COLE, friends since high school, have collaborated on everything from the world's worst porno novel to more film and TV scripts than they care to admit. They stopped counting at one hundred when they suffered the total loss of all bodily hair.

Despite numerous death threats from fans of the STEN series, they have been denied entry into the Federal Witness Program. They are currently in deep cover somewhere between Hollyweird, Martinique and Astoria, Oregon, desperately working on the next adventure.

Also forthcoming is a trilogy to be published by Crown Books and Ballantine. Their highly praised Vietnam novel, A RECKONING FOR KINGS, is available from Ballantine Books.

Allan Cole and Chris Bunch

present imaginative,

suspenseful adventures

for die hard science-fiction fans